MONEY REIGNS

Amanda Zuelo

Midnight Reign Publishing LLC

CONTENTS

DEDICATION

For those who have carried grief and blame like a sentence, may you find a love that rewrites the verdict and teaches you how to breathe again.
This is for you.

EPIGRAPH

"Grief doesn't fade. It just changes shape. And waits
in the silence between heartbeats."

Harper Sawyer

TRIGGER WARNING

Explicit Language: This book contains frequent and un-apologetic use of strong sexual language including cunt, cock, clit, pussy, slut, and more.

Graphic Sexual Content: Open-door sex scenes that are detailed, intense, and *not* plot-drive. They exist purely because the characters wanted them to.

Sexual Power Dynamics: Includes light dominance/submission elements and consensual degradation/dirty talk.

Classism & Wealth Inequality: Themes of power imbalance between billionaire characters and working-class characters.

Alcohol Use: Characters drink socially and during emotional moments.

Emotional Manipulation / Lies by Omission: Characters withhold information or manipulate situations for what they perceive as love or protection.

Chapter One

WAR

The stain is long gone.

But I still see the blood.

Fresh hardwood stretches beneath my shoes, rich, dark, expensive. A stark contrast to the old floors, back when this place was all chipped wood and splinters, rust and rot.

Before I *bought* it.

Before I *remade* it.

Before I *tried* to erase it.

I thought money could sand down the past.

But I remember exactly where he fell.

Noah landed just there. Four stories down.

It was fast.

Final.

But the sound—

The sound still echoes. Not the crash of glass or the scream. Just the sick, wet thud of a body giving up against concrete.

That's what I remember most.

We were just kids. *Thirteen.* All sharp edges and stupid dares.

But Noah didn't get a funeral without cameras. I didn't get to breakdown without headlines.

It was *my* name they splattered across every screen.

The golden boy turned grim tragedy.

The headlines didn't say "grief." They said *"guilt."*

Shame curled around me like smoke.

I never even got to mourn him.

Just got battered and branded.

The Killer Prince.

I shake it off. Doesn't matter now.

I stand in the same spot we used to dare each other to reach. Back when the windows were cracked and we were stupid and alive and thought nothing could touch us.

I was supposed to go first.

I said I'd go first.

But Noah beat me to it.

He always did.

With dares.

With plans.

With dreams.

My hands curl into fists.

The window's new now, tempered glass, braced steel. Renovated to code. Signed off by every city inspector with a pen and a price. I paid them all.

I needed it perfect.

It still looks wrong.

There used to be a spiderweb fracture in the corner pane, barely visible unless the light hit it just right. We joked it looked like a map. Noah said it led to nowhere.

Now it leads here.

The sharp buzz of my phone rattles me back to the present.

Twenty minutes until the quarterly meeting at Beaumont Enterprises.

The machine never stops.

I take one last look at the glass before turning.

The building is almost complete; sleek, rebranded, a monument to reinvention. But I still see him. In the shadows of the frame. In the glint of sun off the glass.

Outside, the city exhales cold morning air. It's brisk and metallic, stinging my lungs. My breath fogs the air. The skyline stretches in front of me like nothing ever happened.

But *I* know.

This place remembers.

The car idles by the curb, matte black, quiet. I slide into the driver's seat. The leather hugs my frame like it knows my shape too well. I press the ignition. The engine hums, a purr of obedience.

Unlike memory.

It roars when you least expect it.

In the rearview mirror, the building stands polished and proud.

Yet the image burns inside me, the boy who didn't get to grow up.

The one I couldn't catch.

The one I never said goodbye to.

I shift into drive.

Let it fade behind me.

Like everything else I've buried.

Time polished the glass.

But it never cleaned the reflection.

Chapter Two

OLIVIA

"Fuck!"

My phone alarm is blaring, the smoke detector is wailing, and I throw open the bathroom door, my hair half-done as I sprint to the toaster.

Bread.

Stuck *again.*

I yank the plug and grab a rag, frantically waving at the smoke alarm before darting back to the bathroom for my lip stain.

I'll apply it in the ride share.

Damn it, I have to order a ride share.

Where the hell is my phone?

Bedroom.

I rush back, grab my heels, and slide them on, making my way to the bathroom.

Where's my lip stain?

In my hand.

Got it.

What am I missing?

Phone!

I sprint back, grab it, and order the ride share.

Ten minutes. Damn it.

I check the time. *I'm going to be late!*

I *can't* be late.

Not for this job interview. Not when I *need* this job to afford my overpriced apartment in this shitty city that hates my guts.

I should move back home.

No.

Nope, Olivia, you will *not* move back home.

I grab my purse and head for the door, almost slamming straight into Broderick; my neighbor and the reason I even have this interview at Beaumont Enterprises in the first place.

His warm brown eyes meet mine, and he smirks.

"Running late again?" he teases.

I sigh, chuckling lightly, feeling the heat rush to my cheeks. Broderick's gaze sweeps over me, just like he does almost every morning these past few months.

"You look good, Baker. Mr. Beaumont will definitely hire you—*if* you make it on time. Need a ride?"

"No," I manage to say, waving my phone at him. "I got a ride share."

"Cancel it," he says smoothly. "Just let me take you."

That glowing smile, the *impeccable* golden brown hair... Broderick is easily the prettiest man I've ever seen, and boy does he fill out a suit.

I hesitate. I *should* say no. I need to be independent. But my ride share won't get here in time, and I can't risk missing this interview.

With a sigh, I relent. "Alright. Just this once. But if I get the job, I can't rely on you for rides every day."

"Of course you can." He smirks, effortlessly taking my purse from me as he leads me to his car.

"Broderick, I mean it," I say as he opens the passenger door for me. His black BMW is sleek and immaculate. He's the kind of man who takes care of his things, probably because he worked hard to get them.

I slide into the car, the leather cool against my skin. The interior smells like new car with a hint of his musky cologne. I inhale deeply, probably a little too deeply, because when I glance over, he's smirking.

"Okay, sure," he says with an unconvincing nod, sliding into the driver's seat beside me. The engine purrs to life, and we're off.

The drive is... disconcerting. It's not that Broderick is a reckless driver, if anything he's annoyingly cautious, but the tension between us is palpable. His gaze lingers at stoplights a little longer than necessary, and every so often, I catch him stealing glances at me.

"Wesley's cool. You'll be fine, I swear," he reassures.

"It's Wesley I'm meeting with, but there's two others, right?"

"Yeah, War and Wilder," he answers as we pull up to Beaumont Enterprises.

"War?"

"Warren," he clarifies. "But friends call him War."

Broderick turns off the ignition and shifts toward me with a grin. "Nervous?"

"I'd be lying if I said no," I admit with a shaky laugh.

He reaches out and gives my knee a reassuring squeeze. An unintentional shiver races through me at his touch, but I shove it away and focus on his words instead.

"Just remember," he says seriously, holding my gaze. "You're more than capable for this job, Olivia. You've got this."

His warmth steadies me. I take a deep breath, offer him a grateful smile, and step out of the car. With my shoulders squared, I stride toward the entrance of what will *hopefully* be my new workplace.

Taking the elevator is easy enough, until the doors slide open.

I step forward and freeze.

Standing directly in front of me, about to enter the elevator, is Santo Amato—owner of NovaRael and grade-A asshole who denied me even an interview.

His sharp gray eyes lock onto mine, cool and unreadable. My stomach tightens. *Of all people.*

For a second, I wonder if I walked into the wrong building, or straight into a trap.

"Am I in the wrong building?" I mutter.

He doesn't say a word.

Beside him, two men I don't recognize step into the elevator with him, and the doors begin to close behind me. I shake off the thought, push down the unease, and head straight for the receptionist.

"Hi, I'm Olivia Baker. I have a meeting with Wesley Beaumont."

Chapter Three

WAR

By the time I park in the garage of Beaumont Enterprises, I'm late. I take the elevator up to the seventeenth floor, *my old floor,* before WesTech needed the space. Now, it's my brother Wesley's domain, and where we have our meeting.

As soon as the doors slide open, the relentless hum of work hits me. Everywhere I look, people are in motion, deep in conversation, hunched over intricate schematics that might as well be written in another language. This isn't my world. My world is real estate, cutthroat negotiations, and making adversaries tremble with a single glance.

Inside the glass-walled conference room, my brothers are already at the table. Wesley is glued to his laptop, fingers flying across the keyboard. Wilder, slouched in his seat, looks up when I enter and smirks.

"War," Wesley greets without looking up.

"Late again," Wilder mutters, shaking his head.

I slide into my chair, stretching out my legs. "Busy morning."

They share a knowing glance before Wesley launches into a rundown of the latest venture they want to pull me into.

My brothers and I run different businesses, but together, we monopolize more than most. I dominate real estate. Wesley owns the tech industry with WesTech. Wilder controls the entertainment world with his production company, mostly based in California, but for now, we have him here in the city.

Wesley dives into the details of some new system he's developing, but my attention drifts. It's not that I don't support them, I do. But their worlds aren't mine. Programming bugs and casting calls are pointless to me. Just like real estate law and city zoning mean nothing to them.

"War?"

Wilder's voice cuts through my drifting thoughts. His brow arches high, expectant. Beside me, Wesley pauses mid-sentence, waiting. I let a beat pass before answering. Long enough to make them think I was considering, not zoning out.

"That's compelling," I reply smoothly, giving nothing away. "Run that by me again."

Wilder rolls his eyes but repeats himself, detailing some issue he's having with a studio space he's looking to buy in Los Angeles. This time, I listen. I offer insights from my experience, suggest alternative solutions.

The doors burst open.

No fucking way.

In walks Santo Amato.

Italian, mafia ties, and a royal pain in my ass; a smug grin plastered on his face.

Of course, he thinks he can waltz in here like he owns the place, two goons at his side.

The temperature in the room shifts the second he steps through, as if his very presence could freeze the air. My hands curl into fists under the table, but I force myself to keep my face neutral. I won't give him the satisfaction of seeing me rattled.

"What the hell are you doing here, Amato?" I spit out, my voice sharper than I intended.

He smiles. That lazy, taunting smirk that's gotten under my skin since the day I met this asshole and his brother. "Is that any way to greet an old friend?" he asks, his tone dripping with condescension.

He's a prick in a three piece suit whose wasted potential is the product of years of criminal activity. My eyes never leaving his as I address him, knowing that even glancing away is a sign of weakness to a man like him

"You're far from a friend," I snap, leaning back in my chair, making it clear I'm not intimidated. "What do you want?"

"I want a building," he says casually, "and I hear you're not willing to budge."

Typical. His words are calm, but his eyes are focused, predatory. He wants me to cave, but that's not happening. Wesley types away on his computer and confirms what we all already know—Santo's after the Parker building.

"You want the Parker building on the east side. Smack dab in the middle of Korsakov's territory," Wesley says.

Maksim Korsakov, head of the Russian mob, the way these sons of a bitches have been trying to weasel, bribe and threaten their way into my businesses pisses me off.

"Gold star for you," Santo replies, as if he's already won. His voice is smooth, *too smooth.*

I cross my arms, narrowing my eyes at him. "No, I'm not giving it up, especially since we all heard about your little alliance with Korsakov. I'm not giving him a damn thing."

Santo tilts his head, looking at me like I'm some kind of joke. "Still in the middle of your little pissing contest with Maks? Pathetic."

The urge to punch him in the face rises, but I resist.

Barely.

"Your brother still kissing his ass? So much so they gave you a bride?" I mention and I watch the way his jaw clenches.

Gotcha.

"How is that little wife of yours? *Vasilisa,* right?"

His eyes darken, his jaw tight. "You don't *ever* say her name."
Good. Got Him.
I smirk. Wilder chuckles. Wesley keeps typing.
I leaned forward. "Would be a shame if something happened to her. Like your—"
Click.
I don't get a chance to finish, the sound of his goons gun cocking cuts through the air.
This son of a bitch.
Wesley's fingers freeze on the keyboard
Wilder lifts his hands in surrender, the idiot he is.
I hold my breath, my eyes on Amato, he lifts a hand to call off his goon, the tension relaxes for a fraction.
But then he's on me before I can even blink. His hand grips my tie, spitting threats about mentioning his wife. I let him, because if I truly let go, I'd crush his larynx before his goons blinked. He doesn't scare me. He only reminds me what kind of men this city breeds.
Monsters in suits.
But I'm the worst of them.
He shoves me back hard. My chair teeters on two legs before I regain my balance.
Then he's gone.
But the stink of him lingers in the air, along with his parting shot: *"Oh, and tell Mandy I'll be seeing her soon."*
Smug bastard.
I slam my fist on the table.
His mention of my sister lights a fire under my ribs.
The only time we ever gave up real estate was when that prick dated her.
She was young. Naïve. Thought it was love. He used her to get property, and we gave it to him, on one condition: he leave her the hell alone.

If he reneges?

I'll bulldoze every damn building he owns.

Wilder chuckles, leaning back in his chair, arms crossed. "Well, that went about as well as expected."

I straighten my tie. "He's got a death wish if he thinks he can use Mandy to get under my skin."

Wesley glances up from his laptop, one eyebrow raised. "What did you expect? He's always been like that. You're not going to hand over the building, and he knows it."

"I don't give a damn about Korsakov or whatever alliance they've cooked up," I say, trying to tamp down the fury burning inside me. "But he's not going to pull that shit with Mandy."

The room falls quiet.

Then the door opens again.

I look up, expecting another hitman or asshole to walk through.

Instead, it's a *woman.*

She's new. And she's impossible to ignore.

Her brown hair falls in loose waves around her shoulders, framing a face that's all big, brown eyes and cherry-colored lips. Not glossy, not overdone, just naturally vibrant. But it's not her face that keeps my attention.

It's her body.

Curves. *Real ones.* A blouse stretched tight over breasts that would look better with my hands on them. A skirt that clings like a fucking invitation, tag still tucked in like she'll run it back to the store after today.

New.

Cheap.

Desperate.

I can smell her need before she says a word. She's not here for ambition, she's here to *survive.* And that makes her interesting.

Because survivalists will do anything. And I want to see what "anything" looks like on her knees.

She's *tempting.*

I force my gaze back to her face, but she isn't looking at me.

Her attention is on Wesley.

I don't like that.

Wesley stands, smiling warmly as he extends a hand. "Ms. Baker, right?"

She nods, shaking his hand firmly. There's a confidence in her grip, even though I catch the slight uncertainty in her eyes.

"Yes. Olivia Baker."

Damn.

Her voice.

I feel it in my chest, low and warm, with just the right amount of huskiness. Like melted honey and something I suddenly want to hear a lot more of.

Her eyes flick toward me, just for a second, before darting back to Wesley. The moment is so brief, I might have imagined it.

But I know I didn't.

I sit up straighter, my interest piqued in a way that hasn't happened in a long time.

Chapter Four

OLIVIA

I don't know what I expected when I stepped into this building.

But it wasn't *this.*

The Beaumont brothers are nothing like I imagined. I assumed I'd be meeting with an assistant today, not Wesley Beaumont himself. My pulse stutters. Surely he doesn't remember me... not after all these years.

He looks... different.

Wesley is striking, all clean-shaven charm and a sharp suit, his blue eyes bright and welcoming. I study his face for any sign of recognition. Nothing. Just professional warmth.

His handshake is firm but polite, like he's careful not to squeeze too hard. A gentleman.

The other two?

Different story.

One is lounging, shirt untucked, a playful smirk tugging at his lips. His eyes, a touch darker than Wesley's and there's a roguishness to him, a casual energy that says *troublemaker.*

And then there's him.

The eldest Beaumont.

I've read about him. Everyone has.

New buildings. Renovations.

He's always in the media, for something.

If it's not business, it's galas.

Auctions.

A different woman on his arm each time.

He's not lounging.

He's not smiling.

He's *watching.*

Dark hair, sharp jawline, eyes the color of ice; and just as merciless. His suit fits him too well, broad shoulders filling it out in a way that makes the air in the room feel smaller. He doesn't just look at me. He pins me down with it. His hand is on the table, fingers drumming slightly, slow, rhythmic, like a ticking bomb only he can hear.

There's tension in his body, a controlled stillness. And his gaze?

It's heavy.

Like he's waiting for me to *notice* that he's noticing me.

I shake Wesley's hand, then pull back quickly, willing myself to focus.

"Thank you for taking the time to meet with me," I say, keeping my voice steady.

"Of course," Wesley says, his hand going to my shoulder as he turns me toward the door. "Let's take this to my main floor."

His eyes flick toward his brothers, but I don't turn to see their reactions. I don't need to.

The weight of Warren's stare drags down my spine, heavy and invasive the whole way out.

Wesley takes me to the elevator and up to the next floor, he talks about his new project and his day to day schedule, what he expects and what he wants.

I just tell myself to keep walking. If he knew, I'd see it—the flicker, the question. But there's only professional ease in his voice.

Wesley stops just in front of a sleek, minimal desk nestled near a frosted glass office door.

"This is where you'll be," he says, gesturing to the workspace. "You've already been set up with a company email and calendar access. Leslie will walk you through the rest."

"Wait, I-I have the job?" I ask confused as I follow him.

Wesley smiles, "You have an excellent resume and glowing references, yes Ms. Baker you have the job."

For the first time since stepping inside, I relax. Maybe he really doesn't remember.

He doesn't say anything else, but his eyes flick, quickly, to the glass wall behind me. A barely perceptible shift in his expression. Like he's trying not to look at something.

Or *someone.*

Before I can follow his gaze, he clears his throat and pulls out his phone.

"I need to step into something," he adds smoothly, already tapping at the screen. "But I have Leslie coming, she's one of our lead systems engineers. She'll help you get settled."

He doesn't wait for a reply. Just disappears, casual but brisk.

A woman approaches a beat later, slim build, a clean ponytail, and an expression that reads efficient but kind.

"Hi," she says, offering a hand. "I'm Leslie Rankin. Ready to get set up?"

"Yes, thank you," I reply, sliding into the desk chair.

Leslie grabs a another chair from an empty cubicle and sits beside me, unlocking the computer and pulling up a series of onboarding systems.

"I'll walk you through the basics; email, calendar, project dashboards, security protocols. Nothing too painful."

I nod. I already know all of the basics.

Things I could handle without Leslie.

Her tone is gentle, her pace slow.

But my focus is elsewhere and the longer I sit there, the harder it becomes to concentrate.

Because I feel it again.

That gaze.

I don't need to turn around to know where it's coming from.

It's not casual or fleeting.

It's deliberate.

Like a spotlight pressed between my shoulder blades.

I click into a training tab Leslie just opened, pretending I'm absorbed in the text. But my breath catches slightly when I hear the low murmur of voices behind the glass.

Wesley and his brother.

They aren't loud, but the cadence is tight. Clipped. Tense.

I feel like a cracked window between two storm systems, exposed and rattling without fully understanding why.

Leslie glances at me, then behind us, and smirks slightly. "Try to ignore it," she murmurs under her breath.

I blink. "What?"

She leans in, typing something on the keyboard as she speaks. "War. He stares. It's a thing."

My chest tightens.

"I wasn't imagining it then," I say quietly.

"Nope," Leslie replies. "He watches everything. *Everyone.* It's how he processes. Creepy at first, then you sort of... get used to it."

I nod slowly, though nothing about it feels easy to get used to.

"So... he just watches everyone?" I ask, keeping my voice low. "Is he, like... Wesley's boss or something?"

Leslie chuckles under her breath. "No. If anything, Wesley's been trying to get War to stop hovering for years."

She shrugs, pulling up a new tab. "Go ahead and enter your password here."

I shift my focus back to the screen and type in: **Bakers_Brood**

A soft laugh slips from me. "My mom used to call us the Bakers Brood growing up because of our last name, Baker. We're not that big, really. Just a family of five, but—"

"Don't use your last name in your password," Leslie cuts in gently, her tone firmer now. "And don't share it. With *anyone.*"

My face flushes hot. "Right. Of course," I mumble, eyes dropping to the screen.

Rookie mistake.

Leslie gives a small nod and clicks into the next field. "Let's go ahead and try a new password."

I pause, hands hovering over the keyboard for a second.

I can feel his eyes.

Then I backspace slowly, each letter of Bakers Brood disappearing one by one, before typing a secure password, one I know no one would be able to pick apart.

I hit enter.

The confirmation screen blinks green.

I exhale.

"...Is he still watching me?" I ask, voice barely above a whisper.

Leslie glances, smirks, and turns back to me.

"Yep."

Chapter Five

WAR

I shouldn't still be watching her.

But I am.

I've been watching her for ten minutes now.

There's a crease between her brows that deepens when she bites her lip, *those lips,* and leans closer to the screen. She's nervous, fidgeting. She keeps adjusting the hem of her skirt, like she thinks it's too tight.

It's not.

It's perfect.

She's nervous. Self-conscious. Probably sweating under that polyester blend she tried to pass off as business casual.

But she's holding it together.

Barely.

That's what makes it interesting.

There's always a moment right before a person breaks, when you see the cracks, the fragility. It's the moment I want to catch, pry open, *keep.* Olivia Baker is teetering there, and it's fucking fascinating. I want to *push.*

I shouldn't care. She's just another name on a file. Another pretty girl in a borrowed skirt.

But then she tucks her hair behind her ear, glances toward the elevator like she's already wondering how hard it would be to run.

Run little doe.

"Cut it out," Wesley mutters under his breath as he steps up beside me, his arms crossed.

I don't answer. Just keep leaning against the glass wall of the conference room, my arms folded, gaze locked on Olivia.

A flicker moves through my chest. Discomfort. Or something worse.

I don't turn to look at him. "Cut what out?"

"You know exactly what," he hisses. "You're burning a hole in her back."

"She can't feel it."

"Warren." His tone sharpens; firm, clipped. *Serious.* No one calls me that. Not unless they want to start something.

I slowly turn toward him.

His expression is taut. Tired. Protective. "You are not sleeping with this one."

"I'm not sleeping with her."

It's a lie.

He knows it.

Wesley scoffs. "Bullshit. You said that about the last one, too."

I shrug one shoulder. "The last one wasn't your assistant."

"She worked for *me.*"

"She also had a thing for being tied up and left begging on her knees, but I didn't see her filing a complaint."

"You left her *stranded* at the fucking docks, "Wesley hisses, jabbing a finger into my chest. "Luckily it only took *twenty grand* to keep her quiet."

I grin. "She wanted the water view."

"She *cried,* War."

"She begged to go again."

"I'm serious, she's perfect, War. I don't need you fucking this one up."

I chuckle. "You're so dramatic. I'm not going to touch her."

Yet.

I already want to touch her in every way that would ruin her. *Wesley thinks 'perfect' means fragile. It means ripe.*

He mutters something under his breath. Probably cursing my name. Then storms off back to Olivia's desk like some righteous office knight.

I wait.

I watch the moment Olivia looks up at him. She smiles. *Soft. Grateful.*

Then I turn, slow and controlled, and head for the elevator.

I take it up to my floor, the elevator doors open, and the scent of roasted coffee hits me before I even step out.

Broderick's already there.

He holds out a to-go cup like it's a peace offering.

"Morning," he says. "Brought your usual."

I take the coffee without looking at him.

Of course he brought my usual.

Because that's Broderick. Fetching, smoothing, smiling. A man who knows how to wag his tail without ever baring teeth.

Always trying to stay one step ahead. Smooth. Polished. *Friendly.*

I don't need a friend. I need someone who shuts up and gets the job done. He forgets that sometimes.

"Thanks," I mutter, heading toward my office, the city skyline stretching wide and glassy beyond the floor-to-ceiling windows.

Broderick follows, talking numbers. Three buildings under contract, one tied up in zoning. I nod when necessary, sip my coffee, let the silence stretch long enough to make him fidget.

"The Parker Estate got another inquiry this morning."

My gaze cuts to him.

"Who?"

He hesitates. "Korsakov."

The name crawls under my skin like rot.

"We're not selling to that asshole."

"I figured," he says quickly. "He offered cash, above asking."

I turn to face him fully.

"I don't give a damn if he offered a blank check and a bow-wrapped yacht. That property stays off-limits."

"Got it."

He knows better than to push. At least on that.

There's a pause. Then Broderick shifts.

"By the way, there's a girl—woman, Olivia Baker. She's interviewing with Wesley today."

I don't answer. He talks too much. Always filling silence like it's his job to keep me entertained.

He keeps going.

"She get the job?"

My jaw tightens. "Yeah."

"She's my neighbor."

That makes me pause.

I glance over.

Broderick shrugs like it's no big deal. "We have apartments next to each other. She made me these peanut butter cookies once when I helped her carry groceries upstairs. Best thing I've ever tasted."

I cut him a look. "What are you, twelve?"

He laughs. "No, just saying. She's a good person."

My gaze sharpens. "You got a crush?"

His smile falters. "What? I'm just looking out. She's new, and she's... you know. Real."

I stare at him for a beat too long.

Because I do know. I saw it the second she stepped into the conference room.

Brody shifts his weight. "Just wanted to make sure she's good. Seems like the kind of person who deserves a break."

The heat in my chest starts to cool. Slightly.

Until he adds, *too* casually, "Plus now that she's officially an employee, I'll have to file with HR if she says yes when I ask her out."

The silence after that is sharp. Tense. Immediate.

I take a long sip of my coffee. Let the quiet stretch.

Then I look at him. *Really* look at him.

"Don't."

I don't tolerate competition. Especially not from my own dog sniffing at the same bone.

Brody blinks. "What?"

"Don't ask her out."

He opens his mouth, then closes it. "Come on, I was just—"

I turn back to the window, cutting him off without another word.

He stands there for a moment, the weight of the warning hanging between us.

Eventually, I hear him exhale and step back.

"I'll get those zoning files updated," he mutters, heading for the door.

I don't respond.

The door clicks shut behind him, and silence fills the room.

I turn back toward my desk, set the coffee down, and wake the screen with a flick of my wrist. Still logged in.

Good.

I open the surveillance system.

Pull up the building feed.

Click the tab labeled 18-*Executive East.* Wesley's floor.

Password required.

Of course.

I smirk, cold and humorless.

Wesley locked me out of live access to his floor's cameras months ago after I *accidentally* caught footage of his last assistant doing unsanctioned yoga stretches between filing cabinets. He called it invasive. I called it preventive liability.

Now I call it inconvenient.

I could try and override it.

But not without leaving a trail.

And I don't need Wesley at my office door.

So instead, I lean back, crack my neck, and open Broderick's employee file. He's been with me long enough.

Quick search. Directory. Address.

Gotcha.

Broderick's apartment is in the West Tower, Unit 5C.

I don't own the building, but I've done business with the property management group before. One call, one favor, and I can see what I need to.

But I don't call.

Instead, I pull up the shared backend portal for local holdings, one of those convenient city-wide real estate integrations my company helped fund back when no one thought to ask why we wanted access.

I click over to tenant data. It's protected, *technically.*

But not from me.

Olivia Baker. Unit 5B.

Next door.

Just like he said.

I stare at the screen for a long beat, fingers hovering over the keyboard.

Then I open a new search.

Olivia Baker.

There's a hit on her work socials. Sparse. Community college. A stack of clerical certs, typing speed, office software, the usual bullshit. The kind of paper resume that says steady, not brilliant.

No real social media presence, just a locked photo account and another account abandoned four years ago.

Clever girl.

Private.

Not Flashy.

I dig deeper.

Age, she's Twenty-seven.

A decade younger.

I shrug. I'll make the exception.

I slide back to the tenant data I technically shouldn't be looking at.

She's been in 5B for two years. No roommate. No car on file. Emergency contact listed as "Mom." No pets.

One late rent notice on record—six months ago. Paid in full the same week.

Then another. She missed this months payment.

Hmm, explains the need to return the skirt.

Quiet tenant. Quiet life.

No one stays quiet in this city without reason.

What's she hiding?

What's she running from?

Or maybe it's the other way around.

Maybe she's running to something.

Her license is on file. I click.

Five-five.

A full foot shorter.

Would've guessed smaller.

Probably because of the way she carries herself, head ducked, shoulders tucked, like she's trying to vanish.

Like she doesn't know how fucking *visible* she is.

Compact. Easy to corner.

But not delicate. Not breakable.

She's lush in all the delicious places, full hips, thick thighs, soft stomach, the kind of curves that make a man's hands feel; made for gripping.

Not fragile. Not fake.

Just real. Real enough to sink into.

I click her file closed and stare at the screen, my fingers still twitching on the mouse.

I should stop.

I should stop.

But I don't.

Because Olivia Baker is now under my roof, close to my brother, and even closer to a man who basks in her attention and thinks peanut butter cookies mean something.

And if she's going to live next to someone who clearly wants her,

If she's going to work inside my family's empire, I need to know exactly who she is, because I've already decided how much of her I'll take.

All of it.

Chapter Six

OLIVIA

Working for Wesley is surprisingly easy. The systems are manageable, and Wesley himself is a hands-off kind of boss, quick meetings, clear expectations, then silence. I fall into a rhythm faster than I expected, and by the time the clock hits five, I barely register the end of the day.

I head toward the elevators, digging through my purse for my phone, and slam into a wall of muscle.

Broderick.

I step back.

"Hey, you," he says with a smile too pretty for how casual he makes it seem, like he knows exactly what it does, flashing those perfect teeth under all that golden-boy charm.

I blink, cheeks flushing before I can stop it.

Focus, Olivia.

"Hey," I say, trying to play it cool as I keep rummaging. My thumb hovers over the ride share app.

Before I can tap it, a hand closes gently over mine.

"Don't," he says. "I'll take you home."

I glance up, hesitating. "Broderick—"

"Brody," he corrects smoothly. "You can call me Brody. We've been neighbors for, what, a year?"

"Two," I admit, a little sheepish.

He laughs softly. "Even more reason to let me give you a ride."

I hesitate again. He's nice to look at, but he's also the kind of guy who probably grew up being voted '*Most Likely to Break Hearts.*' And while he's always been polite in passing, he never really *looked* at me like this before. Then again... I had a boyfriend until a year ago, and he had some girl who practically lived in his apartment for months.

It was never like *this.*

Still. I need this job. I need to stay focused. And saying yes to a ride shouldn't feel like this big of a decision.

"...Alright," I say finally, sliding my phone back into my purse. "But only because the app is surging."

He grins wider. "Sure. Blame it on the app."

The drive is quiet at first, not awkward, just... calm. Brody keeps one hand on the wheel, the other draped casually across the gearshift. His profile catches the evening light just right, sharp jawline, golden-boy cheekbones, and lashes way too long for a man.

I stare out the window, trying to slow my racing thoughts.

I have a job. My first day wasn't a disaster.

Rent extension is due soon and I still have no idea how I'm going to pull that off.

"You settled in okay?" Brody asks, his voice breaking through my spiral.

"Yeah," I say. "Everyone was... nice."

"Wesley's good people," he says with a nod. "War and Wilder are a bit much, but they're not terrible once you get to know them."

I hum noncommittally. I don't know anything about *any* of them. Except that Warren watched me today like he was trying to read my blood type through my clothes.

By the time we reach our apartment building, the sun is dipping lower, casting long shadows across the lobby. We step into the elevator together. The air shifts the second the doors close.

Tighter. *Closer.*

He turns toward me, one hand braced against the wall, angled just enough to keep the mood casual, but it doesn't quite work.

"So…" he says slowly. "Any chance you'd want to grab lunch sometime?"

I blink. "Like, *lunch* lunch?"

He chuckles. "Yeah. The kind with food."

My stomach flips, and not because I'm swooning. Because this is *not* the time. I'm barely scraping by. I just started this job, and *dating?* That's a luxury I can't afford.

I look up at him, my bottom lip caught between my teeth. "Brody… I'm not really looking for anything right now. I just, I need to focus on work, and rent, and…"

He holds up a hand. "Got it. Respect. No pressure."

The elevator dings. We step out into the hallway, that quiet space between our two doors. My hand is already fishing in my purse for my key when he speaks again.

"But how about lunch at the office?" he offers. "You can come up to my floor, eat in my office. No pressure. Just food."

I glance at him. He's leaning against the wall, grinning, not smug, just easy.

Effortless.

Something in me wavers. It's not just the offer. It's the way he's asking.

Like he actually *wants* me there.

Like this isn't a game.

I bite the inside of my cheek, heart doing that stupid flutter thing again.

Maybe this is a bad idea.

But maybe… it isn't. I could use a friend.

"...Okay," I say softly. "Sure. Lunch at the office."

His smile deepens. "Cool. I'll see you then."

He nods, gives me that charming half-grin that makes my stomach twist for a whole different reason, then unlocks his door and disappears inside.

I finally find my key, slip inside my apartment, and close the door with a soft click. The quiet hits me all at once.

I drop my bag, lean back against the door, and exhale.

Lunch.

It's just lunch.

Right?

***

By the time my phone buzzes, the morning is already gone. Work with Wesley is smooth, rhythmic, I've started to find a groove that makes the hours pass without friction.

I blink down at the message:

Broderick

> You still down for lunch? Floor 40. Come hungry.

Floor 40?

My stomach dips a little. Isn't that...?

I press the elevator button and try not to overthink it. Lunch. It's *just* lunch.

But when the doors open on floor 40, the air changes.

Literally, it's colder up here. Sleeker. More expensive. The floors are marble, not tile or linoleum. The walls are glass. It feels less like an office building and more like a throne room.

Wesley's domain is comfortable. *This?*

This is Warren Beaumont's.

I step out, heels clicking, trying to walk with purpose as I make my way toward Brody's office. I remind myself he invited me. That this is normal. I'm allowed to be here.

But that sensation creeps in again.

Eyes.

Watching.

Burning.

I slow, my gaze drifting, against my better judgment, toward the darkened doorway halfway down the hall.

Warren Beaumont stands there, one hand on the doorframe, his posture deceptively relaxed. *But his stare?*

Sharp. Calculated. Assessing.

He doesn't blink. Doesn't move.

Just watches.

I lift my chin slightly and nod; *polite, professional,* but he doesn't return it.

He just keeps looking at me like I don't belong here.

Like he's deciding what to do about it.

I turn away, pulse jumping as I continue down the hall and knock on Brody's door. It opens immediately.

"Hey," Brody says, smiling. "Right on time."

I smile, but it's thinner than I mean it to be. "Yeah... sorry, I almost forgot."

His brow lifts, concerned. "Everything okay?"

I nod, stepping inside quickly.

But I can still feel Warren's stare on my back as Brody closes the door.

His office is brighter than I expected, lots of windows, clean lines, a few personal touches. A leather couch near the corner, a coffee machine that probably costs a small fortune, and two neatly arranged bags of takeout on his desk.

"La Serenata?" I blink in surprise, stepping closer as the scent hits me. Basil, tomato, garlic, and freshly baked bread. "That's my favorite place."

He grins as he unpacks the food. "I know."

My brows lift. "How?"

"You gave me cookies a few weeks ago; remember? The ones in the little white box?"

I nod slowly, suddenly self-conscious. "You noticed the box?"

He laughs softly. "Olivia, I'd notice anything you gave me. But yeah, I recognized the takeout container. It still had the logo stamped on the bottom."

Heat rushes to my cheeks. "Wow. That's... observant."

He shrugs, sliding a soup toward me and setting the sandwich beside it. "Or maybe I just really liked the cookies."

I smile despite myself. "I could give you the recipe."

He leans back in his chair, eyes warm. *"Or..."* he says, drawing the word out, "we could make them together sometime."

My pulse flutters, but I keep my smile in place, soft and noncommittal. "We'll see."

Lunch is easy.

Comfortable. We talk about the city, old jobs, places we've both lived. He tells me a ridiculous story about one of his clients refusing to leave a showing until they lit sage in every room. I laugh so hard I almost choke on my soup.

It's the first time I've felt normal in weeks.

No pressure. No tension.

Just... *good.*

A knock breaks the moment.

Brody glances at the door, then at the clock. "Still got time."

"I can go," I say, standing quickly and brushing off my skirt. "I should get back anyway—"

"It's fine," he says, already crossing the room.

He opens the door.

And my breath catches.

Warren Beaumont.

He doesn't step inside. Doesn't smile.

Just stands there, tall, dark, imposing, his broad frame nearly eclipsing the hallway light behind him. All sharp lines and colder shadows, he towers in the doorway like a warning dressed in a tailored suit.

His eyes land straight on me.

My whole body tenses.

Brody doesn't seem to notice the shift in temperature. "War, what's up?"

Warren's gaze doesn't move. Doesn't blink.

"Didn't know you had company," he says coolly.

The words are neutral. *The tone?* Anything but.

"I was just leaving," I say, already gathering the remains of my lunch, my voice a little too light.

Warren doesn't budge. He's like a skyscraper filling a skyline; bigger than he has any right to be.

His eyes flick to the sandwich wrapper in my hand before landing back on my face. Cold. Calculating.

"Beaumont Enterprises has a very clear HR policy about fraternization during work hours."

The words hit like a slap.

My throat tightens.

"It was just—lunch," I fumble, heat blooming in my cheeks.

Brody steps in smoothly, his voice cool but clipped. "I know the rules, War."

There's something sharper in his tone now. Not friendly. Not deferential.

Warren's jaw ticks once.

Brody turns to me, gently herding me toward the door. "See you later, Liv."

I nod quickly, eyes down, my face hot as I head for the exit.

But Warren still doesn't move.

He's just there, filling the doorway like a boulder in my path.

I hesitate, pulse stuttering. He doesn't say a word.

I have to tilt my head back just to meet his eyes.

His eyes drag over me slowly. Judgmental. Displeased.

I shift awkwardly. "Excuse me."

He shifts slightly to the side.

I edge around him, my shoulder nearly brushing his chest, my breath catching as I finally clear the doorway.

His voice comes, low and barely audible, like a warning meant only for me.

"You've got crumbs on your blouse." His gaze drags lower, slow and deliberate. *"Messy."*

I still.

"Thank you for the reminder, *Mr. Beaumont,*" I say, trying to keep my voice from shaking.

I smooth my blouse, even though it's pointless, the damage is already done.

My fingertips brush over the faint smear of crumbs on the fabric and shame crawls up my throat like a second skin.

He doesn't say anything. He just stares.

Watching me.

Weighing me.

Judging me.

I lift my chin, summon whatever scraps of pride I have left, and walk away—measured, steady, like I'm not unraveling with every step.

Like he didn't just humiliate me with *a few fucking crumbs.*

I don't look back as I walk away.

I won't give him the satisfaction.

Chapter Seven

WAR

R age.

I've felt rage before.

It's a constant companion in my world. Useful. Controlled. Directed.

But this?

Watching her?

This is something else entirely.

A raw, guttural burn that sinks deep into my bones.

Every day she's on my floor.

Every day, she walks past my office with those soft eyes and that tight polite smile like I'm just another fucking suit.

And then she disappears into his.

Door closed.

Privacy implied.

Intimacy assumed.

Took a week of pretending not to care before I had the camera installed. One angle. Hidden. Feeding only to me. She doesn't know yet that when she smiles, it's mine. When she laughs, it's mine. She just shares it with *him* first.

I watch her.

The way she sits, legs crossed delicately, posture straight. The way she tilts her head when she listens, *really listens,* to him.

The way she smiles when he surprises her with more of that goddamn soup from the Amato's Italian place she likes.

I didn't know she liked La Serenata.

Now I know her order.

I know the way she holds the spoon.

I know that she always eats the crust of her sandwich last after peeling it away.

And I hate that he knows it too.

He gets the curve of her lips when they're relaxed in a laugh.

All I ever get is tension.

Fear.

I lean back in my chair, eyes locked on the screen as she hands him a napkin. Her fingers brush his. He doesn't flinch. Neither does she. That subtle touch sends a pulse of something sharp and possessive straight through me. He touches her like it's casual. I'd make her remember my touch for *days.*

I could have her.

Fuck, I want her.

Not just her body—though *Christ,* I think about it too often.

It's the way she walks into every room like she doesn't take up space. The way she tries to blend in. Tries not to be seen.

But I see her.

I *always* see her.

And maybe that scares her.

Brody says something. Her brows lift and she laughs again, head tilting, hair falling over her shoulder like she's in a goddamn romcom.

He mentions a project I gave him in California.

In a few months.

That's *too* long.

That's too much time.

I'll make sure it happens sooner.

And then she does it.

The thing that turns irritation into full-blooded fury.

She asks him, "Are you friends with Mr. Beaumont?"

Mr. Beaumont.

Not War.

Not even Warren.

Mr. Fucking Beaumont.

I taste the name like ash in my mouth.

She'll scream Mr. Beaumont until she remembers it's War; and before I declare it on shit for brains Broderick, I pick up the phone and dial direct to Wesley's office.

"What War," Wesley answers clipped.

"That any way to greet your brother?"

"When you call my direct line and bypass my secretary, yes."

"I want her."

"My secretary?" he asks confused.

"No, Olivia Baker."

"I told you, if you fuck her, just don't fuck it up. I need her to stay, she's doing excellent, she's worth—"

"No, I want her to work for *me.*"

Silence.

"No, War, what the hell do you *really* need her for?"

"I need a personal assistant or whatever."

"No you don't, you literally have a floor full of men because if *you* hire women you fuck them all and they leave!"

"Fine, I'll just call over to NovaRael and hire Evie Mitchell. Steal her right from under Amato"

"...How the hell do you know about her?"

"Your little secret crush? Easy. Also know you've been working with that bastard. I know *everything.*"

"He owes me now, it was an investment."

"Clock's ticking little brother, give me Olivia or I make your girlfriend my new conquest."

"She's not my girlfriend."

"Even better, won't get your sloppy seconds."

"Fuck you War. Take her. I'll tell her about the transfer end of day."

"No."

I cut him off. Sharp. Final.

"I'll tell her. Tomorrow morning."

Another pause.

Then, quieter. "She's a nice girl, she's not like the others, War."

I end the call.

My nice girl now.

***

She's late.

By four minutes.

I know because I've been here eight. Standing in the lobby like I don't own the fucking building. Like I'm not the reason every suit in this place stops to breathe different.

Security nods at me. People glance, then glance away. No one speaks.

Finally.

She walks in through the front doors like she doesn't feel me watching.

Head down. Bag clutched to her side. Not rushing, even though she's late, but not dragging her feet either, just... existing.

Polite. Soft. Invisible.

To everyone else.

But not to me.

My jaw grinds as I watch her.

The moment her heels click against the marble, I feel it in my spine.

She's wearing that same navy skirt. The one that hugs her like a goddamn secret. Hair still damp from the shower. She smells like sugar and warm vanilla.

Like a drug store perfume.

Cheap.

Like she tried to make herself unremarkable.

Like she tried to disappear.

But I see her.

I *always* fucking see her.

Her eyes lift. Find me.

A small hitch in her breath. Subtle. But not subtle enough.

"Good morning, Mr. Beaumont," she says, smoothing her perfect voice into something professional.

It irritates me.

Not the greeting.

The distance.

Mr. Beaumont like I'm just a name on a door. Like I don't think about her when I shouldn't. Like I haven't memorized the goddamn cadence of her laugh when she's with *him.*

Still—I let it go.

For now.

"Good morning, Ms. Baker."

I fall into step beside her without invitation.

She doesn't ask why.

Doesn't look at me.

Just walks toward the elevators with that quiet tension in her spine like she's trying not to spook a predator.

The elevator dings.

We step inside.

She goes to press the button for WesTech.

I catch her hand midair.

Her fingers are smaller than I expected, warm. The skin soft under my palm. For a second I just hold it, the world narrowing to the quiet of the elevator and the steady beat under my thumb.

She freezes.

Gasps quietly, but I hear it. *Feel it.* She doesn't realize it yet, but I'll train her body to make that sound for me.

On command.

Would be delicious to hear having her pressed up against the elevator wall.

I shake the thought and press Beaumont Realty.

Her mouth parts, like she's about to object, to ask why.

"I need to speak with you," I say, voice low and final. "In my office."

The air tightens.

I feel her heartbeat pick up. The tremor she tries to bury.

But she doesn't argue. Doesn't move away.

The doors slide shut.

And in the silence that follows, I swear I can hear her pulse pounding.

Loud.

Uneasy.

Beautiful.

"Mr. Beaumont, if this is about Bro—"

"War."

She blinks. "What?"

"Call me War."

She falls silent, her breath coming in soft shudders.

"Wa-Warren, if this is about—"

"It's not," I clip.

She nods.

Falls silent again.

Warren.

No one calls me that.

The elevator doors slide open and we step out together.

Lapdog Broderick is already waiting, holding my coffee like a good little mutt.

"Morning, War. I got—Liv?" he blinks, dumb and confused like someone changed the script mid-scene.

I don't look at him.

"I have a meeting right now with Ms. Baker. Fill me in on whatever you have later."

I snatch the coffee from his hand and place my other palm to the small of her back. Warm. Steady. Possessive.

She stiffens beneath my touch.

Good.

I guide her past him, toward my office.

The door clicks shut behind us and the silence stretches, heavy and waiting.

She lingers near it. Doesn't step further in.

Like crossing the threshold completely would make this real.

Her hands hover at her sides. One hand clenched on the handle of her knock off purse. Frozen.

But then she moves.

Takes a few careful steps forward, her heels soft against the carpet, and stops halfway into the room like she's unsure if she's invited or cornered.

She lifts her head. Chin up. Eyes wide.

"Mr. Bea—Warren," she corrects herself quickly. "Is something wrong?"

I take a slow sip of the coffee. *It's* wrong. Too much cream. Broderick's an idiot.

I set it down and walk to the other side of the desk. Lean back against it. Arms crossed. Watching her.

"No," I say simply. "Nothing's wrong. But things *are* changing."

Her brows knit. "Changing?"

I nod. "You work for me now."

Silence.

It lands exactly like I expected.

She blinks once. Twice. Then laughs, quiet, nervous. "I-I think there's been a mistake. I work for WesTech. For Wesley."

"Not anymore."

Her smile falters. "Wesley didn't mention any—"

"Because I told him I'd handle it."

She crosses her arms. Defensive.

Cute.

"I wasn't told about any transfer. No one asked me if—"

"You don't get asked," I say, voice flat. "Wesley doesn't mind. And you signed an internal mobility clause when you were hired. Any exec above your current manager can request a reallocation."

She pales. Just a little. Her lips part, but no sound comes out.

I tilt my head slightly. "You didn't read the fine print?"

"I-I thought that was for *departmental* needs—"

"It is."

Her eyes narrow. "What department needs *me*?"

Me.

But I don't say it.

Instead, I move back behind my desk, open a drawer, and pull out a slim folder.

Slide it toward her like we're just talking metrics and quarterly goals.

Not ownership.

"Beaumont Realty has a new internal initiative," I say. "Client interfacing. Lead segmentation. Investor relations, all things you're capable of handling. I've seen the way you organize Wesley's projects. The way you follow up without being told. The way you listen."

I pause, then add, "One of the first projects involves a flagship property, the Parker Building. It's under renovation, but permitting and zoning have stalled the timeline. I want a fresh set of eyes on it. You'll be reviewing reports, investor notes, city filings. If something jumps out, bring it to me."

Her brows knit. "Seen?"

Caught. Brilliant girl.

"*Heard.* From Wesley."

She glances at the folder but doesn't touch it.

I wait a beat. Then:

"I had the office down the hall from mine cleared out."

Her eyes flick up. Cautious.

Round.

Brown.

Perfect.

"It's yours now. New furniture. Updated tech. Fresh paint."

A flicker of suspicion crosses her face. "Why go through all this trouble? There are plenty of qualified assistants already here."

"There are," I admit. "But none of them are you."

Her breath catches. Just slightly.

Good.

She doesn't know it yet, but I've built her a kingdom.

One polished surface at a time.

I know from those little talks with Brody that she likes the scent of eucalyptus in the mornings.

I've seen which pens she uses until they run dry.

I know she prefers natural light. That she gets headaches from overhead fluorescents.

I know everything.

Watched everything.

For a month.

"Let me show you your new office," I tell her.

Welcome to your cage.
Your kingdom.
Your place.
Mine.

Chapter Eight

OLIVIA

This is crazy.

This is batshit crazy.

My *own* office? There's no way I'm getting this lucky.

Then again, it's Warren Beaumont. I'm not *that* lucky. He's been staring daggers at me since I started, and now I *work* for him?

I follow him down the hall in silence. Every step feels unreal. My heart is pounding, loud enough I'm sure he can hear it, but he doesn't look back. Just walks with that confident, predatory calm.

Yet somehow not as scary or intimidating as he usually is.

He stops at the office down the hall to his. Opens the door and steps aside so I can walk in first.

I hesitate before stepping in and can't suppress the gasp that escapes my lips.

It's... *stunning.*

Spacious. Modern. Glass windows that let in soft natural light. A sleek white desk with gold hardware, not a fingerprint on it. Built-in shelves lined with organizational trays and fresh notebooks, like someone knew exactly what I'd need before I even asked.

There's even a small couch along the wall, pale cream, plush, and so pristine it feels like it belongs in a showroom. The kind of thing I wouldn't dare sit on without permission. Like I'd leave a mark.

I've never had anything like this.

Not even close.

I walk further in, eyes scanning the room, breath catching as I spot a glass water bottle waiting on the corner of the desk, just like the one I bring from home. And next to it, a tiny ceramic diffuser, mint green. *My favorite color.*

I pick it up. It's already filled. I twist it gently in my hands, like it might disappear if I'm not careful.

I lift it to my nose.

Eucalyptus.

How did he know?

I almost forget he's standing there until he speaks again.

"There's a pay increase," he says simply. "You'll see it in your next deposit."

I turn, still holding the diffuser in my hand. "I don't understand. Why me?"

His expression doesn't change. It's unreadable. Cold, maybe. Or too calm.

"I told you. I need someone I can trust."

"But you don't even know me," I whisper.

He steps into the room. Closer than he needs to be.

"I know enough."

I nod.

"Enjoy your space. Take a moment to get acclimated, and meet me in my office around lunch, we'll review your initial thoughts on the Parker file. Read what you can, see what jumps out. I'm not expecting a miracle by noon."

"Yes, Mister—Warren," I say before adding. "I'll do my best work."

He raises a brow. "That you will."

And just like that, he's gone.

The door clicks softly behind him.

I stand in the center of the office, still holding the diffuser like it might blow up in my hands if I believe too hard it's really mine.

This is real.

This is mine.

I let out a slow breath and turn in a circle, eyes sweeping over every detail. The matching note pads. The soft light spilling across the desk. The elegant little clock on the wall ticking softly like a countdown to something I can't name.

This is crazy.

Insane.

But also, it's kind of beautiful.

My throat tightens unexpectedly. I blink hard, swallow it down.

There's no time for tears. No space for weakness.

Set my purse down.

Slide into the chair behind the desk and open the folder he gave me.

Focus. Breathe. Work like your life depends on it.

If I'm going to survive this, I have to prove I belong here.

***

The knock on my office door startles me.

I glance at the time.

12:15.

Damn it. I'm late.

"Come in," I call, though my voice barely carries.

The door opens with a quiet click.

I start gathering up papers and open files from my desk as I rise.

"I'm so sorry, Mr. Beau—Warren. I must have lost track of time, but I sent you the—"

I look up.

There he is.

My new boss.

Icy eyes locked on mine.

A chill licks down my spine. I'm about to speak again when I notice the tray in his hands. His sleeves are rolled to the elbows, forearms flexing as he holds the tray like it's a peace offering.

But his stare tells me it isn't.

"I had lunch sent up," he says simply. "But you're *late.*"

I clear my throat as I tap the file against my palm. "I—"

"You tend to *always* be late, Ms. Baker."

My spine stiffens. "I was working, and I sent you—"

He doesn't let me finish.

"The files. I heard you the first time. You'll get better at efficiency." His tone cuts, final. Then he sets the tray down, so close his cologne drags through me like smoke.

"Sit."

My body obeys before my brain catches up. Heat rushes to my cheeks.

"Good." The word lands like a verdict.

What the fuck was that?

He takes the seat across from me, and I glance at the tray.

"I wasn't aware there'd be *actual* lunch," I murmur. "I thought—"

"There is now," he says, lifting the lid.

Grilled chicken, roasted vegetables, jasmine rice, simple, warm, fragrant. Plated like it belongs in a five-star suite.

"Eat."

I lift the fork, unsure why I'm even following his commands.

This man won't even let me finish a sentence.

I eat in silence, the only sound, the soft clink of silverware.

It could almost feel normal, if I didn't feel him watching me chew like he's grading my performance.

Is it how I hold the fork?

How fast I eat?

I can't even taste the food.

I put the fork down.

"Can we go over what I sent you now?"

His lips twitch, so slight, I wouldn't have noticed if I weren't watching him as closely as he's watching me.

"In a moment," he drawls, eyes scanning my face. "You're nervous."

"No," I lie.

He leans in, voice low. "Your hands are shaking."

I fold them in my lap. "You're watching too closely."

"I always watch closely," he says. "That's how I built this empire."

"I'm not an empire," I mutter, too quiet to stop myself.

His lips twitch again. "You could be, Olivia."

My name sounds like a secret when he says it.

Like a leash he's tightening.

"I don't like being scrutinized," I say, straightening in my seat. "You make me feel like I'm under a microscope."

His eyes narrow, deliberate. "Good. That's where you belong. Every move measured. Every flaw magnified. That's how I know who to *keep*... and who to *break*."

My stomach flips. I should stop there. But I don't.

"Then why?" I press, softer. "If I'm here because you *trust* me... why the microscope?"

His answer is quiet.

Cutting.

"Because you make me feel something I don't have a name for."

The words hollow me out. My pulse hammers. I should get up.

I should run.

But I don't.

"Work isn't about feelings," I say, forcing the words flat. "So whatever you think you're feeling—*swallow* it."

His jaw ticks once. Then, like a wall slamming down, his tone hardens.

"Let's go over what you sent."

I wait for a beat as he watches me. "You didn't read what I sent in the email?"

"I reviewed it. I didn't read it. I *expected* a presentation, punctuality *at lunch* so you could recap."

"Right, okay."

I nod, take a breath and reach for the folder even though my hands are still trembling slightly. I hand it to him, pointing to the page I marked in yellow.

"I cross-referenced the zoning archives with historic registries and noticed a clause that stood out," I say, trying to keep my voice steady.

He takes the file. Doesn't look at me. Just flips through it and skims.

I watch his eyes flick back and forth, cold, detached.

But I see it.

That flicker.

A pause.

I press on, "There's a line in the supplemental zoning clause; section 3.4b. It was quietly filed five years ago but never activated, likely overlooked. If it's tied to environmental reinvestment or community innovation, the city will fast-track variances."

He doesn't react. Just keeps flipping pages.

"I double-checked it with the property tax logs. The Parker Building qualifies. You could bypass most of the red tape if you file before the quarter closes."

I stop talking, realizing how fast I'm rambling.

He says nothing.

The silence thickens.

I shift in my chair.

"Sorry, I know that's not really enough. I just saw the discrepancy when I was going through the investor packet, and I thought it might help—"

"You thought?"

His voice cuts me off.

Quiet.

Sharp.

I blink. "Yes. I-I thought that even if you're not final on what you want to use the building for this could still fast track your renovation."

He finally looks up.

And I don't know what I expected, maybe annoyance or maybe dismissal, but what I get is something else entirely.

Stillness.

Tension.

Like a wire stretched too tight.

"You read *all* of this on your own?" he asks.

I nod slowly. "Yes."

"You made the connection. *Alone.*"

My pulse flutters. "I—well, yes. I've been in my office all day. I checked it a few times to be sure."

He closes the file. Smooth.

Careful.

Then he stands.

I brace, suddenly unsure. He paces behind the desk once, then stops at the window, looking out like the skyline holds answers.

A long moment passes.

Then, quietly, he says, "Do you know how many people I've had on that building?"

My throat goes dry. "No."

"Four attorneys. Two consultants. A city zoning liaison with thirty years' experience."

He turns back toward me.

"*None* of them found this."

I sit frozen.

A chill going down my spine.

"I've spent months waiting for something to shift," he murmurs, almost to himself. "A reason. An angle."

His eyes drag across me.

And then, lower. A little colder.

"And you—*you* walk in here in a thrift store skirt and shake the goddamn foundation."

I flinch and his stare hardens.

"Don't mistake me," he says. "That wasn't an insult. That was a *warning.* Because now that I know what you *can* do, Olivia... you don't get to hide anymore."

He places the file in front of me next to the tray of unfinished food, but I don't reach for it.

His eyes stay locked on mine, something unreadable behind them, something I'm only beginning to understand.

"Take the afternoon to draft a summary memo," he says. "Include the tax leverage, the variance opportunity, and the timeline."

I reach for the file, but as I move, I knock my purse on the edge of my desk and it falls.

A few things spill out; pen, lip gloss, my keychain.

I start to bend down, but Warren's already there.

He gathers the items with calm efficiency, slipping them back into my bag before handing it over.

"Careful," he murmurs.

"Thanks," I say quickly, flustered but already too focused on the win still buzzing in my blood.

As he moves toward the door, I set my purse straight and gather the file, my fingers shaking again, but not from nerves this time.

From adrenaline.

From power.

I'd just uncovered something *massive.*

And whatever it means to him...

I did it.

I *found* it.

Pride swells in my chest.

He opens the door, pauses.

Doesn't look back when he says:

"Good work, Ms. Baker."

The door clicks shut behind him.

I exhale now that the air is breathable again.

Warren is no Wesley, but *I can do this.*

Chapter Nine

WAR

I flip Olivia's key over in my hand, the metal warm from my pocket.

Small. *Ordinary.*

But it opens *everything.*

She'll go home tonight and have no idea I've already been inside her world. Her kitchen. Her bed.

Every secret she thought she could keep in that quiet little apartment.

The thought sends a dark satisfaction crawling through me.

My phone vibrates against the desk.

The name flashes across the screen.

Declan Brooks.

Seattle's golden boy.

New money. Self-made.

Smug as hell.

I let it ring twice.

Make him wait.

Then I answer.

"Brooks."

"Beaumont."

"What do you want?" My tone stays flat. Cold.

"I see you're still a pretentious prick," he says, almost amused.

"And you're still trash that learned how to accessorize," I fire back without hesitation.

A low exhale hums through the line. Not laughter. Not anger. Just that flicker of temper I was hunting for.

"What do you want?" I repeat, leaning back in my chair, key turning slow between my fingers.

"I need one of your men. For business."

I laugh once, quiet and sharp. "Let me guess—you want me to hand over one of my men so you can bleed him dry for intel and send him back slower than you found him."

"If I wanted your intel, I'd already have it," he replies. Smooth. Controlled. "It's not exactly locked behind steel. Half the women in your orbit would sell it for a bottle of champagne and a photo op."

My jaw tightens.

"Wrong assumption," I say coolly. "You think I'd ever trust a woman with anything that matters?"

"No," he replies evenly. "I think you don't trust anyone. That's the difference between us."

Silence stretches long. A standoff. Neither of us flinches.

We're both men used to rooms stilling when we enter them. Both men who don't blink first.

I tap the key against the desk, slow and deliberate.

Broderick. Loyal to a fault. Always orbiting where he doesn't belong.

Always too close to things—*and people,* that don't belong to him.

"Actually," I say finally, "I might have someone for you. But what's in it for me?"

"I'll owe you," Brooks says simply. "You'll have my word."

His word. The one thing even I can admit he guards like gold.

I like the sound of it.

"Fine. You can have Broderick."

There's a sharp laugh on the other end. "The puppy?"

"One and the same," I say dryly. "Still up my ass. Still eager to please. If you want him, he'll help you, but don't expect trade secrets. He's as loyal as the dog you think he is."

"Fine by me. Thank you," Brooks says, his voice clean and easy. Like this is just business.

Thank you?

How soft.

Weak.

Here I thought, we were two sides of the same coin.

"Then we're done here."

I end the call.

The silence after tastes sweeter than the deal.

Broderick will be out of my hair. Brooks will owe me.

And Olivia Baker's life is in between my fingers in the form of a single stolen key.

***

The lock clicks too easily.

Her lock.

Her door.

I step inside Olivia Baker's apartment, shutting the door behind me with a soft click.

It smells like her. Not just her perfume, but her skin.

Maybe her soap.

A trace of flowers cling to the air, sweet but thin, like it's trying too hard to be something it isn't.

I move slowly, deliberately, letting my eyes adjust to her space.

One-bedroom. Secondhand couch sagging in the middle. A throw blanket folded neatly on the back, worn at the edges.

Books stacked on the coffee table, spines cracked, pages dog-eared. All lived in.

All *ordinary.*

I cross down the hall into her bedroom and open the closet.

A small row of blouses in muted colors. Black, navy, pale blue. Cheap polyester that will pull at the seams after a dozen washes. A couple skirts that would wrinkle if you so much as breathed on them. Shoes lined up in pairs, scuffed at the toes, worn down at the heel.

Poorly made.

Cheap.

She needs better.

Better clothes. Better shoes. *Better everything.*

I slide open the small dresser drawer, sift through folded fabric. Cotton underwear, plain bras, nothing meant to be seen.

Nothing meant for me.

That will change.

On her vanity, I find it. A bottle of perfume. The kind that comes from a plastic blister pack in the drugstore aisle, shaped like an imitation of the real thing.

One spray and it's gone in an hour.

I lift it, roll it between my fingers. Hold it to the light like it's a joke.

She thinks this is luxury.

She has no idea what *real* luxury smells like.

I'll get her the original.

She needs it.

She'll smell like silk and smoke before I'm done with her.

I set the bottle back down exactly where it was, then take another slow look around.

The cheap linens on her bed. The dented nightstand. The empty picture frames, like she bought them on clearance and never got around to filling them.

This place is a cage, and she doesn't even see the bars.

I imagine filling it with what she should have. A proper bed. Furniture that doesn't creak. Clothes that don't come off the rack at discount stores. Silk instead of cotton. Glass instead of plastic.

My vines are already in the cracks, winding through her life, bleeding like smoke into her walls.

She won't even notice until it's too late.

I turn back toward the nightstand—and freeze.

A picture frame. The cheap kind, metal edging slightly bent. But it isn't empty.

It's her. Younger. Cap and gown. Smiling. Flanked by three men who all carry the same stubborn eyes. Brothers, I assume. Arms looped around her shoulders, standing too close like they'd fight the world to protect her.

Something sharp twists in my chest.

Family.

Her family.

I stare at it too long, longer than I mean to, before setting it face-down.

I breathe once, steady, and step back. The key twirls in my hand as I leave the apartment, locking it behind me.

A voice breaks the quiet.

"War?"

Broderick.

Of course.

He's just stepping out of his own apartment, brows furrowing when he spots me standing outside Olivia's door.

"There you are," I say smoothly, slipping the key back into my pocket. "You left at lunch."

Brody blinks, caught off guard. "Yeah, since you had lunch with Liv, I figured I'd go out for a bit."

Liv.

The way he says it makes my jaw tighten.

I nod once, cutting him off before he can say anything else. "Good. Because I need you to leave on assignment. Early."

His brows lift. "For California?" His voice is full of barely-contained excitement.

I let a slow smile tug at my mouth.

"No," I say, savoring the moment. "Seattle."

The look of confusion on his face is better than any victory won.

Chapter Ten

OLIVIA

By the time I get home, the pride I felt earlier is gone, replaced with the tight, crawling kind of panic that starts in your chest and sinks down your spine.

My rent extension is overdue.

The elevator dings, and I step inside, scrolling through my apps before I even breathe.

If I can just pay it tonight, before the late fee triggers again, maybe I'll still have enough to send something to Mama. Even a little.

The doors slide open on my floor and I nearly slam into Brody.

"Hey, Liv," he says, flashing that tired but easy smile of his.

It takes me a second to notice the sleek black roller bag in his hand, a travel tag flapping against the side.

I nod toward it. "You going somewhere?"

He shifts the handle up. "Yeah. Seattle. War's orders."

My brows knit. "Seattle? I thought it was California. And that wasn't for another month."

"Yeah, well." He shrugs, too casual. "He changed his mind. Wants me to help an associate of his first, then I'll head off to Cali."

I pause. "You okay with that?"

Another shrug. Lighter this time, like he's brushing it off. "Doesn't matter if I am, right?"

There's a flicker of something behind his eyes, resentment, maybe. But he covers it with a grin. "Wish me luck."

"Good luck," I say softly. "And... safe trip."

"Thanks, Liv."

He gives me a wink before stepping into the elevator.

I turn toward my door, digging for my keys, pulse still unsettled.

My fingers fumble through my purse until I find them, sitting in the front pocket.

I freeze.

I never put them there.

A chill licks down my spine, but I shove it off, telling myself I must have been distracted this morning. Still, my hand trembles as I slide the key into the lock.

Inside, the silence hits like a wall.

I drop my purse on the counter, toss the keys next to it, and collapse onto the couch, pulling up the rent app again.

Loading...

System currently under maintenance. Please try again later.

I blink. Tap it again.

Same screen.

What the hell? Since when do leasing apps go down for maintenance?

Annoyed, I open my contacts and hit *Mama.*

She answers on the second ring, her voice soft and warm. "Hey, Liv Bug."

"Hey, Mama," I exhale, rubbing my temple. "Just checking in. Everything okay, how's the inn?"

She pauses, like she's trying to decide how much truth to give me.

"We scraped together enough to pay the quarter," she finally says. "But next one... I don't know, sweetheart. We'll do what we can."

I close my eyes. "I got a raise," I say quickly. "A small one, but it'll help. I'll send some money this week."

Her voice softens. "Livvy, no. You've done more than enough."

"You're my family, mom. Getting money for the inn... it's the whole reason I'm here."

"I'd rather have *you* than your money," she says gently. "You know that, right?"

My heart stutters.

I stare at the apartment, the small chrome kitchen, the white-washed walls, the fancy office shoes still sitting by the door. It all feels borrowed.

Like none of it really belongs to me.

"I know," I whisper. "I just... I'm trying."

"I know you are," she says. Then I hear my brother Dean's voice in the background, loud and teasing.

"Tell her I saved the last of the cobbler!" he shouts. "But only if she comes home and eats it herself."

A small laugh escapes me. "He's still holding me hostage over dessert?"

"He's still got that sweet tooth, that's for sure."

I sigh, my heart ebbing. "I've gotta go. I'll call you later, okay?"

"Love you, Liv Bug."

"Love you too."

I end the call and sink back against the couch, phone limp in my hand.

The app still won't open.

But the pit in my stomach already has.

Something isn't right.

I push myself off the couch, exhaustion dragging at my bones.

Maybe a shower. Maybe just pajamas and lights out.

In my bedroom, I pause.

Something feels... *off.*

The faintest trace of scent lingers in the air, smoky, expensive, masculine.

But it's *familiar.*

My pulse spikes.

Warren.

I shake my head. No. That's insane.

I tug at my blouse and sniff. It's probably his cologne lingering to my clothes.

I cross to the nightstand to plug in my phone and freeze again. The picture frame, my brothers, arms slung over my shoulders at my graduation, lies face down.

I don't remember knocking it over.

A chill crawls up my spine.

I right the frame carefully, staring at our frozen smiles, before forcing a breath past the lump in my throat. "You're losing it, Olivia," I mutter under my breath. *"Losing it."*

I move quickly after that, shed my clothes, shower, slip into cotton pajamas, brush my teeth with shaky hands. The routines help.

Anchor me.

By the time I crawl into bed, I tell myself I'm just overtired. Stressed. That my imagination is playing tricks on me.

Still... the expensive scent clings to the room.

And I leave the lamp on when I finally close my eyes.

***

Warren isn't here yet. Which is... *odd.*

I glance at the clock on my monitor.

8 A.M. Sharp.

For a man who rules this building like a kingdom, his absence feels wrong.

His door stays closed. My inbox pings with a single email.

No greeting. No signature. Just a bulleted list of tasks.

I roll my eyes, but dive in. It's easier to breathe without his stare burning through me.

Easier to focus when I'm not hyper-aware of every flick of his attention.

By the time the clock slides past noon, I've almost forgotten the nerves that usually strangle me. The door opens.

He strides in, silent, sure, carrying a small, sleek black box.

Not files. Not a folder. *A box.*

He sets it on my desk. No explanation. No movement. Just presence. Heavy with intent.

I hesitate. My fingers twitch toward it, then still.

His voice cuts through the air. Low. Calm. Absolute.

"You may open it."

I swallow and lift the lid.

Perfume. *Name-brand.*

The real version of the imitation I've worn for years. My favorite scent, but one I could never afford.

My pulse stutters. "Why... why would you buy this for me?"

He doesn't smile. Doesn't soften. His eyes pin me, sharp and unrelenting.

"Appreciation. For what you found yesterday."

The zoning loophole. The one that made him go still for one impossible second.

"Oh," I whisper. My fingers curl around the cool glass, but it feels heavier than perfume should. Loaded. Like a test I haven't studied for.

"Use it," he says. Not a suggestion. Not even a gift. A command.

My head nods before I can think. "Okay."

Silence stretches. His eyes drag over me, unblinking.

My throat works. "Oh—you mean... now?"

He doesn't answer. Just waits.

Heat floods my cheeks as I pull the cap free, misting my throat. The scent clings instantly; expensive, consuming, undeniably real.

I look back up at him, startled by how intimate it feels.

His lips lift, barely there. Not quite a smile. Something darker. "Good."

He stays standing. Watching me.

And for a moment, I don't know what to do with my hands. My face. My breath.

So I look down.

"Your memo," he says. "The one I asked for."

My eyes flick back up. "I emailed—"

The look he gives me stops the words in my throat.

No softness. Just a slow blink.

I move quick, like a child caught doing something wrong. Fumble open the drawer, grab the printout, and slide it across my desk.

He doesn't sit. Doesn't even glance at the chair across from me.

Just flips the first page open, scans it once, and places it flat again. Closer to me.

"Summarize."

The word lands hard. No lift, no question mark. Just expectation.

"Now?" I ask before I can stop myself.

His jaw moves once. That's all it takes.

I swallow. "Section 3.4b is a dormant clause filed five years ago, it allows a historic-use exemption for the Parker Building. If it's filed under a community reinvestment incentive before the quarter closes, the city will fast-track all variances. I also—"

I stop.

Because he's moving.

Behind me.

His cologne hits first, dark spice and smoke and something ruinously expensive.

Then the warmth of his body.

Then his hand, palm resting on the back of my chair, fingers brushing the fabric right behind my neck.

I stop breathing.

"Keep going," he says.

I force the words out. "I also highlighted a tax deferment opportunity that correlates with the variance if the filing is backdated—"

"Not bad," he murmurs, closer now. I feel it in the shell of my ear. "But not good enough."

He reaches forward. Nudges closer to my keyboard.

"Open your draft," he says.

I do.

The cursor blinks at the conclusion. My hands hover.

"There," he says, and his finger brushes the screen. "You hedge. *'Possibility.' 'Potentially.'* Words for people who apologize when they speak."

I freeze.

"Delete them," he commands.

My chest tightens, I want to push back. To ask why it matters.

But instead... I press delete.

"Better," he says.

He doesn't step away.

His other hand settles, barely, on the back of my chair again. Not touching me. Not quite. But I feel it anyway. Heat pooling low in my belly, tight and wrong and... *addictive.*

"Rewrite the closing," he says, his voice low. "Take out the last sentence. Make the second the last. Add a timestamp."

I type.

He watches.

I feel his breath.

The heat of his body.

His scent consuming me.

I feel his *restraint*.

And I'm unraveling.

Finally, he steps back.

I exhale like I've been holding it in for hours.

"Confidence sells," he says, eyes still on my screen. "Don't forget it."

I finish adjusting the language.

Just enough edge. Just enough polish.

His breath is close behind me, silent, but heavy. *Watching*.

When I click save, print. I wait.

For his approval. For his silence.

I don't know which will be worse.

He doesn't speak right away. Just reaches past me, brushing the edge of my chair as he takes the printed memo from the tray.

Reads it in two heartbeats.

Then:

"Good work."

I take a breath, relieved.

But before I can thank him, his voice cuts again—cool, decisive.

"Let's get lunch."

Chapter Eleven

WAR

The way her lips close around the fork, slow and soft, like she's savoring every bite, makes my blood thrum with heat.

In want.

I want to wreck something.

Tear this place down to give her more.

The food.

The view.

The kind of pleasure that makes her moan just like that, eyes fluttering shut, lips parted, completely unaware of what she's doing to me.

She sits across from me in a restaurant that costs more than her entire apartment building, and somehow she's still trying to disappear. Shoulders tucked. Hands folded. Legs crossed tight under the table like she's afraid to take up space.

And all I want is to give her the whole fucking room.

Her fork clinks against the plate again as she slices a piece of the sea bass. Every move careful. Quiet. *Practiced.*

A woman who was taught to behave.

A woman, that a man like me, was taught to control.

I sip my wine, watching her as she chews. She's still wearing that cheap foundation, the kind that tries to mask what shouldn't be hidden. I can see the freckles underneath. Just a trace. The kind most women laser off.

She has no idea how pretty she is.

No idea how her lips look when she bites them between thoughts.

How her brow furrows when she reads something dense, like she's trying to conquer it by force of will.

No idea how the picture on her nightstand, the graduation one, wrecked me for a full thirty seconds.

"You have siblings?" I ask, too abruptly.

Her eyes meet mine and she brightens like a goddamn sunrise. "Three brothers," she says, smiling. "Logan, Chase, and Dean. Logan's the oldest. He's basically my second dad. Chase is the town heartbreaker who also makes everybody laugh. And Dean's the baby, well *I'm* the baby, but he's the youngest of the boys, thinks he runs the place."

I don't smile.

I just watch her smile.

That joy doesn't belong in this place. It's too clean. Too soft. Too good for the uptight swank and the pressed shirts that say status instead of soul.

But I like it here now.

Because *she's* here.

"They all stayed back home?" I ask, voice smooth.

"Yeah. We grew up in a small town. My parents run an inn. They all help out with maintenance, stuff like that. Chase is in renovation, but does freelance," she shrugs, "whatever keeps the lights on."

She says it like it's nothing. Like it doesn't cost her something every day to be so far from them.

I nod once. "Sounds like a tight knit family."

"We are." She sips her water. "Sometimes too tight. Dean used to go through my phone just to make sure I wasn't talking to anyone the family wouldn't approve of."

I almost smile at that.

Almost.

But the thought of her texting some college boy with baby hands and soft thoughts makes my knuckles itch.

I glance at her plate. "Eat. Don't let that get cold."

"Are you *always* this demanding?" Her brow twitches, the corner of her mouth pulling up like she's deciding whether I'm serious or just an asshole.

"Yes."

She smirks, but takes another bite. When she swallows, she wipes delicately at her lips with the napkin. Still trying to be so fucking poised.

"There's a gala next Friday," I say.

She looks up, surprised. "Like... tuxedos and ballgowns kind of gala?" she asks, her voice light, but I catch the flicker of nerves behind it.

"Yes."

She tilts her head. "You often go to things like that?"

I lift a brow. "You don't think I own a tux?"

"I think you'd wear one like it offended you."

Fair.

Her eyes sparkle with the tease, and suddenly I want to give her every invitation I've ever turned down. Just to see what she'd wear. Just to see how she'd look under chandeliers and too much money and the greedy stares of men who'd never deserve her.

"You're not wrong," I say slowly. "But this one's different. It's at the Halston Estate. Fundraising for the new waterfront development. I'm expected to attend."

She nods, then glances up. "Who are you bringing?"

A question laced with curiosity, *not* jealousy.

Which should settle me.

But it doesn't.

It coils tight, something hungry twisting behind my ribs, ugly and possessive.

"No one."

Her brow lifts. "That's strange. Usually you have a model. Or some actress. I've seen in the tab—"

She freezes, eyes widening. Her fingers tense around her napkin, twisting the edge like she's trying to undo the words.

"Not that I've… read about you, Mister—Warren. I-I'm sorry."

I blink once.

Then let it settle.

The implication.

She *watches.*

She reads.

Maybe not religiously.

Maybe not always.

But enough.

Enough to know who I'm *usually* seen with.

Enough to notice that this time, I won't be seen with anyone at all.

Not unless I change that.

Not unless I want her there.

My mouth curves, slow and deliberate.

Dangerous.

Inviting.

She won't know which until it's too late.

"Didn't peg you as the tabloid type, Ms. Baker."

She flushes deeper. "I'm not. I mean, I don't, it just popped up in a headline once, when I was—"

"Researching the company?"

"Yes," she blurts, too fast.

I lean back in my chair, let the silence do the rest.

Because now I know.

She sees me.

And I haven't decided yet if that makes her lucky…

or damned.

***

Two weeks with Olivia Baker is intoxicating.

Not in the way champagne fizzes in your blood.

No. She seeps under the skin like venom

Sweet. Subtle. Slow.

By the time you feel the burn, you're already addicted.

It starts in the chest, tight and aching. Then spreads.

She doesn't even realize it, how she ruins my concentration just by breathing in my proximity.

Today, I don't need her for much.

But I want her close.

So I make something up.

"Olivia."

She looks up from her desk, hair tied back, pen between her fingers, eyes too bright for this early in the morning.

There's a smudge of ink on her knuckle. I want to wipe it off with my thumb. *Or my mouth.*

"Come to my office."

She blinks. "A new task?"

"Cross-check these vendor invoices," I say, dropping a thick folder on her desk. "I want to know who's bleeding me dry."

"You're being bled dry?" she says, brows lifting. "With *your* net worth?"

My gaze sharpens. My voice drops.

"Researching me again, Olivia?"

I want to see how far she'll go. How deep she's already dug.

She doesn't flinch. Doesn't blush.

She just smiles, soft, smug, *wicked.*

"No. I just do my job. If I'm going to keep this place afloat, I have to know how much water's in the boat, right?"

She watches me a beat longer than necessary, then closes her laptop and begins gathering her things, notebook, phone. Her movements are smooth, efficient, but I still see it. The awareness. The way she straightens her spine just a touch. The way she smooths her skirt before standing.

She knows what walking into my office means: *Get ready to work.*

Good girl.

She follows me down the hall without another word. Heels tapping a beat I already know by heart.

She walks like a song I've memorized. One only I get to hear.

Once inside, I don't move toward my desk.

She goes to sit in the chair across like always.

Instead, I pull my chair back and nod toward it. "Sit."

Her brows lift. "In *your* chair?"

"I have a task for you," I say mildly. "You'll need the monitor."

She hesitates, but only for a second.

Then she rounds the desk and sits.

And fuck if it doesn't do something to me, a twist low in my gut, a possessive thrum in my chest.

Seeing her there, where no one else is *ever* allowed to be. My space. My command post. And she just perches like she *belongs.*

I move behind her, standing close enough to feel the heat off her skin. I don't speak.

I watch.

She moves the mouse. Eyes flicking to the monitor as it flashes on.

A few loose strands of hair fall down her neck. I lean in slightly, breathing in the scent of the perfume I bought her.

She's wearing it.

Like my own personal brand.

Every breath she takes marks her as *mine.*

Warm. Soft. Completely at odds with the steel in her spine.

I count seven freckles on her left cheek.

Eight on her nose.

Three more, barely there, dusted across her collarbone where her blouse dips just slightly.

She doesn't know how seen she is right now.

Her hands move to the keyboard.

Then pause.

"Your password?" she asks, glancing up over her shoulder.

I don't move.

I don't blink.

I just give it to her.

"Parker building, no space, capital P."

She blinks. "Seriously?"

"Type it in," I say simply.

A longer hesitation this time. But she does it.

My password.

My password.

No one has ever had that. Not even my brothers. *Not anyone.*

It's a small thing. A digital key.

But it's hers now.

I watch her fingers move across the keys. Controlled. Light. Sure.

Dangerous.

She's so fucking dangerous.

And she doesn't even know it.

When the desktop loads, she clicks open the folder and starts scanning. She reads quickly; eyes sharp, lips slightly parted as she focuses.

I lean in closer, placing one hand on the back of the chair beside her shoulder.

She doesn't flinch.

She just leans slightly toward the monitor, instinctively adjusting—making space for *me*.

Obedient.

It's not submission.

Not yet.

But it will be.

"I want notes on any discrepancies by end of day," I say, voice low.

She nods without looking up. "Understood."

God, I *like* her.

Too much.

Enough that it's starting to feel like a problem.

She doesn't ask questions. She doesn't second-guess. She doesn't waste time trying to impress me. She just *works.*

And yet somehow, she's the most impressive person I've met in years.

Her phone buzzes once on the desk, screen lighting up.

She hesitates, but doesn't check it.

A single second of doubt. Then discipline.

I smirk.

"Something important?"

"No."

"Then ignore it," I murmur.

She does.

Just like that.

A woman who *listens* when I say no. Who obeys without asking why.

Fuck.

Chapter Twelve

WAR

S he walks in at exactly 8:00 a.m.

Not a second late.

Not a breath behind.

I feel it like clockwork. Like something locking into place.

Good girl.

Always so fucking obedient, without even realizing it.

I'm already standing by the window in my office, pretending to read the same zoning memo I've skimmed three times. But I'm not looking at the paper. Not even pretending, really.

I'm watching her.

Black pencil skirt. Pale blue blouse. Hair pinned back in that loose way that always falls by nine. I watch it fall every morning. Like a promise unraveling. She walks with her head slightly lowered, shoulders squared, like she's holding herself together by sheer will.

That quiet, breakable strength wrecks me so much that I've studied her like scripture.

It makes her so beautiful.

How honest.

She crosses the floor, heels clicking on the marble, and disappears into her office.

I wait.

Ten seconds.

Fifteen.

Then I grab the coffee I got for her this morning and I follow.

I stop at her door. She doesn't hear me. Her back is to me as she sets her bag down, adjusts the monitor, tugs the hem of her blouse like it's not sitting right.

She's always fussing with her clothes, like she hasn't realized yet that they fit her like temptation.

She turns; and startles.

"Oh—Warren." Her breath catches. "Good morning."

Not Mr. Beaumont.

That matters.

I hold out the coffee. Her favorite. Half sweet cream, two pumps hazelnut, no foam. The lid already turned toward her so the mouth opening faces front.

She takes it with both hands, blinking up at me.

"Thank you," she says softly, fingers brushing mine as she grips the cup. "I wasn't expecting..."

She trails off when she sees I'm still watching her.

I don't speak.

I just wait.

Her lips part, then close again. Then finally, eyes still on mine, she lifts the cup to her mouth and takes a sip.

Obedience.

No command.

Just instinct.

Reflex.

Everything in me clenches.

Good *fucking* girl.

"You'll be in my office at noon," I say, voice low, even.

Her brows lift slightly. "Yes, for the... lunch?"

I nod once.

"Yes, Olivia," I confirm. "Lunch."

Her name tastes like a promise I haven't made yet.

I turn and walk away before I let myself say what I really want.

Before I *do* what I really want.

She followed without thinking today.

She came in on time.

She called me by name.

She took the sip.

She's *learning.*

And I'm losing my goddamn mind.

I make it back to my office and immediately pull up the feed.

It flickers to life, clear picture, as it should be. Wesley's newest piece of work.

There she is.

At her desk, shoulders tight with focus, lips pursed in that way she does when she's trying to act unfazed. She sips the coffee I brought her, slow like it's some casual habit, not a command she followed without realizing.

My jaw ticks.

She doesn't know what she just told me about herself. What she just *gave* me.

A map. A rhythm. A window.

I watch her drag her fingers down the side of the cup. Thumb tapping once. Then twice. Nervous energy. A tell.

She has no idea I'm watching, and yet still—she's *performing.* Still trying to be good, *do* good work.

For me.

I lean back in my chair, one elbow hooked over the armrest, the other hand curled tight around my coffee. I don't taste it. Don't care. Not when I'm locked on her.

She shifts in her seat. Her skirt rides just slightly higher.

I shouldn't notice.

But I do.

Fuck, I notice everything about her.

The way she crosses her legs, ankles tight, as if modesty matters when I've already seen her in my head a dozen ways, moaning my name. Not Mr. Beaumont. Not Warren. Just *War*—like a prayer. Like a curse.

She pulls out her pen and starts scribbling in the margins of a printout.

Still using the cheap one.

I already ordered her the set she deserves.

Black lacquer, gold trim. Engraved.

Not because she needs it.

Because she will look fucking beautiful holding power in her hand and still not knowing it's hers.

Yet.

I zoom the feed closer.

There.

9 on the dot.

A single loose strand of hair falls from that twisted knot she tries to pin back every morning. It brushes her cheek. She exhales. Doesn't fix it.

I watch her breathe.

Watch her fucking breathe.

And I swear to God, I could sit here all day watching the way her chest rises and falls, soft and slow, like she doesn't know she's being seen. Touched. Undressed.

Owned.

I shift in my seat, suddenly too hard, too tense, too fucking close to unraveling from a single glance at a woman who still doesn't know she already belongs to me.

But soon.. she'll know and once she does, there's no going back.

My office phone buzzes, I answer swiftly.

"Your package has arrived, sir."

I don't ask which one.

"Send it to Olivia Baker's office."

A pause. "Her... office?"

"Did I stutter?"

"No, sir."

I end the call and lean back in my chair, attention back on the feed.

My sweet, focused Olivia, reading something intently, bottom lip caught between her teeth. If she keeps doing that, I'll forget the whole plan and drag her in here now.

Her hair's completely unraveled now. The collar of her blouse is slightly crooked. Still hasn't noticed.

Then the knock comes to her door, her head lifts.

Cara, the first floor receptionist, enters the frame, holding the box with both hands. Matte black, ribboned, no label. Elegant. Ominous.

Olivia stands slowly.

Brows knit.

Confusion blooming.

She takes it.

Thanks her.

Sets it down on her desk like it might explode.

She stares at it for a beat. Then finally pulls the ribbon loose and opens the lid.

She freezes.

I zoom in slightly. Just enough to catch the flicker of shock on her face. Of disbelief.

Inside:

A custom-fitted gown. Deep emerald green. Structured stretch crepe, a fabric made to flatter every curve, hugging her waist and hips like a second skin, without clinging in the places she tries to hide. Sleek. Sculpted. Regal.

Not silk.

Not soft.

Powerful.

Exactly how she'll look standing beside me tonight.

The note is simple, written in my own hand.

I want her to recognize it. To feel the shift. From assistant… to *chosen.*

You're invited.

Tonight. 8PM.

I'll pick you up

– W.

Her fingers tighten on the card.

Then she sits down.

Immediately stands back up.

Paces.

Pauses.

Moves toward the door, then stops short and turns around.

She stares at the dress again.

Goes to pick up her phone.

Puts it down.

Stares at it again.

Closes the lid.

Carries the box to the small couch in her office and sets it there like she needs distance.

Then she just sits at her desk.

Still.

Like she's trying to regulate her heartbeat. Trying to think.

I smile.

I love watching her unravel.

Quietly. Beautifully. One thread at a time.

Moments later, she stands abruptly and disappears from the camera.

I already know she's on her way and I know what she's going to say.

I already know she'll try to object, to decline, to remind me I never asked.

But I didn't ask.

I don't *have* to.

She's already wearing the scent I chose.

She's already sipping the coffee I handed her.

She's already mine.

A knock comes sharp at my door.

Right on cue.

Chapter Thirteen

OLIVIA

That dress is worth more than every piece of clothing I own. *Combined.*

He can't just buy me something like that.

Invite me to the gala? Fine.

But a designer gown tailored to my measurements, hand-delivered to my office in a matte black box?

No.

That crosses a line.

I stop in front of his office door, hand raised to knock, and hesitate.

I *want* to go. God, I do.

A part of me wants to wear that dress. To be seen like that.

And I don't have anything close to good enough for an event like this.

But still. This feels... *dangerous.*

Why shouldn't I accept it? It's just a gift. Right?

Except it doesn't feel like a gift. It feels like something else.

A claim. A collar made of crepe and emerald.

And maybe I *want* to wear it. That's the problem.

"Damn it," I mutter under my breath, then knock.

"Come in."

I twist the handle and step inside.

"Warren, the dress—"

"Not the right color?" he asks without looking up from his desk.

"What? No, I—"

"I thought emerald would suit your complexion. And your eyes."

I blink. "My eyes are brown."

"When the light hits them," he says, finally meeting my gaze, "they flicker green."

My mouth goes dry.

He leans back in his chair like this is nothing. Like he didn't just casually admit to noticing the microscopic variations in the pigment of my irises.

"If you'd prefer royal purple, say the word," he adds. "Or red. Brunettes always look stunning in red."

Brunettes. Not me.

Not Olivia.

Just a hair color. An accessory.

Arm candy.

I've been here before.

Not with designer gowns or black boxes or cryptic invitations.

But with men *like him.*

Men who smile and flirt and see you as something soft to touch. Something nice to look at.

Something to fuck once, maybe twice, before moving on to the next thing that shines.

That dress—

That dress doesn't say you're invited.

It says you've been chosen.

And not for the gala.

My chest tightens.

Because that's what I've let myself be before, isn't it?

A one-night stand.

A secret worth unwrapping in the dark, but never bringing into the light.

A temporary indulgence.

A beautiful body with no permanence attached.

I clench my jaw.

I am *not* arm candy.

I am *not* a pretty distraction.

I am *not* a body worth dressing up just to be discarded.

"I'm not going to sleep with you," I blurt.

The words fall sharp and clumsy into the space between us.

Warren's brows rise, slow and deliberate, like I've just said something wildly amusing.

"I didn't ask to sleep with you, Ms. Baker."

Ms. Baker.

Sharp. Formal. Like a boundary drawn in ink.

Not Olivia.

My stomach twists.

That's when it hits me.

He's Warren *Beaumont.*

The man who's rumored to sleep with whoever he *wants, whenever* he wants.

The man who always has someone on his arm, but never twice.

The man I assumed this was about.

But this gala is a professional event.

Maybe this *was* professional.

An invitation, not an implication.

And I just walked in here, dripping with my own damage, and handed him a rejection he didn't earn.

Because men like him don't *need* to ask. And women like me don't get invited.

I wince internally.

God. I'm fucking this up.

My cheeks flush. Hard.

"I-I'm so sorry," I start, shaking my head. "That wasn't fair. I shouldn't have assumed—"

He doesn't move.

Just sits there, one arm draped casually over the armrest of his chair, the other resting against his chin like he's considering something.

He's looking at me.

Right at me.

Through me.

Like he sees through the apology, through the panic, straight into whatever cracked part of me expected the worst.

"It's fine," he says finally, voice low and even. "If you don't want to go, you don't have to. It's not a job requirement."

I blink.

No pressure. No guilt.

Just an open exit door.

But I don't want to walk through it.

"No," I say quickly, shaking my head. "No, I *do* want to go. I just... it's tonight and I don't even have time to get my—"

"Hair and makeup are being handled," he interrupts, still watching me like he's memorizing every twitch of my mouth.

"They'll arrive at your apartment by five."

I blink at him. "You...what?"

"My driver will take you home at four," he continues like he's listing facts, not orchestrating every second of my day. "I'll pick you up at eight."

I open my mouth, maybe to protest, maybe to thank him, but nothing comes out.

He lifts one hand. Waves it vaguely toward the door.

Dismissive. Effortless.

But somehow... not unkind.

And for some reason, I obey.

I turn.

I leave.

The door clicks shut behind me and I'm still holding the weight of his words in my hands like something breakable.

He didn't ask.

He *arranged.*

And I let him.

God, what is happening to me?

And why does it feel like falling?

***

The ride is smooth and this is by far the fanciest car I've ever been in.

I don't even know what kind of vehicle it is. It's sleek. Black. The interior smells like leather and something expensive I can't name. The driver calls me "Ms. Baker" and opens the door for me like I'm royalty. No conversation. No music. Just polished silence and tinted glass.

The moment I step inside my apartment, I drop my bag, and immediately hop in the shower, not ten seconds after I'm done, towel wrapped around me, a knock comes.

"Hair and makeup," a cheerful voice calls from the other side.

I open the door to find a woman who looks like she belongs on the cover of a beauty magazine, thin, early thirties, glowing skin, warm smile.

"I'm Isabella," she says, breezing in with a massive case and zero hesitation. "Mr. Beaumont sent me."

I nod and move out of her way.

"I haven't even had time to put on the dress yet—"

Isabella spots the box on the couch and waves me toward it.

"Good thing you didn't try it on alone. Those dresses are a nightmare to wrestle into solo."

She sets her cases down on my kitchen island like she owns the place, then turns back to me, handing over a sleek black box tied with a satin ribbon.

"This is for you. Also from him."

I blink, caught off guard. "The makeup?"

"Nope. This is the first part to the dress." She gestures to the box. "He said you should change into this first, before we do the dress."

I stare at her. "First part?"

She nods expectantly.

My hand tightens around the ribbon of the box.

"You wanna change out here, or in your room?" she asks gently.

I hesitate.

She's kind. Pretty. Bubbly.

Still... a stranger.

"I'll go to my room," I murmur.

"Of course, take your time," she says easily, turning her attention to unpacking a tray of lipsticks like this is totally normal.

I walk slowly to my room, fingers trembling slightly as I untie the ribbon.

When I lift the lid, my breath catches, and I almost drop the box.

Inside: black lace.

Soft. Expensive.

Lingerie.

Not just any lingerie. *My size.*

Perfectly cut for curves.

No tags. No receipt. No notes.

Just... picked out for me.

By my boss.

Heat floods my face.

I want the ground to swallow me whole.

I stand there, frozen, the lace trembling in my hands.

He bought me lingerie.

Not the way I thought. Not just polite invitations and emerald dresses.

He knew my size.

He's thought about this.

About *Me.*

He said he didn't ask to sleep with me. He didn't say he didn't *want* to.

No.

I scoff at myself. Why would he want me? I've seen the women on his arm, sleek, flawless, not... this.

I should stop this. I should call and say this has gone too far.

Breathe.

I take a deep breath.

Toss my towel on the bed

And I slip on the lingerie.

It fits like a glove. Silky against my skin, hugging every soft place I try to hide. I glance at myself in the mirror and have to look away before I fully absorb what I see.

A knock on the door pulls me back.

"Ready for the dress?" Isabella calls.

I look toward my towel and back at myself in the mirror. No point in hiding from her. "Come in."

She enters, holding the gown carefully.

I try not to look her in the eyes, but she doesn't even blink.

Professional. Efficient, as she helps me slip into the dress.

"You look beautiful already," she says, smoothing the gown down my hips as she zips me in. "This man has good taste."

I say nothing.

I try to thank her, but the words get stuck somewhere in my throat.

The dress fits like it was made for me. Structured. Smoothing. Elegant. The emerald green pops against my skin, making me look somehow taller. Bolder.

Different.

Like someone took time measuring a body I've only ever tried to shrink.

Isabella steps back and beams. "Okay, now let's get to work on that gorgeous face."

She guides me into the kitchen and starts setting up products with practiced ease. Her voice is gentle now, like she knows I'm spinning.

"Not used to men like this, huh?"

I shake my head, barely able to meet her eyes.

"He's just my boss," I whisper.

But my body doesn't feel like it believes me.

She lifts a brow, a teasing smile tugging at her mouth.

"Sure he is."

She gets to work, sweeping foundation and blush with expert hands. We don't talk much, which is fine. My brain's a mess of static and pulse and *what the hell is going on.*

It's not until she reaches for the eyeshadow palette that I realize something's off.

"Wait. Is that green?" I ask as she lifts a brush.

"Mhm." She dabs it gently into a muted emerald shimmer. "He chose this. Said to match the tone to the dress. And your eyes."

My breath catches.

He chose the makeup?

I don't even know what to say to that. I barely remember how to breathe, let alone form a full sentence.

Isabella doesn't comment on my stunned expression, just keeps working, humming softly as if this is all completely normal.

Once my face is done, she steps back, wiping her hands. "Time for hair."

I nod, still silent, letting her turn me in the chair. She blow-dries with careful hands, working product through the strands, until my hair is soft and glossy and lighter than air.

I start to relax. Until she pulls out a set of pins.

"What are you doing?" I ask as she begins twisting a section at the base of my neck.

"Chignon," she says, focused. "Classic. Elegant. He said up."

My brows draw in. "Warren wants my hair up?"

Isabella's lips twitch with amusement. "To show off the jewelry."

My entire body goes still.

Of course. The hair. The face. The dress. All pieces to complete the look.

His look.

"I—what jewelry?"

She doesn't answer right away, just keeps twisting and pinning.

When she finishes, she gently tilts my chin so I'm facing the mirror she placed on my kitchen island.

Then she reaches for a sleek velvet box sitting quietly on the counter. I hadn't noticed it before.

She opens it slowly, like she's unveiling something dramatic.

A delicate emerald bracelet sparkles inside, paired with a matching necklace and drop earrings set in white gold. Understated. But not cheap.

Definitely not cheap.

They glitter like promises.

And I don't know if I'm supposed to wear them… or return them with my soul.

I stare.

"That's… that's for me?" I ask softly.

I've never owned anything this beautiful. Not even close.

Let alone had it picked out just for me.

She smiles at me in the mirror. "It's all part of the look, *cariña*."

"I-I can't accept this," I breathe, even as she lifts the bracelet and clasps it around my wrist.

"You have to look the part," she says, her voice gentle now. "He chose them to match the dress. And your skin."

My skin.

When did he start studying me like this?

How long has he been planning this moment?

I don't respond.

Because I can't.

I'm afraid if I say anything, I'll cry. Or laugh. Or both.

Then, as if it's nothing, she pulls out a sleek shoebox and opens the lid to reveal a pair of emerald green stilettos with delicate straps and a pointed toe. They look like something out of a dream.

"Oh," I whisper. "Those are... wow."

"He said you wear a seven and a half," she says, kneeling to help me slip them on. "He was right."

How the hell did he know?

They fit perfectly.

Isabella hands me a silver clutch and I stare at myself.

The woman in the mirror doesn't look like me.

She looks powerful. Soft and sharp all at once.

And she looks like she *belongs* beside Warren Beaumont.

Which is the most dangerous lie I'm starting to believe.

My heart races.

It's just a professional event.

A networking opportunity.

It means nothing. It *can't* mean anything.

This is still just work. I'm *just* an employee.

A pretty one in borrowed power. That's all.

Isabella packs up swiftly, leaving me standing in the middle of my apartment like I've been dropped into someone else's life.

"Have fun," she says with a wink as she leaves. "And try not to fall too hard."

The door clicks shut.

I turn toward my phone. Reach for it.

I can't do this.

I'm not ready.

I'm going to cancel. I'm going to tell him I'm sick.

I stare down at my phone. My finger hovers over his name.

Maybe if I text fast enough, I can get out of this—

Knock knock.

My head snaps toward the door.

Too late.

He's here.

Chapter Fourteen

OLIVIA

The knock echoes like a warning.

My stomach flips. My pulse jumps to my throat. I almost don't move.

I reach for the door handle with trembling fingers.

And there he is.

Warren Beaumont.

Tall, broad, commanding. Just as put together as he is at work, but now—dressed in a tux so sharp it could cut glass, he looks... powerful. His jacket is open, his stance relaxed, but every inch of him radiates control.

He looks like he owns everything he touches. And right now, I feel like one of those things.

His eyes drop instantly to the necklace resting above my collarbone. Then lower. A long, measured sweep down the gown he chose, probably wondering if I'm wearing the lingerie beneath it. My face heats.

His gaze lingers, unreadable, at the dip of my waist.

When he speaks, his voice is velvet and steel.

"Turn around."

My breath catches.

He's not asking.

I hesitate, just for a second, then slowly I turn, spine straight, face burning.

He hums low. Approving. "Good."

The word lands somewhere low in my stomach. Heavy. Warm. Dangerous.

I face him again, stunned into silence.

He doesn't smile.

Instead, he reaches forward, brushes his knuckles against the necklace, his fingers grazing my skin.

"Stunning," he says, voice dipped in something darker. "I knew emerald would suit you."

I try to speak, but nothing comes.

I should say thank you. Or ask him what this is. But I can't do either.

"Hand," he commands, already extending his own.

I place mine in his without thinking.

The second our skin touches, I feel it, that invisible pull. Like I'm being drawn into his world, inch by inch, whether I mean to or not.

"Good," he murmurs, almost too quiet to hear.

My heart stutters. He's already turning, leading me to the elevator, our hands still joined like some kind of claim.

He doesn't speak.

His hand steady in mine.

I remind myself over and over as the elevator takes us down:

This is not a date.

This is not a date.

Then why does it feel like it?

At the curb, a sleek black car waits, engine already purring.

He opens the door for me.

I slide in, careful not to wrinkle the dress.

The seat is warm.

Soft leather.

Screams money. Like I expected.

Warren rounds the car and takes the driver's side.

Breathe Olivia.

He glances at me once as he shifts into drive.

"Comfortable?" he asks, voice low, threaded with something I can't name.

"Yes," I manage.

He hums, as if amused by that. Or maybe by me.

"You wear that dress better than I expected."

My cheeks burn. My pulse kicks. I can't tell if it's a compliment or a test.

"You picked it."

"I pick a lot of things. Doesn't mean they all look like that."

I pause.

I swallow. That pause stretches like it means something.

I want to ask what this is. I need to know what he thinks this is going to be.

"That necklace suits you."

My fingers drift to the emerald at my throat.

"You did a great job picking it all. I'll be sure to return them all to you on Monday."

"Don't."

I shift slightly in my seat.

"But—"

"They're yours."

"Warren?" I ask, my voice quieter. "This was all very kind, but the lingerie—"

His smile is barely there.

"You put it on."

I open my mouth. Close it.

My body heats like he touched me, when all he did was name the truth.

What the hell do I say to that?

He turns onto a main road, headlights painting gold against his knuckles. I regain my resolve.

I steel myself.

"You didn't have to do all this," I say quietly. "It's a lot and I don't—"

"I know."

"You know?"

"Yes. You don't know how to accept them without something in return."

My breath hitches and his lips quirk.

"I make my living reading people Olivia" He says my name like he owns it.

"It's how I make my deals. I can read you too."

I stare out the window.

"I'm just not used to it," I admit.

I feel his eyes on me again, sweeping slowly down my profile before returning to the road.

"You'll get used to it."

His voice is calm. Certain. Like getting used to being spoiled by Warren Beaumont is inevitable.

And that should scare me more than it does.

The car eases to a stop in front of a building that doesn't look real.

I square my shoulders, but nothing prepares me for what I see.

Glass. Light. Music drifting through stone archways.

It's like the set of a movie. Not a place people like me get invited to.

The doorman opens my door and offers a quiet "Ms. Baker."

I step out, heels clicking against smooth stone, my emerald gown brushing over polished floors.

Warren appears at my side, jacket now buttoned, posture impeccable. His hand hovers just above my lower back.

Not touching.

But I feel it anyway.

Warm. Anchoring. *Dangerous.*

Inside, the air is velvet and champagne.

Every detail gleams, chandeliers dripping like constellations, golden trim curling around high vaulted ceilings, servers gliding past with trays of wine and caviar.

I catch my breath.

God.

This is it.

This is the world he lives in.

My heart flutters in my chest, somewhere between nerves and awe.

Warren leans in slightly, voice a brush of silk behind my ear.

"Try not to stare, Ms. Baker."

Heat floods my face.

"Sorry."

He chuckles, not unkindly.

"You're doing fine."

We glide into the crowd, his pace unhurried, his presence magnetic. People turn. Eyes follow.

Warren Beaumont, in his element.

I trail just half a step behind, trying not to look as overwhelmed as I feel.

But I already know—

I'm not walking into a gala.

I'm walking into something I may never walk out of the same.

He stops at a small cluster, two men and a woman dressed in old money and quiet menace.

The kind of people who wield their smiles like knives.

"Ah, and who's this?" one of the men says.

Warren's hand finds the small of my back.

Heavy.

Possessive. Calm.

Like he's claiming me in front of them.

"Olivia Baker," he says smoothly.

"My right hand."

The words hit like a shot of whiskey, unexpected and warm.

He's never called me that before.

"I thought Broderick was your right hand," the woman asks, arching a brow.

Warren smiles, slow and lethal.

"He was. But Olivia's much better looking, don't you think?"

The group laughs, the indulgent kind that only comes from people who haven't worried about money in decades.

I force a polite smile, but my insides are molten.

He goes on, tone breezy, eyes on the crowd as if he's scanning for his next deal.

"She's my new rising star. Brilliant. Smart as hell. Beat out Wesley to get her."

He grabs a drink from a passing waiter and hands me one.

He sips his drink like he didn't just hand me the sun.

"Told HR I wouldn't take anyone else."

Their laughter rings out; light, rich, effortless.

Like power is an inside joke I've just been let in on.

But I can't laugh.

Because I'm still trying to breathe.

Who is this?

This version of Warren, polished, warm, casually charming, unsettles me more than his coldness ever did.

Because he doesn't *try* to make me feel like I belong here.

He just *does.*

He puts me at ease.

And yet...

He's not the man I work for.

That man is sharp-eyed.

Unsmiling.

Cold enough to freeze the air between us.

This man?

This man makes me feel beautiful just by standing next to him.

"Dance with me," he says suddenly, cutting through my thoughts like a knife through fog.

I blink up at him.

"What?"

He takes my drink away and offers his hand.

"We've mingled. Time for the fun part."

Without thinking, I take it.

The crowd parts for him.

Black marble stretches beneath crystal light.

It feels like stepping into a fairytale I wasn't cast for.

Music swells. Something elegant and slow.

He pulls me close, one hand at my waist, the other guiding my hand to his shoulder.

His frame eclipses mine, even in heels, I feel swallowed by him.

Like gravity bends toward him.

Our bodies fall into step like we've done this before.

Like we've always done this.

Like we were always *meant* to.

The scent of him wraps around me.

His hand is warm. His hold, steady.

And those eyes... they don't look anywhere but me.

Like I'm the only thing he *wants* to see.

I glance up, unsure.

He frowns. Just a little.

"I told Isabella not to cover them."

I blink.

"Cover what?"

His thumb brushes gently across my cheek.

"Your freckles."

My breath stutters.

"Oh."

He says nothing else.

Just keeps looking.

Holding.

Leading me across the floor like we're the only two people who exist.

My body hums.

My thoughts snarl in velvet knots.

And in his arms, for the first time, I don't feel like I'm pretending.

I feel *seen.*

Claimed.

And I'm terrified of what that means.

***

The hallway feels quieter than usual.

Maybe because my heart's still pounding from the dance. From the champagne. From the way he looked at me like I belonged in that world.

I pause at my door, still smiling.

Tonight was...

Perfect.

More than I ever expected and Warren was....

"I had an amazing time," I say softly. "Thank you. For everything. The dress, the jewelry, the car... I mean, I don't even have words for how—"

"Unlock your door."

His voice cuts in. Sharp. Commanding.

He hands me my clutch he was holding.

My heart stutters.

I blink. "Oh. Right."

I fumble for my keys, fingers clumsy with nerves. The lock clicks.

I turn back to him.

"I just wanted to say I really appreciate—"

He leans in.

My heart leaps and I don't think. I just move.

My lips press against his. Soft. Grateful. Hopeful.

But he doesn't kiss me back.

His body stays still.

My heart stalls.

Oh God.

I pull away like I've been burned, breath catching in my throat, but he doesn't react.

Doesn't flinch.

Just reaches past me and opens the door.

The air leaves my lungs.

He wasn't leaning in to *kiss me.*

He was just *opening the door.*

Chapter Fifteen

WAR

She moves like she's been struck.

Eyes wide. Lips parted.

A single beat of silence passes as she realizes what she's done—

What I *let* her do.

She kissed me.

Soft. Hopeful. Sweet.

A mistake.

I wait for it.

That telltale shift in her posture. The horror blooming behind her eyes.

The way her mouth parts to scramble for an apology she doesn't owe me.

There it is.

She starts to speak, I grip her chin.

Firmly, but with care.

Exactly the way women like *her* want.

Her words die on her tongue.

I pull her toward me.

And I kiss her like I've earned it.

Like I've waited for it.

Because I have.

My mouth claims hers, hard, deep, hungry.

She gasps and I devour the sound, tasting the moment like a man finally getting what's his.

Her lips part under mine and I take it all—

The sweetness.

The surrender.

The heat.

One hand stays curled around her jaw, thumb brushing the corner of her mouth.

The other fists in the fabric at her waist, pulling her tight until I feel every breath, every tremble, every fucking inch of her soft body pressed to mine.

She clutches at my jacket like it's the only thing keeping her upright.

She whimpers into my mouth.

Fuck.

That sound—

It's mine now.

I don't just kiss her.

I savor her.

Drink her in.

Memorize the way she tastes, the way she gives, the way she doesn't pull away.

Not once.

She *melts* for me.

Exactly how I knew she would.

I could fuck her right here.

Right now.

Against this door, the necklace still on, that lingerie I bought her underneath, *waiting.*

But I don't.

Because this isn't indulgence.

It's discipline.

Control.

Training.
I pull back.
Her lips are kiss-bitten.
Cheeks flushed.
Eyes dazed.
Perfect.
"Go inside, Olivia," I say quietly.
She blinks. Swallows. Her breath hitches.
And she listens.
She *obeys.*
She turns. Walks into the apartment.
The door closes with a soft click.
I wait.
A beat.
Then another.
The lock slides into place.
Good girl.
I turn, the corner of my mouth lifting.
Step one: complete.

***

My weight room is empty, just how I like it.

No distractions.

Just the hiss of my breath through my nose, the rhythm of the rope slapping concrete, and the burn in my arms that keeps me from thinking about her lips.

Not that it works.

Her taste is still on my tongue.

Her face still seared behind my eyelids.

Flushed. Breathless. *Embarrassed.*

Mine.

The door creaks.

Wesley walks in like he owns my fucking place, flipping on the overheads without asking. Light floods the space, slicing across my bare chest, the sheen of sweat and the scowl already forming.

"I told you before," I grit, not breaking rhythm, "if you're not here to work out, leave."

He doesn't.

Instead, he walks over and slaps something onto the weight bench near me.

A fucking newspaper.

And there she is, *Olivia.*

Eyes wide, lips parted, glowing like a goddamn debutante.

Caption: **Beaumont's Mystery Girl.**

I drop the rope.

"The gala, War? Seriously?" Wes says, tone sharp. "What the hell are you doing?"

"It was a networking event for work. She *works* for me."

He scoffs. "You took her to the fucking *Trust Gala* at the Halston Estate, not a networking lunch. She's in the goddamn tabloids."

"So?" I grab a towel, drag it over the back of my neck.

"She's not built for this world."

"She'll learn."

I'll make sure of it.

Wesley stares at me like I've lost my mind. "You're not serious about her. Tell me you're not doing this *again*."

I pause. "She's different."

"Yeah," he snaps, "so don't put her through your stupid step program or whatever the hell you call it. She's not some project, Warren."

I smile, slow and sharp. "It'll work with her."

"It broke the others"

I shrug. "And yet I'm not in low supply of women They always come back."

"Until they don't," he fires. "Until one doesn't. And then what? You gonna break, too? You gonna be human for once in your fucking life?"

The gym goes quiet.

My smile fades.

I step toward him.

He backs up.

He *always* backs up.

Wilder throws fists.

But Wes?

He plays chess. Strategy, analysis, pattern.

He sees me better than anyone.

And I fucking hate that.

"Stay out of it," I say coldly.

Wesley crosses his arms. "You're a disappointment."

I tilt my head. "Heard that one before."

He flinches. Just slightly.

"Get out," I say.

He hesitates. One last look, pity or warning, I can't tell.

Then he leaves, and I'm alone again.

The door slams behind him, echoing like a trigger pull.

The one person who sees me clearly just called me a disappointment. And walked away.

Good. Let him.

I stare down at the newspaper.

Her face.

Her fucking smile.

I crush the paper in one fist until the edges cut into my palm.

If Wesley thinks this ends the way it has before...

He's wrong.

Olivia is different.

And I'm *not* letting her go.

***

This building is both my legacy and my curse.

It's like my soul stayed behind when his left.

The Parker Building stands half complete. Still with exposed wires like grief left too long untouched. I don't know why I came here tonight. Maybe to think. Maybe to bleed without anyone noticing.

Renovation halted six months ago.

But I need it done. Complete. *Clean.*

For me.

For Noah.

I stand in the middle of the room, the same place he and I used to sneak away with my brothers when we were kids, pretending we'd rule the world from up here one day.

He was the good one.

Better than me in every way.

Now look at us.

One's buried.

The other's too fucked up to move forward.

The air smells like stale paint and cold regrets.

I shut my eyes and she flashes to mind.

Olivia. She found the solution no one else did.

My salvation that may get this place clean. Finally complete.

Wes thinks she's step one in another goddamn plan.

He thinks I'll break her like all the others.

He's wrong.

I walk toward the massive floor-to-ceiling windows that overlook the city.

The skyline winks in the distance, sharp and golden. Below it, the world goes on, unaware that I'm up here, trying not to fall apart.

My gaze trails down.

A hammer.

Discarded. Left when production of my rebuilding halted.

I grip it.

Tight. Controlled.

But the glass doesn't care about control.

It wants the truth.

It wants pain.

I slam it into the window once.

The vibration rocks through me.

I hit it again, Right in the corner.

Harder.

A crack forms. A spiderweb across the pane.

I should stop.

I don't.

One more blow and it shatters, jagged edges gleaming in the moonlight, a rush of wind pouring in like a scream.

I stare down at the street below.

So far.

So close.

Wes thinks Olivia will break.

Thinks she's just like the rest.

Delicate. *Temporary.*

He doesn't see her.

Not the way I do.

She walked into my life for a reason.

She doesn't ask why, she just moves.

She works.

She *obeys.*

She *learns.*

Fuck, I think I *need* her.

I press my palm to the jagged edge of the broken frame, blood beading instantly.

I welcome the sting.

It's real.

She's real.

Not a step.

Not a pawn.

Not a project.

She may be the only one who can handle me and what it cost to stand by my side.

And I'm not going to let her fall.

I stare out into the night, city lights blinking like distant stars, and make my vow right here in the ruins:

She won't break.

She'll fucking rise.

And when she does, she'll do it as mine.

Chapter Sixteen

OLIVIA

All weekend I've been sick over this.

Replay after replay in my head, like I'm some masochist who can't stop pressing on a bruise.

Why did I kiss him?

Why did I lean in like some wide-eyed intern, practically begging for my boss, *my boss,* to kiss me back?

Stupid. Reckless. Dangerous.

I should have known better. I *do* know better.

This job is my lifeline, and I cannot, *will not,* lose it. Not over a man like Warren Beaumont. Not over lips that taste like wine and power.

My heels click on the marble as I walk through the lobby, and every step feels heavier. Head down. That's the rule. Keep my head down, do my work, blend in. No one has to know I spent two nights staring at my ceiling, wondering if I'd ruined everything.

The elevator dings. I force my lungs to keep working, force my spine to stay straight. The doors open to my floor, and I walk fast. Too fast. Past Brody's empty office. Past the buzzing phones and the low murmur of the staff already at their desks. Past *his* door.

Closed.

Thank God.

I don't let myself look. Not even a glance.

I go straight to my office, twist the handle, and slip inside like I'm being chased.

The door shuts behind me with a click, sealing me into the only place I think might still be mine.

Then I turn.

And my heart stops.

He's here.

Standing at my desk, broad shoulders filling the space, his hands tucked into his pockets as he looks out my window like he owns not just the skyline but the air in my lungs.

Warren Beaumont.

I move like I've been struck. The breath punches right out of me.

Eyes wide. Lips parted.

My brain stutters through every possible reaction—apology, denial, excuses, but none of them make it past my tongue. Because the only thing louder than my panic is the truth that rushes back in a flood.

The feel of his mouth crashing against mine.

The way my body melted, helpless.

The sound I made. God, that humiliating whimper.

And now he's here.

In my space.

Waiting.

I grip the edge of the door behind me like it's the only thing holding me upright. My throat works, but no words come.

His voice is smooth. Deep. Lethal.

"I figured you'd try to hide," he says, not turning around. "So I waited here."

My stomach drops to my knees.

He knew.

He gestures toward my desk with a tilt of his head.

There's a coffee cup, still hot, still steaming and two sleek matte black boxes.

More gifts.

My heart thumps painfully.

I should leave. I should run. I should tell him this is inappropriate and unprofessional and a million other things I'm too terrified to say.

But I don't move away.

I move toward him.

Like gravity. Like instinct.

Like I never stood a chance.

I reach for the coffee first, needing something to anchor myself. The cup is warm against my fingers, my name scrawled on the side in sharp black ink. I take a sip, and the perfect ratio of hazelnut and espresso coats my tongue.

His gaze sharpens, mouth curving the slightest bit. "Good."

The warmth doesn't stop at my mouth. It spreads down my throat, into my chest, radiating through limbs that had gone cold the second I saw him.

"Sit."

It's not a question.

My chair squeaks faintly as I lower myself, the leather too soft against my rigid posture. He gets closer, his hand brushes over the first box, sliding it toward me.

"Open it."

My fingers tug at the ribbon. The lid lifts. Inside, nestled in velvet, are pens, sleek black with gold trim. My name engraved in delicate script. *Olivia Baker.*

My chest tightens.

"They're beautiful," I whisper.

"So you'll stop using those cheap ones that smudge," he says smoothly. "You always end up with ink on your fingers."

Heat explodes across my cheeks.

He noticed that?

I glance up, but his expression is unreadable. Cool. Calm. *Too* controlled.

Before I say anything, he taps the second box. "That one, too."

I obey, lifting the lid. My breath catches hard.

A watch.

White gold. Delicate, expensive. The band gleams with diamond accents that wink beneath the light. Not just jewelry, a statement. Something I could never dream of affording, not in three lifetimes.

I make a sound, barely audible, but he hears it.

"I can't Warren, I don't—"

His eyes flick to mine, silencing me with a single look. Not cruel. Not cold. Just... firm. Immoveable.

"Did you want yellow gold instead?" he asks, like that's the problem. "Or platinum?"

I blink. "I don't understand why I'm getting gifts."

Why me. Why now. Why this.

"The watch," he says, "is a reward. For coming in on time lately."

My lips part, but no protest comes.

Because beneath the embarrassment and confusion, there's *pride.*

Stupid, helpless pride that he *noticed.*

So I nod.

I swallow.

And I say softly, "Thank you."

I can't breathe.

He lingers for half a second too long once it's secure. Then lets my hand go.

But his voice doesn't waver.

"I'm going to HR this morning," he says.

The bottom drops out of my stomach.

I blink up at him, throat tightening so fast I nearly choke. "What?"

A whisper. Fragile. Shattered.

He watches me, unreadable as ever.

I scramble to explain, to fix this. "I didn't mean to, it wasn't, please don't—"

"It's not a report," he says, calm as glass. "It's a notice."

I blink, pulse roaring in my ears. My voice barely works. "A notice... why?"

He steps in.

Close.

Too close.

"Because that kiss," he murmurs, gaze fixed on my mouth.

His hand lifts, fingertips brushing beneath my chin, tilting my face up to his.

The other settles on the arm of my chair, caging me in with quiet authority.

And then he's kissing me.

No hesitation. No doubt.

His mouth crashes against mine, hot and commanding, like he's claiming the air in my lungs. The chair presses into my back. My fingers scramble for something, anything, but all I feel is him. His lips, soft and warm. His breath, sharp and clean. His scent, smoke and wealth and a danger I'll never outrun.

My lips part on instinct.

He deepens it.

A low sound leaves me, helpless and soft.

He tastes like power. Like control wrapped in temptation. Like every rule I've ever tried to follow unraveling all at once.

His hand slides into my hair, gripping gently but firmly, keeping me exactly where he wants me. The other stays on the chair, anchoring us both, like he's holding the whole world steady through the point of contact between us.

And just when I think I'll forget my name, he pulls away.

Not far. Just enough.

His thumb grazes my bottom lip, swollen and tingling.

"And this one, will continue to happen," he finishes, voice low and certain.

A sound escapes me. Half gasp, half stupid whimper. My throat constricts.

"Any interoffice relationships have to be reported," he says, eyes dragging over me. "We're just being... *compliant.*"

My lips part, but I can't find a single word.

He straightens, steps back like he hasn't just set my whole world on fire.

"You should start using your new pens today," he says. "You'll want to look sharp. Big client meeting at noon."

Then he turns toward the door.

Just before he opens it, he glances over his shoulder.

"And Olivia?"

I swallow hard. "Yes?"

"That lipstick shade from the gala."

His eyes flick to my mouth.

"Wear it again."

The door clicks behind him, and I sit there, watch wrapped tight around my wrist, coffee gone cold on my desk, heart thundering like I just survived a car crash.

Only I didn't survive.

I surrendered.

Chapter Seventeen

OLIVIA

This is the moment.

His meeting is over, War's in his office.

Perfect.

Now I'll talk to him.

Now I'll say it out loud: we kissed, but I didn't say yes to dating you or being in a relationship. This... *us,* it's not anything.

I step into his office, nerves twisted so tight I can barely breathe. He's standing at the window, back to me, phone to his ear.

"Yes."

A pause.

Another.

And then he laughs.

The sound is rare enough to make my breath hitch.

"Send the confirmation to my email and Olivia Baker's. Yes. I want the crew mobilized by next week."

He hangs up, turns around, and smiles.

Smiles.

And I feel it like a punch to the sternum. That rare, easy joy on his face. That lightness. It softens something brutal in him and slices something fragile in me.

"What happened?" I ask.

"The Parker Building," he says, voice rich and warm. "It's back on. Your summary notice... it worked."

I blink. "Wait. Really?"

My heart leaps.

I did it.

He nods. "We're clear to move forward. Construction resumes next week."

I smile before I can stop it.

Pride swells in my chest. Not just for the work. For the way he's looking at me now, like I genuinely helped.

Then he's moving.

Fast.

I let out a yelp as he grabs me by the waist and lifts me off my feet like I weigh nothing. He spins me once, laughing under his breath, and I can't help but laugh, too, sharp and surprised.

"Warren!" I gasp.

"You smiled," he says, like that's justification enough. "I like when you smile."

He kisses me.

Not rushed. Not gentle.

Just sure. Like I'm already his and I just haven't accepted it yet. His mouth claims mine, tongue sliding deep before I can protest. My heels wobble when he lets me go, and I stumble back against the desk.

I blink, dazed, mouth parted. He scrambles my brain when I know what I need to do. I should end this.

Even if I don't want to.

"We need to—"

"Get on the desk," he says, low and certain.

My brain stalls.

"What?"

"I said," he steps in, hand wrapping around my waist, voice like a fucking commandment, "get on the desk."

I hesitate.

He tsks.

"You were doing so well before," he murmurs, brushing a strand of hair behind my ear. "Listening."

And then he lifts me again, sets me down on the edge of his desk.

My breath catches.

No one lifts me.

The wood is cool beneath my thighs. My skirt rides up with the angle of my legs, the slit sliding high on one side. His eyes drop to it.

To what's peeking just under.

The lace panties he bought me. The ones from the gala. I wore them without thinking.

His eyes flare when he sees them. "*Oh, sweet girl.*"

I flush, humiliated. "I washed them over the weekend and I—"

"You wore the panties I bought you." His voice is pure gravel. "That little nervous stammer you do is fucking adorable."

His hand slips under the skirt, fingers skating up my inner thigh, slow and torturous.

"Warren—"

"Shh." He kisses my neck. "I've been thinking about this since the second I left your office this morning."

My whole body locks.

"You were sitting there, legs crossed, trying so hard to stay professional... when you were already soaked for me, weren't you?"

I shake my head, breath shaking. "I wasn't—"

"Tell me to stop," he says, his finger tips grazing the lace.

I don't. I can't. I don't want to.

He hooks a finger under the lace, dragging it aside.

"See, you were," he growls, sliding two fingers through the mess of me. "And *fuck.* You are now."

I moan, helpless, soft, broken.

He kisses me again, harder now, mouth devouring mine as his fingers start to circle my clit, slow and controlled. Not teasing.

Training.

"You like this," he murmurs against my lips, "being touched as I watch *every* reaction?"

I nod, gasping. "Warren—"

"Say it."

"I-I like it," I whisper.

He grins. "Of course you do. You're *perfect* like this."

Two fingers slip lower, slick with me, and presses inside.

"War!" I gasp, my hands shooting to his shoulders.

"Shh, I've got you." He kisses my jaw, thumb brushing my clit now while his fingers pump slow and deep. "You're doing so fucking good for me. *So* good when you say my name."

My thighs tremble.

"That's it. Just like that. Let me feel you."

His other hand spreads across my stomach, holding me still as I start to shake.

"I can feel your pussy fluttering already. Gonna come for me like a good girl?"

My hips jerk. My body spirals.

I bite my lip to keep from crying out, but he doesn't let me hide.

"Don't hold it in," he growls. "Let go. Right here. On my fingers."

I fall apart, *utterly, fully, violently,* back arching, breath shattering, thighs shaking. My moan escapes, hot and raw as my orgasm crashes over me like a goddamn tidal wave.

His fingers stay deep until I stop pulsing.

Until the last tremor fades.

Then, slowly, his fingers leave me.

My head falls forward, forehead resting against his chest, skin flushed and aching.

He brushes his lips against my temple, one hand cupping the back of my head.

"You're mine now, Olivia," he whispers against my skin.

"That kiss wasn't a mistake. That was a fucking promise."

I pull back to look at him, my lips part, a breathless sound catching in my throat.

"War—"

Before I can finish, his slick fingers slide up, pressing against my lips.

Then past them.

Slow and deliberate, his fingers brush against my tongue.

I don't pull away. I don't want to.

"Suck."

A single word.

Dark velvet. Commanding.

I do.

I close my lips around his fingers, tasting myself on his skin, warm and dizzy and too far gone to pretend anymore.

His icy eyes lock on mine.

"Good girl."

The praise is low, rough, and it sinks straight between my legs.

Then softly, almost gently:

"Tell me to stop."

I freeze.

Everything in me screams that I should.

That this is wrong. Dangerous. Inappropriate.

That I work for him. That he's my boss. That this isn't how things are supposed to go.

But I shake my head.

Small. Subtle. Barely there.

Because I don't want him to stop.

I want more.

More of this.

More of him.

His fingers slide from my mouth, slow and sticky, and he wipes them across my lips like he owns the moment. Like he *owns me.*

"You can freshen up in my bathroom," he says, stepping back just far enough for me to breathe again. "We're going to lunch."

I blink. "Lunch?"

His mouth curves.

"Yes. You've earned it."

He walks around his desk, already picking up his phone like nothing happened.

I sit there for a moment; wrecked, panting, soaked through, with my panties still twisted beneath my skirt, trying to understand how this became my life.

And somehow, lunch with Warren Beaumont feels more intimate than the orgasm he just gave me.

Chapter Eighteen

WAR

Olivia Baker is easy.

Easy to command.

Easy to redirect.

Easy to make come.

She's also the most *enticing* woman I've ever met.

She thinks she's overwhelmed. Thinks this is all too much. But I know better.

I felt the way her hips rolled for me, the way she sucked my fingers like she was made for it.

She's spiraling.

Overthinking.

She *always* does.

I lean back in my chair, phone pressed to my ear, pretending to check a message that doesn't exist. My eyes track her as she rises from my desk; unsteady, flushed, wrecked in the prettiest fucking way.

She smooths her skirt. Adjusts her blouse.

But she doesn't know I can still see her panties, the back of her skirt still up. Showing *my* lace across that plump gorgeous ass.

She crosses the room toward the bathroom like she's walking into a courtroom, her shoulders squared, mind racing.

She's thinking too hard again.

I put the phone down without a word and follow.

Her hand is on the bathroom door when I catch up.

She turns, startled. "Warren—"

I don't let her finish.

I nudge her inside, shut the door and grab a cleansing wipe from the counter top.

"Lift your leg," I say.

She blinks. "What—?"

I don't repeat myself.

I just drop to a knee in front of her.

Her mouth opens, maybe to protest. Maybe to plead.

But she swallows it.

Good girl.

She lifts one leg, heel anchored on my shoulder, skirt sliding up automatically.

The lace is soaked. *Ruined.*

"You made a mess, Olivia," I say, voice low, hands already sliding the fabric aside.

She gasps, just once, as I drag the wipe through her.

Slow. Precise. *Thorough.*

"Warren—"

"Shh."

I clean her like it's my right. Like it's expected.

Because it is.

She let me take her apart, and now she'll let me put her back together.

When I'm satisfied, I slide the panties back into place and smooth her skirt down.

Then I rise.

Toss the wipe and then turn back to her.

Her eyes are wide. Breath uneven.

Like she's not sure whether to slap me or drop to her knees.

I tilt my head.

"You ready for lunch now?" I ask, my eyes dragging down her perfect form. "Or do you need another minute?"

***

She eats like she's being hunted.

Fast. Small bites. Eyes down. Shoulders tight.

Like a baby deer caught by a predator.

I lean back in my chair, sip my espresso, and watch her in silence.

God, she's beautiful like this. Wrecked and pretending she's not.

"Slow down," I say.

Her eyes lift to mine, wide and startled.

I can't help it, I chuckle.

"Yup," I murmur to myself, "definitely a little doe."

She swallows hard, cheeks pink, and lowers her fork.

A beat of quiet passes between us. She fidgets with her napkin before finally asking, "The Parker Building... is it really back on?"

I nod. "Construction starts next week."

"I've never seen you smile like that before," she says softly. "You looked... *happy.*"

Something in me stills. A *need* takes over.

A need to tell her.

"It's where my best friend died," I say simply.

Her shoulders drop. "What?"

"Noah," I murmur. "He and I used to sneak into that building as kids. It was our little fortress before it became a Beaumont asset. One day we dared each other to get close to one of the windows. He beat me to it, leaned too far. The window cracked and he fell."

Olivia's eyes soften. "Warren..."

"Don't," I say, voice sharper than I mean. "It was my fault."

Her brows knit. "It wasn't. You were a kid. You were both kids. No one could have known."

I shake my head, but she leans in slightly.

"If you had beaten Noah to that window," she says gently, "it would've been you. That's not your fault. That's an accident."

I freeze.

No one's ever called it that before.

Not the police. Not my father. Not even me.

An accident.

My parents called it a scandal.

Said I embarrassed the family.

That I shouldn't have been anywhere near a run-down building on the "poor side" of town.

Not as a Beaumont.

And here she is, brushing crumbs off her napkin, talking about accidents. Like I'm still innocent.

I look away. Just for a second.

Then I collect myself and move on.

"With renovations back up," I say smoothly, "I think you'd be perfect as my permanent assistant."

Stunned, she hesitates. "But...what about Brody?"

"I have other plans for Broderick."

She tilts her head. "Warren..."

"I'm serious," I say. "You're efficient. Precise. Smart. I trust you."

There's a pause.

Then her eyes drop to the table. Her voice comes out small. "I don't want special treatment."

I arch a brow. "Special treatment?"

She gestures vaguely between us. "Because of... whatever this is."

I smirk.

"Oh, sweet girl." I lean forward, voice low and dangerous. "You don't get special treatment. You're just mine."

She flinches.

Just slightly.

"Warren," she says, her voice a breath, barely above the clink of silverware around us. "I don't think this is… appropriate."

Ah. There it is.

The panic.

The guilt.

The urge to be *good.*

But her pupils are blown wide.

Her breathing is shallow.

I'm sure her thighs just pressed tighter together under the table.

Her mouth says no, but her body?

Her body is already mine.

I stare at her, drinking her in, long and unblinking, watching the way her fingers grip the edge of the table like she needs something to anchor her.

"Tell me you don't want this, then," I say softly. "Tell me to stop pursuing you. Tell me to *stop.*"

She opens her mouth.

Closes it.

"Warren…"

A beat.

"But—"

That's all she gets out.

Her voice dies in her throat.

I sit back slightly and gesture around the restaurant with a slow sweep of my hand.

"We're in public, Olivia. I won't make a scene. You won't be fired. If you want to go back to working for Wesley again…" I pause, let the weight settle. "I'll move you back myself."

Lie.

I'll bulldoze Beaumont enterprises to the ground before I give her up.

She swallows.

Hard.

Her eyes flick around the restaurant, the linen tablecloths, the couples laughing softly over wine, the weight of my gaze pressing into her from across the table.

Then she looks back at me.

And I see it.

Not fear.

Not disgust.

Not even confusion.

Hunger.

Want.

Buried deep, but rising.

So I say it one more time, voice lower than before, just for her:

"Tell me to stop."

Her pulse jumps under the weight of my stare. She exhales, slow, deliberate, like she's making a choice she already decided in her mind.

"I can't," she says at last.

"Then stop fighting it, Olivia. Let me show you what being mine means."

***

She said she couldn't tell me to stop.

And now she's unraveling exactly the way I knew she would.

The screen on my desk glows softly.

I watch her pace.

She's whispering, but the camera still picks up her voice.

"What is happening," she mutters. *"What the fuck did I do?"*

She stops. Starts again. Fingers running through her hair, tugging at the collar of her blouse like it's suffocating her.

Good.

Let it drown her.

That's how she'll rise, with my name in her mouth and my rules in her blood.

Her throat bobs. Her fingers fall away. She stares like she's looking at something indecent, like desire itself snuck in and dared her to touch it.

Because this is what surrender looks like, even if her brain hasn't caught up yet.

The knock on her office door makes her jump.

She straightens and take a breath before opening the door to reveal Angelique, my personal stylist, expression crisp and pleasant as always, flanked by two interns dragging in tall rolling wardrobes

Olivia freezes.

Angelique smiles. "Mr. Beaumont wanted to ensure you had everything you need for your new role. You're welcome to pick anything from the collection. We'll have your selections delivered to your apartment by this evening."

Olivia's jaw drops.

She stares at the wardrobe like it might bite her.

My chuckle is low and private.

I lean back in my chair and watch her approach the rack slowly, fingers brushing over silks and cashmeres and pressed Italian collars. Her touch is hesitant, reverent.

She mouths something to herself.

Looks around the room like someone's playing a joke on her.

But no.

This is real.

She *deserves* this.

I've never loved my money more than I do in this moment.

Then Angelique slides the last panel to reveal the final collection—delicate lingerie in blacks, creams, blood reds. Lace. Straps. *My taste.* Hand-picked. Made for *her.*

Olivia freezes.

Completely still.

Not breathing.

Then, without a word, she turns and walks out.

I turn off the feed.

I don't need to check the hallway camera. I already know where she's going.

I steel myself.

Fold my hands on the desk.

And wait.

Three...

Two...

One—

Chapter Nineteen

OLIVIA

It's one thing to establish a relationship.

To sneak kisses.

Report to HR.

Fingering in the workplace... not the best idea, but it's not on display, it was a *one time* thing.

But lingerie on display in *my* office?

Warren Beaumont is a piece of work.

Those fabrics? Gorgeous.

I'd be a liar if I said I didn't want them and yes I'll take them if he wants to gift them, but *lingerie.*

No.

Hard no.

I don't knock, I open his office door and shut it so hard his eyes lock on mine.

I didn't *mean* to slam it.

My breath hitches at the look on his face.

I can't tell if he's angry or annoyed.

"Can I help you?" he drawls.

"Lingerie Warren? *Lingerie* in the office?"

"You need a complete wardrobe Olivia... or do you want to keep returning and repurchasing the same three outfits?"

My jaw drops and my face heats.

"That—"

"That?"

I exhale. "It isn't HR appro—"

"HR knows you're mine now, and I *own* HR. It's just legal protection for us both and neither will need it."

"Warren I don't—"

He stands.

Just that.

Not a word. Not a raised voice.

But I step back anyway, breath catching as he rounds the desk, slow and deliberate, like a predator that knows the prey won't run far.

"You burst in here," he says, voice low and smooth, "because a few scraps of lace made you blush?"

He's in front of me now.

Close.

Too close.

My back hits the door and I realize I've cornered myself.

"That's not—"

His hand lifts. Just a single finger, pressed beneath my chin.

"Do you think I haven't noticed what you wear under those skirts, Olivia?"

My throat tightens.

"You think I don't know you wear those cheap cotton things every day?" But today you chose to wear the panties *I* bought you?"

I gasp.

He leans in, lips brushing the shell of my ear.

"You moaned in them."

A pulse of heat floods my cheeks, and lower.

"Warren—"

"Do you know what I see when I look at you?" he whispers.

I shake my head.

"I see a woman who doesn't know how to accept being taken care of. Who flinches every time something's given to her. Who spirals the second she's seen."

His lips brush my jaw.

"Too fucking bad, sweet girl."

My breath shudders.

"You said you can't tell me to stop," he drawls. "So don't try to draw new lines now."

He pulls back, eyes sharp and icy and utterly in control.

"Take the lingerie, Olivia. Wear it. Or don't. But don't storm in here like you've forgotten who you belong to now."

I exhale my hands trembling by my side.

"Now go. Pick out something pretty. And when you try them on... bring me your favorite."

I am not going to do that.

My brows furrow as he pulls away and sits at his desk.

He chuckles darkly.

"Stop thinking. Go. before I fuck the thoughts out of your mind and that's not how I want our first time together to go."

I take in a shaky breath.

This man.

I don't stomp out.

That's the worst part.

I want to. I should slam the door and mutter something biting under my breath, but I walk out like I've just been dismissed from a meeting, calm, composed... owned.

I get back to my office and smile politely.

Angelique is still waiting. Unbothered.

She greets me like nothing happened.

"Shall we continue?"

I nod. Wordless. The heat still clinging to my skin.

We go piece by piece. Fabric against fingers. Price tags I don't want to look at. Everything tailored and pristine, clothes meant for someone with power. Someone with presence.

Someone like him.

But Angelique hands me things like I deserve them.

Like I'm not faking this.

I try on the first outfit.

It's a navy silk blouse and high-waisted, cream wide-leg trousers with gold buttons. Not something I ever would've picked for myself. Not something I ever could've afforded.

But when I look in the mirror?

I don't look like a mess of nerves. I don't look like the girl who panicked in the elevator on her first day. I look...*elevated.*

Put together.

Beautiful.

My throat tightens.

This is amazing.

And terrifying.

Ugh. Part of me likes it.

The next few pieces blur. Tailored coats. Belts with subtle branding. A pair of sleek, minimalist heels that somehow make me feel taller than anything else I own.

I keep the trousers and blouse on. I don't want to take them off.

I stare at myself for a beat too long, then glance toward the hallway.

No.

Absolutely not.

I am *not* giving Warren Beaumont a fashion show.

But I want to know what he thinks.

Just one outfit.

Just a peek.

Just...

God, I'm so stupid.

I open the door and make the walk back to his office, palms sweating even though my outfit looks like it belongs on the cover of Forbes.

I knock this time.

A soft, single rap.

His voice comes from behind the door.

"Come in, little doe."

Little doe?

The nickname hits like a brand.

I breathe in, steady, shaky and open the door.

He's at his desk, leaned back, arms resting lazily on the chair's arms like a king on a throne. But his eyes, *icy, assessing,* go molten the second they land on me.

A slow smile curves his mouth. Dangerous. Knowing.

"That's the one," he says simply.

My pulse kicks.

He doesn't stand.

Just lifts two fingers and curls them. A quiet summons.

"Come here."

I move. Against everything in me, I move.

He slides his chair back an inch as I stop in front of him.

"Spin."

The command is soft. Velvet.

I hesitate, just long enough for my skin to prickle.

But I do it.

Slowly. Carefully. I turn. His eyes track every inch of movement like he's memorizing my silhouette.

When I face him again, his gaze is darker. Fixed.

"That outfit looks incredible on your shape," he murmurs. "Tailored like it was sewn for you."

My breath catches.

He shifts, rising fluidly from his chair. One hand gestures, fingertips grazing the edge of the desk.

"Up."

I swallow.

And sit.

The desk is cool beneath me. He's warm. Close. Towering without crowding.

His fingers slide into my hair, gentle but firm, and I feel my shoulders drop. The tension releases, just a little.

He leans in, lips ghosting down my jawline. Lower. Beneath my ear. My breath hitches as he presses slow, open-mouthed kisses to the side of my neck.

Then lower.

His fingers find the first button of my blouse.

Pop.

Then the next.

Pop.

His mouth moves lower, over the newly exposed skin of my collarbone, trailing fire in every press.

I'm trembling, hands curled into fists on my lap, brain barely functioning.

Then he whispers against my skin—

"I can't wait to unwrap you, Olivia."

A quiet, wrecked sound escapes me.

My spine tingles.

He pulls back just enough to meet my eyes.

"Dinner. A date," he says. "This Friday. Say yes."

I don't hesitate this time.

"Yes."

***

Tuesday

I'm learning the rhythm of War's world.

How I fit in it.

My coffee order appears before I ask.

By noon, I'm pinned against a wall between back-to-back calls.

Where I come on his fingers with my mouth pressed against his shoulder to muffle the sound.

He doesn't take more.

Just gives.

Cleans me up.

And gets back to work.

Like nothing happened.

Like it's routine.

And maybe it is.

Before I leave, he hands me a box.

A new phone. Sleek. Expensive. Mint-colored case already wrapped around it.

"It has a stylus," I say, blinking. "I don't need a stylus."

"You do," he replies. "To take notes. And it has a location share."

I roll my eyes. "You want to know where I am?"

"No," he says simply, gaze steady. "I *need* to know where you are."

The air shifts. My stomach flips.

I try to play it off. "Do I get to know where you are?"

He nods. "You have access to mine too."
My heart stammers.
I stare at the mint case. I love it.
Damn it.

Wednesday

Lunch arrives at my desk before I even think to order.
Exactly what I wanted.
I stopped questioning how he knows.
He sends food to my apartment.
Groceries. Wine. My favorite snacks.
Little things I don't remember mentioning, if I ever did at all.
It should feel invasive.
But it doesn't.
It feels like he's inside my life now.
Like he's always been there.
At night, I open the pantry and spot the bag, barbecue chips.
The exact kind. The exact brand.
My weakness.
I smile before I can stop myself, curl up on the couch, tear open the bag, and dial his number.
"How did you know I love these?" I ask, licking the flavor from my fingers.
He doesn't miss a beat. "I know everything about you, Olivia Baker."
I freeze.
Not sure whether to be flattered or afraid.
But all I ask is, "Why?"
"Because I wanted to," he says. "So I learned."
Just like that.
No apology.

No explanation.

Just… him.

We talk for hours.

About nothing.

About everything.

And at some point, I fall asleep with the phone still pressed to my ear.

His voice the last thing I hear.

Thursday

I don't flinch when his hand grazes mine as he passes a report across the table.

I don't question the way he watches me during meetings, like he's memorizing my posture.

Every blink. Every shift. Every line of my mouth.

I don't even protest when he adjusts the strap of my blouse and says—

"You need to look polished if you're going to represent me."

Because that's what I am now, isn't it?

His assistant

His possession.

His.

Later, he walks into my office with a box tied with gold ribbon.

My heart stutters.

"This is…?"

"Open it," he says.

Inside is a white Prada purse.

Soft leather. Real gold hardware. One I've stared at in department store windows but never let myself touch.

I trace the logo with my finger.

"My old one was fine."

"It wasn't good enough."

"Oh yeah?" I ask, forcing a light tone. "Because I represent you?"

His gaze cuts into me, dark and unwavering.

"No," he says. "Because you deserve the best."

I look down at the purse.

At him.

I don't say anything.

But when I walk out that evening, the Prada bag is over my shoulder.

And it feels like more than a gift.

It feels like a *claim*.

Friday

He never takes.

Never needs to.

He just *knows*.

When to look at me.

When to touch me.

When to own me.

What I need.

And somehow, it still doesn't feel real.

Maybe because no one else notices.

Or maybe because he's so good at making it feel like it's always been this way.

I tell myself it's temporary.

That he'll move on.

That this will burn out as fast as it started.

But then I remember the way he looks at me.

The way his voice goes low when we're alone.

The way he makes me feel—

Seen.

Shaken.

Worshiped.

And *owned.*

And the part that scares me most?

I like it.

God help me, I like it.

I get home a little after five.

Everything is just as I left it.

The lamp in the corner casts the same warm glow.

The scent of the vanilla candle I forgot to blow out this morning still lingers faintly in the air.

My shoes are by the door. My mail is on the counter. The hum of the fridge is soft and familiar.

It's calm. Safe.

Mine.

But somehow, it doesn't feel like mine anymore.

Like I left, and someone else moved in.

Someone who wears Prada.

And gets her own office and a new fancy phone.

I toe off my shoes and drop my bag by the couch. Move on autopilot.

Rent. I need to pay rent.

I pull up the app on my phone, expecting the usual anxiety to grip me as I check my balance, as I pray the page loads.

Only this time...

It loads instantly.

And the screen reads:

Paid.

My heart stutters.

I check again.

Paid. For the *entire year.*

A tight, cold coil winds in my stomach.

It had to be him.

Of course it was him.

I never told him I was behind.

Never asked.

Never even mentioned rent.

But he knew.

And just like everything else, *he didn't ask.*

I step into my bedroom.

And freeze.

There's a box on my bed.

Black. Sleek. Tied with a bow.

A simple ivory envelope sits on top.

My name in bold gold lettering.

I sit down carefully, like the box might explode.

I lift the lid.

A dress.

Casual, but expensive. The fabric is soft, light, the color perfect against my skin. Effortless, but luxurious. A dress designed for someone who doesn't need to try hard to be stunning.

I don't even want to know the price.

But what I *do* want to know how the hell it got in here.

I glance around the room like I'll find the answer. I won't.

My phone buzzes.

A single notification.

His name.

WARREN

> My driver will be there at 7. See you soon.

My stomach flips.

I don't respond.

But I stand up and get ready anyway.

Chapter Twenty

WAR

I finish pouring the wine.

The table is already set. Minimal. Elegant. Intimate. The kind of setting I never bother with because no one ever comes here.

Until her.

My phone buzzes.

My driver letting me know Olivia is on her way up.

I place the phone face down, adjust the napkin, and move toward the entryway.

The elevator doors open.

There she is.

She steps off the elevator and into my foyer like she has no idea she's the most exquisite thing I've ever seen.

Hair down. Freckles bare. Lips painted that same deep wine-red from the gala.

My favorite.

She smooths her dress, eyes flicking to mine, and I can tell she's trying not to fidget.

Good. A little nervous. That means she knows where she is.

My space.

My home.

My *rules.*

I extend a hand, and when she places hers in mine, there's a subtle tremble. Barely there. But I feel it.

Perfect.

"You wore the lipstick." My voice drops as I draw her inside.

Her eyes lift, curious. "Isabella left it behind," she murmurs, almost *too* quietly. Then, a smirk. "I'm guessing per your orders."

I don't answer right away. I just look at her, *really* look.

The way her mouth moves when she tries to hold back a smile.

The way her dress hugs her curves without trying too hard.

The way she always teeters between wanting control and craving to give it up.

I step closer. My fingers trail a soft path beneath her jaw.

"That shade *belongs* to you now."

Her breath hitches—and I want to swallow it.

So I do.

I press my mouth to hers, not rushed, not hard. Just enough pressure to remind her that I own this moment. Her lips part without hesitation and I deepen the kiss, tasting the quiet gasp she gives me.

She leans into me, pliant and yielding, her fingers brushing against my chest like she doesn't even realize she's reaching for me. Every soft sigh she lets slip makes me want to push further, take more, ruin the careful evening I've planned.

But I force myself to rein it in. *Not yet.*

When I finally pull back, her lashes flutter against her cheeks, and her lips are still parted, swollen from mine. I drag my thumb across the corner of her mouth, savoring the sight of her undone and breathless, and fight the savage urge to wreck her dress before dinner.

Instead, I slide my hand down to the small of her back, claiming that small space of skin through fabric, and guide her toward the dining room.

She follows, quiet, curious, every step a test of my restraint.

The dim light overhead casts a golden glow across the room, warm and decadent.

I pull out her chair.

She sits.

And for the first time in my life, I find myself *hoping.*

Hoping she likes this place.

My penthouse. My clean lines. My perfectly curated world.

Because Olivia doesn't belong in a hotel like the other women I've used and tossed aside.

She belongs somewhere permanent.

She belongs *here.*

She lifts the lid on one of the covered dishes and her whole face lights up at what's inside: handmade tagliatelle in saffron cream sauce, layered with paper-thin ribbons of zucchini and crispy prosciutto, a touch of lemon zest curling in the steam. The kind of dish you can't find just anywhere, not unless you know exactly what to ask for.

She takes a bite, her eyes flutter closed, and then she lets out a soft hum that curls low in my stomach.

"La Serenata?" she finishes, looking up at me through those lashes like I've just handed her the moon.

"Yes."

Her fork stills. "That's...my *favorite* place."

She doesn't say thank you. Just like I expected, she gets quiet. I watch her across the table, the candlelight dancing across her cheekbones.

Most people can't stand silence. They scramble to fill it. She doesn't. She just withdraws into it like armor.

But I know better.

I see the woman who's afraid to be seen, yet dying to be claimed.

"You're quiet," I state, swirling the wine in my glass.

She shrugs, tries to hide behind another bite of food. But her throat works a little harder to swallow this time.

"It's just…" She sets her fork down, eyes locked on her plate. "It's weird. How much you know. My favorite restaurant. My coffee order. My dress size. What snacks I keep in the back of the cabinet."

I take a slow sip of wine. "And?"

Her eyes flick to mine. "And…*how?*"

I let a beat pass.

Take in her honest eyes.

And then I answer.

"When I want something," I say slowly, deliberately, "I make it my business to know everything about it."

Her breath hitches. Just barely. But I catch it.

Everything about her, the freckles on her nose, the smudge of lipstick on her wine glass, the way she crosses her ankles under the table like she's trying to ground herself, every bit of her is cataloged in my mind.

I don't say all that out loud.

I just watch as she looks away again, cheeks flushing pink.

Good.

Let her wonder how much more I know.

Because she's right.

It's not a coincidence.

It's obsession.

"Eat," I say taking a sip of my wine.

She swallows hard and takes a breath before she complies.

We eat. The silence isn't awkward, it's taut, charged, the kind that makes every scrape of silverware on porcelain feel like a gunshot.

Finally, she breaks it.

"It's still strange, and I *need* to talk about it," she says slowly, "you know so much about me, but I don't even know your favorite color."

I set my fork down, lean back, and let her think she's gotten the upper hand.

"It's the exact shade of your eyes."

Her breath catches. She blinks at me, stunned.

"And yours," I continue smoothly, "is mint green."

Her lips part. "How do you—"

"Like I said," I interrupt, voice low, measured, "when I want something, I notice everything."

Her fingers knot the napkin in her lap, her eyes searching my face. She doesn't even realize I'm feeding her breadcrumbs, leading her exactly where I want her.

Ask me.

Ask me what you really want to know.

She straightens and meets my gaze.

"You left the dress in a box on my bed," she says finally, eyes sharpening, "How?"

A dark chuckle escapes me, curling around the rim of my glass as I sip.

"Don't ask questions you already know the answer to."

"You've been in my apartment."

"Yes," I say without hesitation.

She stares, like she's waiting for me to backtrack.

I don't.

I expect anger. I expect her to push back. Storm off. Make me chase. I'm already ready to stop her if she tries.

Instead, she swallows, voice quieter now. "Did you pay my rent?"

"Yes."

Her gaze narrows. "In exchange for...whatever this is?"

"In exchange for being *mine?*" I correct, my tone sharper, decisive. "No. I take care of what's mine. So I took care of you."

She nods once, slowly, lips pressing together. Then she wipes her mouth with the napkin, movements careful, precise. "A year. You paid a year."

"Yes."

Her eyes lift back to mine, wide now.

"That's how long I expect it to take you to move in here instead. Though..." I let the pause stretch, savoring her pulse quickening across the table. "I plan on moving you in sooner."

She gasps.

"That's madness," she says with a nervous laugh. "We've only known each other a little over a month. We've worked together what—two weeks?"

I lean forward, elbows on the table, voice dropping into something darker, rougher.

"Since I saw you," I correct, "and claimed you for myself, one month, twelve days, nine hours..." I glance at my watch. "...and thirty-seven minutes."

Her mouth opens. Closes. Opens again.

No sound comes out.

Perfect.

Her throat works as she swallows, a nervous flush creeping up her chest. She's unraveling exactly on schedule.

"Come with me."

I push back from the table, my chair scraping against the polished floor. She looks up at me, still caught between resistance and intrigue, and I don't give her time to choose. I stand, extend my hand.

When she hesitates, I arch a brow. "Olivia."

Her pulse flutters at her throat. She places her hand in mine.

I pull her chair back for her, guiding her to her feet. Then I lead her toward the glass doors at the far end of the room, my palm steady against the small of her back.

The night air is cool when I open the doors, brushing over her skin. The city hums below us, restless and alive, but up here it's quiet. Just us and the stars.

"Look," I say quietly, steering her to the edge of the balcony. "Watch them."

She grips the railing, eyes lifted. I step up behind her.

She exhales, soft. Almost relaxed.

Then I lean in and press a kiss to the curve of her neck.

Her body jolts, *subtle*, but there.

I brush her hair out of the way with my hand and do it again, slower this time, my lips brushing over her pulse, my breath teasing the fine hairs at her nape.

"You think too much," I whisper against her skin. "I can see it."

My hands slide down her waist, coaxing, claiming.

"You've built your entire life around doing the right thing. Following the rules. Staying in control."

Another kiss, just below her jaw.

"But this," I nip gently, soothing the spot with my tongue, "has nothing to do with control."

She trembles.

"Shut it down, Olivia," I breathe into her ear. "Your logic. Your guilt. All that noise in your head trying to keep me out."

I lower my mouth to her shoulder, exposed beneath the slip of her dress. She tilts slightly, *just* enough.

"Let me in."

"What do you want?" I murmur, mouth dragging along the line of her jaw. "Not what you've been *told* to want. Not what's *safe*. Not what's rational. What do you—" my teeth graze her ear, just enough to make her shiver, "want?"

She grips the railing like it's the only thing keeping her tethered. But it's not enough. Not anymore.

Her breath stutters with every word I press into her skin.

"I want to hear it from your lips," I coax, soft but unyielding. "Say it. Tell me."

I kiss the spot just below her ear, slow, claiming.

"Don't think." Another kiss, lower, harder. "Just feel."

Her body sways back against mine, as though pulled there by gravity.

She turns in my arms, breathless, pupils blown, all pretense gone.

"You," she breathes out. "I want you."

I smile, slow and dangerous.

Step Two: Complete.

Chapter Twenty-One

OLIVIA

His mouth is on mine before I can take the words back, hard and consuming, his tongue sweeping in like he owns every part of me already. One minute I'm outside in the cool air, the next I'm stumbling backward, his hands unrelenting on my waist, steering me until the world blurs. My back slams against the bedroom wall, a gasp catching in my throat as he cages me in with his body. His hand pins my wrists high above my head, the other gripping my hip, dragging me flush against the thick, unmistakable ridge straining his slacks.

The contact rips a moan from me, shameful and needy, and he swallows it like it feeds him.

My dress strap slips. Cool air hits the bare line of my shoulder, and I flinch, tugging against his hold. I know what comes next. The strapless bra beneath, the one that always makes me feel too exposed, too soft. My body isn't the kind men like him want stripped bare under the lights.

He feels the hesitation instantly. His grip hardens, his mouth dragging lower, hot against my throat until his teeth scrape the sensitive spot that makes me tremble.

"Don't you fucking hide from me," he growls, rough and dangerous, every word vibrating against my skin. "You think I don't know what's under this dress? I've imagined every inch of you.

Every curve. Every soft place I'm going to sink into. You were made to be devoured, my sweet girl."

He releases my wrists and steps back. Just enough to make me ache from the loss of contact.

"Strip," he says, voice low and final. "Then lie on the bed. I want to see you."

My heart skips. Shame flares up fast, what if he sees the softness of my stomach, the dip at my waist that I always try to disguise?

"Now," he adds, eyes dark. "Unless you want me to tear it off *for* you."

That jolts me into motion. I take a breath and turn toward the bed, the air cool against my flushed skin as I ease the side zipper down. I don't dare look back. Not when I can feel his eyes on me like heat, like hunger, like punishment.

The dress falls and I face him.

Air skims my skin; every inch feels awake.

His gaze drags over me, slow and consuming until I forget why I ever tried to hide.

I climb onto the bed slowly, nerves alive and sparking. Lying there in just a bra and panties, I feel exposed. *Too much. Too soft. Too everything.*

But then he moves.

War peels off his shirt like he's undressing for a ritual. His pants follow. His cock strains thick and heavy behind his underwear, and when his eyes land on me, they go molten.

"Fuck," he breathes, his voice rough now. "Look at you. Laid out like temptation itself."

My breath shudders.

"Take it off," he says.

I blink.

"The bra. I want it gone."

My hands shake as I reach behind me and unhook the clasp. The cups fall away.

He lets out a low, dangerous sound that shoots straight between my legs.

"I knew those would be perfect," he mutters, crawling onto the bed like a man possessed. "Fuck, Olivia."

He palms one breast, then leans in to suck the nipple between his lips, teeth grazing it just enough to make me gasp.

"That's it," he groans. "Make those sounds for me. Let me hear what that perfect body does when it's finally getting what it needs."

His mouth moves from one breast to the other, tongue flicking over the hardened peak before he sucks deep, possessive. My hands tangle in his hair, holding on, my thighs shifting restlessly beneath him.

"War—"

"You're perfect." His voice is low, wrecked. "These tits were made to fill my hands. They're mine now. You hear me?"

I nod, breathless.

"No." His teeth graze my nipple, sharp enough to make me gasp. "Say it."

Heat rushes to my cheeks. "They're yours."

His cock jerks against me through the fabric between us, and he groans like the words undid him.

"Damn right they are."

His hand drags down my body, large palm skimming over my soft stomach, my hips, until his fingers press between my thighs. The thin fabric of my panties does nothing to hide how wet I am.

"You're soaked." His voice is a dangerous rasp. "All this just from a little praise? From me telling you what's mine?"

A helpless sound breaks in my throat when his thumb circles my clit through the damp fabric.

"Talk to me, sweet girl. Tell me what this greedy cunt needs."

"I-I don't—" I whimper. "I don't know."

He lifts his head, eyes narrowing. "You do. You're just *shy*. But I'll drag it out of you."

He slides lower, his mouth blazing a trail down my stomach, lips brushing the edge of my panties. When he kisses just above the waistband, my whole body jerks.

"Perfect little mess," he mutters. Then his fingers hook under the band, and in one sharp motion he rips the panties down my legs and tosses them aside.

He stares for a beat, gaze dark and hungry. "*Fuck.* Look at you. Glorious. And all mine."

I try to close my thighs, too bare, too raw, too *big*, but his hands clamp around them, forcing them open.

"Don't." His growl vibrates straight through me. "You don't hide from me. You keep these thighs parted and let me see what's mine."

And then his mouth is on me.

I gasp, choking on the sound, as his tongue circles my clit in a hot, wet stroke that rips the air from my lungs. My hips jerk on instinct, before I can stop them, but his hands clamp down hard on my thighs, pinning me to the mattress.

"Stay still," he growls against me, his breath hot over my pussy. "You don't grind on me. You take what I give you."

And then he devours me.

His tongue lashes over my clit in ruthless strokes, sucking it into his mouth, releasing it, then doing it again until I'm gasping his name like a prayer. My hands claw the sheets, reaching for anything to hold on to, but he doesn't let up. Every flick of his tongue, every hard pull of his mouth is calculated torture.

"War! Oh fuck—" I sob, the plea ragged.

A dark groan vibrates from deep in his chest as he pushes two fingers inside me, thick and unrelenting. The sudden stretch rips a cry from me, my body clenching helplessly around him.

"Fuck," he rasps sucking hard on my clit while his fingers thrust deep. "Tight little cunt's desperate for me already. You feel that? That's mine. Every squeeze, every drip; *mine.*"

The wet sounds are obscene. The slick thrust of his fingers, the greedy suck of his mouth, the rough growl vibrating against my most sensitive spot, it's filth and hunger, raw and consuming.

I thrash, trembling, my orgasm clawing up fast, wild.

He pulls back just enough to rasp, "You don't come until I tell you. Do you understand?" His fingers still, buried inside me. His hot breath hovers over my clit, tormenting me with absence.

I whimper, shaking my head, desperate. "Please—"

His teeth graze my clit, sharp enough to make me cry out. "Say it, Olivia. Say you'll hold it."

"Yes!" My voice cracks, high and frantic. "Yes, I'll wait—"

"Good girl."

And then he's on me again, tongue relentless, fingers thrusting, curling just right until my back arches clean off the bed. He controls every second, dragging me higher, forcing me to teeter right at the edge without falling.

I know I won't last. He's destroying me, orchestrating even the way I break.

His tongue is merciless, dragging me higher with every flick, every rough pull, his fingers pumping inside me until I'm trembling, begging. My nails rake at the sheets, desperate for something to anchor me.

"War, please, I can't—"

"Yes, you can," he growls into me, mouth sealing over my clit again. His words vibrate against me, dark and consuming. "You'll hold it until I give you permission. You'll take it because I said so."

I'm shaking, my body betraying me, walls clenching hard around his fingers. The pressure is unbearable, my orgasm begging to break free.

"Beg for it," he rasps, pulling back just enough to torment me with air. "Tell me exactly what you need."

"Please!" My voice is high, frantic. "Please let me come!"

"Say my name while you beg for it."

"War, *please,* I need it, I need to come—"

He growls like the sound feeds him. "Beautiful. *Now* give it to me."

His mouth latches back onto my clit, tongue ruthless, fingers curling deep; just right, and the dam bursts.

I cry out, my body trembling, as wave after wave tears through me. His mouth doesn't relent. He rides me through it, owning every spasm, every helpless cry, until I'm nothing but a trembling wreck beneath him.

When he finally pulls away, I melt into the sheets. My chest heaves. My mind blanks. I'm still gasping for air when the mattress dips beneath his weight.

He crawls over me, heat sliding between my thighs.

I keep my eyes closed, trying to catch a breath, until his hand grips my jaw, *firm, commanding,* and tilts my face to his.

"Look at me."

His voice is gravel. Rough and unrelenting.

My lashes flutter open. He's there, above me. Pupils blown with hunger. His cock thick and heavy between my thighs.

My cheeks burn hot, shameful and exposed, and his lips twist into a filthy smirk.

"There it is," he rasps. "That blush. That sweet little look that says you know you're mine. Don't hide it, Olivia. Wear it for me."

Before I can even form a thought, he pushes inside me.

The stretch punches a gasp out of my lungs, sharp and visceral, my hands grasp at his shoulders, my nails digging into his skin as he fills me; thick, deep, *relentless.* I haven't had sex in over a year, and it feels like my body is splitting open, reawakened, *alive.*

"Oh!" The word rips out of me, broken.

He stills, buried deep, eyes locked on mine. "Breathe with me."

I do. In. Out. Slowly. The ache softens. The pressure shifts to pleasure.

"There she is," he growls as he begins to move.

His mouth is at my ear, his tone dark and triumphant.

"That's it. Take it. Feel this cock owning you, opening you up. You're *mine* now. You hear me?"

I nod frantically, lost in the ache, the fire of being stretched and claimed.

He thrusts harder, deeper, forcing me to feel every brutal inch.

"Say it," he hisses. "Say you're mine."

"You—I'm yours," I choke, voice shaking.

"Good girl." His pace quickens, fucking me harder, his hold unyielding, as he keeps my eyes on his. "Don't you dare look away. I want you red-cheeked and wrecked, staring at the man who owns this pussy now."

My face burns hotter, my body helpless under his, and I never want to be anywhere else. This is exactly where I want to be.

His cock drives deeper, relentless, and I can't breathe. My body feels split apart, every nerve ending sparking, my pulse pounding in my ears. A year of nothing, and now this—*him,* and it's too much, it's everything, it's exactly what I didn't know I'd been starving for.

"Fuck," he snarls, hips slamming into mine. "This pussy is meant for me. Perfect, tight, wet; gripping me like you've been waiting for my cock to claim you."

I moan, shameful and wrecked, my cheeks blazing hotter with every filthy word.

"There it is," he growls, watching my face. "That blush. You can't hide how much you love this. Being filled. *Owned.* Fucked just like this body deserves."

My nails claw uselessly at his shoulders, at the sheets, at anything I can find to ground me. He doesn't give me a chance. Every thrust is sharp, pounding me into the mattress, dragging me right back to where he wants me.

"You feel that?" His voice is low, dangerous, his grip firm so I can't look away. "That's me. Every inch. Every thrust. You're not running from it, Olivia. You're taking it. You're mine."

"Yes," I sob, my voice breaking. "Yes—"

His breath hot against my ear, his words filth pouring straight into my bloodstream with every thrust.

"Say it again. Say you're mine while I fuck you open."

"I'm yours!" I cry, my body clenching tight around him. "War, I'm yours!"

"Good girl." The praise is rough, almost guttural. "Now come for me. Milk this cock like the desperate little slut you are."

The word hits me like a lash, *slut,* and instead of flinching, something in me tightens. My body responds before my brain can catch up, pulsing around him so hard it drags a groan from his chest.

Heat floods my cheeks. I don't know what shocks me more, that he said it, or that I *loved* it.

"Oh," he growls, fucking me deeper, "you *liked* that."

My breath shudders. My blush blooms deeper. I can't look away.

"Didn't you, Olivia?" he presses. "You like being called my little slut?"

I moan, shameless and wrecked, the need in me so sharp it hurts. "Yes," I gasp. "I-I loved it."

The confession rips something loose inside me. My orgasm slams into me with brutal force, my body shaking, back arching, walls clenching so tight around him it hurts. I scream his name, incoherent and undone, as he fucks me through it.

He doesn't stop. His thrusts riding the convulsions of my body, groaning in my ear.

"Look at you. Falling apart on my cock. *Mine.* Every whimper, every blush, every messy little spasm. *It belongs to me now.*"

I can barely see, barely think, but the way my pussy clutches around him drags a savage groan from his chest. His thrusts turn rougher, almost frantic, and then he breaks, driving deep, grinding hard as he comes inside me.

The heat floods me, hot and claiming, his cock pulsing with every release. He releases my jaw and holds me pinned, buried to the hilt, making sure I feel every drop.

His forehead presses against mine, his breath ragged, his grip tightening. His eyes burn into me, dark and feral.

"You're ruined, Olivia," he rasps, still throbbing inside me. "No one else will ever have you like this. No one else gets this pussy. It's mine now. Understand?"

I nod breathless, cheeks flaming, body limp beneath him, still trembling from the aftershocks.

I've never wanted to belong to anyone more.

Chapter Twenty-Two

WAR

She's still asleep.

Sprawled in my bed, wrapped in the scent of sex and sweat and her perfume still clinging to her skin.

Olivia.

My Olivia.

I've never liked waking up next to anyone. I usually don't. I leave. Or make them. Most don't even make it past midnight. But this—

This feels...different.

Dangerously so.

Her cheek is pressed to my pillow, lips slightly parted, lashes still fluttering like she's dreaming. There's a faint pink flush across her chest. Her hair's a mess, her body still glowing from last night, and I can't fucking look away.

She took *everything* I gave her.

Every inch.

Every word.

Every order.

Perfect.

My jaw flexes. I should let her sleep. Should let her rest. But part of me wants to wake her just to hear her say my name again, wrecked and breathless and *fucking mine*.

My chest tightens as I watch her, like something inside me is shifting, re-arranging itself in the space she's already started to claim.

I'm not used to soft.

But with her, it's effortless.

Natural.

Right.

She deserves more.

Not just orgasms and control. Not just this penthouse or a weekend in my bed.

She needs more designer dresses tailored to hug her curves. The kind of luxury that turns heads the second she walks into a room.

She needs hair products and makeup laid out for her every morning. Creams, palettes, the perfect shade of lipstick I'll fuck off her lips before she finishes her first sip of coffee.

She needs her favorite perfume always stocked.

Purses. Shoes. A whole fucking store.

Whatever she wants, it's mine to give her.

She needs to move in.

Soon.

I could have the closet cleared out in an hour. Drawers emptied. Security updated. Her name on the elevator list. Done before she even finishes brunch.

She might just be...

No.

I stop the thought dead in its tracks.

Because if she's mine permanently...

That means being a Beaumont.

And Beaumont's don't love clean. We ruin. We *rot* from the inside out.

If I keep her, if I make her mine the way I want to, it won't be long before the blood of my name starts staining hers too.

I'll destroy her just by letting her love me.

And I don't know if I'll care enough to stop it.

My name can't be trusted with anything good.

Especially not someone like her.

I shake it off and slide out of bed, careful not to wake her. My feet hit the cool floor, and I head for the kitchen, grabbing a glass and filling it with water like it'll wash the thoughts away.

It doesn't.

I glance over my shoulder toward the bedroom, my jaw tightening.

She'll be hungry when she wakes up.

I grab my phone, already typing.

Room service won't cut it. She deserves the best. I find her favorite breakfast spot and order everything she loves. *Extra.* Enough to make her smile, to make her feel spoiled.

Because she is.

She's mine now.

And I'm going to make sure she never forgets what that means.

I order everything she needs and I wait.

The tray of food sits ready by the bed, steam curling in the air. Truffle eggs, croissants, roasted potatoes, a seasonal fruit compote I had them remake twice until it looked good enough for her.

Only the best.

And next to it, the bags. Clothes delivered at dawn. Dresses, shoes, makeup, everything she should have at her fingertips. Everything I'll give her without hesitation.

I sit in the armchair across the room, shirtless, sweatpants low on my hips, watching her.

Hours pass, and I don't move.

Can't.

I wait for the scent of breakfast to wake her.

Her chest rises and falls in slow, steady breaths. Her lips are parted, swollen from my kisses.

I begin to catalog.

Every curve I worshipped.

Every sound she made when she broke beneath me.

Every soft, greedy clutch of her cunt on my cock.

I want it again.

Now.

But I force myself to sit, to watch, to starve in silence. Because the ache in my chest, the hunger crawling under my skin, is almost sweeter than the release.

Almost.

She looks fragile like this. Breakable. But mine to break or protect and I haven't decided which—maybe both.

No one else will *ever* get this view.

Her lashes flutter. She stirs. A soft sound escapes her throat, and I lean forward in the chair, pulse kicking like I've been waiting a lifetime for her to wake.

Her eyes crack open.

Wide, startled, doe-eyed.

Perfect.

"There she is," I murmur, voice rough from disuse.

She startles hard, jerking upright in bed.

The comforter drops.

And there *they* are.

Her breasts, soft and flushed and perfect, bouncing slightly with the movement. The blanket pools at her hips like an invitation.

She gasps and reaches for the comforter, trying to drag it up.

"Don't." My voice cuts sharp across the room.

Her breath hitches. Her fingers still.

Good.

I rise from the chair, slow, deliberate, and cross to the bed. She watches every step like she can't decide whether to run or melt into it.

That's good. Fear and hunger look beautiful on her.

When I reach her, I set the tray across her lap, the legs sliding neatly into place.

"Eat," I order.

She hesitates, *always so hesitant, always* second-guessing, but then she picks up the fork, testing a bite. Her lips part on a soft hum as she chews, and the sound knots low in my gut.

I don't comment. I don't need to. She'll learn in time that everything she loves will always be provided.

As she eats, I cross to the closet and pull out the bags delivered this morning. Designer. Tailored. Every detail chosen because I've already memorized her size, her style, her preferences. Dresses. Shoes. A silk blouse the color of her blush.

Her fork slows as she watches me lay each piece out.

I pick up the mint green cashmere sweater.

"This." I hold it up. "With the cream skirt and heels. You'll wear it today."

Her throat works as she swallows, fork paused halfway to her lips.

I smooth the fabric once before laying it neatly at the foot of the bed. Then I add the silk lingerie beneath it, the straps delicate, designed for me to peel off her later.

Her brows draw in as she takes in the clothing on the bed, but she says nothing.

Good.

She needs to understand what this is.

"You don't need to worry about what to bring next time." My voice stays even, controlled, the way I give orders at work. "Everything you need is here now. Clothes. Makeup. Shoes.

Perfume. Your sizes, your colors, your preferences; I've taken care of it."

Her lips part, but no sound comes out.

"You'll be staying the weekend," I tell her, calm but deliberate.

Her fork clatters softly against the tray.

"This morning a walk through the Conservatory Garden. You'll like it. Roses, fountains, quiet paths where no one will bother us."

Her lips part like she wants to argue, but I don't let her.

"After that, an art exhibit. Something I want you to see. Tonight, dinner. No parties. No noise. Just us."

I let the silence stretch until she finally looks at me. Then I pin her there with my eyes.

"And after this weekend," I murmur, leaning forward, "you'll leave with me every morning to work. You'll come home with me every night. And by the end of the week, Olivia, you'll be moved in."

Her breath hitches.

I smile. Slow. Dangerous.

Inside, my chest is a riot. Because the thought of her here—*permanently,* sets something loose I've never let myself feel before.

But she doesn't need to know that. Not yet.

All she needs to know is this:

Her life belongs to me now.

Chapter Twenty-Three

OLIVIA

The sex? Amazing.

This food? Phenomenal.

Warren Beaumont pulling out clothes, lining them up like soldiers, and telling me I'm moving in?

No.

No.

No.

NO.

I move the tray off my lap, every nerve suddenly screaming wrong, and gather the comforter up to cover my chest as I swing my legs off the bed.

I need out.

I need air.

I need to think without him watching me like he owns every breath I take.

I spot my dress on the floor. My underwear. I grab both in one frantic motion and step into the panties like I'm on fire.

He's still watching.

Warren fucking Beaumont takes a seat, shirtless, in a chair like a king watching a prisoner try to escape. His eyes are molten steel, pupils blown wide, and still, *still* he doesn't move.

I pull the dress over my head.

Fuck the bra. I don't care.

I just need to get out of this bed, this tower, this trap.

"Olivia."

One word. Just one. And it stops me.

His voice slices straight through the noise.

I freeze, halfway to the door.

"I'm not doing this," I say quickly, not looking at him. "I'm not playing house in your penthouse. I'm not your girlfriend of the month."

Silence.

No footsteps. No outburst. Just pressure. His silence is heavier than most men's screams.

"We had fun," I push, my voice rising. "We had sex. That's all this was. You don't get to order my clothes and plan my calendar and decide where I live like I'm one of the properties you buy and control."

Still nothing.

I can feel his stare on my back like heat.

My throat tightens. I hate the way my voice wavers next.

"I don't want to be in your loop of women, Warren."

Finally, I hear it. The soft creak of the chair as he rises.

My body locks up.

"I said—"

"You're spiraling," he says, voice calm. Too calm. "I can hear the thoughts bouncing around in that pretty head of yours, and not a single one of them is real."

I turn to face him, and it's a mistake.

He's close. *Too close.*

"Stop talking *at* me," I snap. "You don't know what I'm thinking—"

"I do." His eyes flash. "You think I recycle women. You're right. I do. But not you."

My breath gets caught in my chest.

"But, there's something more Olivia. Maybe you think this is too much. Too fast. You don't deserve it. That if you stay, I'll *see* too much. That I'll figure out you're not the polished, perfect woman you think I want."

I swallow hard. He's half right.

"Tell me I'm wrong."

I open my mouth, but nothing comes out.

He steps closer.

"Tell me," he demands, "what are you so scared I'll find out?"

My heart stammers. My pulse is everywhere.

"Nothing," I whisper.

"Liar." His voice softens, darkens. "What are you hiding?"

The air thickens between us.

I weigh my options. If he's serious about this. About me. Maybe he could...

No.

No one else gets dragged in to my family shit.

"I just have a lot going on."

Warren exhales slowly. "I'll figure it out, Olivia." He smirks.

"You know I will. Now take off this dress. Take a shower and change. We leave in twenty."

I don't move.

He watches me, waiting.

Ten seconds feel like ten years.

But then, I turn.

Wordless.

Obedient.

Furious at how much I want this.

Want him.

***

The garden is quiet.

Not silent. There's the hum of the city beyond the hedges, the crunch of gravel beneath my shoes, the flutter of wings near the rose beds, but quiet in a way that feels rare.

Rare and...*intentional.*

Warren walks beside me. No suit today. Just slacks and a white button-down, sleeves rolled, the top undone. A watch still gleams on his wrist, subtle yet stupid expensive.

He looks like he walked out of a billionaire magazine spread titled: *Undress Me With Your Eyes.*

Unfortunately, my eyes are traitors.

He hasn't said much since we arrived, just kept pace beside me as we followed the winding paths. The conservatory garden is lush, overgrown in the best way, with high hedges and arched iron gates and blooms that look like they were painted instead of grown.

My brain should still be in fight mode. Still pissed. Still storming out.

But he handed me a coffee I didn't ask for, my order, perfect, *of course,* and led me through this secret pocket of the city like it was a gift.

I hate how easily my heart flutters.

"You brought me here to win me over," I murmur, half a step ahead of him now, dragging my fingers through a cluster of soft pink petals.

Warren's voice comes low behind me. "No. I brought you here so you'd stay long enough to see I'm not trying to win. I'm *claiming.*"

My stomach flips.

I whirl on him. "What do you want from me, Warren?"

He doesn't answer right away. Just steps closer. Eyes on mine. Not devouring like earlier. Not demanding.

Just...seeing me.

"I want you," he says quietly.

"That's not an answer," I snap, voice too breathy.

"It's the only one that matters." Another step forward. So close his cologne permeates my senses. "You can ask why."

I do.

My voice comes out softer. "Why me?"

His gaze drops to my mouth and then lifts again. And when he speaks, it's a whisper, meant just for me.

"Because you're the only woman who seems strong enough to survive me."

My heart stutters. Hard.

Before I can say anything—*before I can breathe,* he lifts a hand and brushes a petal from my hair like it was interrupting his view.

"What's your favorite flower, Olivia?" he asks softly.

I blink, still rattling.

"What?"

He repeats it, even softer. "Your favorite flower."

The question guts me in a way I'm not ready for.

No one's ever asked.

Not once.

Not in all the years I've bought them for myself and pretended it didn't matter.

I look down, then back up.

"Peonies," I whisper. "Blush pink ones."

Warren nods once. "Noted."

And I don't know why, but I believe him.

That he'll remember.

That I'll come home one day and they'll be there.

Waiting.

My heart shouldn't flutter.

It does anyway.

We walk in silence for a while, the gravel path winding beneath our feet. The wind teases a loose strand of hair into my face, and I tuck it back, needing something, *anything,* to keep myself grounded.

So I ask.

"So when you renovate the Parker Building... are you going to do something with it?"

His gaze shifts, but he doesn't stop walking.

"Like what?" he asks.

"I don't know. A plaque, maybe. Something for Noah?"

He hums. "Maybe."

Then, after a pause:

"Perhaps."

It should be a non-answer, but something in the way he says it feels loaded. Like the thoughts behind it are heavy. Sharp-edged.

He stops near a bench tucked beneath a weeping cherry tree, pink blossoms raining down around us, and sits. I stay standing.

"You know," he says, eyes fixed forward, "you and my brothers are the only people who know the truth about the Parker Building."

I frown, sitting beside him now, the breeze curling around my legs.

"I mean, I know of it," I say gently. "I know it was a tragic moment for you. But I'm not sure I understand the full significance."

He's quiet for a moment.

Then:

"It's the biggest stain I ever left on my family's name."

I blink. "What do you mean?"

His jaw clenches. His hands are resting on his thighs, but I can see the tension crawling up his arms.

"*'Beaumont's child gets foster kid killed in abandoned building on the outskirts of town.'* That was the headline."

I feel my breath catch.

"Foster?" I whisper.

He nods.

"My parents fostered a lot of kids. Not for money. Not even because they cared. It was for optics. To look like good billionaires." He scoffs. "As if any of us are."

I stay quiet. I can tell he's somewhere else now, eyes distant, mouth a hard line.

"That was my first taste of the media, sharp, bitter, and ruinous." he murmurs. "My family's faces plastered across every paper. Talk shows. Lawsuits. The whispers. My parents were livid, but I—" His voice falters for the first time. "I was the disappointment. Out of control. The one who didn't care about the family name."

The wind rustles through the trees, scattering petals like a silent kind of mourning.

I don't speak. I don't know what I could say.

He turns to me slowly, the sadness still there, but something else building underneath.

"So the Parker Building? Renovating it?" He gives a small, sharp smile. "That's my penance. A monument to my failure. It's more than I deserve."

He reaches for my hand. Gathers it carefully, like he's holding something breakable. Then he leans down and presses a kiss to my knuckles.

Soft. Reverent.

"But you," he says, eyes lifting to mine, "you're the one who brought that renovation back."

My breath stutters.

"You're the hope in the ashes, Olivia Baker."

And just like that, I forget how to breathe.

He straightens, still holding my hand.

"Come on," he says. "Let's get lunch. Then we'll head back, get ready for the exhibit tonight."

I nod, wordless, and let him lead me through the garden.

Not because I'm his.

But because, for the first time, he feels like mine too.

WAR

The room buzzes quietly, low murmurs, the occasional click of heels, the clink of crystal against glass.

I should be paying attention to the art. The patrons. The artist.

But I'm not.

I'm watching Olivia.

She's in the dress I picked.

Red.

I told her once brunettes look stunning in red.

And I was right.

It hugs her in all the right places. Soft flare. Smooth chiffon that moves when she walks like it's obeying her. Her hair's pinned up. Lips painted to match the fabric clinging to her hips.

She doesn't realize it yet, but this entire gallery was curated to echo her.

Bold. Classic. Unapologetically gorgeous.

Her fingers graze a canvas. Her head tilts. She's biting her bottom lip in concentration, like she's trying to decode something sacred.

She has no idea what's waiting for her at the end of this hallway.

I nod once at the gallery owner as we pass, and she smiles knowingly. The last room, the spotlighted alcove, has been cleared.

Every patron has been redirected elsewhere.

This moment isn't for them.

It's for *her.*

And me.

We turn the corner.

She stops walking.

Dead still.

Her breath catches.

And I feel it.

The moment she sees *herself.*

Emerald green crepe. The slit high, the shadows deep, her figure half-tucked into the crook of my arm, her smile soft and bright. The same photo that Wesley slammed onto my weight bench with a warning.

Only now, it's paint.

Rendered in soft strokes. Vivid. *Intentional.*

Framed in gold.

Her glow immortalized.

She doesn't speak.

Her lips part like she's seeing herself for the first time. Like she can't quite believe she's beautiful enough to hang in a gallery.

She is.

But it's not just the painting I'm looking at. It's her *now.* In this light. In that red dress.

The neckline dips just enough to tease. Her shoulders bare, her hair swept up and away from her face like a gift being unwrapped. A flush blooms across her chest, high on her cheeks, and I don't know if it's from the lighting or the attention, but it's fucking stunning.

But her eyes, her eyes give her away. Wide, uncertain, reverent.

She doesn't know how to stand in this kind of spotlight.

So I step closer. Become her anchor.

"It was taken after the gala. The photo went viral. Tabloids ran it for days. Wesley hated it."

A pause.

"I didn't. It was the best piece of media about me in years."

Her eyes flick to mine, hesitant.

"I needed something good," I murmur. "Something I could look at and remember that not everything about my name is stained. So I commissioned it."

Her voice is soft. "You commissioned a portrait of me?"

"Of us."

She turns toward the canvas again, lips parting slightly.

I step closer, my tone dipping.

"Do you like it?"

She swallows. Nods. "It's... beautiful."

"Would you like to keep it?"

Her head snaps toward me. "What?"

I lift a brow. "We can hang it in our bedroom."

Her whole face flushes.

"I'm not moving in with you," she stammers, breath catching. "I never said yes."

I smirk, stepping even closer. "Then tell me no."

Her lips twist.

Turns to look at the portrait.

Then at me.

Then back again.

And then—

A breath.

A blink.

A choice.

"No," she breathes. "I don't think I want to tell you no anymore."

The ache in my chest tightens. Spreads.

And for the first time in years...
I feel fucking whole.

***

She says she doesn't want to tell me no anymore.

So I don't give her the chance.

As soon as the bedroom door shuts behind us, I've already got my hands on her. One at the back of her neck, the other at her waist, walking her backward toward the bedroom like I'm leading her straight into surrender.

The moment her calves hit the edge of the bed, I push her down.

She falls with a gasp, flushed and breathless, red dress bunched high on her thighs. Her lipstick's still intact, *barely*, and I plan to ruin that next.

"I've been hard since the gallery," I growl, dropping to my knees between her legs, dragging my palms up those perfect, plush thighs. "Every time someone looked at you, I wanted to break something."

Her breath catches. "Warren—"

"Shut up." I lean in, bite the inside of her thigh. Not gentle. Not soft.

She yelps, back arching.

"I'm done being patient."

I drag her dress higher and tear her panties down her legs, no ceremony, no warning. Just possession.

"I had you painted in green," I growl, gripping her thighs to spread them wider. "But tonight, I want red."

Then I devour her.

No build-up. No teasing.

I lick and suck like I'm starving, tongue punishing, hands locking her open as she writhes. She tastes like she's been waiting for this all day. Like the words she said at the gallery were already a promise.

She doesn't want to say no anymore?

Good.

Because I won't let her.

She claws at the sheets, whimpering, already close, but I don't slow. I don't give her the chance to breathe.

"Come," I order against her clit, voice low and savage. "Now."

And she does.

Hard.

Her hips buck, thighs shaking, cries sharp and wrecked as she falls apart on my tongue.

I ride her through it, holding her down, drinking in every spasm like a fucking addict.

When she's limp and panting, I rise, wiping my mouth on the back of my hand like I just won a war.

She looks up at me dazed. Ravaged. And I haven't even started.

"On your knees," I demand, already unbuckling my belt.

She moves slowly, *too slowly,* so I yank her by the wrist and pull her to the edge of the bed, forcing her down to her knees.

"You want to be good for me?" I murmur, brushing my thumb across her bottom lip. "Then show me. Open up."

Her lips part. Her eyes wide.

I shove my cock past them.

No warning. No easing.

She gags around the thickness, but I don't stop. I hold her there, her throat stretched, her lips red and ruined.

"Good girl," I groan. "Take it. Take all of it. Show me what that mouth was *made* for."

She sucks like she needs me to believe it. Like she's desperate to be wrecked. Her tongue slides along the underside, her hands gripping my thighs, and when she moans around me, I nearly lose it.

I pull her off with a growl, cock glistening.

"Enough."

I pull her up roughly by the waist, tossing her back onto the bed, but I don't follow her down—not yet.

She's gasping, flushed, lips swollen and slick from sucking my cock like her life depended on it. *She's too damn good at it.*

I crawl up slowly, taking my time, watching the way her breath hitches with every inch I close in.

"You want me, Olivia?" My voice is low and steady as I press her into the mattress. "Then you'll obey me. You'll wait for me. And when you finally come, it'll be with my name in your mouth and feel of my cock stamped into your soul."

I lean down, lips brushing her ear. "No coming until I say. I don't care how close you get. I want you trembling. Desperate. Holding on by a thread. Can you do that for me, sweet girl?"

I pull back just enough to see her eyes, voice like silk over steel. "*Say it.* Say you'll obey."

"Yes," she breathes, pupils blown wide. "I'll obey."

"Good girl."

The praise is rough and reverent, a filthy reward in itself.

I press my forehead to hers. "You don't come until I tell you. No matter how full you feel. No matter how much your pussy begs me. You wait for me. Understand?"

She nods.

"Words, Olivia."

"Yes, War. I'll wait. I swear."

"That's my girl."

I drag her dress down her shoulders and off her arms, ripping it straight down the middle.

She gasps.

"Warren!"

"I'll get you a new one," I mutter, pressing her wrists into the mattress. "Looks better on the floor anyway."

I line up at her entrance.

"Please War," she breathes out.

"Fuck," I growl, the sound ragged with restraint snapping thread by thread. "That's it, *beg* just like that."

I grip her jaw, forcing her gaze to stay locked with mine. "You have to earn it, Olivia. Every inch. Every thrust. Every praise-laced command." I press forward, slow and deep, until I'm fully inside her, filling her just like she begged; just like she was made for.

She cries out, loud, wrecked, guttural. Perfect.

"Warren! oh god—" she gasps, nails clawing at my back as her hips lift instinctively, chasing every brutal inch.

"Yeah," I grit, driving deeper. "That's what I fucking wanted."

She claws at my back, hips jerking beneath mine, and I don't let her find a rhythm. I pin her down and take. Hard. Relentless. My cock splitting her open, dragging filthy sounds from her mouth every time I slam into her.

"You want the truth?" I snarl in her ear. "You're the only woman who's ever made me lose control. The only one I've ever wanted to fuck until I break."

She cries out, nails digging deep, legs wrapped tight around me like she doesn't want me to leave even if I tried.

"You're wrecked for me," I growl, hips slamming into hers. "Owned and open, just the way I want you."

"Please, don't stop," she pants. "I-I need it. I need all of it."

She sobs my name, begging for more, and I give it to her, deeper, harder; fucking her like a man who's finally accepted his goddamn fate.

Her pussy clenches around me like she was made to be fucked stupid.

And I plan to keep going until she is.

Until her voice is wrecked from screaming my name. Until her thighs are shaking so hard she can't stand. Until every inch of her body remembers who she belongs to.

Me.

Only me.

Her nails rake down my back as I pound into her, unrelenting. Her cries are high, broken, and desperate, but she's not telling me to stop.

She's telling me to take more.

"Look at me," I growl, hand gripping her jaw as I slam in deep.

Her eyes flutter open, glassy and wide. Red-cheeked. Wrecked.

There it is.

That fucking look I'll never get tired of.

"Say it," I snarl. "Say what I want to hear. Say this body obeys me."

"Yes," she gasps, voice cracking. "It does—I do!"

"That's my good girl."

I shift her legs higher, spreading her open, burying myself even deeper, so deep she chokes on a sob and grabs for anything she can find.

"Too much?" I hiss, voice dark, cock still driving hard.

She shakes her head. Whimpering. Eyes wild.

"Good girl."

Her breath stutters. Her walls clench again, tight, soaked, gripping me like her cunt knows it's about to be claimed.

"You gonna come for me again?" I rasp. "You gonna soak my cock like a filthy little toy?"

"Yes," she cries, legs shaking. "Please, Warren—I need it, I need to come!"

"Not yet," I whisper against her lips.

She whimpers frustrated as I slow my movements to punishing strokes that build heat and torment in equal measure.

Her hand leaves my back to snake between us, but I catch her wrist and pin it above her head, "No sweet girl, be a good for me, and wait."

Her hips buck.

My other hand wraps tightly around her waist, anchoring her to every sharp, slow thrust, halting her movements.

"You hold it," I grit out. "No matter how good it feels. No matter how much your body wants to give in."

I watch every flicker of emotion in her eyes, desire, desperation, worship, and my voice softens. "You're doing so good for me, baby... letting me use your body like it belongs to me. Because *it does. You* do."

My pace deepens, rougher now, and I murmur into her ear, "Hold it a little longer, just for me. Let me watch you break trying to be good."

"Please, War," she whimpers, trembling beneath me, her walls fluttering in warning.

I growl low in my throat, the sound dark and primal. "You're close again, aren't you?"

She nods frantically, eyes wide and glossy. Desperate.

I slam in deep, dragging a gasp from her throat. "You think begging makes it easier? No, my sweet girl. It makes it harder. Because now I know how bad you want it."

She sobs my name again, body arching.

But I don't let her go there.

Instead, I grip her jaw tight and make her look at me. "You want to come?"

"Yes," she chokes out. "Please, Warren, I've been good, I held it—I *need* it."

My voice drops low, hot against her lips. "You did. You held it like a perfect fucking toy."

I slam in again, slow but brutal. "But I'm not done watching you fall apart."

She cries out, guttural and wrecked.

Her hips fight to move, but I keep her still, my grip on her waist tightening

"You're doing so fucking good for me," I rasp. "Trembling, dripping, obeying like you were made for this."

"I'm trying," she whimpers, voice breaking.

Her breath stutters, her whole body locked tight. Such a defiant desperate look in those gorgeous eyes.

"Good girl," I breathe, voice thick with dark praise. "Fucking *so* good baby... taking it so well, holding back even when you're dying to fall apart for me."

Her fluttering walls clench around me, her body quaking with need, and I groan, low, feral, drunk on how perfectly she obeys.

"Look at you," I rasp, my lips brushing hers, "so desperate to come, but still listening. Still giving your body to me, exactly the way I want it."

Each thrust now is precise and brutal, angled to wreck that sweet spot, again and again, dragging you to the very edge. "You feel that? That pressure? That ache? That's me. That's what I do to you and you'll never forget it."

"Never," she chokes out.

Perfect.

"You've earned it. Come for me. *Now.*"

I thrust deep. Once, twice, hard enough to make the bed slam against the wall.

"Come for me. Show me what I fucking own."

She shatters.

Loud.

Tearing the room apart with her cry as she breaks beneath me, her body convulsing, spasming, milking my cock like it's begging me to fill her.

"Fuck," I growl, undone by the way her body seizes around me, tight, hot, perfect.

The sound of her gratitude, her desperate pleas, the way she sobs "Thank you, War!" as she comes hard for me, it's everything.

My control fractures.

"You're so welcome my sweet girl," I snarl, thrusting deep again, my voice breaking with how proud, how possessive, how fucking wrecked I am by her. "You feel what you do to me, Olivia? You feel how tight you are? How fucking perfect?"

"Yes, War—please, fill me."

Her voice is desperate, trembling, soaked in need, and it ruins me.

Her begging, it *fuels* me.

Drives me feral.

A curse rips from my chest as I slam into her one last time, burying myself to the hilt, cock throbbing, every muscle locking tight as I let go with a brutal, guttural groan.

I spill deep inside her; hot, thick, full, claiming her the way she begged. The way I was *always* going to.

Pulse after pulse.

Possession pours into her body like it belongs there.

Because it does.

She gasps my name again, breathless and dazed, and I can't stop pressing into her, grinding deeper, *needing* her to feel every drop. Needing it *branded* into her.

I still, finally, the pulsing ebbing.

But I don't pull out yet, I stay wrapped in her warmth, breath catching as I slowly come down, panting, utterly fucking ruined.

My grip loosens and I cradle her face with both hands. She's flushed, radiant, trembling beneath me—and *still*, she smiles like she's never known anything better.

My fucking undoing.

"My sweet girl," I whisper against her mouth. "So fucking perfect for me."

She blinks up at me, eyes half-lidded, lips kiss-swollen, glowing.

"You fucking ruined me," she whispers with a light chuckle, lips parting in a breathless smile. "I want you to do it again."

"Oh, I will. I've never felt this before," I murmur, forehead pressed to hers. "This *need* to stay buried. To never pull out. To keep you like this until you forget what it felt like not to have me inside you."

Her breath stutters.

"And you will," I vow, voice low and raw. "Because you're mine now, Olivia. Cuffed to this. *To me.* To everything I just gave you and everything I still fucking will."

I kiss her, slow and possessive.

A brand.

A promise.

I'm never fucking letting her go.

I brush my thumb over her mouth. Her lips are swollen, red, maybe I was too harsh.

"Too rough on your mouth?" I ask, voice low.

She chuckles. A ragged, breathless sound that makes my chest tighten.

"I loved it," she whispers.

I exhale slowly, resting my forehead against hers.

"Good."

I slide my hand from her face through her hair, easing off her body slightly.

"You're everything I never thought I deserved," I murmur. "And now that you're mine..."

I press a final thrust into her, making her gasp one last time.

"I'm never letting go."

Step three: Complete.

Chapter Twenty-Five

OLIVIA

By the time we pull into the garage at Beaumont Enterprise, my body feels like it's been through a war. *A very good war.*

Every muscle aches, sore in places I didn't even know I could be sore, but it's the kind of ache that makes me smile to myself. Like I'm carrying the proof of him inside me, everywhere.

Every step reminds me of him. Every ache sings the same name. *Warren. Warren. Warren.*

It's embarrassing how much I like it.

The elevator dings, and he's standing beside me, suited and smug. He didn't even touch me this morning, just kissed my forehead and poured my coffee like it hadn't taken me twenty minutes to walk straight. Like he didn't fuck me so thoroughly over the weekend I'm probably glowing through the tinted glass.

The lobby doors part, and we walk onto his floor like it's just for us.

He reaches for the small of my back as we walk toward the executive wing. My heels click. His hand is warm.

He's in a good mood. Whistling, even. The sound rattles in my chest, softening me, making me forget how nervous I was to agree to move in.

It's all normal.

Until it's not.

Because no matter how many nights I spend in his penthouse, no matter how many times he calls me his… I'm still keeping my apartment.

Just in case.

Because Warren Beaumont makes my heart race.

But I've lived long enough to know that doesn't mean he won't break it.

We stop outside his office. He kisses me, just a brush of lips and the whisper of a smile.

Then his palm swats my ass.

"Don't miss me too much," he murmurs, already walking backward into his office.

I roll my eyes and turn toward mine.

I barely make it two steps in before I see them.

Peonies.

A full, lush bouquet sitting on my desk, blushing pinks and creams like the inside of a love letter. My breath catches.

I walk to them slowly, fingers grazing the soft petals before I spot the card tucked inside.

Scrawled in dark, slanted handwriting.

For the woman who makes my walls worth rebuilding.

We'll add soundproofing to the bedroom.

—W.

I sit down hard, heart in my throat, and chuckle.

He's infuriatingly good at making me blush.

My lips curve before I can stop them. I press the card to my chest for a second too long, then set it down and open my laptop.

There's work to do.

The Parker Building is finally under renovation, and our new hotel chain, *Beaumont Luxe*, is moving from dream to blueprint. I spend hours sorting through floorplans, confirming room re-designs, checking on contractors, and linen vendors, and digital keys.

I get so deep in the numbers I forget where I am, until the knock comes.

Three soft taps.

My heart leaps.

Warren.

I smile, already halfway to standing, when the door opens—

And it's not him.

It's a *her.*

Tall. Thin. Blonde. The kind of blonde that glints almost white under the office lights. Her body is lean, sculpted, perfect. The kind of perfect that doesn't happen by accident.

She smiles politely, though it doesn't quite reach her eyes. "Sorry, I was told this was Warren Beaumont's office. Reception must've gotten it wrong."

My stomach drops.

Her voice is smooth. Confident. The kind of voice that doesn't apologize much.

I force a smile I don't feel. "His office is the next one over."

She thanks me, teeth flashing, then turns and walks down the hall, heels clicking sharp against the tile.

Something ugly twists in my chest.

I follow her.

I don't mean to.

But I do.

I step just far enough out of my office to watch her knock on Warren's door. Hear his deep voice invite her in.

She smiles.

And shuts the door behind her.

Panic hits like a slap.

I freeze.

Do I interrupt? Knock? Pretend I didn't see it?

I glance toward my desk. My laptop is still open to his shared calendar, the one I manage for him. The one I check every morning before I pour my own coffee.

No meetings today.

No woman listed.

Which means she's *personal.*

Not business.

My stomach knots. The bouquet suddenly feels stupid.

I sit down. Hard. Try to focus. Try to breathe.

His door is still closed.

I keep it in my periphery. The hallway is quiet.

My clock ticks.

Five minutes.

Ten.

Fifteen.

Maybe she's a lawyer.

Maybe this is about the Parker Building.

Maybe she's married. Maybe she's a cousin. A PR rep. A—

Shut up, Olivia.

Twenty minutes.

I get up. Pace once.

Sit down.

Stand again.

Twenty-five.

I open my phone. Nothing. No message. No calendar change.

Twenty-eight.

I lean closer to the screen, eyes glued to the hallway.

Thirty.

The door opens.

She walks out, polished and perfect, phone in hand, no lipstick smudged, no dress askew. She smiles at someone down the hall. Hair still intact. Nothing on her face to betray anything.

But it doesn't matter.

Because my brain doesn't care about evidence.

My brain only cares about the way her hand brushed the doorknob, the way her head probably tilted back in a laugh I couldn't hear, the way Warren *didn't tell me* she'd be here.

I'm already sure.

I barely notice when Warren appears in my doorway.

"You okay?" he asks, brow furrowing. "You look sick. Are you feeling alright?"

I look up.

He looks the same.

Pressed shirt. Belt buckled. Nothing out of place.

But he has a bathroom in his office.

One he cleans me in.

And probably her.

I swallow the panic clawing its way up my throat.

"Yeah," I say. "I'm fine."

He tilts his head. Doesn't believe me.

But he doesn't press.

"Come on," he says instead. "It's time for lunch. We'll talk about whatever's going on in that head of yours."

He walks away.

And I follow.

But inside?

I'm unraveling.

***

The food tastes like sand.

I stab at the salad, force a bite past the knot in my throat, chew until my jaw aches. Every swallow burns, like it has to claw its way down. Warren talks, his voice low and smooth, but I can't hear a damn thing.

My brain is too loud.

The image of her: tall, blonde, perfect, sitting in his office with the door shut. The clock ticking. *Thirty minutes.*

My stomach churns with every second I remember.

And then I hear it.

"Her name is Katya."

My head snaps up, breath frozen in my chest. I wait for it. For the kill shot. For him to execute me right here in this glossy restaurant with nothing but the truth. To rip out my stupid heart for daring to believe I could be more than another girlfriend on his roster.

Katya.

Even her name is pretty. Sharp edges softened by silk.

I want to ask.

I want to demand.

Why didn't you tell me you had an unscheduled meeting? Why did you call me yours all weekend if you already belonged to someone else? Why move me into your penthouse only to shred me with this?

But the words knot in my throat. The same knot that's been strangling me since that door closed behind her.

So I swallow hard and manage the smallest sound.

"Oh."

I go to lower my gaze, to hide before I break. But his voice slices through.

"Don't."

The command snaps my head back up. My eyes lock with his. His gaze is steady, dark, unflinching.

We're in public. People are talking around us, glasses clinking, silverware scraping. I don't want to cry here. Not where he can see it.

But he leans back, casual, controlled. Watching me unravel.

"You're spiraling about her instead of just asking, aren't you?"

The lump in my throat tightens. My chest constricts. I nod, small and weak.

His jaw ticks.

"Words."

I shake my head once, because I can't. I can't breathe past it. The knot is suffocating me, choking me, and yet he sits there, calm, expectant, waiting.

The silence presses. I break.

My voice scrapes out, ragged. "Who is she… to you?"

And then he smiles.

It knocks the breath right out of me. He's not angry. Not defensive. Just smiling like I passed some kind of test.

"Good," he says.

Confusion rattles me. *Good?*

He leans forward, forearms braced on the table, voice dropping into something that coils around my spine. "Her name is Katya Korsakov."

The name hits me like a punch. I frown, blinking. "Maksim Korsakov's sister? I thought you hated him?"

My mind races. Pieces spinning too fast to catch.

"Was she here to get the Parker Building for him?"

Warren chuckles, low and sharp, like I'm amusing him. "Slow down."

I flush hot, biting my lip.

"She doesn't dabble in her brother's business," he continues smoothly. "She has her own."

His hand dips into the inside pocket of his jacket. When it comes back up, he sets a small, sleek white box on the table between us.

My pulse stutters.

"Open it," he says.

My fingers shake as I lift the lid.

Inside, nestled against velvet, is a cuff bracelet. Gold, delicate but strong. Etched with peonies—tiny, intricate blooms carved in sweeping detail. The metal catches the light, petals shimmering like they're alive.

It's gorgeous. Staggering in its beauty.

"She custom makes them," Warren says quietly, his gaze fixed on me, not the bracelet. "Carves the designs by hand. It's truly an art."

I run my thumb over the engraving, breath caught in my throat for an entirely different reason now. The flowers seem to bloom under my touch, like she knew exactly what they meant to me.

Peonies.

My peonies.

The knot in my chest loosens.

"She's not a threat, Olivia. No one could be."

My breath catches. The bracelet still cradled in my hands. "I just wish you would have told me."

His expression doesn't change. "And spoiled the surprise? No. You just have to remember that I wouldn't betray you. I don't want to."

I flinch.

But he doesn't say it to wound.

He says it like truth.

Simple. Unadorned.

Then he leans forward and lowers his voice.

"Next time you're spiraling, do me a favor."

"What?" I breathe.

He leans in just a bit closer. Taking the bracelet from my hands and slipping it on my wrist.

"Come to me. I'll clear your mind."

His thumb strokes once over the cuff as if sealing the words into my skin.

Chapter Twenty-Six

WAR

The days blur in to weeks.

Not in a way that dulls.

In a way that *deepens.*

In a way that seeps into me.

She sleeps in *my bed* every night. Curled into my side.

My house doesn't echo anymore.

It's *full.* Of her.

She moves through it like she's always been here. My shirts in the hamper, tangled with her dresses. Her hair ties on the bathroom counter. Her book face-down on my nightstand, spine cracked where she fell asleep mid-sentence. Her scent on my pillows.

We wake up together. I watch her stretch, soft and sleepy, lips parted, skin warm with the kind of heat I put there.

I feed her. Wine. Berries. Her favorite chocolate. My fingers.

Whatever I can press past her lips.

She works just down the hall, focused and sharp, bossing men twice her size with that quiet authority that makes me want to bend her over my desk and fuck her until she forgets how to speak.

I let her have her independence.

But she knows.

Every door she walks through is one I opened. Every task she handles is a weight I allow her to carry, because I trust her.

I trust her.

I keep her healthy.

Draped in couture.

Satisfied.

Wrecked.

There are days I fuck her before breakfast, make her wear my marks under her blouse. I whisper in her ear before meetings just to watch her squirm in her chair, breath shaky, thighs clenched.

There's control in that.

In owning her mind. Her body. Her schedule.

But I know she still keeps the apartment.

Because I bought the building.

So I let her.

She'll give it up on her own.

Eventually.

Because what we have...

It's not temporary.

It's not casual.

And it's sure as fuck not optional.

I'm happy.

For once in my life, I'm *truly* happy.

For a man like me, that's gold.

Worth more than money.

And in my world, money reigns supreme.

Not for me, not anymore. Money is now my tool to watch that smile burst onto her gorgeous face.

Olivia Baker has me.

Fuck.

My phone lights up.

One name. One man.

And a rage I haven't felt in a long time roars to life.

I answer.

"Hello, Father."

"Dinner this weekend. Your mother is expecting the three of you. Make it happen."

The call ends.

Something old claws up my throat; I swallow metal.

My jaw's tight. My knuckles tighter.

Dinner.

A summons.

Clipped words that actually mean: *Just shift things around, War. Drop everything. Fly to Paris.*

Make it happen.

Fuck him.

I drop the phone face-down on the desk and scrub a hand over my jaw. The anger pulses like a second heartbeat. My first instinct is to go alone. Handle it. Get in, get out, survive the emotional minefield of their table, their smiles, their fucking expectations.

But then I glance at the door.

She's here.

In my life now.

In everything.

I can't just *leave* her behind. Can't pretend the thought of sleeping in a cold hotel bed without her doesn't already grate.

But how do I bring her to Paris and leave her in some hotel room like luggage while I go sit through a dinner that's guaranteed to crack open everything I've buried?

I don't have an answer.

Not for Paris.

Not for them.

Not for how the fuck I'm supposed to sit through dinner with ghosts while the one person I actually care about is a continent away.

A single knock and the door opens.

I look up.

She steps inside, hips swaying, wearing that little smirk that tells me she's in the mood to make me lose control.

"Mr. Beaumont," she purrs. "You've been teasing me all day."

She crosses the room slowly, unhurried.

"I'm here to collect."

I don't say anything. Don't smile.

I can feel the tension radiating off me like static.

She stops in front of my desk, eyes narrowing slightly.

"What's wrong?"

"Nothing," I mutter.

Flat. False.

And she knows it.

She rounds the desk before I can stop her, sliding between me and the edge, planting herself right in front of me, her legs brushing my knees.

"You look pissed," she says, voice soft but firm. "Talk to me."

I shake my head once.

Sharp. Dismissive.

I don't want her near this part of me.

The part that still flinches at my father's voice, that still fights old shadows.

She leans in and kisses me.

Soft at first. A whisper of lips. A question.

Then deeper.

One hand slides into my hair, the other gripping my jaw—not gently.

She kisses me like she means to snap me out of it.

Like I'm not allowed to disappear inside myself.

Like I belong to her the same way she belongs to me.

Her mouth parts against mine, tongue slick and sure, tasting the anger still caught in my throat and swallowing it whole.

When I don't kiss her back fast enough, she bites my bottom lip. Just enough to sting.

Then pulls back, barely.

Close enough I can still taste her.

She murmurs, low and firm, right against my mouth:

"Let me help."

She drops to her knees.

And just like that, the noise in my head starts to quiet.

She doesn't rush.

Doesn't say anything.

She just looks up at me with those big, knowing eyes and undoes my belt like she's unwrapping peace.

Like she knows exactly what I need.

Exactly how to take me apart and put me back together.

I lean back in the chair, legs spread wide. Watching. Waiting.

She frees my cock from my pants and wraps her hand around the base, slow, confident.

I'm already hard.

I've been hard since the second she walked in.

Pissed or not, this woman is *everything* that turns me on.

"Fuck," I mutter. My hand fists in her hair. Not a tug. *An anchor.* "You look so fucking pretty like this."

She smiles. Then lowers her mouth.

The second her lips close around me, I groan.

Head falling back.

Eyes shutting.

Warm. Wet. Heaven.

Her lips are tight around me, tongue teasing just under the head.

She takes her time.

Works me slow. Controlled. Her hand stroking what her mouth can't take, spit slicking me up like she wants it messy.

Like she wants me undone.

I look down at her.

Her lips stretch around me, cheeks hollowing, eyes locked on mine like this is worship.

Like she's showing me who I belong to.

"*Good* girl," I grit, tightening my hold in her hair. "Just like that."

She moans around me—*soft and sinful*—and the vibration punches straight through me.

My jaw locks. My thighs tense.

But she doesn't stop.

Doesn't flinch when I buck my hips.

She just takes it.

Deeper.

Her eyes water. Mascara smudges.

And I lose it.

I fuck her mouth.

Slow, then faster. Controlled thrusts that have her gagging softly, spit dripping down her chin.

She lets me.

Lets me use her.

Because she knows.

Knows this isn't just about pleasure.

It's release. Control. *Peace.*

And she gives it to me like it's hers to offer.

"Look at you," I breathe. "So perfect. So fucking perfect for me."

Her hand cups my balls. Rolls them just enough to make me groan again, my head spinning.

She moans as I fuck deeper, more ragged now, my body tight, my grip savage.

I'm on the edge, choking just at the turning point.

She pulls back just enough to suck hard at the head, her tongue swirling, hand stroking, mouth wrecking me like a fucking queen.

"Olivia! *Fuck!* I'm gonna come—"

She moans again, eyes glassy.

Inviting.

Demanding.

And I give it to her.

My orgasm slams through me like a wave breaking open.

I groan, deep and hoarse, spilling into her mouth as she swallows every drop.

She doesn't stop until I'm empty. Until my breath is uneven and my legs are trembling.

Only then does she pull off, licking her lips.

Smiling like sin.

My chest rises like I've come back from war. Like she exorcised something with her mouth.

I stare down at her, panting. Stunned.

Cleared out. *Grounded.*

She rests her hands on my thighs, chin tilted up. "Better?"

I run my thumb along her jaw, wiping the last trace of me from her lips before pressing it between them again, because if she's going to take me, she'll take all of it.

"Come to Paris with me this weekend," I say breathless, still looking down at her, on her knees, wrecked and radiant, mine in every fucking way.

She grins. "I was *that* good?"

I grab her wrist and pull her into my lap.

My mouth finds hers.

"You're perfect my sweet girl," I whisper against her lips. "But it's for dinner...with my parents."

***

I would've hired someone to pack.

Had them lay out wrinkle-free slacks and collared shirts I'll never wear. Steam a suit. Fold ties I won't use.

Hell, I would've flown a stylist in just to make sure Olivia had everything she needed for Paris.

But no.

She insisted we do it ourselves.

So here I am, tossing shirts into an open suitcase like a college kid late for his flight, while she trails behind me, huffing under her breath as she refolds everything I just crumpled.

"You know," I say, watching her smooth out a black button-down, "we don't even have to pack."

She looks up, arching one brow. Skeptical. So I continue.

"I'll have everything you need there. If not, I'll buy it."

She rolls her eyes. Not in the annoyed way.

In the Olivia way.

The way that makes me want to pin her to the bed and kiss every sarcastic comment off her lips.

"We can be normal even if you have money, War."

Fuck, I love that. Love her saying my name like it belongs to her now. Like she branded it.

The way she says normal. The word doesn't exist in my world, but she says it like maybe it could.

I sit on the edge of the bed, watching her fold one of my sweaters, one she stole three nights ago and slept in.

"You won't like them," I say quietly.

She pauses, eyes flicking to mine. "Your parents?"

I nod once. "My mother will act sweet. Smile. Ask questions. But every word's a knife wrapped in velvet. Every sentence, an underlying critique."

Olivia folds slower now.

"And my father…" My jaw tightens. "He'll try to gut me. Gut me and my brothers without ever raising his voice. He doesn't need to."

Her face softens. "I can handle it."

I believe her.

She's tougher than she looks.

"If you get uncomfortable," she adds gently, "we can leave. Or I'll stay at the hotel and explore Paris on my own. I don't mind, War."

That fucking bothers me.

The thought of her wandering Paris alone while I sit at that table in their home, while they try to break me, burns through me hotter than the rage in my chest.

"No."

My voice comes out sharper than I meant, and she looks up in surprise.

I stand, crossing to her in two strides. My hands slide around her waist, pulling her close until she's right against my chest.

"You stay with me," I say, firm. "You don't get left behind. Not by me. Not *ever.*"

She stares at me, wide-eyed. Her fingers curl into the hem of my shirt.

"They may as well get used to you being around," I add.

Her brows furrow. "Used to me being around?"

I nod.

"Yeah, Olivia. You're not mine for a season. You're mine forever."

Silence stretches between us. Thick. Heavy.

A word I never said to anyone before yet feels completely *normal* to say to her.

Forever.

No take-backs. No apologies.

I mean every word.

She blinks once. Then again. Her lips part, but no sound comes out.

And fuck—

There it is. *That look.* The one I want to wake up to for the rest of my life. A mix of awe and hesitation, like she's terrified to believe in something good, but wants to anyway.

Wants me.

"I have to pack the sweater," she finally says softly, like she needs to say something, anything.

I laugh under my breath and kiss her. Gentle. Deep.

I pull back slightly, brushing my nose against hers.

"You bring whatever you want, my sweet girl. Just don't forget that you're already mine."

Her phone buzzes on the nightstand. The sound is sharp in the quiet, cutting through the warmth between us.

Olivia glances at the screen. Too quick. Too careful.

Her face shifts, barely, but I catch it.

She presses a kiss to my jaw and slips out of my arms. "I'll take this in the kitchen."

My heart drops.

Kitchen.

Not here.

Not in front of me.

Something cold claws its way through my ribs as I watch her disappear around the corner. My jaw tightens. I try to tell myself it's nothing

But I'm not the kind of man who ignores instinct.

And right now, my instinct is screaming.

I stay frozen for a beat.

Then I'm moving. Following.

My heart's pounding harder than it should, heavier than it ever had, like every instinct in me already knows whatever waits in that call isn't something I'll like.

Not one fucking bit.

Chapter Twenty-Seven

OLIVIA

I lean against the counter and swipe to answer.

"Hey, Mama."

"Hi, Liv Bug," she says, her voice warm and tired all at once. "You haven't called in a while. Are you alright?"

Guilt punches me square in the chest.

She's right. I haven't called. Not since... not since Warren. Not since my whole life shifted into his orbit.

"Yes, I'm good," I say quickly, forcing a smile she can't see. "Is everything okay with the inn?"

There's a pause, a little sigh. "Yes, we're fine. Next quarter is coming up, but we may just make it. Chase is picking up some renovation work in the next town over, he's going to put that money toward what we need."

Relief and shame crash together in my gut. They're scraping by, counting on my brother's side jobs, while I've been—what? Laying in silk sheets? Forgetting to call? Forgetting why I even came to the city in the first place?

"I'll transfer funds today," I blurt. "I have it."

"Liv, no. Don't you dare. You keep that money for rent. We'll figure it out."

Rent.

My stomach knots.

Rent that's already paid. For the whole year. Because of *him.*

And I've been so wrapped up in Warren Beaumont, his world, his hands, his everything. I forgot.

The job. The paycheck. The reason I left home.

To keep it standing.

"No, Mama," I whisper, throat tight. "I got it. I'll send it."

She sighs again, softer this time. "I love you, Liv Bug. Be good. Be safe."

"I love you too. Tell Daddy I love him."

We hang up, and I stare at the dark screen, guilt burning holes through me.

"Your family needs money?"

My heart lurches. I spin around.

He's leaning in the doorway, arms crossed, eyes sharp.

Watching me.

I swallow. "Yes. The inn... it's tight right now."

The look in his eyes makes my chest seize. Calculating. Decisive.

I know that look.

"No." I shake my head before he even says it. "Don't. Don't even think about it. You are not sending them money."

His jaw flexes, that dangerous silence stretching between us.

One look. That's all it takes to make me want to give in. To let him fix it. To let him be who he is, powerful, unstoppable.

But this is my family. *My* responsibility.

Finally, he exhales through his nose, almost like he's humoring me. "Fine."

Then he moves.

Pushes off the door.

And cages me in against the counter.

One hand planted on either side of me, his body crowding mine.

He towers over me like a threat and a promise, six-foot-five of heat and control.

The counter bites into my back. His chest blocks out the rest of the kitchen.

I can feel the tension rolling off him in waves.

"Then explain," he demands, voice low. "What's going on?"

I lick my lips, trying to steady myself.

"They've been... wanting to renovate the inn. Sell it eventually. But between the mortgage and everything else, they can't keep up with payments and renovations at the same time. So, yeah."

I force a small laugh. "They're in a pickle."

It's only half the truth.

I can't possibly tell him everything. Not about Ronnie. Not about the threats.

Not about how close my parents are to losing the place for good.

He'd march in and fix it his way, with money and intimidation, and that could probably get him killed.

"A pickle?" he repeats, lips curving like he's tasting the word.

"Yeah," I say, trying to sound casual. "It's what we say back home."

His gaze sharpens. "And where exactly *is* back home?"

I hesitate. Just a beat too long.

"Brokenwoods," I say finally, naming the small town that raised me. Not even a dot on most maps.

He hums, thoughtful, and it vibrates against my chest, where he's still crowding me in.

"We should go visit. Maybe after Paris."

I freeze.

Warren Beaumont in Brokenwoods?

The billionaire storming Main Street, standing in my parents' inn?

Oh, that would never work. He'd stick out like a diamond in a gravel lot.

My palms tingle just thinking about it.

"Maybe," I chuckle, trying to brush it off.

His eyes narrow like he knows I'm dodging, but then his mouth is on mine before I can think.

And just like always—I melt.

Melt and hate myself for it.

Leave it to me to turn into the girl who gives in to the billionaire.

***

The Beaumont plane. *Air Beaumont*, apparently; is beautiful. Polished leather seats, dark wood trim, the kind of opulence you only ever see in magazines.

I should be staring at everything. Maybe joining the mile-high club with War. But it's awkward because of who's sitting across from me.

Wesley.

And Wilder.

Wilder catches me looking and smirks, like he knows exactly what I'm thinking. I force a polite smile. "I didn't know you flew back in from California."

"Yeah," he says easily. "Just last night. With Brody."

Warren scoffs beside me. Low. Sharp.

"Brody's back?" I ask, before I can stop myself.

Warren's hand finds mine, grips tight. A warning.

"Yup," Wilder drawls, eyes glinting. "Figured why not fly with my big bros since we're taking a family trip to Paris? Didn't know we could bring our girlfriends."

"You have a girlfriend?" I ask, genuinely curious.

"Nope." He grins, wolfish.

"Wilder." Wesley's tone is flat. "Cut it out."

Wilder leans back like a cat who got the cream. "Where's Evie Mitchell, hmm? Wesley?"

"Shut up, Wilder."

My head jerks toward Wesley. "You're dating Evangeline Mitchell? She beat me out for a job with Santo Amato."

Warren stiffens instantly. His eyes cut to me, sharp enough to slice. "You applied to work for *him?*"

I nod slowly. "Yeah. I was late for the interview, though, so... I didn't get it."

"Good." His jaw flexes. "Don't ever mention that bastard's name again."

Wilder chuckles. Wesley shakes his head like this is normal family turbulence.

"So why didn't you bring Evie?" I ask, softer this time.

Wesley exhales hard. "I'm not dating Evie. Yet. It's—we will. Just... not right now."

"Aww, Wesley." Wilder smirks. "Still saving yourself for marriage?"

"Shut the fuck up, Wilder."

"Are you?" The question slips out of me before I can think better of it.

"No!" Wesley's voice is sharp, defensive.

Wilder bursts out laughing, the sound filling the cabin. Even Warren's mouth curves, a rare crack in his armor.

"No," Wesley mutters again, scrubbing a hand over his face. "I just don't fuck anything that moves like they do."

The words hang in the air, heavier than the jet itself.

He pushes up from his seat before I can even process the sting, muttering something about needing a drink.

His footsteps fade toward the bar at the back of the plane, leaving behind a silence that feels sharp. Exposed. Too much.

Wilder exhales through his nose, shaking his head. "He didn't mean you, Livvy. He's just an ass."

His smirk fades. His voice dips; lower, almost regretful.

"Wes is… complicated. Always has been."

I nod, but the smile I force doesn't reach my eyes. "It's fine."

But it's not fine. Because it scraped something raw inside me. Something I've been trying not to think about since the moment Warren pulled me into his world.

Warren's past.

The headlines. The gossip. The *women.*

And here I am, just another one, sitting on his family plane.

The thought makes my stomach twist until warm lips brush my temple. Warren's voice, low and rough, chases the spiral away.

"Stop over thinking," he whispers. His grip on my hand tightens, solid, grounding.

I close my eyes, leaning into him even as my pulse hammers.

"You're it for me, Olivia Baker."

And somehow, even surrounded by his brothers, I believe him.

***

The hotel is unreal.

Crystal chandeliers drip light. Velvet drapes sweep the floor. Everything touched in gold.

I can't stop smiling, can't stop spinning like a kid, because *Paris, actual Paris,* is all around me.

I press my palms to the glass, forehead against it as I stare out at the skyline. And there it is. The Eiffel Tower.

Not a postcard. Not a screensaver. Right there in front of me, lit up against the night.

My chest tightens, hot and giddy.

I've wanted this since I was a little girl. Paris. Romance. The dream.

And War promised we could stay the weekend. That after all this, we'd come back for Christmas too.

Christmas.

My heart squeezes. I should go home for Christmas. Back to Brokenwoods, to my parents, to Baker's Inn and the people who actually need me. But Paris... Paris feels like a once-in-a-lifetime wish I never thought I'd get.

Arms slip around my waist. Strong. Certain.

War's chest presses against my back, solid and warm, and then his head dips, lips brushing the curve of my neck. My breath catches.

He smells expensive and intoxicating and something darker, sharper. *Him.*

"You look divine," he murmurs, voice low against my skin. "Like a goddess."

Heat curls through me. My reflection in the glass catches the Givenchy dress he picked, sleek and perfect, hugging curves I usually try to downplay. For once, I don't feel out of place. I feel... beautiful.

His mouth grazes my ear, a tease that makes me shiver. "We'll go to this dinner," he promises, his tone roughened with hunger. "Smile. Survive. Then come right back here..."

His hands skim down my waist, over my hips, anchoring me. "...so I can peel this dress off you myself."

My pulse stutters. My body answers before I can speak.

Paris outside.

Warren Beaumont wrapped around me inside.

And for one dizzying moment, I don't know which one is more dangerous.

***

The car slows, tires whispering against smooth cobblestone. My breath catches as the wrought-iron gates rise in front of us, tall and black and gleaming like something out of a period drama. Beyond them, stone. Not just a house. A mansion.

An hôtel particulier, I think I heard Warren call it. But that doesn't prepare me for this.

The gates swing inward and the driver eases us through. The courtyard opens like a secret garden, perfect rows of trimmed hedges, white roses climbing the walls, every detail manicured within an inch of its life.

My chest tightens. It's beautiful. Gorgeous. But there's nothing warm about it. Even the flowers look like they've been told how to bloom.

I lean closer to the window, whispering, "This doesn't even look real."

Beside me, Warren doesn't move. His hand rests over mine, solid, unmoving, but his jaw is tight. Too tight.

The car stops in front of wide stone steps. I tilt my head back to take it all in—the tall windows, the carved balconies, the crest above the massive front doors. It looks like it was built to outlast time itself. Built to judge anyone walking through those doors.

I suddenly feel small in my fancy dress. Like a girl playing dress up who has no business being here.

The driver gets out, circles the car. Warren beats him to it, opening my door himself. His hand extends, palm up, commanding and protective at once.

"Olivia." His voice is low. A reminder. A promise.

I slip my hand into his, and the second my heel hits the stone, his arm comes around my waist. He pulls me in, grounding me before I can spin too far into my own head.

"Breathe," he murmurs, lips brushing the shell of my ear. His scent curls around me, sharper here, against the cold Paris night. "Remember what I said, we go in, smile, eat their dinner, then we're gone. Back to the hotel. Just you and me."

I nod, though my stomach still twists.

Warren leads me up the steps, his hand firm at the small of my back. The massive doors swing open before he even reaches for them.

A butler stands there, tall, gray, and impossibly formal, bowing just enough to make me feel like I've stepped into another century. "Monsieur Beaumont. Mademoiselle."

The foyer unfolds like a cathedral—soaring ceilings, marble floors that gleam under the light of an enormous chandelier, and portraits on the walls that all seem to look down their noses at me.

I'm still trying to take it in when she appears.

Vivienne Beaumont glides into the room, tall, thin, every movement deliberate. Her hair, dark chestnut with not a strand out of place, frames a face that's sharp in a way beauty can be when it turns to intimidation.

She doesn't look at me at first. She goes straight to her son, kissing Warren once on each cheek. "You're late," she says, her voice soft, but laced with disapproval sharp enough to cut. "Your brothers arrived twenty minutes ago."

Then her eyes trail to me. Assessing. Calculating.

"And who is this?"

Warren doesn't flinch. His arm tightens around my waist. His voice is steady, deliberate.

"Olivia Baker. She's mine."

The words steal the air from my lungs. Not a label. Not a definition. Just possession, plain and irrevocable.

My face heats and his mother's eye brows raise slightly.

Vivienne extends her hand. "Vivienne Beaumont."

I slip mine into hers. Her fingers are cool. Her grip is feather-light. Dainty. The kind that makes you feel clumsy just for existing too loudly.

"Thank you for allowing me in your home," I manage, my voice steady even as my pulse races.

She smiles then. A curve of lips without a hint of warmth. No crinkle in her eyes. Just calculation, dressed up as civility.

I already know.

This house wasn't built to let people like me breathe.

Chapter Twenty-Eight

WAR

The table is long. Too long.

Silverware glints under the chandelier. Porcelain plates, pristine and untouched.

I can barely taste the food. Olivia's taken only a few polite bites, her fork stalling every time she feels eyes on her. My hand hasn't left her under the table, anchored on her thigh, thumb stroking, keeping her with me.

But I see it.

The way my father keeps looking at her. Not leering; *worse.*

Assessing. *Judging.*

Like she's another balance sheet, another acquisition to pick apart. It's making her uncomfortable, and I fucking hate it.

"How did you and Warren meet?" my mother asks suddenly, voice smooth as silk, but sharp as the knife hidden beneath it.

Olivia turns to answer, but Wilder beats her to it.

"She was Wesley's before she was Warren's."

Wesley chokes on his drink, coughing into his napkin.

My blood goes molten. Seething.

Wilder chuckles. Smug. Careless.

My mother blinks. Her expression sharpens. "Excuse me?"

Olivia clears her throat. Her voice is steady, bless her. "I worked for Wesley. But now I work for Warren."

My mother nods once, lips pressing thin.

My father's eyes narrow. Cut to me like a blade.

"Dating your subordinates, Warren?"

I drag my gaze to Wilder.

Heat radiates off me.

He only shrugs. Unconcerned.

"I wanted Olivia to work for me," I say evenly, my grip on her thigh tightening.

"So now she does."

I leave it there. Final.

But my father doesn't look at me. He looks at her. "How old are you, Olivia?"

My mother's rebuke is quick.

"William, we don't ask a woman her age."

"It's okay," Olivia says softly.

She glances at me before answering.

"I'm twenty-seven."

My mother hums.

That sound.

That disapproving hum I grew up drowning in.

My father leans back, eyes still fixed on Olivia. "And where are you from?"

Before she can open her mouth, I cut in. My voice is steel. "Enough. She's not here to be interrogated. I brought her here for dinner. We're having dinner. Then we're leaving."

The air snaps tight.

My father scoffs, shaking his head. "Still the same."

Across the table, Wilder sighs loudly and downs his drink. "Here we go."

Wesley mutters, "You had to start it, didn't you?"

My eyes snap to my father, burning.

Olivia's thumb brushes over my knuckles, grounding me.

The only thing keeping me from slamming my fist into the table.

"And what do you mean by that, Father?"

I bite it out, jaw tight enough to crack.

His eyes slice into me. Cold. Unflinching.

"Still the same boy. Reckless. Disobedient. Always needing to make a scene."

The air freezes.

My blood turns molten.

"You want to lecture me at your dinner table?"

My voice drops lower. Darker.

"Then do it. Stop dancing around—say what you want to say."

My father's mouth twists. His gaze flicks to Olivia.

"You don't think we've known about *that* one?"

He gestures toward her with his glass, casual.

Like a blade.

"The small-town bumpkin. Keeping your little gold diggers in the city to warm your bed is one thing, Warren. But to present one to *us*?"

He shakes his head slowly, like I've spat on the family crest.

Olivia's face flames red, her shoulders stiff.

My chest roars. "You're so afraid of gold diggers, yet everyone knows how you met Mother."

The room gasps.

My mother's hand flies to her chest. "Warren."

"Watch your mouth," my father snarls, the mask slipping for the first time.

"You whine enough for someone who's had everything handed to him. But no, you're still chasing shadows. Still clinging to *weakness*."

His eyes narrow. Sharp. Merciless.

"I didn't think you could disappoint me more, until I hear you're restoring the Parker Building. Still chasing what? Redemption? Over the death of some orphan?"

The word hits like a blow.

My breath turns to ash.

"Don't."

My voice tears through the silence. Raw. Jagged.

My hand crushes Olivia's under the table.

"Don't you dare bring him into this."

Wesley's chair scrapes back.

His face is red. His composure cracking. "That's enough, Dad."

"Quiet," William snaps, turning his fury like a blade.

"You—" He points at Wesley, disdain curling his lip. "You've always been the weak one. You hide behind your computers and gadgets, yet nothing of use has come from it."

Wesley's jaw flexes.

He doesn't move.

But the wound is written all over him.

"And you." William turns on Wilder.

His tone laced with venom.

"Reckless. Careless. Squandering every advantage, every opportunity. Do you think your name will shield you forever? Through every flop you create?"

Wilder's smirk is gone.

He stares at our father with ice in his eyes. "Fuck you."

I shove back from the table.

The chair legs screech against marble.

My hand finds Olivia's, firm, pulling her up with me. "We're done here."

The three of us move as one.

Me. Wesley. Wilder.

Storming from the room like a front breaking open.

But his voice follows.

Sharp. Final.

"Just once, Warren, I wish you didn't disappoint me."

I stop.

Every muscle locks.

Rage claws up my spine, tearing through me.

He still thinks I'm chasing shadows.

But Olivia's hand is in mine, and for the first time in my life,

I'm walking toward something real.

I don't look back.

We walk out.

***

I sit on the edge of the bed, the drink I'd been nursing abandoned on the nightstand, fury still burning low in my chest.

My father's words echo.

The look on her face at that table.

It guts me.

I can still see the way her shoulders tensed, the flush of shame rising to her cheeks, shame that wasn't hers to carry.

I wanted to put my fist through his skull.

But worse than that... I let it happen.

I put her in his path. Let his poison touch her.

And I don't know if I'll ever forgive myself for it.

The shower cuts off. A curl of steam escapes through the cracked bathroom door. Then Olivia steps out.

Her face is fresh, bare. No armor.

Just those wide, beautiful brown eyes that undo me every time.

She's wearing my sweater, the one she stole without asking. It drapes over her curves, clinging to them when she moves, loose in others.

She's perfect.

And I sent her in there like cannon fodder.

She crosses the room to me, quiet as a breath, and stops.

Her fingers slide into my hair, soft and tender. The simplest touch, and it nearly undoes me.

My eyes close.

"Are you okay?" she asks softly. Her voice catches. "I know that's a dumb question, but... are you?"

I open my eyes, look into hers—and every wall I've ever built starts to crack.

"I'm so sorry," I whisper. The words drag out of me like a confession. "I should've let you stay here. Explore Paris. Instead, I dragged you into that circus and let them...*berate* you. Interrogate you."

My chest tightens, splitting open.

I've taken fists to the face. Dealt with monsters.

But nothing, *nothing,* has ever cut me like watching her sit at that table and take their judgment with her chin held high.

She deserved candlelight. Roses.

Not to be treated like a fucking transaction.

And I brought her there.

She exhales, shoulders dipping. "It's okay."

I shake my head. Hard. "No. It's not. I should've known better."

My hand slides along the curve of her hip. I squeeze, grounding myself in the feel of her. "They don't *deserve* you."

A pause.

"Hell, neither do I. But you're mine."

Her breath catches. Her lips part.

That's all it takes.

I rise, pulling her with me, my hand anchored at her waist. Our mouths meet slow; deep. I turn and guide her down onto the bed.

She sinks into the sheets, eyes locked on mine, chest rising and falling like she's waiting for proof that I meant every word.

I strip us bare between kisses. The sweater slides up and over her head, her skin revealed inch by inch.

My shirt gone.

Her hands on my belt.

My pants shoved down.

Soon, there's nothing between us but skin and heat and the gravity that pulls me into her like the tide.

I settle over her, kissing down her throat, her breasts, her stomach—worshipping every curve until she's trembling.

My hands roam her thighs, her hips, her back.

Owning.

Devouring.

Claiming.

When I guide myself to her entrance, I pause, pressing my forehead to hers.

Her eyes, wide, glassy, shining, undo me all over again.

Slowly, I push inside.

She gasps.

Her body clenches around me, welcoming me in, taking me deep until I'm buried to the hilt.

My jaw locks; my chest heaves.

This isn't hunger.

It's not rage.

It's something else—deeper, quieter.

More dangerous.

I start to move.

Slow. Deliberate.

Each thrust feels like a vow carved into stone.

My past burns away in the heat of her body, in the softness of her hands gripping my shoulders.

Every scar.

Every shadow.

I rewrite all of it inside her.

She's not my escape.

She's my future.

She's everything.

Her lips brush my ear, her breath hot and trembling.

"I love you."

The words tear me wide open.

I choke on a groan, driving deeper, clutching her like I'll lose her if I let go.

No one's ever said those words to me and meant them.

Not like this.

The truth rips out of me, raw and unguarded.

"I love you."

I say it again, harder this time, desperate.

"I fucking love you, Olivia."

Her nails dig into my back, her body trembling around me as she breaks—gasping my name, clinging to me.

And I follow.

Spilling into her with a guttural sound, holding her through it, clutching her like a man drowning who's finally broken the surface.

When the waves fade, I stay inside her.

Our foreheads pressed together.

Our breaths tangled.

My chest raw. Stripped bare.

But clean. Free. *Hers.*

The words fall out again, quieter now. A broken whisper against her skin.

"I love you."

Not a declaration.

A vow.

A prayer.

A truth that will never leave me.

I am forever hers.

Step Four: Complete.

Chapter Twenty-Nine

OLIVIA

Paris feels like a dream I was never meant to touch.

Too soft. Too glittering. Too *beautiful.*

Yet, here I am.

The city glows around us like something out of a movie. The Eiffel Tower sparkles in the distance. The Seine ripples with light. And Warren's hand is wrapped around mine, warm and solid, like he's tethering me here on purpose.

We stop at a little café tucked into the corner of a cobblestone street. The kind with tiny round tables, flickering candlelight, and chipped menus no one bothers to read. He doesn't glance at it anyway, he orders in low, confident French that makes something flip in my chest.

When the waiter returns, he sets down two flutes of champagne and a plate of delicate macarons, lavender, pistachio, rose. They look like jewels, soft and breakable.

Warren picks one up and holds it out. "Open your mouth."

Heat prickles up my neck. I should roll my eyes, say something sarcastic, anything, but his stare is too intense. Too smug. *Too him.*

I part my lips, and he feeds it to me, slow and deliberate, watching every second like he owns the moment.

"Sweet?" he murmurs, thumb brushing my bottom lip.

"Mhm." I swallow carefully. "But not as sweet as hearing you speak French. Since when do you do that?"

His mouth curves, the kind of smile that always makes me forget how to breathe. "Since I learned it."

I raise a brow. "And how many languages *have* you learned, exactly?"

"Four." He says it like it's nothing. Like it isn't drop-dead sexy.

"Four?" I blink. "You don't exactly scream *'secret linguist'*"

He leans back, eyes unreadable. "Andras Academy. I got shipped off there for high school."

I frown. "Never heard of it."

"You wouldn't have." He nods once, sharp and final. "Mostly kids of high-profile men. Or mobsters."

That last word hangs in the air. Heavy. Quiet. Meant to be left alone.

But I can't.

My fingers tighten around the stem of my glass. "How close are you to them?" I ask carefully. "The mafia?"

He doesn't blink. Doesn't shift. Just watches me for a long, weighted beat. Then he sets his glass down with a soft clink.

"We're not in business with them," he says finally. "But we've had dealings. My sister... she dated Santo Amato for a time. Denies it now, but it happened."

The name punches through me.

Of course I know the Amatos.

Unfortunately, so.

Warren's jaw tightens. "When it ended, the only way to cut him off clean was to give up a property he wanted. A trade. It kept him out of her life. And out of ours."

His tone is level, but I see the tension in his shoulders. He's still carrying it.

Still angry. Still protecting.

"So you're not..." I trail off, unsure where the line is.

"Mafia?" he says, a bitter little smile tugging at his mouth. "No. But we've been close enough to know better. Close enough to protect what's ours."

I take a slow sip of champagne, hoping the bubbles will settle the coil of guilt twisting in my stomach.

My secrets.

My lies.

At least now I know Warren's not working *with* them.

But when I glance back at him, he's already watching me. Eyes sharp. Curious. Dangerous.

"Why are you asking me this, Olivia?" His voice drops low. Like silk stretched tight.

My pulse skips. "No reason."

He leans in, so close I feel the heat of him. His breath brushes my cheek, but it's his voice that pins me in place.

"Don't lie to me." His words are quiet. Lethal. "I'm very close to figuring it all out. And I *will.*"

It isn't a threat.

It's a promise.

A warning wrapped in devotion.

The worst part?

I want to tell him.

Everything.

***

The car slows in front of a quiet, lamp-lit street tucked behind the Seine. All the shops are dark. Except one.

A soft golden glow spills from its windows, catching on beaded fabric and crystal cases. There's no sign on the glass. No crowd. Just the hush of silence and the hum of my heartbeat.

"They're closed," I murmur.

"Not tonight," Warren says, already moving to open the door. He doesn't wait. Just holds out his hand like it's a formality.

I take it anyway.

Inside, the air smells like silk and secrets, like champagne and the kind of wealth people pretend doesn't exist. Spotlights float above curated mannequins. A string of chandeliers drip from the ceiling like frozen fire. Racks of couture line the walls in gentle curves, guarded by velvet ropes and glass panels.

The place is empty.

Not a salesperson in sight.

"I had them clear the appointments," he says, like it's nothing. "Didn't want anyone else breathing the same air as you while you tried things on."

I laugh, nervous. "That's dramatic."

"No," he says, voice low. "It's not."

He watches me drift toward a row of gowns in gold and cream and blood red. My fingers skim the fabric. Each dress is a universe. Hand-beaded, laced, feathered. They look like they belong on a red carpet or in a museum.

"I don't even know what to try," I breathe. "They're all—"

"Exquisite," he finishes. "Just like you."

I glance at him, heat blooming low in my belly.

"Pick one."

"War—"

"Pick three," he amends.

Then he pauses.

"No. Hell, pick them all."

A disbelieving laugh escapes me. "You can't be serious."

But when I look up, his expression doesn't waver.

"I am," he says. "We'll find a reason for you to wear them. Let's ship them all."

He steps closer, eyes burning through me.

"But I want to see you in something now."

I look around for a dressing room, already fumbling with a protest, when his hand brushes mine and stills me.

"Here," he says.

I blink. "You want me to change here?"

He gestures to a velvet couch, sleek and deep blue. "I'll wait."

I glance up, scanning the space for a camera. "Warren. There are probably a dozen—"

"They're off," he says smoothly.

I raise an eyebrow. "And how exactly do you know that?"

He doesn't answer right away. Just smirks, lazy and smug.

"You own this place," I whisper.

He shrugs, unapologetic. "Didn't want to wait on someone else's rules."

My pulse stutters.

The room feels suddenly warmer.

My fingers tremble. Slowly I peel off my dress. I should feel exposed. Should be shy. But his gaze intense stays on my form, heating me.

Watching me.

Devouring me.

His eyes don't leer.

They see.

Heat and love, want and reverence, all tangled together.

When I step into the midnight-blue gown, it's heavier than I expected. Soft. Liquid against my skin. I struggle with the zipper until his hands are suddenly there, brushing my bare back.

"I've got you," he murmurs, fingers grazing my spine as he slowly zips the dress closed.

The moment stretches, quiet and intimate, before he steps back.

His voice cuts through the silence, firm and low. A command wrapped in praise.

"See?" he says. "You're a vision."

I turn.

The mirror steals my breath.

It's me. But it isn't.

The dress clings like it was born on my skin. The color, midnight and starlight, makes my eyes darker; my curves bolder. I don't look out of place.

I look like I belong.

Like I was meant for this life.

War steps closer, slow and sure, until I feel the heat of him behind me. His hands settle at my hips—firm, grounding.

Then he leans in and presses a soft kiss to the back of my neck.

I shiver.

Our eyes meet in the mirror.

His locked on mine, steady and dark.

"You see it," he says, voice velvet and steel. "You see what I see. *Finally.*"

Another kiss, this time to my shoulder, warm and reverent.

My heart flutters. Hard.

"You see why I'm never letting you go," he says, his mouth brushing skin, his gaze still holding mine in the glass. "You're made for me, Olivia Baker."

And he right. I am made for him.

Finally.

I believe him.

***

I wake up tangled in his sheets, wishing we were still in Paris.

The sunlight here isn't soft like it was there. It's bolder, whiter, too real. The city sounds different too; no bells, no water lapping against bridges. Just the hum of traffic several stories down and the low murmur of Warren's voice somewhere in the penthouse.

His bed smells like him. Clean. Expensive. A little bit like the cologne. I run my hand over the empty space beside me, still warm.

We're not in Paris anymore.

But I wish we were.

I sit up slowly, the silk sheets slipping down my bare skin. The lingerie I'm wearing, the pale mint green set he surprised me with when we landed. It clings to me like second skin. Soft. Barely there. Just the way he likes.

He walks in just as I stretch, two coffees in hand. His eyes dip to the curve of my thighs, linger, then lift to meet mine with a look that says he already knows exactly what I'm thinking.

"Keep that on," he says, voice rough with sleep and satisfaction. "We're working from home today."

I arch a brow. "We are?"

He hands me my coffee, then leans down to press a kiss to my shoulder. "Jet lag. And I want to look at you in that all day."

My stomach flips, heat crawling up my spine.

Breakfast arrives.

Croissants, fruit, and the soft scrambled eggs he knows I love. He nods at the delivery guy, barely cracking the door.

We eat at the long marble kitchen island, both barefoot, both quiet. He answers calls, his tone shifting depending on who's on the other end. Sharp and short with one. Warm and commanding with another. His voice is low but firm. Everything about him feels in control. Untouchable.

And then there's me. Sitting across from him in lace and silk, pretending I can keep my own secrets when I'm in the middle of falling in love with him.

So in love.

I said I loved him and I meant it.

But *damn* am I still falling.

I open my laptop and transfer the money I've been putting off sending. My brother's text flashes across the screen, short, a little goofy, and grateful. I close the window quickly.

War looks up from his phone. "You okay?"

I smile, small and practiced. "Yeah. Just paying bills."

He watches me for a moment too long, then returns to his phone. "Parker Building renovations are going smoother than I expected," he says, sounding almost... surprised. "It's going to be beautiful when it's done. Fit to honor him."

The softness in his voice guts me.

I stare at him. At the way his brow creases when he's deep in thought, the way his thumb taps against his glass absentmindedly. He's not smiling, but his eyes are brighter than I've seen them in weeks.

And my mind can't stop screaming it: I love him.

God, I *really* love him.

War answers another call and I get back to work.

Or try to.

I try to focus.

I really do.

He's talking; something about permits and square footage, insurance clauses and structural engineers. I should be deep in numbers, reviewing projections for the new hotel site.

But instead, I'm watching him.

Lounging at the other end of the kitchen island, barefoot, shirt half-open, casual command incarnate. One hand cradles his cup, the other gestures sharply as he speaks.

He's so in control. So effortlessly in charge.

All the while, I'm drowning in him.

I adjust in my seat, trying to cross my legs. His eyes flick to me. One glance. That's all. But it hits like a warning.

I look away.

He finishes his call, murmurs a clipped goodbye, then scrolls through something on his phone. His thumb pauses.

"You're not working."

My head jerks up. "What?"

"You've been staring at me for fifteen minutes," he says without looking up. "And you've typed nothing. Not a single key."

I feel my face flush. "I was—thinking."

"Mm." His gaze lifts now. Sharp. Knowing. "Thinking about what?"

My mouth opens. No words.

He straightens.

My pulse stutters.

"You wore that set all morning like I asked," he says, voice low. "You sat there in it. Crossed your legs in it. Shifted just enough to make sure I noticed."

I blink. "I didn't—"

He's already crossing the room.

"I've let you play office," he murmurs, coming to a stop behind me. "Let you pretend that I don't see the way you squirm in that chair every time I speak."

"War..."

His hands settle on my shoulders. Warm. Heavy. Possessive.

"You said you loved me," he whispers. "But right now, I want you to *show* me."

His mouth finds the curve of my neck. I shiver.

"I want you bent over the arm of that couch in the next ten seconds," he says, lips brushing my skin. "Or I'll put you there myself."

I stand so fast my chair scrapes back.

His chuckle is low, dark, full of satisfaction. "Good girl."

The lace clings to me as I walk, every inch of me aware of him behind me. I barely reach the couch before he's there, pressing me forward, spreading my legs with his knee.

"Do you know what you do to me?" he murmurs, lifting the lace above my hips. "You think I can sit across from you all morning and not take what's mine?"

His hand slides along the silk of my panties.

"War—"

"Quiet."

It's not cruel. It's a command. One my body obeys instantly.

"You were so good not changing from last night, letting me enjoy watching you in this," he praises.

His fingers slip beneath the silk, tugging the panties to the side. The fabric drags along my skin, exposing me inch by inch.

I gasp.

"You're soaked." He groans softly behind me, like he's losing patience with himself. "All for me?"

"Yes," I breathe.

I hear his belt come undone. The quiet clink. The slide of leather.

Then, the head of his cock presses against me, thick and hot, teasing.

I gasp, hips pushing back instinctively, aching for more.

"Please," I whisper, breathless. "I need it."

"You waited so well," he says, one hand bracing at my lower back. "Now I get to reward you."

He pushes inside. Slow. Deep. Thick. Until he's fully seated and I'm trembling, braced against the couch arm with nothing to hold onto but the fire building inside me.

I cry out, needy, breathless, aching.

"That's it," he grits. "Take it, sweet girl. Take every inch of this cock. *You earned it.*"

He pulls back, then thrusts in harder. My body jolts with the force of it. My moan breaks open in the quiet room.

"You like when I use you like this?" he growls, fucking me harder now, his hand gripping my hip like a brand. "Bent over in our penthouse? Wearing what I bought you, just to get fucked in it?"

Our Penthouse.

"Yes, War! yes—"

"You're mine, Olivia. Say it."

"I'm yours," I gasp. "All yours, *please* don't stop."

He doesn't. He pounds into me with ruthless rhythm, every thrust sending shockwaves through me. My pussy pulses around him, desperate, greedy. My nails dig into the upholstery. I'm shaking, my orgasm so close it hurts.

His hand slides up my back, into my hair. He pulls gently, just enough to arch me back toward him.

"You gonna come for me?" he murmurs against my ear, voice rough silk. "You gonna milk my cock like the good girl you are?"

I shatter.

It rolls through me fast and hard—pleasure so sharp I scream. My whole body clenches, hips jerking as he holds me in place, thrusting through every wave until I go limp in his grip.

And still he doesn't stop.

He growls my name, slams into me once more, and spills deep. My body pulses around him, greedy for it. Welcoming every drop.

We stay there, tangled. Sweaty. Spent.

His hand loosens in my hair, trails down my back. He bends, kisses my shoulder, then my spine.

"Thank you for wearing it for me," he murmurs again, softer now. "You're perfect."

I melt.

Because I am completely his and *fuck,* I love when he makes me feel like this.

I never want us to end.

Chapter Thirty

WAR

I've never been this happy in my life.

With Olivia beside me, I don't just own the building, I own the whole fucking world.

She's glowing.

Mine.

Every inch of her stamped with me.

The bracelet glinting on her wrist? I bought it.

The clothes hugging her curves? Mine.

Even the shimmer in her hair and the color on her mouth, I put those there.

She's mine from head to toe, and she doesn't just accept it.

She *loves* it.

And fuck, I love her for it.

I steal a kiss and swat her ass as she slips into her office. She glances back, cheeks pink, and my chest tightens so hard it almost hurts.

I can picture it—

A ring on her finger.

My last name stamped across her future.

Forever.

By the time I settle into my chair, I already know what I want: emerald-cut, platinum band, flanked by two diamonds, clean and bold and timeless. Just like the look in her eyes when she calls me hers.

I pull up jewelers, scanning bands, cuts, clarity. Visualizing how it'll shine on her hand as I pin her wrists.

The wedding can be in Paris... though I don't want my family around.

Then I pause.

Her family.

She told me that their inn was struggling.

That she didn't want me involved.

The little twist in her voice when she tried to get me to drop it.

She didn't ask for help.

She probably wouldn't want it.

But I can't sit back and watch her carry that weight alone.

I dig. Searching the inn's records.

Nothing.

No mortgage holder.

No clear chain.

Like it's been intentionally buried.

My jaw tightens.

So I open her employee file. Scroll. Stop at the line marked Emergency Contact.

Her mother.

Before I can second-guess it, I hit dial.

The line rings once, twice.

"Hello?"

Her voice is warm. Weary. The sound of years lived in the same place, carrying the same weight.

"Mrs. Baker," I say evenly, leaning back in my chair. "This is Warren Beaumont. I'm calling about the inn."

A pause. "I—what? I'm sorry, who did you say?"

"Warren Beaumont," I repeat. "Olivia's... boyfriend."

I hate that fucking word.

Boyfriend.... it's juvenile.

Another beat. Then a smile in her voice. "Oh! Well. Liv Bug didn't mention she was seeing anyone."

Liv Bug.

A low chuckle. "Aren't you her boss?"

"Technically," I say smoothly. "But that's because I own the company. She's more like the best right hand I've ever had."

A soft hum, somewhere between amused and curious.

"That is our Liv, always a hard worker."

I push forward before she asks more. "I wanted to talk about the inn. I'd like to pay it off."

Silence. Then a careful, "Pay it off?"

"Yes. Whatever's owed—I'll send a check today. Just tell me the number."

There's a long pause on the other end.

"Mr. Beaumont... it's not quite that simple. It's not a loan we're paying down. It's more of a... quarterly debt."

My brows pull together. "Quarterly?"

She hesitates again. "Yes. We don't really own the property in the traditional sense. We just... keep it. In exchange for payments."

I tilt my head. That hesitation wasn't casual. The way she says it makes me want to pry further.

Red alarms ringing.

Understanding hits slow and cold.

Her mother is just as evasive as she is.

"How much?" I ask tightly.

"Ten thousand a quarter," she says softly. "It's always been that way. Since before Olivia left home."

"I'll have it handled today. You'll get a check, and a contact to deal with going forward."

"Oh... Mr. Beaumont. Liv wouldn't want—"

"This is between us Mrs. Baker."

A pause.

"You can call me Jillian."

I nod, even though she can't see it. "Thank you, Jillian."

And I mean it.

Because she's just given me another piece of the puzzle.

One Olivia didn't want me to find.

But I found it anyway.

And I'll fix it. Quietly.

Thoroughly.

Permanently.

I hang up, lean back in my chair, and stare at the screen still open to solitaire jewelers.

I'm going to put a ring on her finger.

Wipe every shadow from her past.

Give her a life so far from that debt-soaked inn she'll never have to look back.

She'll never carry anything alone again.

Knock knock.

"Come in," I call.

The door opens.

Broderick steps inside.

And he looks...*pissed.*

Which throws me.

His jaw is tight, hands clenched, something burning behind his eyes. He crosses the room and slams something onto my desk.

A camera.

Not just any camera.

The camera.

The one I had planted in his office when he and Olivia were having those daily lunches for a *full fucking month.*

I stare at it.

Then my eyes meet his.

I don't say a word.

Just lean back, calm and silent, letting the tension fill the room like smoke.

Break puppy.

And he does.

"You planted this," he snaps. "Without my knowledge. Without *anyone's* knowledge. That's illegal. Unethical."

I let the silence stretch until the air feels thin. Then, low and even, "My building. My rules."

His mouth twists. "You think I'm going to what? HR? No. Fuck no. I'm going to the *press*." He jabs a finger at the camera. "Voyeur War Beaumont spies on his employees without their knowledge. Front page. Everyone gets to see the empire's golden boy fall."

That pisses me off.

My name. Dragged through mud. Smeared. Not because I give a fuck about public opinion, but because it would touch *her*.

I stare at him. Silent.

He shifts under it, but keeps his chin up. For once, he doesn't look like a grinning puppy. For once, he bares his teeth.

Since when did Brody grow a backbone?

My voice drops. Dangerous calm. "What do you want?"

And just like that, the rage in his eyes flickers.

Confusion seeps in.

There he is.

The puppy.

My puppy.

All bark, no bite.

Holding leverage he doesn't know how to use.

His brows pull together, lost.

He came in here with something that could break me.

And no idea what to ask for in return.

He fumbles, lips parting, trying to find an answer he doesn't have.

And then *her* voice cuts in as she opens the door.

"War? I think—"

Fuck.

Olivia steps in, tablet in hand, eyes flicking up from the screen, and freezes.

"Oh. Sorry," she says, gaze bouncing between us. "I didn't see a meeting on your calendar."

My jaw tightens.

I didn't want her walking into this.

Didn't want her anywhere near *him.*

But before I can say anything, she lights up.

Eyes softening, lips curving.

"Oh my God, Brody!" she says brightly, crossing the room. "It's so good to see you."

And then she hugs him.

She hugs him.

Her hands on him.

His hand resting low on her back like he's used to touching her there.

That's my hand's spot. *Mine.*

Brody chuckles, slipping back into that golden boy charm. "It's been a *lot.* But I can tell you all about it later."

My fists curl at my sides.

Too close.

Too familiar.

Too fucking comfortable.

"Olivia," I snap.

She startles, pulling back from Broderick and looking at me, brows furrowed.

I stand, closing the space between us, taking her hand, *my hand,* and tug her gently but firmly to my side.

"I was just telling Broderick," I say, eyes locked on his, "that he'll be taking over the California flagship."

His face twists in confusion.

"Wait, what?"

"Yes," I say smoothly. "He's been showing a lot of promise. Broderick's on the path to becoming the next me."

A *lie.*

A gamble.

One I hope the golden retriever understands.

Broderick blinks once. Twice.

Then, slowly, a smile spreads across his face. "Yes. That works perfectly." His gaze cuts to mine, sharp. "No need to tell the *press* about it. I'd prefer a quiet climb up the ladder."

Smart puppy.

Olivia beams. "Wow, congratulations!" She starts to move toward him again. *Again,* but I tighten my grip on her waist.

She falters. Looks up at me.

Confused. A little breathless.

Good.

"Broderick, you should go," I say without looking at her. "I'll have a contract drawn up and sent your way soon."

He nods, but lingers.

"Thank you again, War," he says, stepping toward the door. Then he pauses, smile smug. "*And* for the *pay raise.* Really generous."

I smile.

Tightly.

"Of course."

He leaves.

The door clicks shut.

Silence.

I turn to her.

My eyes drop to where her chest is rising just a little too fast.

She's breathing harder now.

Nervous.

Mine.

"You don't hug him like that again," I say, voice low, dark, final.

Her lips part. "War—"

"No," I cut her off. "No excuses."

I back her toward the desk, step by slow step.

"You. Are. Mine. Say it."

She looks up at me, rolls her eyes, tablet clutched against her chest like a shield.

I take it. Rip it from her hands. Toss it onto the desk.

"War!" she snaps, hands flying to her hips, eyes narrowing.

I step closer, looming. "Say it."

Her chin tips up. Defiant. "Say what?"

I arch a brow. "That you're mine. Or do you need a reminder?"

Her eyebrows lift. And then I see it—the flicker.

Not fear.

Curiosity.

Heat.

She *wants* the reminder.

Good.

I grab her wrist, spin her, and press her front against the glass. The floor-to-ceiling windows stretch across the skyline, city glittering beyond them. My chest pins her back as my hands drag up her thighs, grip, lift. Her skirt rucks up high.

Her breath hitches. "*War*, someone could—"

My hand drops to my belt. The sharp snap of it coming undone fills the silence. I unzip, shove my pants down just enough to free my cock, heavy and aching for her.

"Could what?" I growl, fisting myself once before yanking her panties aside. "See?"

I thrust into her in one brutal, unyielding stroke. No preamble. Just me, buried to the hilt in one slick, hot, perfect push.

She cries out against the glass, palms flattening, body jolting forward from the force.

Fuck.

Tight. Wet. *Mine.*

I groan into her hair, grinding deep, savoring the way her cunt grips me like a fist.

"No one's watching, Olivia," I murmur against her ear. "And even if they were? I assumed you *liked* the attention."

Her heart pounds so hard I can feel it through her back. Her breath fogs the glass. She squirms, hips jerking, torn between restraint and need.

I slam into her again, hard enough to make her cry out.

"You're squeezing me so fucking tight," I snarl, dragging my cock out slow, then driving it back in, deep and rough. "You like this. Don't you? Being *reprimanded.* Pinned here where anyone could see."

Her pussy clenches around me, fluttering.

I laugh, low and dangerous. "I can feel how much you like it. Your cunt doesn't lie, Olivia. It's *begging* for me."

Her head drops forward, forehead pressed to the glass, a broken sound spilling out of her.

And I don't stop.

Won't stop.

Not until she says it.

Not until she remembers she belongs to *me.*

Chapter Thirty-One

OLIVIA

The cold glass shocks against my skin, but it's nothing compared to the shock of him inside me. No warning. No gentleness. Just him. Thick, unyielding, filling me to breaking.

I can barely breathe. Every thrust pushes air from my lungs in ragged gasps.

He pulls out.

A long, slow drag that leaves me desperate, empty.

I whimper. My hips push back without permission, chasing him.

"Yeah," he groans behind me, his hands gripping my hips like a vice. "That's what I thought. Hungry little cunt can't stand to be without me."

He slams back in. Hard. Ruthless.

Giving me exactly what I wanted.

My cry fogs the glass.

"Fuck, War—"

"Say it," he snarls into my ear, pulling out again, inch by inch, until I'm trembling with the ache. Then he slams forward, filling me to the hilt. "Say you're mine."

My eyes squeeze shut. My heart is racing, adrenaline and heat tangling together. The thought of someone in the other building seeing us, *watching me spread open like this,* makes my stomach twist.

"What if someone—"

"I told you, no one can see." His voice is a dark rasp against my ear. "But even if they could? You'd love it."

My stomach flips. Shame tangles with heat.

Because he's not wrong.

The filthy thought of someone, anyone, in another building watching me pinned to this glass, skirt shoved up, panties torn aside... my pussy squeezes around him so hard it hurts.

He groans, low and triumphant. "See? I can feel it. The way you're clutching me. You fucking love this, Olivia."

My cheeks flame. My body betrays me, pulsing around him, soaking him.

Every thrust is brutal, owning. His cock splits me open again and again until my legs tremble and my palms squeak against the glass.

"This is punishment," he snarls into my hair. "For *touching* him. For hugging him."

"I wasn't—" My protest melts into a moan as his cock drags deep and my walls spasm around him.

"Just say it," he orders, hips slamming into mine, his hand gripping my jaw, forcing my face against the glass. "Promise that you're mine."

I choke on the words. Half shame. Half need.

His fingers circles my clit, sharp and relentless, while his cock pistons into me with punishing force.

"Promise me, Olivia." His voice is a rough. "Or I'll fuck you until you can't walk back to your office. Until every man out there knows exactly who you belong to."

My head tips back, a sob tearing from my throat as pleasure builds too fast, too sharp.

"I promise," I gasp, trembling, thighs quaking. "War, I'm yours!"

His growl vibrates against my spine, dark and primal. *"Louder."*

"I'm yours!" I cry, the words tearing out of me.

"Fucking perfect," he groans, hand fisting in my hair, yanking my head back as his thrusts grow ragged. "You're gonna come for me. Right here. With my cock so deep inside you everyone will know you're mine."

My vision shatters. Pleasure detonates through me, raw and devastating, my pussy spasming around him, clenching, dragging him down into my release.

"Yes! Fuck, Olivia," he groans, pounding once, twice more before he buries himself deep and comes, filling me until I feel it spill down my thighs. His roar shakes the air, primal, savage.

I collapse against the glass, trembling, spent, panting.

He doesn't move right away. Just holds me there, cock still inside me, chest heaving against my back, his lips brushing my temple.

"Mine," he murmurs again, softer now. "Always mine."

He eases out of me with a hiss, tucking himself back into his pants. He grabs tissues from his desk, wipes me gently, then fixes my panties, smooths my skirt down over my thighs. He doesn't say a word while he straightens me out, just does it quietly, reverently, like I'm something priceless he's putting back in place.

Then he pulls me toward his chair, sinking down and tugging me onto his lap.

I freeze. "War, I'm too—"

His mouth covers mine before I can finish, a kiss that steals my protest and turns it to a sigh. When he pulls back, his hand slides into my hair, brushing it back, his thumb stroking along my cheek. His eyes lock on mine, fierce and soft all at once.

"You're perfect here," he murmurs, thumb brushing my cheek. "Exactly where you belong, sweet girl."

My throat tightens. My pulse pounds so loud it drowns out everything else. He looks at me like I'm the only thing in the world worth holding.

"I can't stand it," he admits, voice rough as he presses a kiss to my neck. "Any other man near you—it makes me see red. I need you all to myself. Because I love you. Because I fucking *crave you.*"

The words dig into me, hot and heavy, and something inside me melts under the weight of them.

Before I can answer, his tone shifts, casual, like flipping a switch. "What do you want for dinner tonight?"

I let out a shaky laugh. "You know what I'm going to say—"

"La Serenata," he cuts me off, lips twitching. "Yes, yes. You love that place."

I roll my eyes, reaching to grab the tablet he tossed onto the desk earlier. "Yes, I do. But I actually came in here to show you something. The Luxe property? It's actually right near a transitional home for kids aging out of foster care. They're struggling financially and it gave me an idea... maybe the Parker Building could become something like that. A place for kids who need stability, like Noah once did."

For a second, he just stares at me. Then his mouth curves, slow and sharp. "That's brilliant. And we'll make sure that center nearby is taken care of, too. We'll donate."

"*We?*" I arch a brow.

"Yes, we." His voice is final, possessive. "What's mine is yours. And *you* are mine."

The heat that line sends through me leaves me speechless.

Only he could go from wrecking me against a window to domestic bliss like it's the most natural thing in the world.

That's Warren Beaumont.

Ruthless. Obsessive. Unpredictably tender.

And I never want to fight it again. I want to always be his.

Chapter Thirty-Two

WAR

The gates swing open at the press of my thumbprint.

Iron. Stone. Legacy.

The estate rises ahead like something carved out of another century; miles of manicured hedges, columns built to intimidate, glass that gleams like the whole place is watching you.

I've never brought a woman here. Not once.

Not for dates. Not for flings. Not even for the long weekends when I hosted charity events just to prove I could play the part of Beaumont heir.

This house is a cage dressed in gold.

And yet, tonight, it feels like something else.

Because she's beside me.

Olivia.

Her hand rests in mine across the console, warm, steady. She doesn't see the ghosts in the walls, the history pressed into stone. But I do.

And I've decided it's hers now.

Just like everything else.

My chest tightens as we roll up the circular drive. Staff are already waiting—security at the perimeter, house manager by the door, even the chef in her whites. Their faces are polite masks, but I can feel the shift in the air.

They know.

They know she's not just another guest.

I bring women to the yacht, to hotel suites with blacked-out windows and plush bedding. I fuck them. Use them. Toss them a gift and order them a ride share.

But I never bring them here.

This is the endgame.

And Olivia?

She's *the one.*

I step out first, buttoning my jacket, covering nerves I shouldn't have. I've done deals with men who could kill me with a word. Stared down my father across tables sharper than knives. Never flinched.

But bringing Olivia here?

That makes my pulse hammer in a way nothing else does.

I circle to her side, open the door myself, and hold out my hand. "Olivia."

She takes it, slipping out in that soft dress that clings in all the places I want to keep my hands. Her eyes go wide as she tilts her head back, taking in the mansion. "War... this is... wow."

Her awe makes something break open in my chest.

"Welcome home," I murmur.

Her gaze darts to me, startled. She laughs lightly, like she thinks I'm joking. But I'm not. Not even a little.

The staff line up as we enter the grand foyer. The marble gleams. The chandelier drips light like fire. Normally I hate it—too perfect, too cold.

But tonight, with her hand in mine, it feels right.

Like this place was waiting for her.

I lean down, voice low against her ear. "This house has been empty for years. Never meant anything to me. Until now."

Her lips part, eyes wide, like she hears what I'm not saying.

I squeeze her hand, anchoring myself. "Let me show you what will one day be yours."

The staff here, my chef, my groundskeeper, my house manager, even the night security, aren't faceless names on a payroll. They've been with me for years. They know my tells, my moods, my silences. They're the closest thing I've ever had to a real family.

And tonight, I'm bringing Olivia into that circle.

Which makes me more nervous than any Paris dinner ever could.

Her fingers tighten on mine as we walk though the doors. She looks up at the vaulted ceiling, wide-eyed, her lips parting in wonder. She probably thinks I'm watching the marble or the chandeliers. I'm not.

I'm watching her.

The house manager, Margaret, steps forward first. Gray hair, sharp eyes, the kind of woman who once barked at me to eat more vegetables when I was twenty and living on whiskey and spite.

"Mr. Beaumont," she says, formal as always. Then her gaze softens. "And this must be Olivia."

Olivia blinks, surprised. "Yes... hi."

Margaret actually smiles. "Welcome, dear. Dinner's nearly ready. We've all been looking forward to meeting you."

We.

Not I.

We.

Olivia glances at me, startled, and I can already see it in her eyes—the difference. Paris had been ice and metal. This... this is *warmth.*

One by one, the others greet her. My chef insists she'll have her favorite dessert ready "next time." The gardener offers her a tour of the rose beds. Even old Thomas, the night guard, gives her a rare nod that means more than any bow.

And Olivia?

She glows.

Her glow floods the shadows of this house like sunlight pouring into a mausoleum, chasing out ghosts I thought I'd live with forever.

The flush in her cheeks. The soft curve of her smile. The way her shoulders relax, like for the first time since Paris she isn't bracing for judgment.

They treat her exactly as she deserves.

Better than my family ever could.

And standing there, watching the only people I trust welcome the only woman I'll ever love—

I know I was right.

This is the next step.

This is her home now.

Ours.

She takes it all in with wide eyes, and for a moment I don't move. I just...watch.

Her hand brushes along the polished banister, fingertips tracing the carved wood like she's afraid it will vanish. She pauses to admire the chandelier, then laughs softly when Margaret fusses over her like she's already part of the family.

It hits me all at once.

This house; cold, cavernous, silent for years, has never looked more alive.

Because she's in it.

I walk her down the hall, past the portraits I've avoided since I was old enough to hate the faces in them. She doesn't flinch at them. Doesn't tense. She looks at me, not them, and suddenly those shadows don't matter anymore.

When I unlock the gallery—the collection I've never let anyone linger in—she goes still. Her eyes roam the canvases, the sculptures, the chaos I've surrounded myself with over the years. Pieces chosen for their sharpness, their violence, their edge.

She takes her time, quiet, moving from frame to frame until finally she turns to me. Her voice is steady but soft.

"War... it's beautiful. But it feels lonely, like you've been waiting for something that never came."

I almost laugh, except my chest is too tight.

Because she's right.

Then she says the thing that guts me.

"I can understand it though. I've been in survival mode for so long, I don't know what to do with myself now that I can breathe."

The words sink into me like a blade.

Because it's my truth too.

I've spent my whole life clawing through shadows, fighting my name, chasing redemption, drowning in ghosts. And here she is. The first clear breath I've ever taken.

I pull her in, kiss her slow, reverent. She tastes like everything I'll never deserve but will never stop keeping.

And in that kiss, my mind steadies—finally letting me see everything I've never dared to want.

Her in white, walking toward me.

A ring on her hand, my name tied to hers forever.

Her belly rounded with our child, those wide brown eyes passed down, paired with my sharp grin.

Little footsteps echoing in these halls that have only ever known silence.

Her laughter would burn itself into the walls, softening every sharp edge this place was built on.

I want it.

All of it.

Sooner than she could ever guess.

When I finally pull back, her smile wrecks me. She doesn't even know. Doesn't know she's already burned herself into every wall, every room, every part of me.

This estate isn't mine anymore.

It's hers.

And one day soon… I'll make sure the world knows it.

I cup her face, my thumbs brushing her cheeks, and watch her eyes melt.

"What's one thing you've always wanted, Olivia?" I murmur. "If money wasn't an issue… what would you choose?"

Chapter Thirty-Three

OLIVIA

The question lands like a pebble in a still lake, small, then ripples everywhere.

What would *I* want?

Financial freedom is a dream I've never really thought possible, definitely not in the form of a man.

But that's not what this is.

My mind shuffles through the lists of things I've never been able to buy, *own.*

I can feel him watching me, thumbs resting at my jaw like he's holding the moment steady so I don't have to. It should be easy. People always have answers for this, right? A dream, a plan, a list.

"What do I want..." I echo, and hear my own voice drift in the high, honeyed light of his gallery.

Back home, wants were practical. Fix the porch steps before they swallow another ankle. Stretch rent into groceries. Keep the lights on at the inn. In the city, wants were smaller still—quiet, manageable. A coffee I didn't have to do mental math to justify. A pair of black slacks without a shiny seat. Survival wants. *Never* dream wants.

I pull back a little and War lets me, his hands sliding down to mine, fingers lacing like he's content to hold the question with me. No pressure. No rush. Just... space.

"Can I…" I swallow, suddenly embarrassed. "Can I think about it?"

His mouth tilts. "You can take forever."

The knot in my chest loosens, just a notch.

We wander.

He shows me every room, but we stop at the library last. It's not fussy or dark or male on purpose; it's small, tucked away, quiet. I touch the spine of a book I've only ever checked out from a library that smelled like lemons and old wood polish. Here it smells like paper and wool and the faintest echo of cedar from the built-ins.

"Pick something," he says. "Anything."

I run a hand across the shelf until my fingers land on a slim collection of letters. "This one."

"Read me a line," he says, settling on the window seat like a man who can bear to be still.

I open to the middle and read whatever my eyes find first: "I don't know what to do with a day that isn't spent searching for the exit. But if I stand still long enough, perhaps a door will appear that opens somewhere softer."

The words hit too close. I close the book and press it to my sternum like that might keep it from cracking me open.

He notices. He *always* notices.

"Tell me, what's going on in that beautiful mind," he says. Not an order. An invitation.

"Like I said I've been in survival mode so long," I say, staring out the window at the lawn where the light turns the grass to coin-colored silk. "It's like my lungs don't remember how to hold anything but panic."

He nods once, like he recognizes the ache by name. "Me too."

I look back at him. "You?"

His jaw works, and something unguarded flickers. "Until you," he says simply.

Something inside me goes warm and heavy, like a soft stone I want to keep in my pocket forever.

I exhale and place the book back on the shelf.

"I think," I say finally, choosing my words like thread, "when you grow up counting pennies and favors, your wants get small on purpose. You don't ask for the big things because you learn not to want what you can't carry."

"And now?" He ask, his eyes watching me, patient.

"Now…" I breathe out. "Now my life is bigger. *You* are a very big thing in my life. And it's terrifying and beautiful. I don't know what I want yet. Not exactly. I just know I *want* to want. I want the chance to figure it out without worrying if the floor will disappear."

His eyes go molten at that. Not hungry. Proud. Like I've said the bravest thing I could say.

"Then that's your first want," he says quietly. "Room to breathe."

I huff a small laugh that turns into something wetter than I intend. He doesn't call me on it. He stands, reaches for me, cups my face, and kisses me soft. Not a brand, not a claim. A promise.

"Let's have dinner," he murmurs against my lips before taking my hand and leading me to the dining room.

Marta, the chef has laid the table like a postcard, linen that begs for elbows, silver that catches candlelight instead of scolding it. The seat beside mine holds a sprig of rosemary tucked under the napkin ring.

And to my surprise the staff sits with us.

Like a family.

Like this is *his* family.

The conversation is easy. Thomas tells a story about a fox who keeps stealing gloves from the gardener's shed and War pretends to be scandalized, which makes Ana, the gardener laugh hard enough to wipe her eyes. Someone mentions the first frost coming early this year, which segues into preserves, which segues into the time the generator failed and the entire house ate ice cream for dinner rather than let it melt. It's ridiculous and real and I'm so full of it I could cry.

After dinner, War brings me on to the terrace, the air is colder. I tuck myself into War's side and he tucks me tighter, like he's been rehearsing the motion in his sleep for years. The hedges breathe. The stars blink. Somewhere inside, music plays, the soft, old kind that knows how to live in a house without disturbing it.

He kisses my hair and doesn't speak. He just walks me through the dark by staying close.

The silence is perfect, intimate, freeing.

"Olivia," he murmurs, fingers brushing my waist. "One day soon, I'm going to marry you."

My breath stumbles, sharp and uneven, like his words knocked the air out of me. *Marry me?* It sounds absurd, impossible, something girls like me don't dream about. Survival, yes. Scraping by, yes. But this? To a man like him?

I look up, ready to laugh it off, to shield myself with disbelief.

But his gaze doesn't waver. It's steady. Fierce. Certain.

And suddenly the ridiculous weight of it shifts, sinking into my chest until it feels less like a fantasy and more like a promise. Terrifying. Beautiful. A vow already carved in stone.

***

Weeks blur, fast and golden.

The kind of golden that tastes like honey and sex and warm coffee War never lets me finish.

I'm curled up on the couch, laptop balanced on my thighs, catching up on the mountain of emails he's neglected.

The morning is still on my skin. My thighs ache from the way he wouldn't let me up, from the hours he kept me caged under him, moving inside me like the world could burn and he'd still be buried there.

He'd ignored it all.

His meeting. His calendar. An investor call he should've taken.

Now he's at the dining table, shirt sleeves rolled, the very picture of control—as if he didn't spend half the morning fucking me senseless on that same table, ignoring the phone that lit up again and again.

He only came up for air when I started shaking. And even then, it wasn't to stop.

Now I'm the one answering his neglected emails, my inbox window bright with tasks that should've been his. He can talk strategy with associates later. For now, I send polite words in his name, cleaning up his mess.

I snort quietly to myself and refocus on the inbox.

No distractions. My fingers fly over the keys, one email, then another, while the clatter of his keyboard behind me fades to background noise.

I'm dressed today. On purpose. Jeans. No skirts, no dresses, nothing soft for him to slide a hand under and distract himself with. Not after the way this morning went. I smirk at the thought, at the ridiculous lengths I have to go just to keep him contained.

I type fast, clearing out everything flagged as urgent. Drafting responses. Cleaning up the wreckage he leaves when he's too obsessed with touching me to remember his own business empire.

The last email flies out with a soft chime just as a shadow cuts across the screen.

I jolt, glancing up.

He's standing over me.

No sound. No warning.

Just *presence.*

Heavy. Possessive. I hadn't even noticed he'd ended his call.

He doesn't clear his throat. Doesn't announce himself. He just stands there until I feel it in my bones, that heat he carries everywhere, pressing down on me.

"Make me peanut butter cookies," he says. Not asks. *Demands.*

I look up arching a brow at him. "*Make* you cookies? No please? No thank you?"

His gaze locks on mine.

Dark. Direct. Possessive.

Then, flat as stone:

"You made Broderick peanut butter cookies."

The laugh punches out of me before I can stop it. "*Oh,* so this is about—"

His mouth claims mine before I can finish, hard and hot, the kiss stealing the rest of the sentence, erasing the name.

When he pulls back, his breath scorches mine.

"Don't say his name."

His words hang there, rough and final, and I'm still half breathless from the kiss when I snap my laptop shut with a click.

I tilt my head, eyes narrowing. "How do you even know I made him cookies?"

His stare doesn't flicker. No games, no dodge. Just brutal honesty.

"He told me."

I blink. "So now *you* want them?" My laugh is half incredulous, half teasing. "Are they even your favorite kind?"

"No." His jaw flexes, his gaze burning through me. "But I want to be the last man you *ever* make peanut butter cookies for."

Something in my chest flips, heat tangling with ridiculous amusement. I can't help the chuckle that escapes me. "*Okay...* but what's your favorite then?"

He hesitates in the way he does when he's about to give something away.

Finally, low: "Oatmeal chocolate chip."

The laugh bursts out of me, softer this time, warm. "That's my favorite too."

His mouth curves, sharp and smug, like he'd been waiting for me to say it.

I push up from the couch, brushing past him toward the kitchen. "Fine. I'll make them. *Both.*"

His hand snags my wrist, pulling me back into the weight of him, lips ghosting my temple before he lets me go.

"Good girl."

Chapter Thirty-Four

WAR

I hate when Broderick is right.

But fuck, Olivia does make the best peanut butter cookies. And now they're all mine.

Forever.

She's mine.

No other man will ever taste these again. Not a single goddamn crumb.

I lift one to my mouth, savoring the warm, golden center like I just conquered a kingdom instead of a kitchen.

She's curled on the couch beside me, 'workday' officially sacrificed at the altar of butter, sugar, and me being a jealous bastard. She chuckles, soft and unbothered, and curls deeper into my side.

"I make them for my brothers every holiday," she says, nuzzling my shoulder. "I can't exactly deny them, War."

Damn it.

I want to say yes, fine, family exception.

But instead—

"They can have some of my stash."

She twists toward me, blinking like I just declared war on the Department of Cookie Distribution.

"What?"

"You make a batch for *me*," I clarify, biting into another cookie. "We can *share* from mine. But the cookies belong *to me*."

Her brows pinch together, confusion written all over that gorgeous face. "Are you serious?"

Deadly.

I meet her gaze, unflinching.

"Yes."

Because it's not about the cookies.

It's about claiming something no other man gets.

It's about the way she sings off key when she bakes, the little dance she does in my kitchen, the way she presses the fork into the dough just so before sliding the tray in the oven.

It's about her feeding me with her fingers and grinning when I groan like she just made me see God.

Those moments?

They're mine.

And if it takes hoarding cookies like a lunatic to make sure every man on this earth knows it?

So be it.

Her laugh bubbles out, light and sweet, and it grates on me because she's laughing *at me.*

"You're ridiculous," she says, shaking her head as she curls closer, crumbs still on her fingers. "Cookies, War? Really?"

I grit my teeth.

She doesn't get it.

It's not about the damn cookies.

It's about her.

The soft flush on her cheeks when she caught me staring at her while she mixed the dough like she'd just rewritten the laws of gravity.

Broderick had that.

Once.

And I'll never fucking forgive it.

She tips her head, eyes gleaming with mischief. "Okay, fine. What about *your* brothers? Can they have my cookies?"

My whole body goes still.

Wesley.

Wilder.

The thought of them biting into something she made with those soft, perfect hands makes my vision haze. My first instinct is the only one that ever lives in me: No. No one touches what's mine.

I open my mouth, ready to snap it out, final, but then—*fuck.*

Maybe once.

Just once.

So they *understand.*

So they know.

So they taste exactly what they'll never have again.

A sample.

A warning.

A boundary drawn in sugar and fire.

"Yes," I bite out. "Once. And only once. So they understand what they'll never touch again."

Her laugh bursts out louder, bright and delighted, like I just told her the most romantic thing in the world.

It pisses me off and wrecks me at the same time.

She thinks it's funny. I mean every word.

***

She's sitting on my desk like a temptation I can't touch.

Crossed legs. Tilted head. One brow arched like she's already bored with me.

"This is ridiculous," Olivia says, gesturing around the office. "You brought me in here just to sit on your desk like some executive paperweight?"

"Not a paperweight," I murmur, finishing an email. "A prize."

She snorts. "Even worse."

My eyes cut to hers, sharp enough to make her spine straighten.

"*Careful,* Olivia." My voice drops, stern, the kind of warning that settles in her bones. "You're not here to mock me."

Her lips part. A flush rises in her cheeks, quick and guilty, but her eyes still spark with defiance.

I let the moment stretch, my gaze steady until I see the shiver run through her, the awareness clicking back into place.

Fuck, I love that fire.

The way she pushes just enough to *make* me remind her who she belongs to.

The way she blushes when I do.

I ease back into my chair, deliberately calm.

"Give me a minute."

I hit send, then turn to my secondary screen. The one I never use for business. Only her.

Three images are pulled up. High-res mockups from the jeweler I had on retainer.

She watches me, confused, until I pivot the monitor toward her.

"I have three designs in progress," I say. "I didn't want to wait, but I also didn't want to get it wrong. So pick. Which do you prefer?"

Her expression softens, but something flickers behind it. A pause. A hesitation.

"War..."

That single word slices through me.

Not because it's soft. But because I know what it might mean.

She's going to say no.

She's going to say she's not ready, that this is too fast, that I'm too much.

I brace myself for the rejection like I've braced for boardroom betrayals and family knives.

But before she can finish—*before she can say anything else,* I cut her off.

"I'm marrying you." My voice is low, even. Final. "But I have to ask first. So pick a style."

Her shoulders relax. The tension bleeds from her spine like a held breath finally exhaled.

She leans forward. Looks.

And I look at her.

Her freckles catch the light now that she isn't hiding them behind makeup anymore. Her skin glows, clear and soft and perfect, because I made sure of it. The conditioner I bought her makes her hair shine like glass in the sun. She smells like warm vanilla and summer wind because I ordered another bottle of the perfume she loves before she even ran out.

She's healthy now. Rested. Fed. Touched.

Loved.

Owned.

This is all I ever wanted.

To give her the version of herself she was never allowed to be.

She hums thoughtfully, pointing to the second image. "That one."

It's the ring with a cushion-cut center stone, thick claw prongs, and a hidden halo beneath the setting. The band is gold. No pave, no distractions. Bold. Timeless. Hers.

I study it, nod once. "Fitting."

Her gaze lingers on the design, then flicks back to me. A flicker of hesitation crosses her face.

"One thing," she says softly.

My chest tightens. "What?"

"When you propose... I don't want a surprise. I hate surprises. I want to know it's coming. I want to be ready for it."

She means it. No teasing, no edge; just truth.

For a beat, I say nothing, already filing it away. She thinks she's asking for a condition. What she's really done is hand me the perfect solution. A way to give her everything she wants and still make it mine.

The best idea I've ever had starts forming, sharp and flawless, like the diamond she just chose.

"Done," I murmur, brushing my thumb over her hip.

Her shoulders loosen, the tension easing out of her spine. She relaxes fully, trusting me.

Inside, I'm already smiling. She won't see it until it's too late.

I hook my hands around her waist and pull her off the desk, settling her onto my lap where she belongs. Her gasp cuts through me as her weight presses down, warm and perfect, anchoring me in a way nothing else ever has.

I kiss her like she just gave me something I never thought I'd have.

Because she did.

She gave me the future, right here, in a single choice. My future.

When I pull back, my forehead rests against hers, our breaths tangling.

"Thank you," I murmur.

And for once, it doesn't feel wrong to say it.

Not soft.

Not weak.

Just honest.

Because I'm grateful for her.

I always will be.

Step Five Complete

Chapter Thirty-Five

OLIVIA

A ring.

Warren Beaumont was serious.

A fucking ring.

I just chose a ring.

A laugh claws out of me, too high, too sharp, bubbling hysterical as I rush down the hall. My office door clicks shut behind me, the slam ricocheting in my bones as I press my back to the wood, chest heaving.

I squeeze my eyes shut, my breaths jagged, shallow, useless. I try to breathe. I try to think.

What the hell just happened?

Then suddenly, I feel it.

A prickle along my skin. The faintest shift in the air. The scent of something familiar, a cologne I haven't smelled in weeks.

I open my eyes.

Brody is inches away.

His hand clamps over my mouth before I can scream.

"Shh," he whispers, urgent. "Stay quiet."

My whole body jerks, panic a wildfire in my chest, but I nod, stiff.

He waits a beat, then slowly pulls his hand away.

His voice is low, urgent. "When I was in Seattle, helping Declan Brooks I started noticing weird shit that got me thinking about War. About the way he is. All these billionaires, Liv. They're the fucking same."

He glances around the room like it might be wired.

A scoff slips out before I can stop it. "Don't you want to be one of them?"

He shrugs, jaw ticking. "Not so sure anymore. When I came back, I searched my office. Found a hidden camera. War didn't even *deny* it when I confronted him, just offered me that California position instead. The contract comes with a bonus, bigger apartment. Clean slate. You interrupted us, remember? That's what it was."

My stomach twists. I *do* remember. War's voice. The tension. The way he looked when I barged in.

"I figured... if he did that to me, someone he barely gives a shit about, then what the hell has he done to you?" Brody's voice lowers. "And I *found* it. A camera in *here*. In your bookshelf."

My gaze jerks toward the shelf.

Brody's fingers snap lightly against my chin, turning my head back. "Don't look." His voice drops. "I know you two are close. Maybe he's forcing—"

"No." The word rips out of me, hard, immediate. "He's not forcing me."

He studies me like I'm speaking a foreign language. "You don't even seem surprised about the camera."

I shrug, the weight of it sitting heavy in my chest. "That's just... War."

Silence falls like a stone.

Brody takes a step back, like he's been burnt, nodding slowly. "Oh. Okay..."

He reaches behind me for the knob.

"Well, I guess all that's left to say is goodbye, Liv. I'm leaving today. For good. Got all my stuff shipped last week. I just wanted..."

His voice trails off. "

I step aside, suddenly hollow. "I'll miss being neighbors."

He pauses, hand on the knob. "We haven't been neighbors in a while, Liv."

That one hits deeper than I thought it would.

"I—Hey, I know I said I wasn't ready for anything when you asked, but—"

"But I'm not War Beaumont," he says, not unkindly. Just final. "I get it, Liv."

He turns the knob, opens the door, but glances back once more.

"I just hope you realize the cage he's put you in... before he throws away the key."

And then he's gone.

The door clicks shut behind him.

Silence rushes in.

Thick and immediate.

I don't move. Not yet.

Just breathe, Liv.

I press myself back to the door, hands still curled at my sides like I'm bracing for something else to crash through. My lungs sting with the breath I haven't let go.

A camera.

In the bookshelf.

I close my eyes, try to center myself, but all I can smell is the faint trace of Brody's cologne, sharp and familiar in the space War has carefully constructed for me.

My pulse stutters, the words he left behind rattling in my chest. *Cage. Key.*

I should check.

I should tear every book off that shelf and find the thing he swears is there.

But I don't.

Because I already know.

If Brody said it, it's true. War wouldn't deny it. He'd look me straight in the eye, unapologetic, and say of course I put a camera in your office Olivia.

Of course I need to see you when I'm not there.

I push off the door, legs shaky beneath me, and make my way to the desk. My laptop is still open, cursor blinking like nothing just shattered the illusion of privacy I never even realized I was clinging to.

My fingers hover over the keyboard.

Focus. Just... work.

I open my inbox. Drafts. Deadlines. Numbers I'm supposed to care about. But the words blur, crowding into one long smear of static.

A camera.

He watched me.

He *wanted* to watch me.

A cold ripple moves through me, then another that's not quite cold. It sits low in my belly, heavy and humming.

Because War didn't install that camera to monitor.

Not in the way Brody meant.

He's not the kind of man who watches out of boredom.

He watches out of *want.*

Possession. Hunger. That restless, obsessive burn he never even tries to hide.

The camera hums at the edge of my awareness, louder than the keys clacking under my fingers. I can almost feel it now, tucked in the spines of the books beside me, glass eye unblinking.

And maybe I should feel angry. Or violated. Or betrayed.

But mostly I just feel...*known.*

Seen in the way only he sees me. The way he always has.

Of course he'd do this.

It's not paranoia, not cruelty. It's War.

His obsession is oxygen.

Control wrapped in gold.

I breathe out slowly, pulse still jagged as I lean into the screen, telling myself I'm fine. That I can focus. That I can work.

Even while I know I'm being watched.

My gaze drifts again, unbidden, toward the shelf.

I don't let it land.

Not yet.

I don't know what unsettles me more, the violation.

Or the fact that I don't feel violated at all.

My thighs cross. My pulse kicks. I shake myself.

Get a grip, Liv.

My thighs press tighter, my pulse hammering. I tell myself to focus, but every word on the screen blurs into nothing.

Because all I can think is that he might be watching.

Right now.

I shift in the chair, angle my body just slightly toward the bookshelf. My breath catches. The thought coils hotter the longer I let it sit.

What does he see when I'm like this?

Does he sit back in that leather chair of his, silent, smug, taking me in? Or does he lean closer, hungry, restless...

Heat pools low in my belly. My fingers drift, almost without permission, to the hem of my skirt.

Slowly, deliberately, I tug it higher.

Just a few inches. Just enough for him, if he's looking, to know *I know.*

My pulse stutters. I pause, hold still, daring the silence to break.

Nothing.

Which, somehow, makes it worse.

I slide the fabric up further, baring my thighs to the cool air of the office, to the glass eye I can't see but feel all the same.

My breath turns shallow. My hand slips lower.

I shouldn't.

But the thought of him watching… of War sitting somewhere with that sharp, possessive gaze fixed only on me, sets my skin alight.

"Are you watching me?" I whisper.

The words aren't for me. They're for him.

And even though there's no answer, no click or glitch or red light—

I feel it.

I spread my legs wider.

Let him have this.

My fingers trail down between my thighs, sliding beneath lace, finding heat and slick and pulse.

I gasp, but I don't stop.

This is surrender.

To War.

To the way he wants me.

To the way I want to be seen.

Chapter Thirty-Six

WAR

The line clicks dead.

Another pointless meeting.

I lean back in my chair, exhaling slow, watching the city burn gold beneath the windows. Four thirty. Almost time to leave.

My mouth curves, sharp with satisfaction.

She chose a ring.

Our ring.

For a man who owns half this skyline, I've never felt more like I own the world.

I could pack it in now. Go to her office, collect what's mine, drive us home. But habit pulls me sideways. One last check.

I toggle the feed. The bookshelf camera blinks alive.

And the air leaves my lungs.

Olivia.

Her chair angled just so. Her skirt hitched high. Her thighs spread wide, soft and bare under the office light.

And her voice—low, breathless.

"Are you watching?"

My heart slams once, brutal, dropping to the floor.

She knows.

She knows about the camera.

For a split second panic rips through me, then the truth clicks in, sharp and savage.

She knows and she's touching herself anyway.

Touching what belongs to me.

My cock strains against the confines of my slacks as I watch her fingers disappear beneath lace. Her gasp carries through the speakers, broken and sweet, and I grip the edge of my desk hard.

Fuck.

She's wet. For me. For the thought of my eyes on her.

My good girl.

The sight of her surrender hits like gasoline on a fire. Every instinct in me screams to break distance, to end the delay, to take back what's mine.

I close the feed with a vicious swipe, stand, and shove my chair back.

Because if she wants to be watched...

I'll watch her up close.

And if she wants to give me her body like this—then I'll take it.

All of it.

I leave my office, steps sharp, certain.

Time to collect.

The hallway disappears under my stride, every step a beat of possession hammering through me.

She thinks she can tease me.

Angle herself to my camera, spread her thighs, whisper into the lens like it's my ear.

She thinks she can touch what's mine without my permission.

I shove her office door open without knocking.

She jerks, startled, fingers flying away from where they were pressed against her pussy. Her skirt is still bunched high on her hips, thighs slick, lips parted, chest heaving like she's been caught in sin.

She has.

My Olivia.

Her eyes widen when she sees me, shame and heat battling in her face. She goes to tug her skirt down.

With a smirk.

A smirk.

Oh my girl knows what she's doing.

"Don't," I growl. The sound rips out of me, sharp and absolute.

Her hands freeze.

I stalk across the room, slow, deliberate, eating her with my eyes. Every inch of her is trembling from being caught. From knowing I saw.

"You *knew.*" My voice is low, dangerous. "You knew about the camera."

Her breath hitches. She nods.

"And you touched yourself anyway."

Another nod, smaller this time, her lips trembling.

Hunger knot inside me, burning hot, tearing at my ribs. "That's my pussy, Olivia. Mine to touch. Mine to ruin. Mine to keep wet. And you thought you could take that from me?"

My hands catch her waist and lift her straight off the chair. She squeaks, weightless for half a second, before I plant her face-down against her desk, hands flat to brace herself.

The chair topples behind us.

"W-War—"

"You *wanted* me to watch," I say, my voice a low growl in her ear as I press into her back. "You spread your legs for the camera. You whispered for me."

She whimpers. "You didn't tell me about the camera."

"I don't have to tell you when I'm watching what's mine."

I push her skirt higher over her hips, baring the soaked lace beneath. I palm the heat of her cunt through it and hear her breath catch. "Didn't think I'd come take what's mine?"

She doesn't answer. *She can't.*

Not when I hook a finger beneath the ruined lace and rip it clean down the middle.

I drop the torn fabric to the desk like a receipt.

"Hands flat. Stay down."

I unbuckle my belt with one hand, the sound harsh in the quiet room. My cock is already hard, leaking, aching.

"Did you come?" I ask, dragging the head of my cock through her soaked pussy. "Before I got here?"

"N-no."

"Good."

My hand fists in her hair, yanking her head back so her mouth falls open on a gasp.

I drive into her in one brutal thrust, burying myself to the hilt in that wet, gripping heat.

She screams, sharp and stunned. I slap a hand over her mouth.

"This office isn't soundproof," I murmur roughly. "But you know that, don't you?"

She nods, trembling.

"Then stay quiet while I fuck you," I say. "Like the good little slut you are."

I fuck her hard, brutal, claiming.

Each thrust pushes the desk forward an inch. Papers scatter. Her moans muffle under my palm.

She's soaking me, her cunt clenching tighter with every slap of skin.

"You think I wouldn't find out?" I bite at her ear. "You thought I wouldn't see you?"

Her eyes roll back as I hit deep again, again, grinding against the spot that makes her sob.

"I see *everything*, Olivia."

I drop my hand from her mouth, grab her wrists, and pin them behind her back. Her cheek is pressed to the desk, lips parted and gasping.

"Fuck," I groan, driving deep, grinding my hips against her ass. "So tight, *baby*. Always so fucking tight for me."

Her pussy grips me, wet and hot, clenching around me like she's begging me to stay buried forever.

I pound into her, ruthless, relentless, each stroke jolting her perfect body against the desk.

"You're mine," I growl, every word a thrust. "This cunt. This body. Every sound out of your mouth. All mine."

She sobs, broken and needy, "Yes! War; yours!"

"Say it louder."

"Yours!" she cries, voice hoarse, body shaking under the force of me.

Her thighs tremble, her breath breaks, and I feel it; the quick, desperate flutter inside her.

"Come on my cock, Olivia," I command, my fingers finding her clit, circling in time with my thrusts. "*Now.* Let me feel you."

She shatters with a moan, her body convulsing, cunt spasming around me, soaking me with her release.

The heat drags me under. My thrusts turn savage, each one harder than the last until I bury myself to the hilt and let go.

"Fuck, baby" I groan, spilling into her, filling her so deep it leaks around the base of my cock.

She moans through it, her body clenching around me like it needs every drop.

When I finally still, my body drapes over hers, my breath ragged in her ear, I whisper:

"You wanted to be watched."

My lips graze her shoulder.

"Next time, I expect you to wait for me."

She shivers beneath me with a chuckle. "Yes, sir."

I pull out slow, loving the hiss she makes as I slide free. My cum spills from her, dripping down her thighs onto the floor.

I tuck myself back into my slacks, then smooth her skirt back down, fingers grazing the mess I made between her thighs.

She flinches, over-sensitive. Spent.

Wrecked.

Beautiful.

Ruined by me.

Exactly how I like her.

She slays limp, breath hitching, and I steady her with a hand at the base of her spine. My other hand pulls a cloth from the drawer behind her desk, one I placed there myself months ago. For moments just like this.

I clean her carefully. Slowly. Thoroughly.

Because she's mine.

Once she's decent, I help her stand, I steady her with a hand at the base of her spine, then reach for her coat hanging by the door; the long wool one I bought her last month, dark green, soft as sin. I hold it open and ease it over her shoulders, one arm, then the other. She's still shaky, so I pull her close as I button each one for her, slow and sure, like she might unravel if I rush it.

"You shouldn't have worn the skirt," I murmur, adjusting the collar so it sits right against her throat. "It's starting to snow."

She groans softly, smiling up at me. "War, the car is literally in the parking garage. It's always warm. I'll be fine."

My brows lift. I give her the look; the one that means she's not winning this argument. Then I wrap her scarf twice around her neck, tucking the ends in, my knuckles brushing her jaw.

"You're mine," I say quietly, pressing a kiss to the tip of her nose. "I take care of what's mine."

Her lips curve, soft. "I know."

I cup her cheek once more before letting go

Then I glance over my shoulder at the bookshelf.

At the red light still blinking.

Still watching.
Just the way I planned.

Chapter Thirty-Seven

WAR

I wake her with sugar.

A cupcake, the kind she likes from *Smash and Sugar*. Perfect swirl of frosting, edible gold flecks on top. A single candle burning down, flame small and steady in the dim of our bedroom.

She blinks awake, lashes fluttering, confusion turning to warmth when she sees me standing there with it.

"Happy birthday, my sweet girl," I say softly, setting the plate on the nightstand so I can lean in and press kisses across her face. Her temple. Her cheek. Her lips.

She laughs softly, voice still heavy with sleep. "War…"

"Blow it out," I say against her mouth.

She sits up, hair mussed and perfect, and leans over the candle. Her lips part, a breath, and the flame snuffs out in smoke.

I take the plate back, set it aside, and tip her chin up. "What'd you wish for?"

Her smile tilts, sly and secret. "If I tell you, it won't come true."

I chuckle, low in my chest. "Doesn't matter. You'll get it anyway. Whatever it is." My thumb strokes along her jaw, steady, reverent. "Because I'll make sure you get whatever you want for the rest of your life."

Her eyes soften, and something in my chest pulls taut.

I've had everything. Power. Money. Sky-high glass towers with my name on them. But nothing—*nothing*, has ever filled me like this woman curled in my bed, candle smoke still hanging in the air between us.

I've had women in my bed, in my head, but *never* like this. Never in the space between my heartbeats.

She's perfect.

And for the first time in my life, so is everything else.

My heart has never felt this full.

Life has never felt this good.

She swings her legs out of bed, stretching with a sleepy sigh, and pads toward the bathroom. I pull open the closet, and slide a hanger free, laying her blouse across the duvet, smoothing the fabric flat with my palm. Her skirt follows. Stockings. The soft click of her heels as I set them neatly at the foot of the bed.

Behind me, the sink starts running. The muted scrape of her toothbrush against her teeth. I picture her in the mirror, mouth full of foam, hair mussed from sleep, and my chest tightens.

"We'll leave work early," I call, my voice carrying through the sound of running water. "Two instead of four. Come back here, get ready, and I'm taking you out for the best evening."

The faucet clicks off. Silence. Then the faint swish of the brush against porcelain, the metallic clang of it being set down.

I straighten the skirt with a precise tug, fingers dragging across the fabric like every crease offends me.

I chuckle under my breath, thinking of the theater at the estate. Staff already prepped, the screen queued with the little film we made. Maybe we'll make another. I want her to watch herself, watch that perfect face go soft and desperate when I'm deep inside her.

"War…"

Her voice pulls me out of the thought.

She's leaning in the doorway, brushing her hair, the strands catching the light as they fall over her shoulder. Her eyes are cautious, soft.

"I don't want a big thing tonight," she says. "Just us. No fancy restaurant, no—"

I cross the room in three strides, catch her wrist before she can lower the brush, and hush her with a kiss. Slow. Sure. My mouth sealing over hers until the rest of her protest dissolves into a sigh against my lips.

When I pull back, I press my forehead to hers, my hand sliding down to rest against the dip of her waist.

"Get dressed, sweet girl. We'll work, and then tonight is *just us.* Me celebrating another year of the most beautiful woman being alive."

She rolls her eyes, but the pink rising in her cheeks betrays her. She tries to turn back, but I catch her chin, make her look at me.

"Okay," she murmurs, cheeks warm, lips curved as she trails her fingers down the hard line of my jaw. The touch is light, but it jolts through me like a live wire. My pulse kicks, brutal and fast.

"Thank you. I love you."

The words are soft. Casual. Like she doesn't know they gut me every time.

I swallow, kiss her again, slower this time, tasting toothpaste and her warmth, and whisper against her mouth:

"I love you too, Olivia Baker."

And it's the truest thing I've ever said.

I trail my fingers down her arm slowly and glance over at the skirt I laid out.

It's thin.

Too thin.

My jaw tightens.

"I told you," she says with a knowing smirk, watching me notice. "The car's warm. I'll be fine."

"No," I mutter, already turning toward the drawer. "You're wearing fleece-lined stockings today."

"War—"

"No arguments, Olivia." I toss them onto the bed beside the outfit. "You *insist* on wearing skirts even in the dead of winter when you have brand-new fitted trousers. So if you won't dress warm, I'll do it for you."

She groans, flopping back onto the mattress dramatically. "You're so bossy."

I arch a brow. "And you're going to tell me you're not cold? I see *everything* Olivia."

She mumbles something into the comforter that sounds suspiciously like *"You're lucky I love you."*

I lean down, kiss the crown of her head, then whisper against her hair, "I am. So lucky. And I'll keep you warm however I have to."

***

The door bursts open without a knock.

I don't flinch.

Wesley's the only one who does that.

Even my Olivia knocks once before opening the door.

He strides in, eyes lit up like I've never seen, suit rumpled like he's been pacing half the city instead of sitting behind a desk.

"The mob is fucking crazy!" he blurts.

A laugh rumbles in my chest, low and amused.

"Still spending time with the Amatos?"

He shakes his head, pacing across the rug before spinning on his heel to face me.

"You have no idea. I helped the mob."

I arch a brow.

"We don't get involved in that shit. You want to smear our name all over the media in blood and concrete?"

"Relax." Wesley exhales hard and drops into the chair across from me, running a hand through his hair like he doesn't know what to do with the energy crackling off him.

"I helped save Santo Amato's wife."

That gets my attention.

I lean back, steepling my hands.

"You?"

"Yes, me." His chin lifts, indignant. "Don't look at me like that."

I can't help it; a bark of laughter breaks out of me. "*You* held a gun?"

He scoffs, straightening his tie like he's about to give a board-room pitch.

"No. I figured out who was after her. I was an intricate part."

"Congratulations?" I drawl.

He leans forward, hands braced on his knees, eyes sparking.

"It has me thinking—"

"No."

My tone sharpens, final.

"We won't work with them. We won't sell to them. And we sure as fuck won't build our own criminal empire if that's where you're going."

Wesley shakes his head quickly.

"Not that. Just... maybe they aren't all that bad."

My jaw ticks.

He's playing with fire, and he doesn't even see it.

I swivel my screen toward him.

One click brings up the article I've been tracking.

"The mayor's son, Jude Olsen, is missing. Last anyone heard, he went back to Seattle. *Supposed* to be back on campus."

Another click.

"He hasn't shown up. His last notable appearance?"

Click.

"A gala with Vasilisa Popov... now known as Vasilisa—"

Wesley's mouth curves. "Amato."

"Exactly."

I level him with a stare.

"Do *not* get involved with them, Wesley. Not their games. Not their wars. Not their women. I don't care how bright it looks when you're standing in the dark. You step into their world, you won't walk out."

He exhales, sinking back in the chair, some of the fire dimming, but not gone.

Wesley's always been the level one.

Steady where I'm sharp.

Controlled where Wilder's reckless.

But now...

The Amatos lit something in him.

Or maybe they're weaving their webs around him, pulling threads I can't see.

And that worries me more than I'll admit.

Chapter Thirty-Eight

OLIVIA

My phone doesn't stop buzzing on my desk. Between Mama and Daddy, my brothers, and Ella, my best friend, it's been a steady stream of birthday wishes.

Dean even sent me a picture of my favorite strawberry cake Mama baked in my honor.

He plans on eating it.

I roll my eyes, but the ache slips in anyway.

I miss them.

I want War to meet them. To see the people who made me. To know I had a life before him.

But with Ronnie always hovering at the inn, I can't risk it. If War knew, he'd get involved. And I can't let him shoulder that weight for me.

I fire off another email, try to refocus, but my mind drifts to tonight. What War has planned. He's been restless all day, that sharp glint in his eye like he's holding a secret in his fist.

I should be excited.

Instead, I stare at the clock and think about the box of things I left behind at my old apartment. The clothes Mama bought me. My album of family photos. My grandmother's heirloom necklace tucked in the top drawer.

I told myself I didn't need them when I moved into War's penthouse. That I wouldn't be at his place long. I had no idea that we would become so much more.

But on my birthday, the weight of it presses down harder.

I want something that's *mine* on my birthday

Just a piece of home.

I get up before I can stop myself, before War whisks me away on whatever plan he's plotting.

I grab my keys and head out.

Just a quick trip.

***

This was *not* a quick trip.

I don't know how War does it. We always make it back to the penthouse in like five minutes, this rideshare took forever to get me home.

Well, my *old* home.

I should probably get rid of this place.

I look over at Brody's door.

So weird that that apartment is empty.

I shake off the thought and unlock the door

The lock clicks, the door swings open.

And I freeze.

This... *isn't* my apartment.

It's the same layout. The same walls. But nothing else belongs to me anymore.

The sagging couch is gone, replaced by a brand-new sectional in soft gray, pillows plump and perfect. A coffee table gleams in the center, glass so clean it looks untouched. Matching end tables. A rug that actually matches the curtains.

Even the kitchen catches my eye from here, new stainless-steel appliances humming quiet, a toaster so sleek it looks like it could toast a slice of bread without charring it black.

My throat tightens as I step inside, my shoes whispering against the rug I never bought.

Down the hall, the frames I left empty are filled.

I stop, my hand catching on the wall for balance.

Photos.

From Mama's albums. My brothers laughing on the porch. Daddy covered in flour at the inn kitchen. Ella grinning with a braid half undone.

My family. My life. Hung up in frames I never filled.

I stumble into the bathroom, my chest tight.

Everything is different.

The counter lined with bottles, my favorite shampoo, the perfume I thought I'd run out of, the exact face wash I used to hoard because it was too expensive to buy twice. Fresh towels, fluffy and white.

"War," I whisper, my voice catching.

I rush to the bedroom.

And stop dead.

The bed is new. Larger. Covered in fresh linens. A dresser stands where my chipped secondhand one used to lean crooked against the wall.

The closet door is cracked, just enough for me to glimpse inside. Fabric in colors and textures I don't recognize—silk, cashmere, lace. New clothes hanging neatly, tags glinting in the dark.

My breath hitches, jagged.

Why?

Why would War do this?

Was he planning on letting me go?

Was this some kind of birthday surprise?

Or did he want this place furnished, waiting, just in case I decided to leave him?

The thought twists sharp in my chest, too heavy, too much.

I sit down on the edge of the brand-new bed, staring at the life he built for me here, in *secret.*

At first, it feels like too much to hold in my chest.

Something soft.

My fingers press into the comforter, plush and new, and I let my eyes drift to the closet door again. New clothes. New life.

Maybe he wanted this for me.

My heart flutters. Maybe War meant this place to be ours too, another *nest.* Somewhere closer to my favorite food haunts, the places I've forced him to order from a hundred times. Maybe this was his way of saying, *I see you.* I know what you love.

For a dizzy second, I let myself believe it.

My phone rings. The sound breaking my thoughts

I fumble it out of my purse, heart still fluttering, until I see the name on the screen.

Mama.

I swipe, breathless. "Hey, Mama."

"Hey, my Liv bug," she coos, warm as sunlight. "Happy birthday, baby girl. Is Warren around?"

I freeze.

"...Warren?"

My phone vibrates. War's name flashes. I decline it.

"*Yes, Liv bug,*" she answers teasingly. "We all know about Warren Beaumont."

From the background, I hear my brother making obnoxious kissing noises.

My stomach plummets. "How?"

"Because he called," Mama says, matter-of-fact. "And we want to thank him, Liv... he paid for the Inn for the rest of the year! He—"

Her voice is bubbling with joy, but my heart drops so fast it hurts. I don't hear her anymore.

My phone vibrating in my hand, his name flashing as my mother sings his praises.

No.

No, *no, no.*

He wouldn't.

He wouldn't go behind my back after I asked him not to. He wouldn't snoop.

"Did you... did you tell him about Ronnie?" My voice splinters on the name.

Silence.

Then Mama, quietly answers. "No, Liv bug. I figured that's something *you* should do."

My chest tightens. The edges of the room blur.

"Mama, I-I have to go," I choke, and hang up before she can say more.

My phone slips from my hand onto the comforter. I press both palms to my face, breathing sharp and erratic.

There's no way War hasn't figured it out.

No way.

That's why he did this. Why the apartment is redone. Why every inch feels like a replacement life waiting for me.

My chest feels tight.

Too small for my ribs.

For my breath.

For the ache clawing its way up my throat.

This isn't freedom.

It's fallout.

That's why he did this.

Why every inch of this apartment feels curated, clean, safe.

Perfect.

Because it isn't mine.

It's his.

A replacement life waiting for me to step into it.

Not a gift.

A cage.

Brody was right.

And I was too blind to see it.

Too lost in War's voice, his hands, the way he said my name like a prayer he owned.

My breaths come faster.

I can't be here.

I shove to my feet and rip the closet door open. My suitcase is still there, mercifully untouched, waiting in the corner.

I drag the suitcase out of the closet and start throwing clothes inside, shaking so hard I can barely hold onto anything.

My vision tunnels, corners blackening.

I have to go.

Before I lose the nerve.

Before he finds and talks me into forgiving him.

The thought alone cracks something open inside me. Because part of me—

God, part of me wants to go to him.

The phone buzzes on the bed.

War.

My body stills.

The sound is soft, but it detonates through me.

I just stare at it, frozen, watching his name flash over and over.

My pulse hammers so hard it shakes the air.

My heart is a traitor, pounding faster, louder, like it still believes he's the safe place it remembers.

My throat burns.

Tears sting my eyes, hot and stupid.

He can't fix this with that voice.

He can't make this better with a word.

I shouldn't.

I know what happens when I do.

He'll say my name, and I'll fold.

He'll sound sorry, and I'll forget what he took from me.

But the silence is worse.

It presses against my chest, heavy and endless.

My hand trembles as I reach for the phone.

I shouldn't.

But I do.

I swipe the screen, breath hitching.

My voice comes out small, cracked, betraying everything I wanted to hide.

"Why?"

Chapter Thirty-Nine

WAR

I shut down my screen at two sharp. Time to leave. Time to get her.

I stride down to Olivia's office, push the door open. Empty. Her chair still tucked in, her laptop closed.

I frown.

Maybe the bathroom.

I check the staff restroom down the hall. Nothing.

I double back, step into my own office, push open the bathroom door.

Maybe she slipped in without me noticing.

Empty.

The unease settles deeper.

I head to the front desk. "James," I snap. "Where's Olivia?"

He blinks, surprised. "Uh… she left about an hour ago, Mr. Beaumont."

The words hit like a blade sliding between my ribs.

Left? Without me?

I pull my phone, dial her. It rings, and rings.

Voicemail.

I stab at it again as I walk, long strides carrying me into the elevator. The doors close. I call again.

No ringing this time. Straight to voicemail.

My stomach drops like stone.

Her phone is off?

The elevator dings. My blood runs cold, then hot. My mind snaps to the only possibility.

Wesley working with the Amatos.

They want the Parker Building.

I storm his floor, my thumb hammering Olivia's number again and again, each time met with the same empty voicemail.

By the time I reach his office, my blood is pounding loud enough to drown out thought. I throw the door open without knocking.

And freeze.

Evie. Blonde. Plump. In Wesley's lap, her mouth swollen from a kiss.

I can barely register, I only see red.

"What the fuck did you do?" I snarl, voice sharp enough to slice the air.

Wesley jerks back, face flushing. "Evie, give me a minute."

She scrambles up, cheeks flaming, and slips past me, closing the door.

Wesley snaps at me, breathless. "What the hell is wrong with you? What are you talking about?"

"I'm talking about Olivia," I bark. My hands fist at my sides. "She's not here, and when I call, it goes straight to voicemail."

I charge toward his desk.

"*And you* were working with Santo Amato. You've got his fucking secretary in here like what? Your paid whore—"

"Hey!" Wesley snaps, standing. "She's not—"

"What did you do?" I roar, the words tearing out of me raw, desperate.

"Nothing!" Wesley shouts back. "I helped Amato, he was grateful. Said I could hire Evie. He has his *wife* as his secretary now, okay? That's it. We may do a collaboration in some surveillance releases, but that's all. They wouldn't touch Olivia."

I drag in an uneven breath, chest heaving. My fists ache from how tightly I'm holding them.

Wesley exhales, shoulders dropping. "Did you go home? See if maybe she's there? Maybe her phone died?"

The suggestion lands like a slap.

Stupid.

Of course I didn't check.

But I don't let him see that.

I step in close, my shadow swallowing him whole. "Stay away from the Amatos. We don't do business with them. *Ever.* Do you understand me?"

His throat bobs, but he nods. "Yeah."

I leave without another word, my pulse still hammering, every step echoing with the same thought.

Olivia.

Where the fuck are you?

***

"Olivia!" I call the second the elevator doors slide open. My voice ricochets off glass and marble, too loud in the silence of the penthouse.

No answer.

The kitchen. Empty.

Living room. Empty.

Bedroom. Empty.

Bathroom. Empty.

Each room I check hollows me out further. I stalk through the space like a predator, but there's nothing to catch. No sound. No movement.

My chest is tight, breath coming sharp as I throw open the closet. Her clothes are still here. Dresses lined neat, shoes in their rows. I yank open drawers, half-expecting them to be bare, but her things are folded inside.

I stumble into the bathroom. Her perfume is on the counter, cap askew like she used it this morning. Her toothbrush, her face cream, all of it waiting.

She's not gone.

But she's not here.

I drag my phone out, thumb shaking as I hit dial again.

She answers on the second ring.

"Why?" she whispers.

The sound hits me like a punch.

Her voice, soft, broken, the sound of something coming apart.

"Where are you?" I manage. It comes out rougher than I intend, almost a growl.

I can hear her breathing, the faint hitch like she's trying not to cry.

"Why did you pay for my family?" she asks.

I exhale hard, drag a hand through my hair. "Olivia... baby, I had to help. I couldn't just—"

"No," she cuts me off, voice trembling but sharp enough to wound. "I *asked* you not to get involved."

"*Olivia,*" I try again, softer this time, pleading. "Just meet me at home, okay? We can talk. I'll explain."

"No."

The word is quiet, final.

"War, I can't do this."

The line clicks dead.

For a second, I just stand there, phone to my ear, listening to nothing.

Then I look down.

She hung up on me.

The floor tilts.

She wouldn't.

Not Olivia. Not my sweet, stubborn girl who always obeys.

I hit redial anyway. The call doesn't even try to connect.

Blocked?

My stomach turns to ice.

She wouldn't turn her phone off.

She wouldn't block me.

Not with me.

Not ever.

My hand fists against the marble counter, the crack of skin to stone echoing.

I press my knuckles to my mouth, breathing hard through the burn in my throat.

I will *not* lose her.

I cannot.

Then, an opening. A thought.

Location sharing.

I swipe hard across the screen, find the icon, log in with muscle memory.

The little circle loads.

Come on. *Come on.*

Her last known location populates the map.

I stare, blood pounding in my ears.

Her apartment.

Of all places.

Why the fuck would she go there?

***

I don't even remember leaving the penthouse, just the slam of the door and the growl of the engine as I tear into the street.

My knuckles ache against the wheel, white-knuckled, every red light nothing but an insult.

Her apartment.

I'd had it decorated for her. Every detail. Every piece of furniture chosen because I knew what she deserved. Fresh clothes in the closet, her favorite toiletries, frames filled with her family's photos. If one day she chose to move out of the penthouse, I was going with her. There was no version of reality where she lived here alone, without everything she needed.

It was supposed to be a surprise.

Maybe she saw it. Maybe she *hated* it.

The thought tears through me like shrapnel.

By the time I reach her building, I'm shaking with it. The elevator drags to get down to me, crawling between floors like it's mocking me. I don't wait. I bound the stairs, three at a time, lungs burning.

Her door is in front of me. I yank out my copy of the key and shove it into the lock, twisting hard.

"Olivia!"

The word rips out of me, harsh and desperate, echoing down the empty hall.

Silence.

I stalk inside. The air smells faintly of her perfume, a sweet trace that punches me in the chest.

Bedroom.

The sheets are rustled at the edge, like she sat there, like she thought. Like she planned.

The closet door hangs open. A few clothes are scattered on the floor.

No.

No fucking way.

I step closer, chest clenching so hard it feels like it might collapse.

Her suitcase is gone.

My throat locks. My vision blurs.

She left me.

She *left me.*

Without a word. On her *birthday.*

She just—

Something snaps.

I lunge for the closet, rip the clothes from their hangers, hurl them across the room. The dresser drawer slams against my fist, wood splintering as I tear it out and dump it. Her perfume bottle shatters against the wall, scent exploding, choking me, burning me.

I tear the sheets off the bed, the mattress skidding half off the frame. My hand slams through the mirror, glass raining down, blood streaking across the shards.

I destroy it all.

Because it's mine.

Because she was mine.

And she walked away.

The rage is white-hot, animal. But beneath it—beneath it is something worse.

Hollow.

The kind of hollow that swallows men whole.

I drop to my knees in the wreckage, glass biting through slacks, blood dripping from my knuckles. My chest heaves. My throat burns.

"Olivia," I rasp, the word breaking, useless.

She left me.

And I don't know how to breathe without her.

Chapter Forty

OLIVIA

Changing in the airport bathroom was a choice.

The heater blew weak warmth into the freezing tiles. I had to rub my arms just to pull on the sleeves of my sweater.

Standing in line for a ticket was a choice.

Boarding a three o'clock flight while knowing War was probably tearing apart half the city looking for me?

That was a choice too.

My choice.

Because for months, Warren Beaumont has been making all the choices for me.

But crying in my first-class seat next to the nicest stranger alive? That wasn't a choice.

The woman beside me slid a tissue into my hand without a word, then pressed her unopened snack into my lap like it was medicine.

I should have went home to him, talked to him. Should have asked him what he knew. Or told him everything. That the mafia owned my family. That Baker's Inn was theirs, and I was tangled in something I couldn't undo. That I'd be a liability to a man like him.

But instead, I hung up on him and I ran.

I inhale a shaky breath, try to swallow it down.

"You feeling any better?" my seatmate asks softly.

I nod, wiping at my eyes. "Yeah. Thank you. I'm Olivia, by the way. Olivia Baker."

She smiles; kind, warm, steady. "Selena Nandez. But you can call me S.J."

Her hair is glossy brown silk, her hazel eyes bright with something sharp behind the gentleness. A book rests in her hand.

With her name on the cover.

"You're an author?" I ask, surprised.

She chuckles, lifting the book and wiggling it. "Guilty."

"That's amazing," I murmur, almost forgetting the ache in my *chest.*

She tilts her head, *studying me.* "Are you headed home?"

"Something like that...and you? Headed home or headed out?" I ask, desperate to shift the focus off me.

She smiles. "Oh, this? Just a connection. I'm on my way to California."

I nod, fiddling with the tissue in my lap. "Work or play?"

"Work," she says, lifting her book with a little grin. "Always work."

Her expression softens into something that feels dangerously close to pity. "What's his name?"

I blink. "Excuse me?"

"It's always relationship issues," she says gently. "So what's his name?"

"...Warren."

"And what did Warren do?"

My throat closes. The truth burns at the back of my tongue.

"Nothing," I manage. "That's the problem. He just... gave. And gave. And before I knew it, I was swallowed up by all his things. *His* choices. His world. I didn't realize he'd locked me in until I couldn't see the way out."

S.J. is quiet for a long beat, just watching me. Then she leans closer, her voice low but steady.

"Here's the thing, Olivia Baker," she says. "A man can give you the world. He can build you castles, hand you keys, lay down his empire at your feet. But if he never asks you what you want, it stops being a gift. It becomes a prison with gold bars."

My chest tightens. She sees right through me.

She squeezes my hand, her grip warm and grounding. "You don't need to run forever. You just need to figure out what's yours. What you want. And if the man loves you—*truly loves you*—he'll want that too, even if it scares him."

Her words lodge deep, sparking something small and dangerous in my chest.

Hope.

***

The terminal feels too bright, too loud, too busy. I keep my head down, clutching my bag like it's armor as I walk through the sliding glass doors.

And then I see them.

Logan, tall and gruff in his Baker's Inn fleece-lined jacket, the logo stitched just above his heart, arms crossed like a sentinel against the cold. Chase, the only sandy blond in the family, bundled in a flannel and puff vest, jeans still dirt-stained, crooked smile already tugging at his mouth as he opens his arms wide. And Dean; messy brown hair peeking out beneath a knit beanie, the tallest of the three, barrels past them, the strongest as always.

"Baby sis!" Dean shouts, scooping me up before I can even breathe. My bags drop to the ground as he spins me, planting a noisy kiss against my cheek. I can't help laughing through the sting in my eyes.

Chase is next, pulling me into his arms, squeezing tight. "Happy birthday, Livvy," he murmurs against my hair.

Logan doesn't say much. He just grabs my bags like it's nothing and hauls them to the truck. When he comes back, he opens the back door for me. For a second, his gaze pins mine.

"You good?"

The shame crashes over me like a wave. They know. Of course they know. I'd called Dad in the rideshare on the way here, sobbing like a child. God, what a loser.

I climb in anyway, sliding onto the bench seat. Chase slips in beside me, wraps an arm around my shoulders, and tugs me against him until my head rests in his lap. His hand strokes slow and steady through my hair, the way he used to when I was little and scared of thunderstorms.

Dean climbs into the passenger seat, already fiddling with the radio. Logan takes the driver's side, all silent focus as the engine rumbles to life. Music fills the cab, something upbeat, and we pull away from the curb.

The windows fog a little from our breath, the heat blasting, but I still can't seem to get warm.

My chest aches and I wonder if I made the biggest mistake of my life.

Or maybe... maybe this is better.

Maybe I should just stay here.

I haven't been home for two Christmases.

Two whole years of excuses. Work. Life. *Warren.*

Being back in Brokenwoods feels strange, like slipping into a sweater that used to fit but now hangs differently.

Dean's the one who breaks the quiet. "We're out of the city."

I push up, straightening in the back seat, and press my hand to the window. The world outside changes, slower, softer, familiar.

Main Street rolls by, every shop stubbornly the same. The florist with the crooked sign. The bakery where I used to spend my last five bucks just to buy a single lemon square.

The restaurant where I had lunches with Ella every Saturday, where we thought coffee and fries were rebellion.

The truck slows, turning down our street, and my breath catches.

The park, dusted in snow. The swings still rusted. The bench where I had my first kiss at thirteen with a boy who smelled like bubblegum and too much body spray.

My chest twists.

Across the street from our house looms the Inn.

Baker's Inn.

Our whole messy legacy.

It looks the same. Exactly the same. As if the years I spent away didn't happen. My heart drops heavy in my chest.

"Mom's watching the front desk for me," Logan says gruffly as he kills the engine.

"And Pops is in the house," Chase adds, turning with a crooked grin. "Waiting for you, Livvy."

I swallow hard, nerves scraping my throat raw as I hop out.

I glance at Dean, the only one still watching me instead of the Inn. "Could you come with me?"

He doesn't hesitate. Just nods. "I'll get your bags."

Chase and Logan head across the street, already slipping back into their rhythm, shoulders squared to carry the weight I dropped.

Dean falls into step beside me, solid and steady, as I walk toward the front porch of the house I swore I'd never need again.

My knees shake. My lungs burn.

But I keep moving.

Because my dad is waiting.

And I don't know if I'm ready.

Dean turns the knob for me and swings open the door as I climb the patio steps, the wood groaning under my weight like it remembers me.

As soon as I step inside, I smell it.

The strawberry cake.

My cake.

The air is thick with sugar and vanilla, warm and familiar, and for a second I'm ten years old again, skipping through this hallway with sticky fingers.

I pass the living room.

The couch is still here—ten years old now, maybe more, sunk in the middle, still wrapped in Mom's favorite color. Periwinkle. A ridiculous shade for a couch, and somehow even more ridiculous that she fought to keep it all these years. The fabric is frayed at the arms, faded in the sunlight, but it's ours.

Photos line the walls, frame after frame. School pictures with bad haircuts. Family Christmases. Mama and Daddy on their wedding day. Chase holding my hand on my first day of kindergarten. The faces are frozen in time, smiling, laughing, alive in a way I don't feel right now.

I make it to the kitchen doorway, and stop.

He's there.

My dad. Standing by the counter, the strawberry cake waiting behind him like it's been holding its breath for me.

The sight of him cracks something wide open. The tears come fast, hot, spilling down my cheeks before I can even try to stop them. A sob rips out of me, ugly and raw, but it doesn't matter because the weight that's been crushing me for months lifts in an instant.

"Daddy," I choke, the word breaking as I stumble forward.

His arms are already open. I run into them, burying myself against the safe, solid wall of him. He smells like flour and coffee. Like *home.*

He hugs me tight and rocks me, the same way he used to when nightmares sent me running to his room. Safe. Untouchable.

"You've got four layers of protection," he used to whisper. *"If anyone wants to get to you, they've got to go through your brothers first. And then me. And no one, no one, is getting through me."*

My chest shakes as I cling tighter, the years between us evaporating.

"I messed up again," I sputter against his shirt, ashamed, broken.

He presses a hand to my hair, gentle, firm. No judgment in his touch, none in his eyes when I finally dare to look up.

"Well, you're home, my Ollipop," he says, voice steady as bedrock. "You can hide out here as long as you need."

Chapter Forty-One

OLIVIA

One Month Later

The smell of peanut butter fills the kitchen, warm and thick, clinging to the air the way memories cling to me. I stand over the mixing bowl, wooden spoon in hand, fighting back the ache in my chest.

I remember the way War leaned against the counter in his shirt unbuttoned just enough to look human, watching me scoop dough onto the tray.

"I want to be the last man you ever make peanut butter cookies for," he'd said, dead serious, like it was some blood oath instead of a batch of cookies.

I'd laughed at him then. Called him ridiculous. But I went along with it, because the way he looked at me while biting into one, like I'd given him something rare and holy, made me feel like maybe I had.

Now the memory burns. He was supposed to be the last. And here I am, back in Brokenwoods, apron dusted with flour, baking peanut butter cookies for no one.

I slide the tray into the oven, shut the door with a dull clang, and press my palms flat against the counter. My heart aches with the ridiculousness of it all.

"Smells good in here."

Dean's voice snaps me out of it. He saunters into the kitchen, hair damp from a shower, hoodie sleeves pushed up, worn jeans tucked into thick socks like he's still thawing out. Before I can warn him, his hand snags a cooling cookie from the tray on the counter.

"Dean—"

Too late. He takes a huge bite, crumbs falling onto his hoodie.

The sight shouldn't hurt. But it does. Watching him bite into it feels like he's taking something that doesn't belong to him, something that should have stayed War's.

I look away, chest tight, pretending it doesn't matter. Pretending I didn't bake them for a ghost.

I force a smile as Dean chews, but the sting hits my eyes before I can stop it. I turn back to the counter, wiping at them quick, hoping he doesn't notice.

"Mmm," he says around another bite. "Haven't had these in forever. You spoil us."

I swallow hard. These weren't supposed to be his.

Dean leans his hip against the counter, licking a crumb from his thumb, completely oblivious to the way my chest is unraveling.

"So," he drawls, voice light, teasing. "When's Mr. Moneybags rolling into Brokenwoods to apologize and whisk you away? Because I gotta say, I'd pay to see that show."

My hands still.

Maybe never, I think.

Maybe not at all.

The words scrape my throat as I say them aloud. "Maybe never."

And God, it hurts. Hurts more than the fight. Hurts more than leaving. Hurts because the truth is uglier than I can stand, because I unblocked his number a week after coming home. I waited. Still wait. And he hasn't called. Hasn't texted.

Not once.

I grip the counter tighter, holding myself together while Dean keeps talking like it's all a joke.

Dean snorts, finishing his cookie. "Maybe I'll just kick Mr. Moneybags' ass for you. Guy needs it, don't he?"

Before I can answer, boots thud in the hall.

"Kick whose ass?" Chase asks, shaking snowflakes from his flannel like he walked through a blizzard to get here. He swipes a cookie off the tray without hesitation.

My heart seizes. Watching him bite into it, *War's cookie,* feels like someone's wringing me out from the inside.

"Livvy's ex," Dean says with a wicked grin. "We'll rough him up a little. Teach him a lesson."

Chase grins back, already balling his fists. "Oh yeah? I'd get him so good—"

Dean bounces on his toes, pretending to duck a punch. "One left hook. Bam! He'd never know what hit him."

They laugh, sparring in the kitchen like idiots, tossing fake punches and snickering about how they'd make War sorry.

I can't breathe.

Quiet. *Please.*

"Stop it," I whisper, clutching the counter.

But they don't hear me.

"Stop it," louder this time, my throat tight, eyes stinging. "Stop it—"

"SHUT UP!" The shout rips out of me before I can swallow it down.

The room freezes.

"Olivia Lynn Baker!" Mama's voice scolds, sharp as she steps in with a basket of folded laundry balanced on her hip. Her eyes narrow at me, shocked.

I crumble, tears threatening again. "Sorry, Mama. Can you take my cookies out of the o-oven?" My voice cracks on the last word.

Before anyone can stop me, I dart past her, past the stunned silence of my brothers, and race up the stairs.

My old bedroom swallows me whole. Mint green walls everywhere, the same ridiculous bedspread, the same stuffed bear propped on the dresser. Frozen in time, like the girl who used to sleep here never left.

I shut the door, chest heaving. I press my back to the door. My cheeks are flushed from the sting of cold air seeping in through the old windowpanes.

I grab my phone off the nightstand.

My thumb hovers over his number. Unblocked. Waiting. *Still* waiting.

But I don't press it.

I can't.

Instead, I scroll, find Ella's name, and hit call.

"Pick up," I whisper, tears slipping hot and heavy. "Please, just pick up."

"Liv?" Ella's voice crackles through the line, softer than usual, a little sad around the edges. "What's wrong?"

The sniffle gives me away. My throat works, and before I can stop myself, the words spill out in a rush.

I tell her everything.

All about Warren Beaumont.

How he made me work for him. Gave me an office. Bought me everything I needed. How he made me feel loved, seen, wanted. How he made me pick out a ring, promised forever. How there were cameras. Secrets. How he did things without asking. How he paid for the Inn behind my back. How I'm still hiding the truth about Ronnie.

And worst of all, how I left without seeing him.

How it's been a month. How I unblocked his number. How he hasn't called. Not once.

It all comes out too fast, tripping over itself, choking me, until I'm empty.

On the other end, Ella is quiet for a long moment. I can hear her breathing, steady, patient, the way she always is.

Then she sighs. "Well… why haven't you been honest, Liv? What's scaring you? If everything he was doing made you feel safe and seen, why wouldn't you tell him everything?"

I roll my eyes, wiping at my wet face. "God, I forgot my best friend's a shrink."

Ella exhales, then says gently, "Do you want friend Ella or psych degree Ella right now?"

"Friend Ella," I mutter, curling into my mint-green comforter like I can hide inside it.

"Okay, friend Ella says: what the hell is wrong with you? That man is a billionaire—who loves you. He designed a ring for you, Liv. Yeah, the camera in your office is creepy, but you said you liked it. He paid for the Inn… so what? You think he doesn't already know about Ronnie and just hasn't said anything yet?"

"I don't know," I snap, then soften. "He hates the mob, Ella. They're literally trying to steal a building that's important to him. He doesn't do business with them. And what? The woman he wanted to marry is tied to them? How does that even work?"

"It works with communication," she shoots back, sigh heavy with exasperation. "God, it's so annoying when people don't just fucking talk."

"Hey," I whisper, a small protest.

She chuckles, the sound light but tired. "You asked for friend Ella, not professional Dr. Marsh."

There's a pause, then her voice drops, quieter. "Did you break up with him before you left?"

My stomach twists. "…No."

"Does *he* know that?"

"Why?" My voice edges sharp with panic.

"Check the tabloids, Liv."

My hands shake as I put Ella on speaker and open the browser, typing his name. *Warren Beaumont.*

And there it is.

War.

In a restaurant.

With a blonde.

The photo is crisp, *cruel.* He's leaning in close, suit jacket off, tie loosened, looking like the man who used to come home to me.

Above it, the headline blares:

"War Beaumont's New Mystery Woman?"

My breath catches, sharp and shallow.

The phone slides from my hand, landing facedown on the comforter.

And just like that, every cookie, every promise, every whispered forever tastes like a lie.

Chapter Forty-Two

WAR

The whiskey burns down my throat, but it doesn't touch the hollow inside me. Curtains drawn, leaving the penthouse in heavy, self-made darkness. I sit slumped on the couch, glass loose in my hand, staring at nothing.

The elevator pings.

My heart jolts, wild and stupid. *Olivia.*

I shove upright, hope pounding in my chest.

The light clicks on.

Not her.

"Damn," Wilder says with a chuckle, taking in the scene. "This is what you're doing?"

"Go away, Wilder." My voice is raw, sharper than I mean it to be.

He steps further in, rolling his eyes. "I just got back from Cali. Went to the office. Heard you haven't been in for a week. What's going on? This still about Livvy?"

"Don't call her that."

Wilder snorts. "Oh, for fuck's sake. Get the fuck up and go get her."

I scoff, sinking back against the couch. "I don't even know where she is."

"Yeah, you do." He smirks, all sharp edges. "She's back home."

I sit up, pulse hammering. "She's *home?*"

"Not here, dumbass. Back home. In her little podunk life."

The glass flies from my hand before I think. Wilder ducks, and it smashes against the wall.

"Shards scatter across the hardwood, glittering.

"Throw shit at me again, War, and I'll kick your ass."

I laugh, bitter. "You'd only win because I've been drinking."

Wilder digs in his jacket pocket, pulls out a folded sheet of paper, and tosses it onto the coffee table. "She gave her resignation. She's not coming back."

I snatch it up, scanning fast. Professional. Clean. Final. *Gone.*

"No," I growl. "I'm not accepting it."

"She didn't send it to you," Wilder says easily. "She sent it to me."

I freeze. "Why the fuck would she send it to you? She works for me."

"Maybe because you wouldn't accept it. And if she sent it to Wes, he'd have asked you first, and you still wouldn't accept it. *Me?* Technically also her boss. She knew I'd approve it."

Fury rips through me. I surge to my feet, fists clenched. "You didn't."

"Oh, but I did." Wilder's smirk is razor-sharp. "Let her go. You're not good enough for her anyway."

Red clouds my vision. I lunge.

We crash to the floor, fists flying, grunts filling the penthouse. A jab to his ribs, his elbow digging into my shoulder, my knuckles cracking against his jaw.

"You had no right!" I snarl, teeth bared.

Wilder laughs, grappling, stronger than he looks. "I don't know what you did, but she deserves better."

I grit my teeth, twisting, shoving hard until I gain the upper hand. Fury fuels me. "Damn, you're strong angry," Wilder mutters through a strained laugh.

The fight drains out of me all at once. I shove off him, collapsing back onto the floor, chest heaving. My hands drag down my face.

"I paid for her family's inn," I rasp. "I furnished her apartment. I don't know what I did wrong." My voice cracks, breaking me open. Eyes stinging. "I don't know what I did wrong."

Wilder sits up, rubbing his jaw, and sighs. Then he claps me on the shoulder, solid and brotherly despite the bruises.

"Get cleaned up. Get some sleep. Call your girl in the morning."

I sit up, the fury draining into exhaustion. The glass shards glitter on the floor beside us.

Morning feels a million miles away.

But Olivia...

She's even further.

***

The office smells like burnt coffee and ink. I sit behind my desk, phone in hand, staring at my it like it might blink first.

I should just call her.

Beg her to come back to me.

Ask her what I did wrong.

Tell her I'm sorry.

A harsh breath tears out of me. I drag a hand through my hair, jaw tight.

But I'm *not* sorry.

I took care of her. Gave her everything she needed. Made sure she had more than enough.

Why the fuck is she angry?

The phone slams down against the desk, rattling the papers scattered there. The sound is sharp, final—until it starts buzzing in my hand.

Unknown number.

I answer anyway. "War Beaumont."

A steady, gruff voice: "Mr. Beaumont, this is Logan Baker. Olivia Baker's eldest brother."

I freeze, blood turning to ice. The first thought in my head, something's happened to her. "Is she okay?"

"She's not your concern," Logan grunts. Then, after a beat, "But I'm about to be."

The warning in his tone grates. I sit up straighter, every nerve on edge. "What can I do for you, Mr. Baker?"

"I'm calling to thank you for paying for the rest of the year at the Inn," he says flatly. "But we've got it from here. We've got *Olivia*, from here."

My jaw locks. "She wasn't some kind of payment to keep your Inn afloat. I love her."

Logan doesn't flinch. "Then prove it. You come here, face us, and make it right."

I scoff, sharp and bitter. "Face you? Listen, Logan, the only person I'll ever explain myself to is Olivia. And I don't know what she told you, but—"

He cuts in, voice iron steady. "I'll level with you. How long did you plan on paying off the Amatos for us? A year at a time? Forever? For as long as you and Olivia stayed together?"

The name slams into me like a freight train. *The Amatos?*

My grip tightens. "The Amatos are who you pay for the Inn?"

"You didn't know?" Logan's voice is flat, edged with disbelief.

"No." My pulse spikes. "*How?* How the hell did *your family* get tangled with them?"

"It's been generations," he says. "Ronnie is who we deal with. He takes quarterly payments. They used to use the place as a hideout back in the day. Now it's our curse, passed down. Always has been."

My chest hammers. *That's why Olivia was secretive. That's why she hid it. She knows how I feel about the Amatos.*

"I'll handle it," I snap, cutting him off. I hang up before he can say another word.

The silence after the call feels heavier.

I start listing my options.

Call my lawyer?

A lawyer against the mob? What the fuck would I even do with that? Draft a contract that says *let my fiancée's family go?* They'd laugh me out of the room.

A harsh breath tears out of me. *Fiancée.* I never even got to ask her. Never put the ring on her finger. She just... left.

The memory slices through me. She was hesitant sometimes, just a flicker, quick, like she didn't quite trust the ground under her feet. I told myself it was nerves, told myself she'd settle into me, into us.

She listened so well. Always *so fucking good* for me. But maybe... maybe she only listened because I forced it. Maybe she didn't really want any of it.

The thought rips at me, jagged, unbearable. I shake my head hard, rejecting it. No. That's not true. She wanted me. *She was mine.*

Was.

I grip the edge of the desk until my knuckles go white. There's only one way to handle this.

In person.

But which Amato?

My stomach turns, fury and disgust burning up my throat. I don't want to deal with either fucker.

Both brothers are pieces of shit.

But if Olivia's family is tied to them, if they're the reason she slipped through my fingers—

Then I'll face whichever bastard I have to.

Chapter Forty-Three

WAR

I hate walking into NovaRael.

Outside, it's freezing. Inside, it's worse.

Santo Amato's technological empire. Bought with a marriage contract like it was still the fucking Middle Ages.

How archaic.

How tactless.

But what else do you expect from barbarians like them?

The glass lobby hums with quiet efficiency, polished marble floors, sleek chrome edges, people in suits pretending they don't feel the weight of the Amato name pressing down on their necks. My shoes hit sharp against the tile as I cut straight to the private elevator.

By the time I reach his floor, the shadow of a guard steps into my path.

"Beaumont," he says with a smirk.

"Goon," I bite back, brushing past him toward Amato's office.

His hand snaps out, fingers locking around my arm. My jaw ticks, fury biting up my throat. "Don't touch me."

He releases instantly, smile sharpening as he extends a hand instead. Up close, I see the bulge at his hip under the jacket. Gun. Obvious. Deliberate. He wants me to notice it. Wants me to think twice.

"I'll play nice. Name's Romeo Romero. And the boss doesn't like unexpected visitors—*especially* when his wife is here."

He rounds me, smirk lingering, his stance casual but his eyes anything but. "Since I'm one of her guards, I have to ask... what business do you have here?"

"Seriously?" My laugh is humorless, teeth bared. "Does it look like I'm carrying an arsenal? I need to make a deal. An exchange. It's none of your fucking business, and I don't plan on being here longer than I have to. So shoot me, or get the fuck out of my way."

I shoulder past him.

Click.

The unmistakable cock of a gun.

"I choose option one," Romeo says lightly.

Staff gasp, ducking behind desks, heels skittering against the floor. Papers scatter. Someone yelps.

Goddamn it.

"Romeo," a voice cuts through the chaos, calm, even, but striking like a blade. "Put it away."

I turn.

Santo Amato stands in the doorway of is office, all dark suit and darker eyes, the kind of monster who doesn't need teeth bared to remind you he'll eat you alive.

I step toward him. "I need to make a deal."

He stares me down for a beat, silent, weighing. Then: "Fine. Come in."

I walk away from Romero, jaw tight, and step into the office—

And stop.

A woman's here.

Small. Delicate. Skirt with tights, highest heels I've ever seen on someone so short. Lush blonde hair, eyes too big for her face. Striking, sure, but not in the way everyone else probably thinks.

No, this is the kind of girl you *sell* to a man like Amato. **Fragile. Breakable.**

Before I can make sense of it, Amato strides past, grabs her by the wrist, and pulls her into his lap like she's a doll he just bought off the shelf. My gut twists. *Definitely* an arranged marriage.

She smiles at me, kind, like she doesn't realize she's sitting on the lap of a devil in a Brioni suit.

He gestures to the chair opposite. I sit, stiff, uncomfortable.

The office isn't what I expected. Not wood and steel, not mobster chic. Shelves of books line the walls. Art; *real art*, hangs with deliberate placement. And in the corner, a smaller desk, fitted with its own chair. Like it was set up for *her*.

The Amatos are fucking creepy.

"What do you want, Beaumont?" Santo finally asks, voice flat, dangerous in its calm.

"Be nice, Santo," the blonde whispers.

Amato sighs. Actually sighs. His eyes soften when he looks at her.

I'm fucking losing it.

"Yes, Dea," he murmurs before turning his attention back to me, eyes sharp again. "This is my wife, Vasilisa. Dea, this is War Beaumont. His brother is my largest competitor."

She gasps, wide-eyed. "Oh, *Wesley* is your brother? He's very kind."

As she speaks, Amato watches me like a shark scenting blood. I ignore her, leaning forward.

"I need you to let go of the Baker family."

His wife's head tilts.

Santo frowns. "Who?"

"The Baker family. They own Baker's Inn and have been paying you off for generations. That stops today."

"I don't know what the fuck you're talking about, Beaumont. We don't own an inn."

"The Bake—"

"Yes, we do," his wife interrupts in Russian, looking up at him.

His head snaps toward her. "No, we don't," he responds, same language.

Little do they know, I'm fluent.

I lean forward, my voice cutting through. "Da, ty delayesh."

Yes, you do.

Both of them go still.

Vasilisa beams, eyes lighting like I just passed some secret test. She turns back to English, her voice quick, apologetic. "When I was going through files, I found the account. I didn't realize it was still running funds through. I hadn't gotten to the financials part yet."

And that's when it happens. Santo Amato smiles at her.

Actually smiles.

It rattles me more than his gunmen, more than his calm. Because Amatos don't smile. Not like that.

"Vasilisa," he says softly, still looking at her. "Give us a moment alone. Maybe paint me something new for the walls."

She nods, rising gracefully, smoothing her skirt. "Of course." She glances at me once more, politely. "It was nice to meet you, Mr. Beaumont."

Then she slips out, his eyes following her until the door clicks shut behind her.

The smile vanishes from his face like it was never there.

Now it's just me and the monster.

He watches me.

I don't blink.

I don't back down.

I'm not about to break because some mobster glares at me.

"What is that Inn worth to you, Beaumont?" he asks sharply.

My jaw works. He studies me like he already knows the answer.

"You seem interested in the Baker family," he adds, voice cool, probing.

I could lie. I should. But I don't.

"It's for Olivia. Her family owns the Inn and she's mine."

Something flickers in his eyes—brief, telling. He steeples his fingers, leaning back. Then a low, dark chuckle rumbles out of him. "You gave away your biggest weakness that fast?"

Heat spikes through me. My hands fist on the armrests.

"Your biggest weakness just left the room," I snap. "Don't act like we aren't the same here."

His jaw ticks. Just barely. But I see it.

Silence stretches, heavy.

Finally, he leans forward, voice colder than before. "What do we get in exchange for letting the family off our books?"

"How much do you want?" I grind out.

Santo shakes his head slowly, like I've offended him. "We don't need your money. We have our own. You know what we want."

My heart stutters.

The Parker Building.

"I can give you any other property," I counter, grasping. "Any other building."

"We don't want any others." His voice is final.

I stare at him, fury and dread clawing at my ribs. Grapple, calculate, fight; then finally, the word tears out of me. "Deal."

Santo smirks, victory sharp in his eyes.

"But call off Ronnie," I add quickly, leaning forward. "Send his ass back here. He doesn't need to be a lingering reminder."

Santo's brow furrows. "Who?"

The door opens. Vasilisa slips back in, barefoot now, a smear of pale blue paint drying across her fingers. She drifts toward Amato like she belongs nowhere else.

"Ronnie is a guard," she explains gently. "He's the one who collects the funds."

She hesitates, eyes flicking down before lifting again, sheepish. "I started painting, but then I came back... and I was eavesdropping."

Confessing like a child who knows she's done something wrong.

Amato exhales slowly, closing his eyes for a beat. His jaw clenches, then eases. When he opens them, he looks at her with something softer than I thought a man like him was capable of; like even her guilt is something he'll forgive.

It rattles me. *Monsters don't look at women like that.*

He turns back to me, expression shuttered, voice cold as stone. "Deal."

And I don't know whether I've just secured Olivia's freedom... or made the biggest mistake of my life.

There goes Noah's legacy.

And I don't even know if Olivia will ever come back.

But I've got one more thing to do.

Chapter Forty-Four

OLIVIA

Two Months Later

I wake before the sun, the house still quiet except for the pipes knocking as someone turns on the shower down the hall. It's cold, *really cold*; the kind of cold that seeps through the windows and settles in your bones. My chest feels heavy, the way it always does when I've cried myself to sleep, tight, bruised, hollow. I pull on jeans and a soft, thick sweater, twist my hair up, and sink back onto the edge of the bed with my phone in my hand.

No word from War. Not a call. Not a message. Nothing.

The silence hurts worse than the gossip articles I can't stop torturing myself with. His picture with her, glossy and perfect, splashed across the internet. I scroll past them again, just to feel the sting, a self torment. Maybe it's punishment. Maybe it's proof that I was always a fool.

I thought he'd call on Christmas.

When the house was strung with lights and the scent of cinnamon rolls filled the kitchen, I kept looking at my phone. My heart wishing he was here. Imagining his chuckle filling the hallway as my brothers tried to size him up, my mother sneakily adding extra glaze to his plate, like he belonged.

He would've hated the caroling; loved teasing me for knowing every word, but he would've kissed me anyway, twirling me under the mistletoe like it wasn't the first real Christmas I'd ever let myself enjoy.

But he wasn't here.

And not on Thanksgiving either, when I sat at the table, smiling so wide it hurt, pretending I didn't feel his absence in every toast. I kept thinking about how he eats—or doesn't, watching me after every bite I take like it's instinct, and wondering if he'd like my mama's peanut butter cookies better than mine.

And New Year's? *God.*

Midnight came with paper hats and cheap champagne, and my family's cheers rattled the windows, but all I heard was silence. I stood outside under the snow and stars alone, wondering if he was thinking of me. If he kissed *her* when the clock struck twelve.

My thumb hovers over his name. I don't even know what I'd say if he picked up. Confess everything? Tell him about Ronnie, about my family being tangled up with the mob? Ask him point-blank who that woman is? All of it comes out in a jumble when I rehearse it in my head, tangled and messy.

Still, I hit call.

Straight to voicemail.

My heart drops. I try again.

Voicemail.

Again, like maybe my need alone could force him to answer.

Still voicemail. The tears are already stinging hot when my phone lights up with an incoming call.

Not him. *Ella.*

I swipe it up fast, wiping my cheek with the back of my hand. "Hey, El."

"Guess what?" her voice is bright, bubbling with excitement. "I'm in town!"

I shoot up to my feet, pulse racing. "You're *here?*"

Ella chuckles, a familiar warmth threading through the static. "I'm downstairs. Please save me from Chase."

There's a muffled sound and then Chase's low chuckle filters through in the background.

I don't even bother with socks. I jam my feet into boots and shrug into my coat, the lining still warm from the radiator. "I'm coming," I breathe, hope sparking where heartbreak had been.

I jog down the hall and take the stairs two at a time.

At the bottom, Ella stands in the doorway, wrapped in a long camel coat, her suitcase parked beside her, tiny snowflakes clinging to the wool. Chase is next to her, leaning against the wall with that smug smirk that makes everyone in a ten-mile radius want to roll their eyes.

Logan stands off by the couch, jaw tight, arms crossed, a storm brewing in his expression as his gaze cuts toward Chase. Dean catches it, mutters something under his breath, and elbows Logan in the ribs before he can open his mouth. Logan scowls deeper but bites it back.

And then Ella spots me. "Liv!"

I don't even hesitate. I run straight into her arms, squeezing her like she's air after drowning. Relief floods me, sudden and overwhelming, and I cling tighter than I probably should.

"You're here," I whisper against her shoulder, the tears threatening again but softer this time; less ache and more release.

"Of course I am." She pulls back, smiling like sunshine. "And you look like you need pancakes. Let's get something to eat? Murphy's?"

The mention of our favorite diner hits me right in the chest. Cracked red booths, menus always sticky with syrup, the smell of coffee so strong it seeps into your clothes. Comfort I didn't know I was starving for. I nod fast, almost desperate. "Yes. God, yes."

Ella loops her arm through mine, already tugging me toward the door.

"Grab my bags and check me into the Inn?" Ella says to Chase. "Since you want to stay there and stare at me."

"I'll do it," Logan interrupts before Chase has a chance.

Ella's brows lift, surprise flickering before she schools her expression.

He grabs her bag and brushes past us, out the door into the snow.

I slip on my gloves and zip my coat. We follow behind him, breath puffing out in clouds. "Sorry about them," I mutter.

Ella chuckles. "Please. I've known them as long as I've known you. They've been weird since I hit puberty—I'm used to it."

I laugh with her, and for the first time in months, it doesn't hurt so much to breathe.

***

Sue is still here. Of course she is. She's been working Murphy's as long as I can remember, hair pinned up in that messy gray bun, cheeks ruddy from the cold as she moves with the same practiced sway between booths. She doesn't even bother handing us menus, just slides two coffees onto the table and sets down our pancakes with an extra plate of bacon and a wink.

Some things never change, and for a moment it feels like I can finally exhale.

Ella leans back in the booth, cradling her mug between both hands. "So," she says, eyes on me, "any thoughts on War and what you're going to do?"

My stomach knots. I hesitate, but this is Ella. I never lie to her. "I tried calling him this morning." My voice comes out thin, breaking around the edges. "Straight to voicemail. Every time.

So maybe… maybe I'm blocked." Even saying it hurts, a lump rising sharp in my throat.

Ella sips her coffee slowly, gaze unreadable. "Or he's indisposed."

I frown, really looking at her for the first time. Her red hair isn't polished and sleek like usual, it's tied in a messy bun, stray strands framing her face. Barely any makeup. Faint dark circles under her eyes.

"Did you have a breakup too?" I ask gently.

Her brows knit. "No, I'm just not sleeping well. Don't deflect, Liv. What would you have done if War answered?"

I grab a piece of bacon, more for the excuse to stall than the taste, but I chew and force myself to be honest. "I'd tell him everything. About Ronnie, about the Amatos, about how I freaked and ran away. All of it."

Ella nods, encouraging.

"And," I add, pushing the words out, "I'd ask him to stop doing things for me without at least a heads up. I hate surprises. You know that."

Ella flinches. Barely, but I catch it.

"What is it?" I press.

"What?" she says, too fast, lifting her mug again.

"You're lying, or hiding something. I don't know what it is, but all your tells are showing."

Ella sighs, sets her cup down, and folds her hands on the table. Hazel eyes flick up to meet mine, guilt swimming there. "War called me."

My whole body goes still. *War called Ella?* He knows about Ella?

"What did he say?" My voice is a whisper. "Why?"

She bites her lip, then finally admits, "He asked me to come here. To bring you out."

A shiver rolls through me, sharp and electric. "El… why?"

She straightens in the booth, fingers lacing tight together. "Because his flight lands today. And he wants to talk to your parents alone."

"*Ella!*" My palm slaps the table before I can stop myself, the sharp crack drawing stares from nearby patrons. Heat rushes up my neck and I shrink back, mortified. "Sorry," I mutter.

Ella winces but gives me a sheepish look. "Is it worse if I say he paid for my first-class flight here?"

My chest tightens, the swirl of relief and betrayal and dread all crashing at once. He called Ella. He brought her here. *He's in town.*

My town.

I grip my mug, fingers white-knuckled. "Wait." The word comes out sharper than I intend. "So Warren Beaumont is in my house right now? At our crooked kitchen table, drinking from chipped mugs, with baby photos of me everywhere?"

Ella deflates, lifting her mug, guilt written all over her face. "Yes. And more than likely with your brothers around. I... may have warned them."

"Ella!" My stomach lurches, nausea rushing through me, and I press a hand to my middle, breathing deep to hold it back. Then another thought hits me like a punch. The cookies. The stupid peanut butter cookies sitting in the kitchen. War is going to see them, and he's going to know. He'll be so—

No. I cut the thought off viciously. He was with another woman. He doesn't get to be sad.

Ella studies me over the rim of her mug. "Oh, you look angry." Her voice is quiet. "At me?"

I shake my head hard. "No. I'm over here worried about what War will think when he was out with some other woman."

Ella lowers her cup, lips pressing together. "He says he can explain that."

I freeze. My pulse stutters. "How long did you talk to him?"

Ella's mouth twists, like she's weighing how much to admit. "I may have gone into Dr. Marsh mode and... dug through his psyche for a moment."

I gape at her, both horrified and desperate.

She softens, leaning in, her hazel eyes steady on mine. "If it's worth anything, Liv, I'd say hear him out. Be honest. And let it happen."

Ella reaches across the table, her fingers curling around mine, warm and steady. "You've got this," she whispers.

I don't feel like I do. My pulse is too loud, my breath uneven, but I nod anyway. Because what else is there?

We pay the bill in silence. Not tense, just full. Ella doesn't push. She knows the storm inside me is loud enough.

The walk back is quiet too. Snow crunches under our boots, the air sharp in my lungs. A dog barks in the distance, someone shovels a driveway. Life goes on, even when yours feels like it's teetering.

I keep my eyes forward, but my heart trips with every step. He's at my house—War. No more photos. No more what-ifs. Just him.

And I don't know if I want to scream, sob, or run.

By the time we round the corner, my chest is tight, my breath uneven.

The late-morning sun glints off snow-covered rooftops, too bright for how shaky I feel inside. Ella pulls me into a hug, fierce and grounding, then tips her head toward the inn across the street. "I'll be right there if you need me."

I cling to her for a heartbeat longer before letting go. She starts across the road, her hair catching the light, and I watch until she's gone.

Then it's just me.

Me, staring at my family's porch steps like they're a gallows.

I force one breath. Then another. My legs move even though every part of me screams to run, and the creak of the first step echoes up my spine.

War is inside.

Waiting.

With my brothers.

And my dad.

I take a deep breath.

I don't know if I'm walking into forgiveness or ruin.

Chapter Forty-Five

WAR

I should've taken a regular flight. Air Beaumont drew more attention than I wanted, commotion, cameras, a fuss that left me itching to be anywhere else. But when I leave here, it'll be with Olivia, and she deserves the best, whether she wants it or not.

I had to call a taxi to drive me into Brokenwoods, and the ride feels like entering another world. The streets are narrow, lived-in, lined with weathered storefronts that have been here longer than my family's empire. Small. Soft. Quiet. The kind of place that folds in on itself. No wonder Olivia is always trying to make herself smaller, *hidden.* Doesn't think she shines the way she does.

The car pulls to a stop in front of a two-story building with a wooden sign partially cover by snow, **Baker's Inn.** Paint peeling. Porch steps sagging. But there's a warmth to it, the kind of place people return to year after year. I step out, bag in hand, and tip the driver.

I turn, my eyes lift across the street.

Her parents' house. Quaint. Nostalgic. Curtains drawn back just enough to see blurred photos framed in the fogged window. The kind of home that feels like it has roots sunk deep in the earth.

And standing in front of it, three men; in flannels and sweaters, arms folded across their chests like a human barricade. Her brothers, no doubt. Beside them, an older man whose presence is sharper, heavier.

Olivia's father.

I square my shoulders, grateful I didn't wear a suit this time. Wool sweater under my thick coat, dark jeans—casual, but intentional. I was right to go this way.

The men don't move as I cross the street. Arms stay folded. Feet planted. Cold wind cuts down the block, but none of them flinch. A line I'll have to walk through to get to her.

Pecking order matters. *Always.*

I stop first in front of the older man. His shoulders are straight, his jaw set, but his eyes are steady rather than hostile. I extend my hand. "Mr. Baker."

His grip is firm, testing. "Call me John."

I incline my head once. A man like him respects brevity more than charm.

Then my attention shifts to the three brothers.

The eldest is easy to peg. Logan. His narrowed eyes haven't left me since I stepped out of the cab, sharp and calculating, the same way I'd watch a man I didn't trust. He's sizing me up. *Measuring.*

The second steps forward before I can speak. "Chase," he says, extending his hand with a smirk that plays at his lips like he can't quite help it. Dirt streaks his palms, under his nails. He's the Wilder, no question—ready to get under my skin for the fun of it.

The last one nods once, quick, before offering his hand. "Dean."

I study him a beat longer. Younger than the other two, but still older than Olivia. His kind of protectiveness isn't about control or bravado… it's quieter. Older brother, not patriarch. Harder to place, and that makes him more dangerous.

Their clothes tell me as much as their eyes. Logan's sweater is stamped with the Inn's logo. Chase's dirt-stained hands speak of hard labor, the kind that leaves a mark. Dean wears a firefighter's shirt, under his flannel the name stitched over his heart. Solid. Trusted.

I clock it all, every detail filed away.

"Come inside," John says finally, voice even but firm.

I step up onto the worn wooded patio following him in.

Inside, the air is warm, lived-in. The kind of house that wears its years proudly.

"Drop your bag by the door," John says, not unkindly. "Coat can go in the closet."

I do, then follow him toward the kitchen, taking everything in along the way.

The photos. Olivia everywhere. Big smile, crooked braids, arms slung around a redheaded girl I peg as Ella. School pictures. Family portraits. Snapshots in mismatched frames that somehow belong together.

My Olivia.

Raised in safety.

Comfort.

Warmth.

The kitchen table is crooked. The chairs creak when we sit.

And it doesn't matter.

Because I smell them.

Peanut butter cookies.

My peanut butter cookies.

Fresh.

Hers.

Dean grabs the plate and sets it on the table before he sits; easy, like it's nothing.

To me, it's *everything.*

He takes one. Bites it.

Fire licks irrationally at my throat.

John folds his hands, steady eyes on me. "Olivia hasn't told us much, except she felt trapped. My Olivia has always been a strong girl, independent and kind. For her to feel trapped means something. So I'm going to ask you—what *were* your intentions with Olivia?"

The word *trapped* twists in my gut.

Logan leans in, voice cutting. "A man like you going after a girl like her, what was the motive, Beaumont?"

That bothers me more than I let show. *A girl like her.*

I look between them, waiting for more questions. When they don't come, I turn back to John. My voice is even, clipped. "Olivia didn't communicate that she felt trapped. If I had known, I would have rectified it."

I slide my hand into my pocket and pull out a small box. I set it on the table. It lands with a quiet thud. "My intentions are easy. I want to marry Olivia."

Dean chokes on his cookie. Logan's jaw tightens; Chase's smirk stutters.

Good.

I use the moment to fix my gaze on Logan. "And if you ever refer to Olivia as *'a girl like her'* again—as if to imply she's *less* than, I can show you what a man raised in the city can do."

"I didn't. But a man like you, using money as his bargaining chip doesn't—"

"Doesn't *what?* Love?"

Dean recovers enough to speak, his voice rough. "We've seen you online, a different woman on your arm at every function. What's Livvy to you?"

"Everything," I counter.

"Any other questions in your arsenal? Net worth? Number of properties I own? ... No?"

Silence.

"Good. I got the Amato's to relieve you of Ronnie. He won't be in charge of your inn anymore. *You are.* Outright."

Jaws drop. It's so silent I can hear the roar of the wind outside the kitchen window.

I continue, meeting John's gaze. "I want to repair and renovate the inn. I know winter construction's tough, expensive, slow, but I'll eat the cost to get it done. She deserves to know her family has everything whole."

Chase huffs. "You planning to send a fancy city crew out here to gut it?"

"No. Local."

He raises a brow. "Good. Because I'm local. I own my own company. You want it done right, it goes through me."

I consider him. "I get to recruit more men. We finish faster."

Chase narrows his eyes. "But I'm foreman."

"Fine, but *with* a head contractor of my choice and I'll triple your men's salary."

A beat. Then Chase nods.

"Good," I say. "Then we've struck our first deal. Renovations start Monday. The men will stay. But if Olivia will have me; we're leaving Friday."

Chase's smirk wavers. "And if she *doesn't?*"

My heartbeat stutters, but I push through it. My voice stays steady. "If she doesn't, I have a plan set for that too."

I look back at John. "Do I have your blessing to proceed?"

John frowns, gaze narrowing. "The inn is ours?"

I nod once. "As it should be. Paperwork's in my bag."

The men go stock still exchanging glances before John chuckles, *hearty,* his shoulders shaking as he does.

He claps me hard on the back and looks at his sons. "Son of a gun we're free!"

A palpable weight lifts from the kitchen, Dean leans back in his chair. Chase shakes his head Logan's shoulders drop.

They all start to laugh.

"If she'll have you, you have my blessing," John says extending his hand. I take it.

And then I feel her.

I turn toward the kitchen entryway, and there she is.

Pink sweater. Hair twisted up in a rush.

Jeans hugging her perfect hips. Freckles dusted across her nose, just like I remember.

My Olivia.

She looks the same.

And yet, nothing like the woman who left me behind.

God, I missed her. So much it makes my vision blur for a second.

Her eyes meet mine.

Those gorgeous eyes are bright; *burning* with spark of something. Recognition. Maybe even relief.

But then they harden.

And she turns without a word.

Just like that, she's gone.

My chest hollows, a quiet implosion.

I stay seated, controlled. *Always controlled.*

Inside, I'm already chasing her.

Chapter Forty-Six

OLIVIA

I pace my room. My heart hammers, my hands shake, and I can't stop seeing him at that table.

War.

My War.

God, my heart still loves him. I should have expected it, but not like this, not so sharp and sudden. One look and I was back under, drowning in everything I've tried to erase by being here.

But all I can see is *her.* The woman in the photos. The gossip columns. Him with *someone else.* The bile rises, sharp and bitter. I have to ask him. I *need* to ask him.

I reach for the door, ready to demand answers, when a sharp knock rattles it first. My breath hitches. Probably Dean, checking on me.

I pull it open.

Not Dean.

War.

He doesn't speak. Just looks at me. Three months, and all that heat is still in his eyes. The kind that knows me. *Owns me.*

Before I can breathe a word, his hands bracket my face, mouth crushing against mine. He tastes like mint and the faint smoke of his cologne, the scent I used to fall asleep breathing in. The kiss is hard, desperate, breaking me open in an instant. He pushes me back into the room, the door slamming shut behind us.

And I melt.

All the fury, all the questions dissolve under the heat of him; his smell, clean and dark and familiar. His touch, rough but sure. His lips, claiming mine like they never lost the right. A low sound rumbles in his chest, part growl, part plea, and it shreds what little defense I have. My arms fly up around his neck, clinging to him, greedy for more.

My heart. My stupid, treacherous heart.

It's still his.

I should shove him away. I should slap him, scream at him.

Instead, I moan.

He turns us, pressing me hard against the door, mouth still on mine, all fire and demand, and for one reckless second I melt into it, *into him*, until my fury tears through.

"No." The word rips from my throat as I shove hard at his chest. My back hits the door. My palms sting with the effort of pushing him away.

His eyes flash, voice low and brutal. "You left me."

My chest caves, but I throw it back. "You paid for the inn without telling me."

He surges closer, fists braced against the wood on either side of my head, caging me in. "You made them *my* cookies."

The accusation slices, but rage spikes hotter. "You were with her! With that blonde woman, in *every* photo. I saw it, War, *everyone* did."

That stops him cold. His hands drop, he exhales "Olivia—"

"I saw it online," I spit, tears burning my eyes. "In almost every gossip rag."

His brows knit. "That was *Miranda?*"

I falter, the name cutting deep. "That's her name?" My voice cracks.

His head tilts, sharp and disbelieving. "Yes. That's my sister. She isn't blonde—it was a wig to throw off the paparazzi. She hates them."

I blink, the ground tilting beneath me. *Sister.*

"Your sister?"

"Yes, Olivia. My sister."

Shame and confusion crash over me. My legs give, and I sink onto the floor, heart still galloping. He follows, sitting close, close enough that his presence burns.

We sit in silence, the space between us thick with everything unsaid.

"Why didn't you tell me you felt trapped?" he asks, finally.

I stare at the wall across from us, blinking fast.

"Because..." My throat aches. "You take over everything, War. You walk into a room, and it stops breathing until you decide it's allowed to again."

He doesn't argue. Just watches me.

"I didn't even realize how trapped I felt until it all piled up. First working for you... then the apartment, the clothes, the gifts, it was all meant to make me feel seen, and it did... *too seen.*"

I shake my head, the words catching. "You made me feel important. But then I remembered where I came from. Who I was. What my family was. And I *told* you not to pay for the Inn. I begged you. And you didn't even try to talk to me about it. You just did it."

I pause, breath shaky. "And I couldn't find my way back after that."

He's quiet for a beat too long. Then, with a breath that sounds more like a growl:

"You didn't want to tell me about Ronnie?"

I nod. "Because I didn't know how. I didn't know how to explain that I came from something messy. That someone had power over my family. That I wasn't the polished, collected girl you make me feel like I am when I'm with you."

Finally, I turn to look at him.

And he's already staring at me. Those sharp, wild blue eyes I've memorized and missed and mourned all at once.

"I ran," I whisper. "Because I was scared."

His hand finds mine. Warm. Familiar. His thumb brushes over my knuckles like muscle memory.

"Olivia," he says softly, "I come from something messy too. In my life money reigns. You've seen it. It's just... a far cry from what *you* have."

I blink, confused. "What's that supposed to mean?"

He exhales through his nose. Not sharp. Just tired. Tired in a way I feel all the way down to my bones.

"It means I had silver spoons and silk cribs and boarding schools." His lips curl into something bitter. "You had dinners that didn't require backlash and defenses. You had *real* pictures. Not oil paintings in marble hallways."

His eyes sweep the room, *my room*. The slightly crooked book-shelf. The old quilt. The taped-up edges of posters from high school that I never bothered to take down.

"Your family... your home..." he trails off, shaking his head like he can't find the words. "It's lived in. It's *loved*."

I nod, throat tightening. Because it's true. Even under the crushing weight of debt, of desperation, we stick together.

"That's what I saw the first time I looked at you," he says.

"My family?" I ask, surprised.

He shakes his head. "No. *You*. A woman who deserved more."

His voice dips lower. Honest. Bare. "And now I understand why I saw that. It wasn't that you were lacking it *here*. You were lacking it in the city."

I swallow, a lump forming that I can't push down.

"I thought giving you everything I believed you deserved was enough," he says quietly. "The job. The apartment. The wardrobe. The stupid fucking hair products I kept stocking the bathroom with."

His tone wavers. The kind of tone you only use when you're about to ask for forgiveness. I brace for it.

But instead...

"But you had everything you needed here, didn't you?"

I frown. This doesn't sound like a makeup speech.

"War—"

"I don't want you to feel trapped, Olivia." His voice cracks just a little, and I hear it—the edge of goodbye. "You're a diamond in the middle of this small town. And I was trying to rip you out of it. To put you on display in the city. The galas. The commissions. The wardrobe. I kept trying to dress you in glass when you were already carved from stone."

He laughs bitterly, self-directed. "I used money to fill the space between what I felt for you and what I didn't know how to say."

And my heart drops.

No. No. It's breaking. I feel it. Splintering from the inside out.

He doesn't see it. Or maybe he does, and that's why he looks like he's falling apart, too.

He exhales. "The Inn belongs to your family again. I spoke to the Amatos. They've released it."

My breath catches.

"I have a crew coming Monday to renovate. And for the sake of full honesty..." he stands, reaches into his pocket and pulls out a folded paper, laying it gently on the nightstand. "I set up an account in your name. Ten million. It's yours. No strings."

I scramble to stand, I can't speak.

His hand cups my cheek, gentle. Reverent.

"You're free, Olivia." His thumb brushes my jaw. "Your family is free from the Amatos."

Then, softer.

"And you... you're free from me."

Chapter Forty-Seven

WAR

The suitcase handle cuts into my palm, but the real weight is in my pocket. A ring box. Heavy. Hopeful. *Useless.*

If she won't take it.

I keep walking. Across the street.

Every step feels like bleeding. Like I'm leaving parts of myself behind on the cracked pavement; and I don't think I'll get them back. The Inn rises in front of me, worn wood and peeling paint, but alive in a way my glass towers never were.

Inside, behind the front desk, she's waiting. An older version of Olivia, same bone structure, same smile, only green eyes where Olivia's are brown.

"Did my boys behave themselves?" she asks, voice soft, teasing.

I nod. "They did."

Then, without warning, she rounds the counter and wraps her arms around me. I freeze. For a second, I don't even remember how to return it.

But I do. Slowly. Stiffly.

I let this woman, *her mother,* hold me. Anchor me.

And I hate how much it breaks me open. It's so warm it aches. The kind of mother I might have had, if mine hadn't been taught to chase dollars instead of children.

When she pulls back, her gaze sharpens. "Are you staying?"

I clear my throat. "I don't want to leave without her. But she—"

"Needs time," she finishes gently.

I nod once, jaw tight.

She studies me for a long beat, then her voice lowers. "Thank you. Ronnie stopped by before you did, said he was leaving. That's... a freedom I didn't think we'd ever get."

Bittersweet coils in my chest. I incline my head. "You're welcome, Mrs. Baker."

Her lips curve. "Jillian. Call me Jillian."

"You're welcome, Jillian." My voice comes out rougher than I intend. "May I have a room?"

Her brows lift slightly, then she turns and pulls an honest-to-God brass key from the board behind the counter. "Of course. You can have the biggest one—Room 10."

The key drops into my hand, cold and solid. I close my fist around it, nod once, and head for the stairs.

I mutter a thank you, and turn for the stairs. My steps are slow, quiet, creaking with age beneath my shoes.

The hall is narrow, carpet worn thin. Every detail screams of a life lived, not designed. And still... it feels more honest than anything I've built.

When I reach the end, I pause at the brass number on the door. Room 10.

I don't know what I expect behind it.

But it's not this.

Room 10 is bigger than I expected, but it carries the weight of years. The wallpaper's peeling in one corner, a radiator coughs when I set my bag down, and the bed creaks with a protest when I sit. My eyes skim the space automatically, logging what I'll tell the crew to fix; floorboards uneven near the dresser, window frame warped, bathroom tile cracked. Easy repairs.

I stand, cross to the window, and part the curtain.

And I still.

Across the street, her house. Olivia's house. From here, Room 10 looks directly into her bedroom. Curtains wide open, no defenses. She's there, perched on her bed, shoulders bowed, face buried in her hands.

The sight knocks the air out of me. Pain slices clean through my chest.

A thought slips through, slow and certain.

Jillian knew.

She gave me this room on purpose.

This room.

This view.

She knew I'd be able to see Olivia.

To watch.

To wait.

For one reckless moment, I want to storm across the street, to break past the brothers, to lift her chin and force her to see me. To remind her that she's mine, that nothing can cut that truth clean away.

Not even the words I said.

But I don't.

I let the curtain fall back into place. Just enough to remind myself: privacy, not distance. My fists clench, then release.

She needs time.

So I'll wait.

Five days. That's all I can give her.

Five days to hope she loves me enough to not want to be free of me.

And if she doesn't...

I'll let her go.

Even if it kills me.

***

By morning, the place looks like an anthill. Trucks lined along the curb, tools unloading, men hauling lumber and tile. The air smells like sawdust and new beginnings.

I stand on the porch steps, giving Greg the head contractor, my rundown. "Tiles replaced. Fresh paint inside and out. Rotted wood gone. New fixtures. Nothing cheap."

He nods, scribbling notes, barking orders over his shoulder as I talk.

Through the newly installed frosted glass doors, Logan sits at the front desk. He isn't glaring anymore. Just watching. Weighing.

Out front, Chase leads the crew on the ground already with a hammer in hand, grinning like the chaos is a game. He catches my eye. "We'll run short on supplies. The local hardware store will have what we need"

I pull out my wallet, slide a black card free, and hold it out. "Get everything. No limits. Whatever this place needs."

Chase whistles low, pockets the card. "Guess money does grow on *Beaumont trees*." He hops into his truck still smirking.

I turn back to Greg. "The playground down the block, it's a mess. Can you come back here in a couple months?"

Greg scratches his chin. "We can, but that park needs new everything. Slides, swings, benches. Hell, the mulch under that snow is moldy."

"I've already spoken with Parks and Rec," I tell him. "Deliveries start when the snow thaws. I'll cover labor if you can spare it."

His brows rise, then he extends a hand. "You've got yourself a deal, Beaumont."

We shake.

Firm, solid.

I step back inside, the air warmer after the noise of hammers outside.

At the counter, a woman with red hair pulled neat stands. She's dressed well, clean lines, not flashy, not cheap. Middle of the road. Intentional. Hazel eyes catch mine, though there's a sadness tucked behind them, even as her blush gives away that Logan said something she liked.

Logan stiffens the moment he notices me watching.

Noted.

Ella steps forward; poised, careful.

But not afraid.

"Mr. Beaumont," she says, tone dry but not unkind. "The man. The myth."

I smirk, slow. "Dr. Marsh."

Her lips twitch, but her gaze doesn't drop. "You're not scary, you know."

She leans in, voice dimmed to a private whisper: "I can see the crushed little boy beneath you."

A dark chuckle rumbles out of me. "And I can see the sad little girl in you. What are *you* hiding, Ella?"

She falters, just for a beat, before she folds her arms.

I tilt my head. "Where are you going today?"

Her brows lift. "What makes you think I'm going anywhere?"

I take a breath, play along with her obvious banter. "You're protective of her. I get that. So am I. Which means you're going somewhere with *her*. Where?"

She studies me, like she wants to measure how much truth I deserve. "Why?"

"Because I love her."

I don't blink.

"I need to know she has someone with her who makes her feel good. So... *Dr. Marsh.* Will you be with her today?"

Ella exhales, then nods once. "Yes. Just at her house. Call it a therapy session." She chuckles, light but not careless.

I step aside. "Well. Don't let me keep you."

She slips past, Logan's eyes following her until she's out the door.

I turn to him. "How long?"

He blinks, irritation quick and shallow. "What are you talking about?"

"You and the good doctor."

Logan's jaw tightens. "There's nothing going on."

"Doesn't mean there won't be." I lift my chin toward the door. "She's carrying something behind those eyes. Find it. Fix it. That's your way in."

Logan doesn't answer, just glances toward the door Ella slipped through.

I follow his line of sight, the corner of my mouth tugging. I know that look, like a man already lost, *already hers.*

Same look I wear for Olivia.

I leave him to it.

I have my own woman to watch.

Chapter Forty-Eight

OLIVIA

Monday

I'm still in bed.

Still in yesterday's clothes. Still in the same spot I crumpled into last night after he kissed me like goodbye and left.

The curtains are open because I can't help it.

Because I keep looking.

A soft knock. Then the creak of the door.

"Liv?" Ella's voice floats in, careful, gentle.

I don't move.

She pads in anyway, loose strands from her neat bun tucked behind her ears, cashmere sweater sleeves too long, but folded. She smells like chamomile and that clean perfume I always forget the name of.

"You want to catch a movie? Or go walk the town? Something brainless?"

I shake my head into the pillow.

Ella sighs and crosses to the bed. Her eyes sweep over me and land on my hand.

"What's that?"

Shit.

I scramble to sit up, trying to shove the box under the covers. But she's already seen it.

"Wait. Are those... macarons?" Her nose scrunches. "I figured you'd have your signature heartbreak girl snacks, chips, chocolate or jelly beans. Not fancy rainbow cookies."

I sniff, cheeks hot. "They're from France."

I open the box anyway, because it's already ruined, and hold it out to her.

She takes a delicate green one, bites in, chews slow. "Hmm. Not bad."

I smile through the sting in my chest. "He used to keep them in the penthouse. Had them shipped from Paris, just because I liked them."

My voice catches.

"And now... he left a box in my parents' fridge. For me. Like he knew I'd need them. He was *so good* to me."

The tears fall without asking.

Ella doesn't say anything at first. Just chews slowly. Then, with that signature bluntness of hers—

"Then why don't you go to him?"

I blink at her, tears sliding sideways down my face.

"Because..." I swallow hard. "Because he told me I'm free. And I don't know if I want to be or not."

Ella nods slowly, understanding more than I expect her to.

"These are really good," she murmurs, grabbing another one.

I laugh wetly, wiping my cheeks.

Then her head tilts. "Wait. He took you to France?!"

I nod.

The question rips the breath from me. My throat locks as the memory surges; the weekend in Paris. The Seine at night. His hand warm around mine as the city glittered. His mouth on me in a hotel that smelled of jasmine and rain.

I sob, covering my face.

Ella doesn't speak.

Instead, she climbs into bed beside me and curls up like she used to when we were kids, arms folded, warmth offered.

"Shhh. It's okay, Liv." Her voice is soft now, anchoring. "He's at the inn. He's here until Friday. He doesn't want to leave without you."

She brushes her thumb across my wrist.

"You have time, okay?" she whispers. "You don't have to decide today."

And somehow that's worse. Because I'll see him again. And it'll hurt.

But I nod anyway.

Curl into her, like I used to when the world felt too big.

And cry.

***

"Tell me when it's gone, tell me when it's gone!" Ella squeals, face buried in the collar of her sweater.

I laugh, toss another handful of popcorn into my mouth, and mumble, "It's gone."

She peeks out, blinking, then drops her sweater back down.

I shake my head. "I don't know why you insist on scary movies when they scare the life out of you."

She exhales dramatically, smirking as she grabs the bowl. "That's the fun part."

"*What's* fun?"

We both scream, popcorn rains over us, kernels skittering across the blanket.

Dean chuckles from the doorway.

I grab the remote and lob it at him. He ducks easily, flicking on the light.

"Not the big light!" Ella groans, yanking her sweater over her eyes.

I squint at Dean. "What do you want?"

"Pops asked if you could pick up the pies from Murphy's."

I frown. "Why can't you do it?"

Dean shrugs, already halfway back into the hall.

"Busy with the renovations," he says over his shoulder. "Murphy's closes early, so hurry."

He disappears, leaving my door open.

I glance at Ella.

My heart's already tightening.

"War's gonna be there, isn't he?"

She doesn't pretend otherwise.

"More than likely, yes."

I nod once, already bracing for the sting.

Ella shifts, folding her legs under her. "Your family likes him, Liv. But if you don't anymore, then tell them to respect your boundaries. You don't owe them anything."

Her tone is kind, but firm.

"But," she adds softly, "if you do like him... then go. He's probably just going to talk to you. That's it. And it's up to you if you want to talk back. Okay?"

I stare down at the box of macarons on the nightstand.

Colorful. Delicate. Stupid.

I miss him.

God, I miss him.

I nod.

Ella doesn't smile, doesn't press. Just watches as I pull my hair into a low bun and grab the coat I left slung over the desk chair.

Downstairs, Dean is lacing up his boots.

He looks up when I reach the bottom step. "You going?"

"I'll take your car."

He arches a brow but doesn't argue, just tosses me the keys before heading out the front door and across the street, where the inn hums with the sounds of renovation.

The drive to Murphy's is short. Familiar.

The kind of path you could take blindfolded.

But my pulse pounds the whole way there.

The parking lot is mostly empty. The diner glows warm in the fading light. I park, take a breath, and head inside.

The bell above the door jingles.

I scan the booths. The barstools. The corner table where my dad always sits with his paper.

But War isn't here.

My heart sinks, and I hate that it does.

I tell myself it's better this way. That I can just grab the pies and go.

Sue sees me from behind the counter and waves. "Got three ready for pickup, sweetheart. Be right back."

I nod, gripping the edge of the counter to ground myself.

The door jingles again.

I don't even turn at first.

But then I hear it—boots on tile. Slow, steady. A low voice murmuring a polite "Thank you, ma'am" to one of the waitresses.

I turn.

And there he is.

A dark winter jacket half-zipped over a charcoal shirt. Fitted jeans. Work boots scuffed at the toes. His collar dusted with snow melt. Paint smudges streak one hand where his glove must've been pulled off.

He looks...human. Solid. Out of place and yet perfectly placed, like some kind of mirage I summoned with grief.

My lungs stutter. He's too close. Too real.

But he doesn't see me.

He doesn't look at me.

The waitress hands him two bags of food. He passes her a folded bill. I know it's too much, he *always* tips too much. He murmurs a quiet thanks.

Then he turns.

And walks out.

Just...*leaves.*

I stare after him, stunned.

My throat tightens.

Sue sets the pies down on the counter, wrapped and boxed. "Need help carrying those out, honey?"

I shake my head.

Swallow hard.

"No, I got it."

I try not to rush, try not to look like I'm chasing him.

But I am.

I get outside just in time to see him shut the trunk of a sleek black rental.

He gets in.

Doesn't look back.

Doesn't see me.

And drives away.

I stand there on the curb, hands full of pies, heart full of something I can't name.

He didn't even look at me.

Chapter Forty-Nine

OLIVIA

Tuesday

The morning light is pale when I peel back the curtains. It slants through the frost-slicked glass, cool and silver, catching on a swirl of breath that ghosts the window from where I've leaned too close.

Outside, the world is quiet beneath a soft crust of snow. The porch steps of Baker's Inn are still crooked, the sag I used to leap over as a kid now half-buried under a shoveled path. A ladder leans against the side of the building abandoned and two men in thick coats are brushing fresh paint along the doorframe despite the chill. Another is scraping ice from the columns, steam rising from his thermos on the stoop.

And then, movement.

Quick and familiar.

There are *children* out front.

Three boys and a girl, all bundled up in coats and hats, tossing a snowball back and forth with mittened hands too big for their fingers. One kid slips, laughing, before clambering back to his feet with a puff of breath in the cold.

And they are all playing—with *him*.

War stands near the sidewalk, jacket zipped halfway, a knit beanie pulled low over his ears. His gloves are off, stuffed in a pocket, fingers red from cold but nimble as he packs a snowball, loose and soft, before lobbing it gently at Tyler; the boy from two houses down. Tyler shrieks, catches it wrong, and fumbles. War kneels, showing him how to form a tighter one, not too wet. Another kid joins. Then another.

He doesn't make it a show. Doesn't try to win the kids over. He just... *plays.* He ducks when they ambush him, laughs when they get him good, teaches them, quietly, easily, how to aim better, how to pack snow without freezing their fingers. His mouth shapes the words, his breath visible in the cold, his posture relaxed, open.

Something inside me pulls tight. *Too tight.* I stand up straighter, as if that'll help.

It's ridiculous how fast my heart remembers.

It doesn't care about the silence between us, or the heartbreak in this bedroom, or the months we didn't speak. It sees *him.*

My War, in a simple coat, crouching in the snow, teaching kids how to aim without hurting. It sees that, and it leaps.

"Don't," I whisper, palms pressing over my sternum like I can hold myself together. "Just because he's good with them doesn't mean—"

But the lie falls flat.

Of course it means something. I've seen men perform kindness. This isn't that. *This is War being careful with something small.*

God help me, I love him most when he's careful.

He was always careful with me, even when he was rough, I was *safe.*

I step back from the window like it burned me.

I shouldn't be looking.

I told myself I wouldn't.

But he's still here.

A knock at the door breaks the silence. It creaks open a moment later, and my mom steps in, bundled in her fleece cardigan.

She holds a large thermos of cocoa and a stack of paper cups on a tray, steam curling from the spout.

She follows my line of sight to the window, then sets the tray on my dresser.

"I was going to ask you to bring this over to the workers," she says softly. "But if you're not ready yet, it'll be downstairs."

My stomach twists.

I stare at the tray. "Can't Dean do it?"

She lifts a brow. "Dean's already over there. He's covered in paint and snow. You're not."

I hesitate. She softens

"You don't have to say anything to him, Liv Bug. Just hand out the cocoa. That's all."

And then she's gone.

The door clicks shut, and I sink onto the edge of the bed.

The tray waits. So does the window.

But I force myself to move, to choose clothes, to pull something over the ache still living under my skin.

I open the closet.

It's cold out, I should wear jeans. A sweatshirt. Something that says nothing.

Instead... I reach for the dress.

It's sage green, soft, long-sleeved with a gathered waist and a hem that brushes the top of my boots. War filled my closet with dresses like this. I stuffed this one into my suitcase the day I left.

He always used to grumble when I choose skirts in the cold.

Still, I pull open the drawer and grab a pair of fleece-lined pantyhose, shimmying them on before stepping into the dress.

A small rebellion. A quiet compromise.

I glance at the mirror.

The fabric floats as I move, feminine and gentle in a way that feels like remembering who I am. My hair's messy, tangled from laying in bed too long. I braid it over my shoulder with stiff fingers.

Makeup?

No. War always liked my freckles.

But my eyes are puffy, rimmed in exhaustion.

Concealer.

I dab it on carefully, then swipe mascara through my lashes. I pause, staring at the reflection.

Before I know it, I've done the full routine, except my freckles. I let them stay.

Then I eye my jacket.

It's heavy. Puffy. Practical.

And I hate how it feels over this dress. Like armor when I don't want to be armored.

I leave it behind.

I take another full glance.

"You got this Liv," I murmur to myself.

I lift the tray, carefully balancing the thermos and cups, and head downstairs.

The air outside bites immediately, sharp and bracing. Snow crunches under my boots as I cross the street. My breath fogs in front of me, and the chill creeps through the fabric of my dress, but I keep moving.

Voices drift from the porch. Hammers thud. Saws buzz faintly under the crackle of frozen air.

Greg is the first to spot me. "Well now," he says, smiling wide. "Cocoa angel's here."

A few of the men cheer, teasing lightheartedly. I offer a small smile in return, cheeks burning from cold and nerves.

I scan the group.

No War.

The children are gone.

I swallow the lump forming in my throat and set the tray down on a nearby sawhorse. "Hot Cocoa."

They thank me, passing around the cups like it's Christmas again. One of them offers me a cup back. I take it just to keep my hands busy.

I stay a minute longer than I should, pretending to enjoy the drink.

Then I gather the tray and turn to go.

I don't run.

But I want to.

Back in my kitchen, I set the tray in the sink and stare at the single untouched cup. The one I held the whole time. The one I never drank.

I pour it down the sink, watch the chocolate swirl away, and whisper to myself: *let it go.*

***

"This is the worst," I grumble.

Ella chuckles. "Hush, we love romcoms"

Ella thought it would be brilliant to go to the movies, watch something on the big screen, get dressed and go out.

I love Romcoms, but not now, not tonight.

It's sweet. It's funny.

It's unbearable.

Every glance on screen feels like a knife, like the weight of his stare across a crowded room. Every brush of hands reminds me of his palm covering mine. Every kiss, too soft, too staged, pulls me back to the hotel balcony where he kissed me until my knees gave out.

I can't breathe.

Worse—I swear I can smell him. His cologne, threaded with something warmer, something I could never name but always knew. His scent clings to the back of my throat like memory.

I shift in my seat.

Then again.

And again.

My chest is tight, my skin buzzing.

I have to get out of here.

"Bathroom," I whisper, and Ella waves absently, already laughing at the screen.

I slip into the lobby, heart pounding.

It's quiet out here. The hum of a vending machine. The faint chatter of the concession counter. And then, I see him.

Tall. Broad shoulders. Dark hair, immaculate. Jeans. A plain black sweater. Standing with his back to me, weight balanced in that familiar way.

It has to be him.

My pulse stutters, then races. This could be it.

I can tell him I don't want this distance.

I don't want to be free.

I want *him.*

Maybe I can ask him to join us, to sit in the dark beside me, watch the movie and laugh at the predictability. I can already picture his hand brushing mine when we reach for the popcorn at the same time.

I step closer, almost close enough to reach out, to touch his arm—

He turns.

Not War.

Heat slams into my cheeks. "Sorry," I stammer. "Thought you were someone else."

The man blinks, polite and puzzled, before turning back to the machine.

I spin away, mortified, my throat closing around a laugh that never comes.

My feet drag me back to theater, the room is washed in the blue glow of another montage. A song swells. Two actors kiss. A few people in the audience sigh.

I scan the rows anyway as I walk to my seat, certain I'll catch a flash of him, certain I'll smell him again like smoke curling through the dark.

"Stop being weird," Ella whispers, tugging me down into my seat.

I let out a shaky breath, fold into the cushion, eyes fixed on the screen.

But my pulse doesn't settle. My skin still hums. And my heart—

My *heart* is sure he's near.

Even if he isn't.

Chapter Fifty

OLIVIA

Wednesday

The morning drags. Every tick of the clock feels louder than it should, like it's mocking me. I try to read. I try to help Mom with laundry. I try to lose myself in Ella's chatter over breakfast. Nothing sticks. My skin feels too tight, like I'm waiting for something without admitting it.

By late afternoon, I give up. I pull on boots, a thick scarf, and my old coat, tucking my hair into a messy knot before stepping out into the brittle cold.

Brokenwoods in February feels like a photograph drained of color. Frost clings to the curbs, salt streaks the asphalt, and every breath hangs white in the air. The trees are bare skeletons, their branches scraping against a dull gray sky.

Every street is a memory, the cracked sidewalk outside Mrs. Whitmore's house where Ella and I used to ride bikes, the patch of grass on Maple where I fell rollerblading at eleven and Logan carried me home, blood streaking down my knees. Every block holds some version of us frozen in time.

I turn the corner and hear it before I see it: the grind of machinery, the splintering thud of wood, men shouting over the noise.

The park.

It's being gutted. Half the fence is down. The benches are overturned, the play structure half-disassembled. Piles of wood and metal lay scattered like bones. Even the air smells different, cold dirt, sawdust, and rust.

I stop at the corner, my pulse quickening.

My eyes go straight to the far end.

The swing set.

Gone.

My chest hollows. The space where it stood is nothing but churned earth and splintered planks tossed beside the dumpster.

A memory hits so sharply I sway.

Ella and me, twelve years old, racing barefoot through the grass. She gets there first, throws herself onto the left swing, hair flying like fire in the sun. I grab the right one, push off, both of us shrieking with laughter. Our initials carved into the frame with a pocketknife Chase swore we'd get grounded for touching. Cherry popsicle stains on our fingers. The creak of the chains, the dizzy rush of summer.

We used to tell each other everything on those swings; crushes, secrets, stupid dreams. It was our place to be infinite, like nothing outside the park could touch us.

Now it's nothing but dirt.

I stumble back, pressing my hand to my mouth.

It feels like someone ripped a page out of me and threw it away.

Panic burns through the numbness. They can't just erase that. Doesn't anyone understand some things shouldn't be replaced?

I turn and run, boots slipping on the frost-bitten sidewalk, the cold biting at my lungs as I head straight for the inn.

Logan's at the front desk when I push through the door. He looks up, startled.

"What room is War in?"

He frowns. "No, Liv."

I roll my eyes, breathless. "Not for that, I need to speak to him."

Logan hesitates, jaw flexing, then sighs. "Room 10. But he's not here."

My chest sinks. "Where is he?"

"Hardware store. With Chase."

The air rushes out of me.

Too late.

It would have been too late anyway. The swings are already gone.

I nod stiffly, turn away before Logan can say more, and retreat across the street.

Back into the house.

My chest aches as I climb, each step heavier than the last.

By the time I reach my room, tears are already stinging, because it isn't just about swings. It's about *everything*. About him, about me, and about what's gone that I can't seem get back.

***

"You're not eating."

I look down at my plate, Murphy's famous grilled cheese, the one I begged for every birthday as a kid. Three kinds of cheese, golden crust, fries crisped just right. It should taste like home. It tastes like nothing.

"He had our swing removed," I murmur.

Ella exhales, leaning back in the booth. "I'm not dead, Liv. We don't need a rotten piece of wood with our initials to prove it meant something."

"I know." My throat tightens. "But it feels like—like it's gone because of him. Like every time I almost tell myself I want him back, I can't reach him. He's always just... out of reach."

Ella steals a fry from my plate, crunching it slow. "Have you tried calling him?"

The words hit harder than I expect.

"No. Not since the day he showed up here. I figured he blocked me."

She shrugs. "So check. Worst case? You're right. Best case? You're wrong. Either way, you'll stop torturing yourself."

I dig through my purse with shaking hands, fingers closing around my phone like it's a live wire. My heart hammers as I unlock the screen. His number sits there, unchanged, like it's been waiting.

Ella leans on her elbow, watching. "Gonna call him right now?"

I hover, thumb trembling over his name.

"I shouldn't," I whisper.

"Up to you," she says, dry as ever. "But don't pretend the phone's the one holding you back."

My thumb hovers, heart slamming, before I finally press his name.

It rings. Once. Twice.

Click.

The line connects, but there's no voice. No breath. Just muffled sound.

I freeze.

Then I hear it—laughter. Familiar voices. My family.

Dean. My mom. Logan. All bleeding through the speaker like he's sitting in my living room with them.

My stomach drops. I hang up fast, my pulse rattling in my ears.

I look at Ella. Narrow my eyes. "Are you distracting me again? Bringing me here so War could meet with my family behind my back?"

She blinks, startled. "No, Olivia. You asked *me* to go out. What happened?"

I toss cash onto the table, my movements jerky. "War's at my house. I have to go. And I have to run, and I know you hate running, so I'll see you tomorrow."

Ella scoffs, incredulous. "Liv, let's just call one of your brothers. They'll drive us—"

"It'll be too late if we do that," I snap, sliding out of the booth. "And they'll tell War. I need the element of surprise."

Before she can argue, I shove through the diner doors and into the freezing night air.

I hate myself instantly. I hate the way the cold air burns my lungs, the way every extra pound drags like an anchor, the way my thighs scream with every step. But I don't stop. Not until my house is in sight.

I stumble up the porch steps, breath ragged, sweat dripping down my back.

The door flies open under my hand.

Empty.

The lights are off. The rooms silent. My family; gone.

I stagger back outside, heart pounding. The inn glows across the street, warm with lamplight.

I force my aching legs to move, cross the road, push through the door—

And there they are. My family, gathered together.

But not him.

"Where's War?" My voice cracks as I scan the room.

My mom smiles, like it's nothing. "He went to Murphy's."

Defeat crashes over me. "When?"

"Like five minutes ago," Dean says with a shrug. "Ella called Logan to pick her up, but War said he'd do it. We all thought you were with her."

My vision blurs hot. Fury. Humiliation.

Fucking Ella.

I turn on my heel before anyone can see me break, push back out the door, and make the walk back across the street with tears burning in my eyes.

Chapter Fifty-One

OLIVIA

Thursday

One more day. I have one more day.

War is *mine.*

I want to be with War.

Tonight I'm telling him. Tonight he won't pass me by last minute. No more hiding. No more last-second shrug-offs.

No more of this hiding shit.

I watch him from the window.

Like some creepy voyeur.

I chuckle to myself.

He's my voyeur. Always watching me.

Camera in my office. Probably one in the apartment.

Definitely in his penthouse.

But here?

Here he doesn't watch me.

Doesn't command me.

Doesn't take what I *willingly* want to give.

He just waits.

I never thought I'd hate a patient Warren Beaumont. But I do.

I liked the command. The control.

I loved never having to think about clothes, or food, or toi-letries.

Anything I needed, it was just there.

And not just *stuff.*

It was the way he picked it all. Carefully. Expensively.

Like I was something worth curating.

He made me feel like I deserved it.

Never once did I feel less than.

And the *praise.*

God, I miss the praise.

And his filthy fucking mouth.

Damn it, War.

I sigh.

I should be saying *Damn it, Olivia.*

Listening to stupid Brody about cages and freedom and all that bullshit.

I like being trapped.

What woman in this world says, '*No thanks, no billionaires for me, I'm good.*'

I hate that shit in movies.

'*I can't take your money. I just can't.*'

Why the fuck not?

I leave the window. I'm not even watching him anymore.

I'm just brooding.

This is what missing the one you love—*and dick deprivation,* does.

It makes a woman brood.

I flop on my bed, staring at the ceiling. Enough brooding. Enough waiting for him to come to me.

If War were me? He wouldn't sit here, sighing into the quiet. *He'd plan.*

He'd move pieces on the board.

He'd make sure he got what he wanted.

So fine. Tonight, I'm War.

And War wouldn't sit still. He'd sneak. *Scheme.*

He'd get into that inn, no matter who stood in his way.

Sneaking into the inn shouldn't feel like plotting a heist, but with Logan at the front desk it may as well be. He's still got that older-brother scowl, the one that used to catch me sneaking out at sixteen with a boy's address scrawled on my arm. He'd never let me past without an interrogation.

So. Work around him.

I grab my phone and type to Ella quick.

> Distract Logan tonight. Get him away from the desk. At ten. You in?

El

> Do I get to know why?

> No.

El

> Liv! calling Logan to my room is going to be un-comfortable.

> I didn't say call him to your room. I said distract him! Make him go out back.

El

> Fine.

I grin, toss the phone aside. Step one: complete.

I drag my suitcase from the closet onto the bed and unzip it.

I know I left it in here...

There it is.

Lingerie.

I grabbed it in the panic that day, shoving anything from the closet into the case.

Now I'm glad I did.

I lift a green slip between my fingers. Then a blue. Hold them up to the light.

"Green or blue?" I whisper to myself.

Tonight, War's not the only one who gets to set the rules.

***

The slip clings beneath my dress, silk whispering against my skin like a secret. The coat over me does nothing against the freezing night air.

I've been overthinking it all night; green or blue, too much or not enough, what if he doesn't even look at me?

I wore it anyway.

Because tonight *has* to be different.

The frosted glass door of the Inn glows with lamplight. I press my palms against the cool pane, peering in. Empty. No Logan at the desk. Relief spills through me.

Thank you, Ella.

I slip inside, the hush of the lobby wrapping around me. Everything smells *new*—polish, fresh wood, warm paint. My chest tightens. He did this. For my family. For me. My throat aches as I run a hand over the gleaming counter.

Then I freeze.

"Oh, shit."

The old key board is gone. Just sleek little card slots now. My stomach sinks. Of course. War updated the locks. I can't just sneak in anymore.

New plan.

Just going to have to knock and hope he answers.

He's a light sleeper. A knock should wake him.

I take the stairs, heart hammering harder with every step. The hall is spotless, walls painted in soft cream, brass sconces glowing warm. It's beautiful. It's his mark on everything.

I'm happy.

I let out a breath, I'm so damn happy.

But nerves coil sharp in my stomach. What do I even say?

I don't want free. I love you. Let's go home.

Ugh. Too much. Too little. Nothing feels right.

Room ten waits at the end of the hall. My pulse thrums in my ears. I lift my fist.

Knock once.

Nothing. *He's not here?*

No. I saw him come in at eight.

I knock again, softer this time.

Shuffling.

The door swings open, and there he is, hair damp, towel slung low on his hips, chest gleaming warm and bare. Droplets slide from his hairline, trailing down the hard lines of his shoulders. His eyes lock on me, sharp as always, but softer too, like he doesn't quite believe what he's seeing. His brow furrows.

"Olivia?" My name rumbles out of him, rough and husky, like gravel dragged over velvet. It curls low in my stomach, makes my knees wobble. "Are you okay?"

God. His voice. I forgot how much it undoes me, like every syllable has weight, pulling me closer. Like he owns my name, not just me.

Now or never.

I shake my head, "No, I'm not okay."

I press both hands flat to his chest, heat sliding under my palms, damp skin giving way to solid muscle. He's warm—*scalding,* and my fingers twitch, wanting to cling. I push him back, firm enough to shock him into motion. He stumbles a step, eyes flaring, and I slip inside, breath catching as I kick the door shut.

I kick off my boots, the soft thud of leather hitting the floor barely audible over the thundering of my pulse. My feet are cold on the polished wood, toes numb from the walk, but I don't care. I need to feel the ground. I need to feel him.

My arms loop around his neck, desperate, greedy. I drag him down before I can lose my nerve, before reason can drag me back into the girl who hides instead of takes.

I crush my lips to his.

He groans into my mouth; deep, low, feral. The sound vibrates through me, breaks me wide open. My chest caves, my knees buckle, every wall I built between us melting like wax in fire. His taste floods me, clean soap and pure War, and I drink him in like oxygen.

I whimper, pressing closer, clutching the back of his damp neck as if I could crawl inside his skin. His towel brushes my thigh, a reminder of just how bare he is, how close I am to losing everything if he pushes me away.

But he doesn't. He groans again, hungrier this time, and I know—*I know,* he's seconds from taking over.

And I want him to.

I break the kiss, breathless. His lips chase mine, unwilling to let go, his eyes molten as I take one shaky step back. Unzip my coat and let it drop. My fingers grip the hem of my dress. I pull it up and over my head.

Green silk clings to my skin, sheer and daring. His eyes flash, dark and hot, as he takes me in.

I meet his gaze.

"I don't want to be free."

Chapter Fifty-Two

WAR

Her words detonate in my chest. *I don't want to be free.*

For a beat, I can only stare. Green silk, sheer and reckless, drapes over curves I've been *starving* for.

I had seen her pull both pieces of lingerie out of her suitcase. I had hoped to watch her slip one on.

I'm glad she chose the green.

My throat goes tight. My pulse slams.

Then I snap.

I crash my mouth down on hers, swallowing the breath she stole from me. She tastes like defiance, like surrender, like *mine*. My hands drag over her hips, gripping, owning, pulling her flush to me as if I could fuse us together and never let her slip away again.

Inside, a single thought roars, over and over. Finally. *Finally.* She's mine for good. She's never leaving me again.

I walk her backward, lips locked, teeth clashing, until her knees bump the bed. She gasps into my mouth, but I don't give her air—I don't give her escape. One push, and she falls back against the mattress, silk riding high on her thighs.

The towel slips from my hips as I follow her down, climbing over her, bracing my weight on my hands so I don't crush her with the force of everything tearing through me.

My lips drag from her mouth to her jaw, her throat, her collarbone. She arches, shivering beneath me, and I growl against her skin.

"I don't know whether to punish you for leaving," I rasp, voice jagged, "or worship you for coming back to me."

Her nails rake into my shoulders, desperate. "Don't ever set me free again," she whispers, fierce and trembling all at once.

I lift my head, pin her with the full burn of my gaze. "Never." The word is a vow, guttural, absolute.

I seal my mouth over hers, devouring her. My tongue thrusts past her lips, rough, desperate, tasting every shiver, every gasp, every inch of what I almost lost. Her thighs part beneath me, the green silk riding higher, teasing me with flashes of bare skin.

I drag my hand down, fisting the slip, tearing it up to her waist. She arches, whimpering into my kiss, and I groan, low and savage, at the feel of her pussy through the last flimsy scrap of fabric.

"Fuck, Olivia…" My voice breaks against her mouth. "Mine. *Always mine.*"

She writhes beneath me, her nails scraping down my back, hips bucking into mine like she can't stand the space between us. I grind into her, hard and aching, my cock sliding against her through the thin barrier. She cries out, and the sound nearly destroys me.

My cock throbs at the feel of her panties already damp. I rip them aside, don't give a fuck if they tear, and push my fingers deep into her pussy.

Hot. Wet. Mine.

She arches off the bed, gasping into my mouth, her nails digging into my shoulders. I pump my fingers, curling them until she moans, until her thighs start to shake.

"Yes," she whimpers, eyes wide and shining. "War, please."

I bare my teeth against her throat, biting down just enough to make her cry out. "I should make you beg. Make you *fucking* crawl for leaving me. But I can't, because I *need you* too much."

I pull my fingers from her, fist my cock, and line up in one desperate motion. No warning. No mercy. I drive into her in a single thrust that rips a scream from her throat.

"Fuck," I groan, forehead pressed to hers, "so wet, *always* so fucking perfect."

Her pussy clenches around me, dragging me deeper. I slam into her again, hard, punishing, the bedframe rattling under us. She cries out, wrapping her legs around my waist, pulling me in like she'd die if I pulled out.

Every thrust is a brand. A vow. *She's mine.*

She claws at me, moaning, breaking under me, and I can't stop, *won't stop,* until she knows. Until every inch of her knows.

"Never letting you go," I snarl into her mouth. *"You hear me, Olivia? Never."*

I sink into her, deep, relentless, and for a second I think I could stay here forever, just get lost in her until the world ends. But it isn't enough. Not tonight. Not for this.

I need more. I need all of her.

I pull out slow, she clenches around me like she'd drag me back in if she could, and she whimpers my name like a wound. The sound nearly undoes me, but I force myself down, gripping her thighs and spreading her wide.

"War—" her voice cracks. "Don't stop—"

"Oh, I'm not stopping," I growl, lowering my mouth to her. "I'm never stopping."

I taste her. Sweet, soaked, desperate

The first swipe of my tongue makes her moan, head thrashing on the pillows. I groan into her, devouring, licking deep and slow like I can drink back every second we've been apart.

"Sweetest fucking thing I've ever had," I rasp between licks.

Her hand shoots into my hair, knuckles white, fingers tangling in the damp strands. Her moans fill the room, each one a divine plea, music to my ears. I don't let up. I can't. My tongue circles her clit again and again, driven by a thirst that can't be quenched.

My fingers digging into her lush thighs, how could I ever have told her she's free from me.

She will never be free from me.

I need Olivia Baker.

"War!" she cries out as my lips seal around her clit and suck.

The way her thighs tremble and her hips roll make my eyes roll back.

A goddess, that is what she is.

"War," she gasps, thighs clenching around my head. "I-I can't—"

"You can," I growl, voice rough, vibrating against her skin. "You will. For *me.*"

Her back arches, body going rigid as I flick my tongue against her oversensitive clit.

The cry she lets out is one of pure surrender.

Her hand tightens in my hair, pulling as if to yank me away, but I only push forward, my hands on her hips keeping her in place.

There's a sob in her voice when she gasps out my name again, the words shaky, broken. Her body trembles under me as she comes, thighs closing around my head, but I don't stop. I can't.

I savor her taste, the sweet, shivering surrender. I feast on her pleasure, every gasp, every whimper, every twitch of her thighs.

It's intoxicating, addictive. I could live off this alone, her taste, her warmth, the way she looks at me when I give her what we both crave.

"I need you, War," she whispers, a desperate plea. I smirk against her skin, a rough chuckle escaping me.

"I need you more, sweet girl," I growl back, leaving a trail of hot, open-mouthed kisses up her soft stomach, to her breasts, my tongue trailing her nipple before capturing it between my teeth, biting until she gasps. She writhes beneath me, but I keep her pinned down with my weight, my hands holding her hips captive. Her nails dig into my shoulders, a desperate plea etched into her skin.

"War..." Her voice is a broken whimper, and the desperation in it sends a thrill through me.

My eyes meet hers.

"I won't ever leave you again," she promises, brushing my hair back, her gaze locks with mine. Her words are a balm, soothing the raw ache of her absence, the void she left behind.

"Good," I growl, releasing her nipple with a wet pop, grinning at the whine that escapes her parted lips. "Because I won't ever let you."

Her legs tighten around me like chains.

And when I slide back into her, slow this time, deep and aching, she lets out a sound that breaks me clean in two.

A whimper. A sob. A moan that tastes like forever.

I brace my arms around her, forehead against hers. No more growls. No more force. Just breath and warmth and the slick press of our bodies coming back together where they were always meant to be.

Her eyes flutter open, wide and wet, and she stares at me like I'm the sky and she's finally stopped running from it.

"I missed you," she whispers, voice shaking. "Every night. Every morning."

"I know." My voice cracks. "I missed you more."

I rock my hips, slow and deep, dragging every inch of my cock inside her. No rush. No punishing rhythm. Just us. The slide of skin, the sighs between kisses, the creak of the mattress as I make love to the woman who tore me open and stitched me back together with one knock on my door.

She wraps her arms around my neck, pulling me close, her lips brushing mine with every exhale. "You feel like forever, War."

I kiss her like a promise. My hips moving slow, unrelenting. Our bodies already know each other, but this—this is new. *This is real.* There's nothing left to prove. No anger. Just her soft sounds, her shaking legs, the way her pussy tightens each time I whisper her name.

"Say it again," I murmur.

She breathes, "Don't ever set me free."

I thrust once, deep, and kiss the corner of her mouth.

"Never," I whisper against her skin.

She comes quietly this time, her breath catching, her body curling around mine like a secret. I don't stop. I let her ride the wave, rocking into her as I kiss her neck, her jaw, her lips again.

When I finally break, when the heat coils tight and spills from me with a guttural groan into her welcoming body, it's not wild. *It's reverent.*

I stay there for a moment, letting the tremor pass, the world tilt back into place.

Then I ease out of her gently, careful, and she whimpers at the loss, shifting to cling to me.

"Shh," I murmur, brushing her hair back, pressing a kiss to her temple. "I've got you."

She melts into me as I pull her into my arms, her body curling instinctively against my chest. I tuck the blanket around us, my hand splaying across her back, stroking slow and grounding.

She hums, soft and sleepy. "I'm sorry I left."

My heart kicks.

I press a kiss to her forehead. "No more apologies," I whisper, voice raw with truth. "I was never going to leave here without you."

Her fingers slide over my chest, resting above my heart.

"But you didn't watch me this time," she whispers. "You didn't seek me out."

I go still.

Then I huff a quiet laugh, low and dry.

"Oh, sweet girl."

She tilts her head up, blinking at me with those doe eyes, already shining again.

"This room…" I murmur, brushing my knuckles across her cheek, "has a *direct* view into your bedroom window across the street."

Her breath catches. "What?"

"You never close your curtains," I say, voice dropping, disapproving. "Not once. I should spank you for that alone."

Her cheeks flush, and I let my thumb graze the heat blooming there.

"Did you watch me change clothes you voyeur?" she asks with a little laugh, her voice almost shy.

"Maybe. Maybe I hoped you'd notice." I smirk pressing a kiss to her lips.

I pull back slightly, my voice low.

"I saw you go into Murphy's that first day. Watched you scan the diner, looking for me."

I pause. "I walked in, grabbed my order, and left. Couldn't stand to see your face when you realized I wasn't coming to sit down. It was so hard not to look at you."

Her mouth parts in a soft gasp.

"I watched from the rearview mirror," I add, quieter now. "Saw you standing there, bags in hand, still looking after me even when I drove away."

She closes her eyes, her body curling tighter into mine. I hold her through it.

"I also saw you watching me from the window when I was playing in the snow with those kids in the street. Pretending like you weren't. Pretending you were fine."

I feel her fingers grip my chest, her breath shaky against my neck.

"And I almost saw red," I growl softly, "when I watched you walk up to that stranger at the movie theater."

Her eyes fly open. "Wait—you *were* at the theater?"

I chuckle, the sound rough with disbelief. "You think I wouldn't know where you were?"

She blinks, stunned.

"And I heard you were worried about the swing set. I have the rotted piece of initialed wood in my suitcase, we're taking it home."

She smiles, her breath hitching.

My heart thrums.

"When Ella called, I went to Murphy's to pick you *both* up, I thought *you'd* be there."

Her silence is deafening, her smile drops.

"You weren't," I finish. "So I drove Ella back here instead. And spent the rest of the night watching your window like a fucking addict."

"Her eyes shine, glassy with disbelief. "Why not just *speak* to me, War?"

"I needed it to be your choice, my sweet girl. And now it is."

She nods. "You never really let me go then."

"Never," I say simply. "I could *never.*"

She kisses me soft and deep and full of everything I have ever needed.

I hold her tighter; for the first time in months, my lungs don't ache. She's *here.*

She's mine.

Step Six: Complete.

Chapter Fifty-Three

OLIVIA

"Logan is going to see me," I rasp-whisper to War as he ushers me down the steps.

"It's Friday, it's *noon*, and we've spent all night and all morning in bed." His lips brush my neck, heat curling there with his teasing kiss. His hand stays firm on my waist, steering me. "I'm sure your entire family knows where you are."

My face flames.

Ugh. Walk of shame, *family edition.* Exactly what I didn't want today.

"We could always go back into the room." His chuckle rumbles against my skin, wicked and warm.

I whirl on him, grasping at my coat and tugging at the hem of my dress. "No! That makes it worse. I don't even have panties, War." My whisper turns frantic. "You ripped them."

His grin is sinful, bright enough to melt my mortification.

"I don't know why you're whispering, baby. I didn't exactly renovate those walls to be soundproof. And you, my sweet girl, are *very* loud."

My stomach drops as he strides past me down the stairs, laughter trailing in his wake.

"Whether you come down now or later, they already know," he sing-songs, leaving me to groan and follow him toward the lobby.

The lobby yawns open in front of me; mercilessly empty.

No Logan. No family. Not even a stranger lingering by the desk.

Relief punches out of me in a shaky laugh, knees almost buckling as I sag against the banister.

War glances over his shoulder, grin tugging at his mouth. "See? No firing squad."

I narrow my eyes at him, still tugging the hem of my dress down. "You knew."

He shrugs, maddeningly smug. "Maybe."

I groan. "You're insufferable."

"And you're adorable when you panic," he fires back, sauntering toward the doors like the whole inn belongs to him.

I hurry after him, still hot-cheeked, still scandalized, but mostly just *his*.

The relief of the empty lobby lasts all of three seconds.

Because the moment I step outside, the cold slaps me like a wake-up call—and the hammering of the construction crew splits the brittle winter air.

Of course. Still working. Still here. Still witnesses to my walk of shame.

I duck my head, hugging my arms tight as if that can somehow make me invisible.

"Morning, Beaumont," one of the guys calls with a nod, breath fogging in the cold as he lowers his coffee cup.

War lifts a hand in greeting, then leans in to press a kiss to my temple. "Go on, sweet girl. I'll be over in a minute."

War doesn't miss a beat. He slides right into conversation, easy and commanding all at once, his hand brushing my lower back before drifting away.

My heart skips.

So I gather what little dignity I have left, tug my coat tighter against the wind, and cross the icy street toward my family home, praying no one else notices I'm rumpled, panty-less, and wearing last night's sins in the form of a dress.

I slip through the front door as quietly as possible, my pulse hammering in my ears. The living room is blessedly empty.

Then I hear them, voices drifting from the kitchen, low and casual, like any other Friday. My stomach knots.

I dart for the stairs, taking them two at a time. My bedroom door clicks shut behind me, muffling the sound of laughter below.

I sag against it for half a breath before shoving myself into motion. Time to pack, get dressed, and say goodbye to my family.

My heart twinges, but I whisper to myself: *It's okay. I'll be back sooner next time.*

***

By the time I make it back downstairs, the kitchen is full; voices, laughter, the smell of something warm and buttery drifting through the air. And right in the middle of it all, *War.*

He looks completely at ease at my family's table, like he's been here a hundred times instead of once. Logan tosses barbed jokes his way, and he just smirks, firing back with that sharp Beaumont wit that somehow doesn't rub them wrong. They laugh with him, not at him.

I linger in the doorway for a beat, quiet and still, letting the moment wash over me.

War *fits.* Like he's always been here. Like he belongs. He's relaxed in a way I rarely see, a smirk tugging at his lips as he talks to Chase about the next stage of renovations. Mama sneaks extra sweets into foil, muttering that "he should eat more," He thanks her with a smile that transforms his rugged face into something boyish, making her beam like a teenager, and my chest twists with something warm and terrifying all at once, like a sparkler burning too close to my heart.

My heart sings.

Because this—*this* is what I wanted. Not the chaos. Not the tension. Just peace. A morning like this.

And he's here. Loose and light, so different from the version of him I've seen with his family; stoic, strained, always carrying the weight of expectation. Here, he's free. Here, *he's happy.*

Mama looks up and catches sight of me in the doorway. "There she is," she calls, drying her hands. "We thought you two were going to leave without saying goodbye."

"Never," I say, stepping into the room as my chest swells with something warm and full and a little bit aching.

When he catches my eye across the room, his ice blue gaze locks onto mine, and his lips curve into that knowing half-smile that makes my knees weak. He fits here like the last puzzle piece clicking into place.

He stands, bag of treats in his hands. "You ready?"

His voice tender. I nod and look around at my family. My father steps inside from the porch. "Car's here!"

Logan's already waiting by the door, coat on, my bag slung over his shoulder like always. He doesn't say a word, he just gives me a look, the same look he's been giving me since I was old enough to carry a backpack: *I've got it.*

I smile, slipping into my coat as War grabs one more treat from my mother.

I step outside with Logan. My father talking to the driver.

"Ella's not here?" I ask, scanning the porch, expecting her to pop out of nowhere with a hug and sage, sharp advice.

Logan's steps falter—just barely. "She's, uh... not feeling great. Said to tell you bye. She'll call you later."

Something in his voice tugs at me. Too even. Too practiced.

"Uh-huh," I murmur, glancing up at him. "You sure you're okay?"

"What? Yeah." He clears his throat. "Why wouldn't I be?"

"You're *blushing.*"

"I'm not." He adjusts the strap of my bag and keeps walking. "It's cold"

A smile tugs at my mouth. "Right. Of course. Just cold."

He doesn't look at me. Doesn't rise to the bait. But his ears are definitely pinker than before. He puts my bag into the trunk.

I don't push. I just walk beside him, biting back a grin as I glance toward the front door where mom and War come out. She hugs him close.

"You two will come back soon won't you?"

"Jillybean! Let them be," Daddy calls out as he steps up putting an arm around me. "You be good Ollipop and if you need me, I'm on the next flight."

"Me too!" Dean shouts from the doorway, brushing past War and wrapping me up in a bear hug.

I laugh and shake my head my eyes meeting Wars as he heads to the car to place his bags in the trunk.

"We'll be back Jillian, can't keep me away when you make the best pecan pie," War says sure.

Mama beams and Chase emerges with a cookie in hand. He comes down the porch steps ruffles my hair with calloused fingers like I'm still twelve, grinning that obnoxious dimpled grin that's gotten him out of trouble since kindergarten.

"Don't let her fatten you up when she makes you her famous double-chocolate cookies, Beaumont," he warns, patting his own annoyingly flat stomach with a theatrical slap.

I swat at him, but War only smirks. "I like cookies too much to care," he says easily, and Chase barks out a laugh.

"But you'll be back right? maybe Christmas with both of you?" mama asks once more, her voice pleading that it cracks me open.

Daddy steps beside her and holds her close.

I glance at War, uncertain, but he beats me to it. "I promised her Paris," he says, like it's the most normal thing in the world, "but then yes—we'll be stopping by here. Wouldn't miss it."

My mother practically swoons. "Paris? Oh, I would *love* to see Paris…"

War tilts his head at her. "When's your anniversary?"

My face flames. "War, no."

He frowns. "No?"

"June fifteenth," my mother answers, ignoring me completely.

War nods like he's just made a mental note for the ages, while I shake my head, half exasperated, half…so damn full of love I can't even speak.

Mom cups my face in both hands, eyes bright. "Liv bug, I can see it. That little ounce of guilt… you *stop it.*"

Tears burn my eyes. "Mama—"

She shakes her head. "No, Olivia Lynn Baker. You were made for more than just this town. So you go be more."

Her arms lock tight around me, and I break, crying into her shoulder.

"I love you, Mama."

"Love you too, Liv Bug."

Chapter Fifty-Four

OLIVIA

"*War.*" I giggle, *an actual girlish giggle I don't even recognize as mine* as he trails kisses up my neck. "We haven't been in the air five minutes."

"Then that's four minutes too long," he murmurs, his voice a low rumble against my skin. "I've waited months to have you like this again."

His hand slides to my thigh, gripping with quiet possession. "You're not walking off this plane without feeling me still inside you."

My breath hitches. "Plane bathrooms aren't exactly—"

"We're not going to the bathroom This is *my* plane." He tilts my chin, eyes blazing. "Get on my lap, Olivia. *Now.*"

I should say no.

I should remind him that the flight attendant is probably just behind the curtain.

I should breathe.

But instead—I move.

I slide into his lap, my hands trembling, heart full. And the world fades around us, until it's just him and me and everything we've survived to be here again.

***

The car glides away from the hangar, the sky dipped in honey gold as the sun begins its descent. I'm tucked beside War in the back seat, his hand resting on my thigh like it belongs there.

My phone buzzes.

Ella

> Sorry I didn't say bye. I wasn't feeling well.

I glance at War before typing back.

> Yeah. Logan said you were sick. I hope you're okay.

Ella

> I think I caught a cold. I'll rest. Love you.

I stare at the screen too long. Something about her words are too neat. Too distant.

War brushes his knuckles along my jaw. "You okay?"

I sigh. "Yeah, I just…" I hesitate. "I feel like Ella's hiding something."

He leans in, presses a kiss to my temple. Warm. Steady.

"She'll come around," he murmurs. "You've been friends too long not to figure it out. Call her later."

I nod, though the unease lingers, a quiet thrum beneath my ribs.

The car pulls up to the front of the building. War's hand doesn't leave me as we step out, the driver tipping his head before disappearing behind the wheel.

We ride the elevator up in silence, but it's not uncomfortable. It's the kind of quiet that feels full—shared, lived-in.

When the doors slide open, I step into the penthouse.

The familiar scent of cedar and citrus. The clean lines. The sweeping view.

I didn't think this place would ever feel like home.

But standing here now—my suitcase in one hand, War's warmth at my back, it does.

He takes my bag without asking, hauling both into the bedroom like they're nothing. I trail behind him, heart tugging as I watch the quiet strength in his shoulders.

I've been gone for months. How did I survive it?

A whole month without this man, this place, *this feeling.*

Then it hits me, sharp and inconvenient.

"Oh no," I blurt. "I quit my job."

He glances over his shoulder, amused. "You just remembered that now?"

"I had a lot on my mind," I groan.

His smirk is maddening and sweet. "I'll rehire you. But we're renegotiating salary. You've made yourself... *irreplaceable.*"

I drop onto the bed, burying my face in my hands. "I'm sorry. I'll apologize for the rest of our lives if I have to."

He pauses, that smile softening into something real. "I like that. The rest of our lives."

My breath catches. I sit up straighter, nerves twisting inside me, suddenly too aware of how much I want that to be true.

"How were things without me?" I ask. Quiet. Scared of the answer.

He doesn't meet my eyes as he tosses our clothes into the hamper and tucks the suitcases away.

Just says one word:

"Dark."

And it cracks something wide open in my chest.

I force a smile, swallowing the burning lump in my throat. "How's the Parker Building? The renovation must be finished by now."

He stills.

His hands freeze mid-motion, fingers curling into his palms.

"We can talk about work later," he says with practiced casualness that doesn't reach his eyes. "You must be starving. Should we order from La Serenata? Those garlic prawns you love?"

I frown. "*No.* I want to know about the Parker Building. What's going on?"

He exhales slowly, then walks over and sinks into the mattress beside me, the bed dipping under his weight. "The Amatos owned Baker's Inn. They wanted a trade. I gave them one."

My heart stops. "No," I whisper. "War... tell me you didn't."

His voice is steady, but his eyes are full of something raw. "The Parker Building wasn't worth more than your freedom. Your *peace.* I'd trade every brick of it again."

I stand, stunned. *He gave it up.*

"You built that from the ground up," I whisper. "For Noah. You breathed life back into it. That building is *part of you.*"

"And so are you," he says gently, rising with me. "What matters more?"

I blink through the sting in my eyes. My throat tight. "They'll ruin it."

"Maybe," he admits. "But they won't ruin you. *Or* your family. And that's all I care about."

I wrap my arms tight around his neck, burying my face in his chest. "I'm *so* sorry," I whisper. "I hate that you had to choose."

"I didn't have to. I *wanted* to," he murmurs. "That building was never going to love me back. You do."

His words hit bone-deep.

I pull back just enough to look at him.

Frown firmly placed.

"What do the Amatos even need it for?"

He chuckles, amused by my frown. His thumb brushes gently over my pout.

"They gave it to Maksim Korsakov. He's been gunning for it since I got it. Now he has it..."

His gaze softens.

"And I have you. I win."

He smiles, but his eyes are sad.

"Okay," I breathe, my mind already made up as my lips brush against his skin. "But we are *never* buying from La Serenata again. Those bastards don't deserve our money."

War chuckles, the vibration rumbling through his chest and into mine, his breath warm as it stirs my hair.

"*Our* money? Calling them bastards?" He pulls back just enough to meet my eyes. "My, my, Olivia *Lynn.* You are spending *far* too much time with me."

I laugh softly.

"And I'll spend every second of my life with you."

And I will.

I vow it to myself, silent and fierce.

We'll get the Parker Building back someday.

Noah's legacy. War's sacrifice.

I don't know how yet. But I'll fix it.

For the man who has given me more than I could have ever imagined and asks for nothing in return, but love.

It's my turn to do something grand. For us. For love.

For him

Chapter Fifty-Five

OLIVIA

Two Months Later

Being back feels good.

Even with the little eye in the sky watching me from the door.

I glance up at the camera mounted above the office entrance and give it a lazy wave.

"My voyeur," I mutter, shaking my head with a fond smile.

The man who gave up the most important thing in the world for me.

My heart aches. The Parker Building.

It had become something to me.

It was his cross to bear, but it became a sigil for redemption and hope.

Our dream. *Our* legacy.

And now it's gone. Traded. For me.

I never wanted that. Never wanted to be worth more than something that meant everything to him.

I close my eyes briefly, then refocus.

We'll build something else. Honor Noah another way.

This morning, I called the city office. Left voicemails for the director of outreach. Emailed the zoning board. Asked if there's a vacant lot next to Beaumont Luxe we could redevelop. A shelter. A creative arts space. Something bright and safe with Noah's name etched in the foundation.

But none of it stops the anger from curdling in my gut.

This is Maksim Korsakov's fault.

That Bratva asshole.

I don't care what "territory" means in their world. I care that War had to trade our dream for my family's safety because that man wanted the Parker Building like a damn trophy.

I type his name into the search bar again, fists clenched.

Colorful hair? *Really?*

What kind of mobster runs an empire looking like a reject from clown college?

Snake bites through his lip. Ink down his throat. A permanent smirk that makes me want to throw my coffee at the screen.

I click through a few articles. One about The Gilded Ace... his casino, all glass and gold and debauchery.

Another about Exile, some high-profile club in the city I've definitely heard of, but never went.

And then I see it.

Smash and Sugar.

My *favorite* bakery.

"No," I whisper. *"No. No no no—come on."*

Nothing is sacred!

I keep scrolling.

Property deeds, shell companies, all funneling back to Korsakov Holdings.

Do these bastards own *everything* in this city?

I huff and yank my hair into a messy bun.

I need more. Need to know why he wanted the Parker Building. What he's planning.

Maybe I can find leverage.

Maybe I can steal it back.

I open a new tab and pull up an old shortcut.

WesTech Intranet.

I shouldn't...

But this isn't my first time.

Wesley didn't seem to remember me. Not really. But I remember him.

I was sixteen, bored, angry, brilliant; and stupid enough to test a security patch on the new WesTech servers I had read about all the way from my tiny town.

I cracked it in under an hour.

His legal team showed up two days later. Mama nearly had a heart attack.

Wesley didn't press charges. Said he was... impressed.

Paid me, quietly, for a line of encryption I'd built from scratch, something he claimed they'd been trying to develop for weeks.

That check helped save the inn that year.

But Mama made me promise never to touch anything like that again.

Sorry, Mama.

I pull up the WesTech Intranet and type in the credentials.

A beat.

Then: **Access Granted.**

I blink.

"Seriously? "I mutter, "Some things, never change."

We need to work on our offboarding protocols.

I click into the internal systems. Wesley never knew I added myself to the backend dev team as a ghost profile. I was careful—mirrored logins, masked IP, backdoor routed through a dead server in Arizona. Rookie shit, but effective.

Okay, Liv. Time to go hunting.

I route myself through a VPN, then sandbox my browser just in case.

I don't touch anything sensitive. Not technically. Just hover near the financial servers, then pivot into public asset registries.

My fingers fly, tracing breadcrumbs:

Corporation names, subsidiary loops, LLCs hidden inside offshore accounts.

It takes hours, but I find it.

A map of Maksim Korsakov's empire.

And a weak spot.

The Parker Building wasn't just a grab.

It was a homecoming.

I dig deeper. Property records, archived sales, auction history—

There it is.

The Parker Building used to belong to his father.

Alexei Korsakov. Bratva royalty.

Lost the building fifteen years ago in a quiet forfeiture.

The city seized it after a nasty racketeering case tied up in civil litigation.

Beaumont Enterprises acquired it at auction six years later—clean title, no red flags.

War had to have known.

My cursor hovers over the file.

So Maksim didn't want the building because of its location.

He wanted it because it used to be his.

A ghost from his past.

A wound.

A slow grin pulls at my lips.

Personal wounds make for *very* effective leverage.

I keep going.

If his father's loss still lingers... what else does?

I dig into old records, court cases, even police reports from Maksim's adolescence. It's all scrubbed, sealed or encrypted or buried under layers of legal sludge.

But I know what I'm doing.

I crack into a database I'm technically not supposed to still have access to. A private health records aggregator.

Just poking.

Just looking.

I pause, fingers trembling slightly.

Do I really want to do this?

This isn't just petty revenge or city politics.

This is personal.

Still... he took our building.

This isn't just strategy.

It's war.

I enter the parameters. Maksim Nikolai Korsakov. DOB. Known aliases.

A file pings.

Psychiatric evaluation. Age 15.

I open it.

My stomach tightens.

It's not just the aggression scores, or the dissociation markers.

It's the description of the incident that triggered the court-ordered psych hold.

A violent episode.

I exhale slowly, the edges of the report burning into my brain.

Now I understand why he wanted the Parker Building so badly.

I lean back in my chair and stare at the ceiling.

Okay.

Two plans.

Plan A: Strategy. Business.

Plan B: The jugular.

Only if I have to.

Because if Maksim wants to play dirty?

He's not the only one who knows how to destroy people from the inside out.

I glance up at the camera again, its red light blinking in silence.

"Sorry, War," I murmur.

"I have to do this one *my* way."

Chapter Fifty-Six

WAR

Being back in the office feels good.

Being back with *her?* Even better.

I sink into my chair, the familiar leather molding to me like it never stopped waiting. Everything's sharp, humming, under control. Olivia is back under my roof. My penthouse. My office. My *life.*

I pull up the feed.

Her office flashes onto my screen. The camera isn't tucked in her bookshelf anymore, I moved it, right above the door in plain sight, angled to catch her desk. She knows I'm watching.

And I fucking love that she knows.

She sits there, head bent, typing fast, her lips pursed in concentration. Every now and then she brushes her hair out of her eyes. She pauses to stretch, arching her back. My lips twitch as I watch her mouth something under her breath, probably cursing at the program I made her use. I could watch her all damn day.

My chest tightens just watching her. She looks so fucking good here, like she was always meant to be part of this empire.

I sigh, content, and pull the small box out of my drawer. The ring. I'd been ready to put it on her finger in Brokenwoods, but the timing was wrong. She needed to come back here first, fall back into the flow of things. In to *us.* When I do it, it'll be perfect.

The door crashes open; Wilder saunters in first, Wesley on his heels.

I snap the feed closed, jaw tight.

"Is there another writer's strike?" I mutter, not bothering to hide my irritation. "Why are you always here now?"

Wilder just grins, drops into the chair across from me, and swings his feet up onto my desk. "Don't have to be there. You sent Brody over. I've got your little lapdog running my errands now."

"Brody's supposed to be managing *Beaumont Realty*," I bite out. "Not *Wilder Productions.*"

Wilder shrugs like it doesn't matter. "Details. He likes me better."

Wesley sighs and takes the other chair. "Enough. You two argue like children. Glad to have Liv back, I see. I thought you two would be *working from home* forever." His eyes flick to mine knowingly before he looks at Wilder. "You really *should* do your own work. And we have an issue. The *three* of us."

I swat Wilder's shoes off my desk, hard enough that he curses under his breath, and lean forward. "What issue?"

"Relax," Wilder drawls. "It's not that big of a deal. Wes is just pissed it interrupts his little love fest with the chubby girl."

"Hey!" Wesley and I snap at the same time.

Wilder chuckles, hands lifted in mock surrender. "What? I *like* them soft. I wasn't being rude. I just forgot her name."

"Her *name* is Evie," Wesley growls.

I level him with a look. "What's the issue?"

"With Evie?" he deadpans.

"No!" I snap. "What's our issue?"

Wesley straightens. "Miranda wants a meeting."

I blink. "So?"

"I saw her months ago. We had lunch. She's fine. I talked her off that ledge."

"Apparently not enough." Wesley's tone is grim. "She's coming for the building. She wants her cut."

Wilder snorts. "Well, she doesn't get a cut. She can fuck off to Paris and keep playing the golden daughter."

"For once, I agree with Wilder," Wesley mutters.

I lean back in my chair, smirking. "Then let her have her meeting. We'll say no, as *usual.* She'll storm off. In another two years, she'll come back to bitch about it again. Rinse and repeat."

Wesley's jaw tightens. "What if she tells Dad?"

I laugh sharp and humorless. "What's he going to do? Pull his funding? We haven't needed him in over a decade. Let him pull it. He wants to play knight in shining armor for Daddy's little girl, he can buy her her own damn building." I pause, my smirk sharpening. "Oh wait, he already did."

Wilder leans back, folding his arms behind his head, his Rolex catching the light. "She doesn't need a meeting. She needs a man. Someone to keep her busy so she'll leave us the fuck alone."

Wesley actually chuckles. "We should pay someone to do it."

I bark out a laugh, dry and callous. "Do you know how much we'd have to pay for her age?"

Wilder frowns, starts counting on his fingers. "She's twenty-nine. That's not old."

I freeze. "She's only twenty-nine?"

Wesley nods. "Eight years younger than you. Seven from me. Five from Wilder."

"Christ," I mutter. "I thought she was at least thirty-five with the way she complains."

Wilder smirks. "You'd think she came out of the womb filing lawsuits."

"Or monologuing about her *value in the family business,*" Wesley adds with a groan.

I shake my head, half amused, half exasperated. "Maybe we *should* pay someone to date her. Get her to latch onto some poor bastard instead of clinging to Beaumont Enterprises like it's her birthright."

"She's still running that makeup line though," Wilder says, not bothering to hide the surprise in his voice. "What's it called again? Blood Vow?"

Wesley corrects him. "No that's just the lipstick line. And it's actually doing well. I saw the quarterly. Someone must be running it for her."

"She's got vision," I admit. "Just no off switch."

"Or filter."

"Or awareness of her lane."

I lean back, mulling it over. Twenty-nine. Somehow I thought she'd crept further into spinster territory.

I tap my fingers against the desk, calculating. "If she shows up here or corners either of you, just send her my way. She's never had a backbone against me."

"Because you scare the shit out of her," Wilder says, amused.

"She still flinches when you raise your voice," Wesley mutters.

"Good," I reply flatly.

Both of them nod, unspoken agreement sealing the matter. Miranda might be our little sister, but she *is* still a Beaumont—and Beaumont's always find a way to turn family problems into business strategy.

Wesley's phone buzzes.

One glance and he pales.

"Fuck. Shit—*shit shit shit.*"

Wilder sits up straighter, alert.

"What now?"

"We're being hacked," Wesley says, standing, fingers flying over his screen.

I straighten. "*We,* or just WesTech?"

Wesley doesn't look up. "Looks like both. Someone was in the backend. I don't know how deep yet."

"What the hell is happening?" My voice drops an octave. Tight. Controlled.

Then Wesley freezes.

"Where's your girlfriend?"

My heart drops into my stomach.

"Olivia?" I'm already standing. "Is she in danger?"

"No," he says, slowly, dread rising in his tone. "She *is* the danger."

I whirl toward the screen.

Pull up the office feed.

Olivia's office flashes onto the monitor.

Empty.

I blink. Refresh. Still empty.

"She's not in her office," I grit out, already moving for the door.

Wesley steps in front of me, blocking the way. "Of course she's not. She hacked into my system and left."

"What the fuck are you talking about?" I snap. "Olivia didn't hack anything. Someone's using her login, spoofing her credentials—"

"Uh-oh," Wilder laughs grabbing a drink from my decanter, shaking his head.

"You didn't tell him?" he asks glancing at Wesley.

Wesley answers clipped. "Apparently neither did she."

Now I'm getting pissed.

"Tell me what?"

"I told you she was perfect for the job, before you stole her," Wesley says, switching from his phone to my desk. "You think I let her into WesTech because she makes a killer coffee?"

He groans, dragging a hand through his hair. "She's not just a glorified assistant, War. Olivia's a prodigy in my field. Cybersecurity, systems engineering, anomaly detection; she has the credentials and the instincts. She's the one who found the zero-day exploit in our old firewall when I first started the company up by *hacking* it. Anonymous. But I traced it back to her."

He shakes his head. "Her design? I still use."

"She *what?*"

My mind is whirling.

My Olivia?

"She applied to NovaRael, but I called her in as soon as Brody told me she didn't get the job," Wesley snaps. "She knows how to break a system—*my system*. Which is why I gave her limited access and never let her near the core servers, figured I could use her in case of an emergency. But now..."

He trails off, connecting his phone to my computer.

I'm frozen. Replaying conversations.

When she mentioned Santo Amato, I told her not to speak his name again.

She was the only person to find the information I needed to get the Parker Building renovations back up.

She was genuinely confused as to why I needed her up here...

I thought she was being cute.

I never thought—

"So what?" I manage. "She's some kind of tech genius?"

"Yeah," Wesley says without looking up. "And whatever she was looking for, I need to find out before it's too late. If she stole—"

"She wouldn't," I cut him off.

Wilder chuckles.

Wesley lifts a brow.

"She wouldn't steal. She has everything she needs with me."

I say it with more certainty than I feel.

Wilder watches me as he sips my scotch.

Wesley doesn't argue, he just says quietly, "Then let's find out what she was doing."

"I'm calling her," I say leaving my own office and pacing the hall.

I stare at my phone a moment then dial. It rings twice.

"Hi, babe," she answers, all breathy and casual.

My brow furrows. *Babe? She never calls me that.*

"Where are you?" I ask, voice low.

"I went to pick up lunch," she says quickly. *Too quickly.* "I... I couldn't wait."

She's lying.

I can hear it in the tiny hitch of her breath.

"Oh yeah?" I pace, one brow rising. "Where?"

Another beat.

"Not La Serenata," she answers.

Smartass.

"Listen, I'm next," she adds, voice soft. "I'll see you soon."

The line goes dead.

I stare at the dead screen for a second longer, jaw clenched so tight it aches. I force myself to breathe.

She's *not* a thief. She wouldn't run. Not after everything.

No.

She's not leaving. She wouldn't. Not again.

But if she did...

She'd end up back in Brokenwoods and I'd drag her ass back here, kicking and screaming, tie her to my name, and *never* let her leave the damn penthouse again.

"Found it!" Wesley's voice chimes. "She wasn't just skimming. She tunneled straight into asset registries. She was after something specific."

I step back in and walk behind him, Wilder tucks in close to look too.

"Here. This is the search history."

Search Query: **Maksim Korsakov**

Related Entities: Korsakov Holdings. Gilded Ace. Exile. Smash and Sugar.

My blood turns cold.

Korsakov.

Of all the names in this city—

"She was digging on him?" I ask, voice sharp.

Wesley nods grimly. "For hours."

My mind races.

The damn Parker Building.

"She has a fucking death wish," I grit.

I open the GPS tracking app.

Let's see where you went, little doe.

You like being watched, don't you?

Good. Because now I'm coming for you.

I pray I get to you before *he* does.

Chapter Fifty-Seven

OLIVIA

This is stupid.

Lying to War is stupid.

I could die.

They'd probably bury me in some Bratva ditch behind a meat warehouse and no one would ask a single damn question.

I stare up at Exile.

Now or never.

In the daylight, the club still looms, black brick, sharp steel awning, windows masked with thick, matte-black curtains that choke out even the idea of sunlight.

Red neon letters flicker above the door like a threat dressed up as a welcome. The entire building hums with something… dangerous. Coiled. *Waiting.*

The moment I step inside, the temperature seems to drop.

A bald man blocks my path. Built like a bulldozer in a too-tight shirt, his expression screams *'wrong move and I break your jaw.'*

"We're closed."

"I'm looking for Maksim Korsakov," I say, straightening my spine, trying to keep my voice from shaking.

His eyes drag over me, slowly, and a sickly tingle creeps up my spine. I don't flinch, but I want to.

He says nothing. Just pulls out his phone and starts speaking in Russian, voice low and clipped.

I try not to panic.

When he hangs up, a loud bang echoes from above, a door slamming open.

Heavy footsteps descend the metal staircase from the VIP section. I glance up.

A tall man emerges.

White button-down rolled to the forearms. Dual guns strapped in a chest holster. A wicked knife twirling between his fingers like a toy.

He smirks as he reaches the bottom, his dark hair slicked neatly back, jaw strong and clean-shaven, dark brown eyes unsettlingly bright.

He stops a few feet in front of me. He's as tall as War. And if War is fire, this man is ice.

"You can go, Sergei," he says, not looking at the other man.

Sergei disappears behind a side door without another word.

I swallow. Hard.

The man flips his knife once more before sliding it into a sheath in his waist band, then holds out a hand.

"Vaska Morozov."

I hesitate a breath, then take it.

His grip surprises me, *firm,* but gentle. Controlled.

"Olivia Baker. I'm looking for Maksim Korsakov."

He releases my hand, eyes gleaming with amusement.

"Regarding?"

"Business," I say, lifting my chin.

He chuckles, low and amused. "You're determined, *krasivaya.*"

The Russian rolls off his tongue like smoke. Pretty. Dangerous. "But Korsakov isn't expecting any women today."

"I'm an unexpected visitor," I reply. "But I *still* need to speak with him."

Vaska smiles like a man who knows something I don't.

He considers me for a moment, then nods. "Okay," he says simply. "I'll bring you to him."

He turns, and I follow him up the stairs.

Each step feels like a mistake.

A choice I can't unmake.

The farther we go, the darker it gets—velvet curtains muffling light, plush carpet muffling sound. Shadows crawl across the walls like ghosts. The air thickens.

At the very end of the VIP hall, Vaska stops in front of a heavy black door with a gold handle. He opens it without knocking and steps aside.

"After you," he says.

A chill creeps up my spine. But I step in.

The room is sleek and shadowed; glass, concrete, and a massive dark wood desk that looks like it was dragged out of an old-world war chamber.

And behind it, *him.*

Maksim Korsakov.

Blue hair mussed up, snake bite piercings catching the low amber light. Tattoos disappear under the collar his shirt.

He leans back in a leather chair like he owns not just this building but the city around it.

His cold blue eyes rake over me.

Slow. *Intrusive.*

Vaska steps in behind me and shuts the door.

The click of the lock makes me flinch.

I'm trapped.

With *both* of them.

This was a bad idea.

Maksim's gaze lingers, hungry in a way that makes my skin crawl.

"I didn't order a woman today," he drawls. "So what do you want?"

Bastard.

I fight the disgust clawing up my throat and force my voice steady.

"I'm Olivia Baker. I work at—"

"Beaumont," he cuts me off, smirking. "He sends a woman to do his bidding?"

He laughs, low and condescending.

My mouth moves before I can stop it.

"I'm here on my own."

Shit.

His expression sharpens. He leans forward slightly, interest flashing.

"Alone?" he repeats, one pierced brow lifting.

I shake it off. Straighten my shoulders.

He's trying to rattle me. I won't let him.

"I want to make a deal for the Parker Building."

Maksim leans back in his chair, a bored look settling across his sharp features.

"No."

Flat. Dismissive. Like I offered him gum instead of a deal.

I blink. "I haven't even told you—"

"I'm not interested." He waves a tattooed hand lazily. "You can go now, *Olivia.*"

Heat floods my face. Not from embarrassment, but frustration.

Plan A it is.

"What if I offered you something better?" I ask, moving around his desk.

He lifts a brow but doesn't object. Just watches.

I stop beside him, hovering awkwardly. "Could I use your desktop?"

His smile curves, all teeth and arrogance. "Hell, you can sit on my lap while you do it, if you want."

"No, thank you." My voice is tight. Controlled.

He doesn't move.

So I lean over him, carefully reaching for the mouse. His clean, sharp scent, ocean breeze laced with something spicy, fills my nose. It shouldn't smell this good, but it does.

He doesn't look at the screen.

I can feel his eyes on me, not the property listing I pull up. That somehow makes it worse.

Focus, Olivia.

I pull up the maps and blueprints I've prepared. "This is Beaumont Luxe," I say, pointing. "It's larger. Better for what you want to turn it into."

He doesn't look. Not right away.

"What do you know," he says slowly, "of what I want to make it into?"

I glance at him.

Big mistake.

We're inches apart.

My breath shudders.

Then I pull back, standing straight again.

"Whatever you use it for..." I clear my throat. "It has more basement space. And for a man like you—"

He smirks. *"A man like me?"*

His gaze flickers with something. *Amusement?* Threat? Both?

"Ms. Baker, I'm just a businessman."

I fold my arms. My patience is wearing thin.

He's going to say no again. I can feel it coming.

And I'm done playing nice.

I place my hands on my hips. "It's no secret you're Bratva. Matter of fact, you're the head of it."

His smile fades. Just a little.

"You could use the basement for your kills. The upper floors for your fronts—money laundering, illegal shipments, whatever the hell you want. We'll even finish the renovations for you."

I meet his eyes.

"But we want the Parker Building."

Maksim shakes his head, that same smirk playing at the corner of his lips. He's about to dismiss me again.

I speak before he can.

"It's still in your territory," I say, pivoting fast. "Beaumont Luxe... There's a transitional home not too far from it—for kids aging out of foster care."

He doesn't interrupt. But he doesn't look interested either.

"We were going to donate. Make a big thing out of it. Cut a ribbon, get some press coverage. Looks good for the city. And for whoever owns the block."

His eyes finally meet mine.

Cold. Blue. Piercing.

"Why," he says slowly, "would I care about transitional homes? Or kids?"

I hesitate for half a beat.

Then I go for it.

"Your mother," I say quietly. "She was adopted, wasn't she? And your father's—"

"Enough."

The word slices through the room like a blade.

He stands.

My breath stutters. I don't move.

Vaska, still leaning near the door, shifts. Says something in Russian, his tone low, cautious.

Maksim doesn't look at him. His eyes are locked on mine.

"Leave."

Vaska hesitates. "Maks..."

"Leave. Now."

The pause that follows is long and silent.

Then Vaska nods once, his jaw tight. He looks at me on his way out, and something in his expression curls unease through my gut.

He shakes his head, barely noticeable.

Then he's gone.

The door closes with a quiet, final click.

Oh god.

This is how I die.

Why did I say that?

Why did I bring up his *mother?*

I read his psych eval.

I know better.

Why did I poke the bear?

"How do you know that?" Maksim's voice is quiet. Too quiet.

His eyes narrow. "Does Beaumont know?"

"No," I say quickly. "No, just me."

He tilts his head. "So I kill you and no one will know."

The tears come instantly. Hot and humiliating.

A sob breaks.

He sees it. Freezes.

I remember what I read. He doesn't cry. Can't handle it when others do.

"War gave up the building for me and I—"

"Stop that," he snaps, reaching for a tissue from the corner of his desk.

He hands it to me, and it's oddly... gentle.

Like he wants me to stop crying because he genuinely doesn't know what to do with it.

I pat my tears away.

"I need to *keep* the Parker Building," he says.

"For what?" I ask, voice rough.

"That's none of your business."

I take a breath. My voice steadies.

"If it's just to sit there. If you're only holding it because of your father—trying to prove something, make a point about his failure, then fine. Keep it in your name. But let *us* build it. Let us make something good out of it."

He steps back.

His brows furrow so deep they nearly meet. One hand hovers near the gun holstered at his waist.

His voice turns sharper. "How do you know so much about me?"

I swallow, my breath catching in my throat. He hasn't moved, but I feel it. The shift. *The danger.* His hand is on his weapon.

"Maksim—" I try, but his expression darkens.

"Who *sent* you?"

No longer curious. *Suspicious.* I take a step back.

"I just—" I flinch as his fingers twitch, and it bursts out of me. "I did something illegal, okay?"

His head tilts. "Illegal?"

"Yes," I breathe. "I... I pulled tax records. Real estate holdings. Employment history. Your liquor license renewals, everything! It was stupid, I know, but it's what I do when I'm curious. And you were..."

I trail off trying to think of anything appeasing, his silence pressing in.

"You were interesting," I finish lamely.

He studies me for a long moment. The tension lingers between us, sharp as a blade, but his hand leaves his gun.

"So yes, what I did was illegal," I admit. "And yes, I'm the only one who knows. Yes, you could kill me, hide my body, and no one would ever find out."

I pause, taking in a shuddering breath, trying to keep the tears at bay.

"Or...I could owe you."

The words leave my mouth like a death sentence.

"Owe me?" His voice is low. Curious again.

Wrong move Olivia.

He could ask for *anything.*

I nod, slowly. "You need someone to break through a system you can't get into? I'll do it. I'll help. But let us have the Parker Building. You can have Beaumont Luxe. We'll finish the renovations, we'll donate to the transitional home; in your name."

His head tilts.

"You *need* the good press," I continue, my mind racing. "You need to look valid. You've been on law enforcement radar for a few months now."

He freezes.

Then slowly, a crooked smile pulls at his lips.

"You hacked into local law enforcement?"

I nod once. "And your medical records."

That makes him laugh. Full and sharp. Eyes gleaming now.

"So you *know*," he says. "And you still had the balls to walk up in here and face me alone?"

"Yes," I exhale.

Maksim sits again. Slowly. Then leans back in his chair, arms resting wide on the armrests like a king on a throne.

"I'm not taking your '*I owe you*,'" he says, lips twisting. "I won't tie you to the Bratva."

He pauses.

"But I'll take Luxe. I'll take the donation.

And the land under the Parker Building?" He taps the desk once.

"Still mine."

"So *we* get the building?" I ask. "We can make it whatever we want?"

Maksim nods once, slow and deliberate.

"What is it that you're making?"

I hesitate. But I tell him.

He gave me a deal. I owe him the truth.

"A home," I say softly. "For kids who age out of the system. And a scholarship fund... in Noah Hartman's name."

His eyes shift.

Recognition flickers there.

"That kid who died," he murmurs. A beat passes. Then he nods.

He falls silent. Stares at the desk for a long moment. I don't breathe.

"Deal. That'll make my territory a *pillar of the community.*"

"Exactly," I reply, heart still racing.

He extends a hand across the desk.

I stare at it for a second, then take it.

His palm is rough. His grip, firm as he pulls me in hard, eyes locked on mine.

"You keep that mouth shut, yes?"

I nod. "Yes."

The door swings open behind me.

Vaska steps in, face tight.

"You need to move. Beaumont's two seconds from taking a bullet."

My heart plummets. "Oh no—please don't," I gasp, bolting past him.

Maksim's laugh follows me. "Vaska, call Sergei off."

I don't wait to hear more. I tear down the stairs, skipping steps, breath ragged. The second I hit the floor, I see them—War and Sergei, chest to chest, heat rising off both of them like smoke. The air practically vibrates with violence.

Both men are tall, furious, and locked in a verbal brawl, in *Russian.* Words fly like gunshots, sharp and escalating.

I wedge myself between them before I can think better of it, my body the only shield between two men who look ready to kill each other. My heart's about to crack my ribs.

"I'm so sorry," I say breathlessly, eyes wide. "We're leaving. *Now.*"

Vaska appears behind Sergei and mutters something.

Sergei curses under his breath but steps back, clearly annoyed.

I grab War's arm and tug him toward the exit, pulse hammering.

Once we're outside, I exhale hard, relief crashing over me in a wave.

"You speak Russian?" I ask, glancing up at him.

He doesn't answer right away. Just looks at me. Hard. Calculating.

"You hack systems?"

He doesn't shout. He doesn't curse.

But his voice lands like a fucking verdict.

Shit.

Chapter Fifty-Eight

WAR

I'm livid.

Livid and relieved.

That gargantuan bastard could have shot me, but I was ready, more than willing to die if it meant getting my Olivia away from that blue-haired motherfucker.

She trails behind me into the penthouse, her voice, soft, apologetic, beautiful, chasing me through the silence. But I can't hear her.

I can't hear anything except the roar of my own blood in my ears.

I yank open the fridge, grab a bottle of water, and slam it shut. The sound cracks through the kitchen. She flinches beside me.

Damn it.

I drag in a breath. My voice is rough when I turn to her.

"Olivia—"

"War, I'm sorry, okay? I just wanted to get the building back, and I know Wesley may be angry at me, and I—"

"You could have been killed!"

The words rip out of me, sharp and violent, like they've been carved from bone. I barely recognize my own voice.

"But—"

The bottle cap snaps in my hand, water spilling down my wrist.

"But nothing, Olivia." My throat burns. "Men like Korsakov kill women like you for less than what you did. Demanding to see him? Walking into his place of business? *Alone* with him?"

"War, I'm sorry."

Her fingers brush my jaw. That simple touch sends a bolt down my spine, but it doesn't calm me, it only makes me ache more.

"For?" I bite out.

"Scaring you. Upsetting you." Her eyes glisten, her voice trembling but steady. "Leaving without telling you."

I grit my teeth. "Never telling me you have a degree in cybersecurity?"

"I tried to tell you," she whispers. "When you hired me. I told you I worked for WesTech, but I couldn't explain because you kept cutting me off."

The fight drains out of me, caught on her truth.

I swallow my next words because she's right.

I stare at her.

My Olivia.

My brilliant, reckless, infuriating woman.

My pulse is still thundering in my ears, but she's right. She tried to tell me. I didn't listen.

Still—

None of that excuses what she did.

She walked into a den of wolves.

Alone.

My hand tightens around the bottle before I finally set it down on the counter with a sharp clack.

I step into her space.

She doesn't flinch.

Doesn't move.

Of course she doesn't.

She's too damn brave for her own good.

"I should put you over my knee for what you did," I say, my voice quiet and dangerous.

Her breath hitches, but she doesn't break eye contact.

"I was just—"

"Don't," I growl. "Don't justify it."

I reach for her wrist and tug her toward the kitchen island. She lets me.

Her footsteps are hesitant. Her body tense.

Good.

"Hands on the counter," I order. "Bend."

"War—"

"*Now,* Olivia."

She obeys, leaning forward, palms pressed flat on the cold marble.

The hem of her skirt shifting as she moves.

I step behind her and slowly flip the skirt up over her hips, exposing the soft curve of her ass and the soft fabric of her underwear.

She's already breathing harder.

"You don't walk into Bratva territory ever."

My voice is low. Controlled. But barely.

"You don't lie to me."

I raise my hand.

"And you never, ever put yourself in danger like that again."

I bring my palm down hard.

Her soft flesh bouncing.

She gasps—sharp and sudden.

"That's for leaving without a word."

Another slap.

She bites her lip, shoulders curling inward.

"For letting Maksim fucking Korsakov *breathe* near you."

A third strike. Sharper this time. She lets out a soft whimper.

"For not trusting me to handle it."

I pause, watching her back rise and fall as she breathes through it.

"You should be *furious* with me," she whispers, pressing back against me.

"I am," I snap. "But more than that; I was scared. And I don't do scared, Olivia."

I lean closer, my hand resting on the small of her back, holding her down gently.

"You belong to me," I murmur at her ear. "And I don't like when people play with what's mine."

Her fingers curl against the marble.

"I'm sorry," she breathes.

"Not yet you're not."

Another spank, firmer. Her skin pink and hot under my palm.

She chokes out a sound—part pain, part apology.

One more.

Then I grip her waist. Not for control, but to steady her.

"You hear me, Olivia?" I ask, voice low but firm. "You don't go to men like that without me."

"I hear you," she whispers. "I won't. Never again, I swear."

Good.

My hand lingers a second longer, fingers grazing over her soft skin, calming the burn I left behind. She shudders under my touch, and I know she feels it too; *that ache.* The sting. The heat between us that hasn't cooled one bit.

I should walk away.

Calm down.

But I can't.

Not when she's like this.

Not when anger and fear have melted into desire and dominance.

Not when she's bent over for me. Still. Silent. Waiting.

I slide my hand down her thigh, then back up, slow and possessive. My fingers hook under the seam of her panties and tug them to the side.

She gasps.

I unbuckle my belt, unfasten my pants, and free myself, thick and hard and aching to be inside her.

I don't wait.

I thrust into her in one brutal, claiming push.

She moans—high, breathless, hungry.

And I curse under my breath because she's fucking *soaked*.

Clenching.

Welcoming.

She enjoyed her punishment.

I grip her hips hard, grounding myself in the feel of her.

She takes every inch like she was made for me.

Because she was.

Her body shudders.

Defiant. Needy.

And I know what she's thinking.

This doesn't feel like punishment.

My grip tightens.

Chapter Fifty-Nine

OLIVIA

I f War thinks this is punishment... *he's wrong.*

The spanking?

I may ask for that again.

His cock driving into me like this?

His hands gripping my hips hard enough to bruise?

I'd *beg* for this kind of punishment.

I push back into his thrusts, matching his rhythm, my breath catching with every snap of his hips.

He holds me down, tight and unrelenting.

"No, stay still," he growls again, like he can hear my thoughts. "*This* is punishment, Olivia."

I can't help the breathless chuckle that slips out of me.

"It isn't though," I whimper, smiling even as I moan.

My hand slides down beneath my skirt, fingers finding my clit, rubbing in tight desperate circles as he fucks me deeper.

War groans above me—low and feral.

He doesn't stop.

Doesn't let up.

And I don't want him to.

I circle my clit, desperate for release, every nerve sparking under his thrusts, until his hand shoots down and grabs mine, yanking it away.

"Don't," he snarls in my ear, voice guttural. "Don't touch what's mine."

My breath catches.

His pace slows, drags, tortures me. Then he pulls out entirely, leaving me empty, aching.

"War—" I gasp, half protest, half plea.

"On your knees," he orders, his voice rough steel.

I freeze. My body trembles.

Because I know what's coming.

And I want it.

Even if he swears it's punishment.

I turn, my legs shaky, my skirt hiked up around my hips, as I drop to the cool marble floor. My knees hit hard, but I don't care. Not when he's standing over me, his belt loose, his cock thick and glistening from being inside me.

I lick my lips without thinking. His eyes darken.

"Open your mouth," he says, voice low and lethal.

Heat floods my cheeks, my body. I part my lips.

He grips the back of my head, guiding me closer. Not gentle. Not soft.

"This is what happens when you lie to me. When you walk into Bratva territory like you're untouchable."

His tip slides against my tongue, and I moan around it.

"You want to touch yourself, Olivia? You want forgiveness?" His voice is a growl, sharp with restraint. "You earn it. With your mouth. With obedience."

I open wider, moaning when he pushes past my lips.

The thick weight of him fills my mouth, my tongue curling around him instinctively. His grip tightens at the back of my head, holding me still as his hips drive forward.

"Good girl," he growls. "Take it."

I gag once when he hits the back of my throat, but the sound makes his chest rumble with approval. My eyes water, and I moan around him, the vibration dragging another curse from his lips.

He pulls back, then thrusts forward again, harder this time. The salty taste of him coats my tongue, slick and intoxicating. My thighs press together, desperate for friction.

I slide a hand down, sneaking beneath my skirt. My fingers find my clit, already swollen and aching. I circle it, needy, moaning as his cock drives deeper.

He glances down and sees what I'm doing. His eyes darken further, his jaw clenching.

"You want to touch yourself while I use your mouth?" His voice is a growl, dangerous, but not stopping me.

I whimper around him, nodding as best I can.

"Then do it," he orders, thrusting into me again. "Rub that greedy little cunt, while you choke on my cock."

The permission unravels me. My fingers work furiously over my clit, my slick soaking my fingers. My moans vibrate around him, and he curses again, hips snapping harder, faster, as he fucks my mouth.

Tears stream down my cheeks, spit dripping from the corners of my lips. He doesn't stop. He holds me there, fucking into me, his cock hitting deep again and again until I'm dizzy, my whole body buzzing.

"Look at you," he groans, his grip on my hair tightening. "On your knees. Crying. Touching yourself while I ruin your throat."

I moan louder, my orgasm crashing through me, my body shuddering, clit pulsing under my fingers.

He groans, deep and raw, and jerks into my mouth one last time before spilling hot and thick down my throat. I swallow greedily, moaning as he holds me there until he's empty.

When he finally pulls back, I'm shaking, gasping for breath, my lips swollen, my chin wet.

He drags his thumb across my mouth, smearing spit across my cheek, his eyes blazing with satisfaction.

"You'll never walk into danger again," he says, voice low and final. "Not while you belong to me."

I stay on my knees, trembling from the aftershocks of pleasure, my lips swollen, my throat raw, my hand still slick between my thighs.

War breathes deeply above me, eyes fixed on me like I'm the only thing that exists. Then, with a quiet exhale, he tucks himself away and fastens his pants.

He crouches in front of me, his hands slipping beneath my arms, lifting me to my feet.

"Come here, sweet girl," he murmurs. "Let's get you cleaned up."

***

"On one hand, I am proud of you," War says, his voice softer than I deserve. "Grateful you got the building back... even if you did *terrify* me."

He feeds me a bite of pasta from the bowl balanced between us. I take it, and my heart soars at the simple sweetness of it... this man, shirtless in bed beside me, a movie playing low on the flat screen, feeding me like it's the most natural thing in the world.

I shift against him, the silk of the blue set he bought me whispering over my skin. The one he goes feral for, his gaze had already darkened the moment he saw me in it tonight, his hand lingering over my breasts before we ever pressed play.

I swallow, and smile up at him.

"I will say..." I pause for effect, teasing. "Your punishment is ineffective. Because I definitely want it again."

That laugh bursts out of him; the deep, rumbling one that lights up his whole face, that makes the sharp, ruthless man look boyish for just a second. I love that laugh more than I should.

He shakes his head, still chuckling, then turns toward me, cradling my cheek in his large hand. His thumb brushes over my skin, tender, reverent. His forehead leans close to mine.

"I'm in love with you, Olivia Baker," he murmurs, voice rough and unguarded. "*Desperately* in love."

My breath hitches. "War... I know. You've said."

"I've said I love you," he corrects gently, "and I do. But I'm also *in* love with you. So damn much."

My chest clenches. "Why?" The word slips out before I can stop it.

His gaze softens, ice-blue and endless.

"Oh, Olivia. *You.* You are the human embodiment of every star I've been trying to reach and never managed."

Tears sting my eyes. "Warren..."

"You are worth everything," he says, fierce and raw. "Every single thing in this world is tangible—but *you*... you're eternity."

The movie flickers forgotten in the background. His bare chest is warm beneath my cheek as I press closer, holding him like I'll never let go. And I know I won't.

War tilts my chin up, eyes locked on mine.

Then he kisses me.

Not hungry. Not punishing. Just... slow. Deep. Devoted.

The kind of kiss that says I'm yours.

The kind that ruins every kiss that came before.

When he pulls back, his lips curve into a smile.

"You're mine, Olivia Baker," he says, brushing a knuckle down my jaw. "And you're never walking into danger without me again. But..."

His eyes flick down to my chest. The grin deepens.

"You *are* wearing that set again. I'll buy you a thousand more."

Chapter Sixty

WAR

"This is ridiculous," Olivia snaps the moment she steps in, eyes fixed on the second desk opposite mine.

"Do you not like your new office?" I ask, pretending to be offended.

She crosses her arms. "I already have my own office, War."

"And now you have another one. *Here.* With me." I grin, because the little crease between her brows is ridiculous and adorable all at once.

She exhales, all stubbornness and lipstick. "I told you I wouldn't run away again."

"Mhm." I push my chair back, stand, and with exaggerated gentlemanly flourish I grab the visitor chair and pull it out for her. "Sit."

I curl a hand around the back of her chair and lean down, close enough she can feel my breath on her neck.

"See? Isn't this better? Now I won't have to watch you from a screen. You'll be right here." My voice drops playful, soft. "And I get to make sure you don't actually run."

She opens her mouth, looking for a retort, but it dies when my lips press against her pulse point. She huffs, but the edge is gone. "You're impossible," she says.

I ease back into my chair, stretching out, content to just watch her. She opens her laptop, the glow of the screen lighting her face, and for a second I swear she was made for this; made to sit across from me, part of my empire, my life.

God, she looks good sitting there.

Like she was always meant to be here—mine, in every possible way.

The second desk was weird when Amato did it. *Now I get it.* Olivia Baker is a flight risk and a fucking force of nature, and I'm not letting either out of my sight.

My gaze lingers.

I should turn back to work. But I can't stop watching her.

Her hair falls forward as she types, her lips pursed in concentration. and I feel it—how lucky I am to have her here, in this office, in my life. How easy it would've been to lose her. Never thought I'd deserve this kind of love.

She catches me staring.

Without even looking up, she says flatly, "Stop eye-fucking me and go back to pretending you work."

I grin. "Can't help it. You're my favorite view."

She rolls her eyes, muttering something about *ridiculous men and their God complexes,* but I catch the corner of her mouth twitching, like she's trying not to smile.

And *that?* That's how I know she loves it here.

My phone buzzes on the desk.

Olivia's head pops up at the same time I reach for it, her eyes curious. I glance at the message, and a grin spreads across my face before I even realize it.

"Guess what, baby?" I say, turning the phone so she can see the notification. "Time to furnish the Parker Building."

Her eyes go wide, lips parting. "It's finished?!"

Relief slams into me, heavy and sweet, loosening something in my chest I didn't even know was still wound tight. A smile breaks across my face, bigger than I've let myself have in a long time.

"It's finished."

I watch her light up, that spark in her eyes turning molten. She shoots up from the chair like she can't help herself.

The office door creaks open.

"I waited months," Wesley says, stepping inside like he owns the damn floor. He raises a brow at Olivia, arms crossed over his chest. "And yet not one apology."

Olivia freezes.

I stiffen.

Wesley closes the door behind him, slow and theatrical, and levels a stare so sharp it could slice glass. "*Let's see.* Unauthorized login. Accessing a terminated WesTech account. Tracing financial paper trails through archived Bratva holdings. And—my personal favorite, *hacking into Maksim Korsakov's juvenile psych records.*"

"Wesley—" she starts, eyes wide.

"I thought you were better than that," he deadpans. "You left a trail."

I'm already rising from my chair. "If you've got a problem with her, you bring it to me."

Wes throws me a lazy glance. "Relax. She didn't break my company. Just bent it. *Impressively.*" He turns back to Olivia, and his voice softens, not much, but enough. "I should be mad. But I'm mostly just..." He exhales. "In awe, honestly. That was damn near beautiful work. And terrifying, you've grown since you were sixteen."

She blinks. "You're not mad?"

"Mad?" Wesley grins. "I nearly stole you back from War with a promotion. You breached six layers of encryption, rerouted through a dormant honeytrap I *personally* coded after your first little breach, and did it all from a Beaumont Realty laptop that I technically had blocked."

I sit back down, tension easing. "So you're saying my woman's a genius."

"She's a *menace*," Wesley corrects. "But yeah. A genius."

Olivia tries to hide her smile. Fails. "You should really patch that backdoor access."

"I already did," Wesley mutters, then eyes me. "Keep her out of my servers, or I swear to God, War—"

I raise both hands. "No promises."

Wesley turns to go, tossing one last look over his shoulder. "Oh, and for the record? I like the second desk. Makes it harder for her to disappear."

Then he's gone.

Olivia slumps back into her chair, cheeks flushed.

I smirk across the desk at her. "So. You got praised, threatened, and almost rehired all in one visit. Impressive."

She grins back, a little breathless. "What can I say? I multitask."

"And apparently commit multiple felonies before lunch."

Her smile softens. "I just wanted to help. To give something back to Noah. To you."

My throat tightens.

She has no idea what it does to me, to be seen like this. *Chosen* like this.

I stand again, walking around the desk until I'm in front of her. She looks up, blinking.

"Come here," I murmur.

She rises. I wrap my arms around her waist and pull her close. She fits against me like she was always meant to be here.

"I'm proud of you," I say softly, brushing my lips to her forehead. "Grateful you got the building back. Even if you did scare the hell out of me."

She smiles, that wide, teasing smile I crave. "If I'm being honest, getting scolded by Wesley I think means I need another punishment," she muses. "Just to be effective, you know?"

I bark out a laugh, that full-bodied kind that only she can pull out of me.

And right there, with her in my arms and a future in our hands, I know I've never been more certain.

I'm tying this woman to my name.

Chapter Sixty-One

WAR

Four Months Later

The scissors are heavier than I expected. All gold and ceremonial, probably unused since the mayor's last press event.

It's just a ribbon, I tell myself.

But it's not.

It's every memory I've locked behind this building's walls.

Every mistake I swore I'd never repeat.

Every dream Olivia made feel possible.

Cameras flash. Applause rings out.

I take it in; the polished suits, the eager city officials, the whispers of legacy.

And then my eyes land on her.

Olivia, radiant and calm, the kind of calm that steadies me without even trying.

She gives me a small nod. *You've got this.*

And I do. Because she's here.

I cut it.

Clean. Final.

Applause breaks out, echoing off the marble steps of what was once the Parker Building. Now, it's **Hartman's House.**

A home for the ones no one remembers.

A second chance for kids who never got a first.

I step back so the press can get their shots. The banner behind me catches the wind, lifting the name into the sunlight. Hartman's House: A Future Begins Here.

I take the podium, breath steady, voice ready. "This project has been a long time coming. Years of plans. Months of renovation. And today, it's real."

I scan the crowd. Mayor Olsen nods beside me. Olivia stands near the entrance, in soft blue, her eyes already brimming.

"This wouldn't have been possible without Mayor Olsen's support," I continue, "and without Korsakov Industries, who donated the land for this facility." I pause, because I can feel Olivia's smirk from here.

Credit where credit's due, she told me after. *Even if it's to a man with no soul.*

I'd never been more in love.

A reporter raises her voice above the rest. "Mr. Beaumont—do you think this facility will erase the tragedy that happened here twenty-five years ago?"

There it is. The question I've been waiting for.

I still see him.

That damn grin. The busted-up sneakers he refused to throw out. The way we'd sneak to the kitchen just two kids looking to steal the last donut.

I blink hard.

"While we can never erase what happened here twenty-five years ago," I say, my voice catching the weight of it, "we can acknowledge it. We can call it what it was. A terrible accident. And we can build something better in its place." I glance back at the building. "A monument in his memory. A legacy of healing."

Olivia squeezes my hand. Then slips away to greet the kids coming in.

Doing what she does best.

Bridging gaps. Softening edges. Giving kids who've been through hell the one thing no system ever gave Noah: a sense of home.

I watch her beside a girl no older than seventeen, point out the mural behind them, and something in my chest pulls tight.

This is what healing looks like.

And somehow, she gave it to me, too.

"There will also be a scholarship program," I add, voice roughening, "in Noah Hartman's name. Every teen who comes through these doors will have a chance at higher education. Full tuition, housing, a monthly stipend. If you want a future—we'll help you build it."

The applause returns, louder this time.

But I'm not looking at the crowd.

I'm watching her.

Always her.

I take a breath, the weight of everything settling into my chest, not heavy, but grounding.

She did this.

Not just the building.

She cracked me open. Made me softer. Smarter. *Better.*

She made me dream again, and not about buildings or legacies or war rooms. About mornings with her in my bed. Laughter echoing in these halls. Maybe even a couple kids with her eyes and my last name.

I watch her throw her head back laughing with a kid who's already grinning wide.

And all I can think is—I *can't wait* to seal her with my name.

Chapter Sixty-Two

OLIVIA

I love waking up at the estate.

The penthouse is beautiful, sure, sleek and towering and unapologetically War. But the estate?

It's grand.

Quiet. Expansive. Wrapped in warm light and old stone.

Everything I need is here.

Margaret always has everything in perfect order.

Ana even cut fresh peonies for our room this morning; white and blush and soft as a sigh. I set them by the window where the breeze can catch their scent.

War kissed my forehead before he left. Said he had *"a few things to take care of"* and that he'd be back soon.

I have a sneaking suspicion about what that means.

But I didn't ask.

Didn't press.

Just smiled.

Because I trust him.

There's a knock on the bedroom door.

"Ms. Baker?" Margaret's voice is warm and formal as always. "You have a visitor downstairs."

A visitor?

I tug on a soft robe and head down the curved staircase. My bare feet whisper against the cool marble.

And then I see her.

"Ella!"

She spins toward me, smiling wide, dressed in a rose-colored sun dress that flutters around her legs like something out of a spring catalog.

She's holding a small black box wrapped with a gold bow and an envelope tucked neatly on top.

I nearly crush both as I hug her.

"What are you doing here? I thought you were still in Brokenwoods!"

She laughs, holding the box up like a fragile artifact. "Careful! That's probably important."

I step back, eyes wide. "Wait. Did he *fly* you in?"

Ella smirks. "War called last night. Booked my flight. Got me this dress." She twirls, the skirt flaring. "Apparently he had a whole plan."

I stare at the box. Then at the envelope.

"Today's the day, isn't it?"

She shrugs, all faux nonchalance. "I'm just the messenger. I'm supposed to give you this box... and tell you to read the note."

My hands shake just a little as I take the envelope. I slide my finger under the seal, unfold the heavy card inside.

No surprises. Just like you asked.

But don't think for a second I didn't plan every detail.

Enjoy your day.

I'll see you soon.

Today's the day.

—W

I press the note to my chest, heart leaping. A squeal escapes before I can stop it.

Ella chuckles. "Okay, that reaction was definitely worth the flight."

"What are we doing?" I ask breathless.

"We," she grins, "are apparently hitting all your favorite spots. Hair, nails, professional makeup, and a full day with moi."

I laugh, eyes stinging. "He really did all this?"

Ella nods toward the box. "Open it."

I lift the lid slowly.

Inside, folded like a dream, is a white dress.

Short, but not too short. Fitted until it flares softly at the hips. Elegant. Playful. Effortlessly me.

I gasp. "Oh my God, it's perfect."

Ella grins. "Right? You should've seen the sales girl's face when he asked for 'something short, white, and impossible to say no to.'"

I laugh, holding the dress up to my chest and twirling. It sways just enough to feel flirty, feminine, and like something out of a dream.

A War Beaumont dream, at that.

Before I can get lost staring at it, Ella claps her hands together. "Alright, no time to waste. The man made an itinerary."

***

A sleek black car is waiting out front. Inside—cold sparkling water, champagne bottles on ice, even a personal playlist War made me queued and ready.

I can't help squealing, and Ella keeps smirking every time I do. "What's the full plan?"

Ella sips her champagne smug. "You'll see"

The studio we pull up to is already humming when we arrive, mirrors lit like halos, the air perfumed with powder and hairspray, trays of brushes and palettes gleaming under soft light.

"Olivia!" Isabella sweeps over, all warm smile and long, graceful hands. She's dressed in black from head to toe, sleek as always. "I was hoping today would finally be the day you landed in my chair again."

I laugh, hugging her. "You make me sound overdue for service."

"Darling, you are." She snaps her fingers, and an assistant steps forward to guide Ella into the next chair. "This one will take care of your friend's hair and makeup. And I've got someone on nails waiting for you too. Full pampering. Nothing less."

I sink into the chair, already feeling my nerves settle.

"You know," Isabella says as she clips back my hair, "I always knew you two would turn into more."

I blink at her reflection in the mirror. "Oh yeah? Guess you're good at predicting the future."

She shakes her head with a smile. "Not at all. But I know Mr. Beaumont. He's only ever hired me as a gift for coworkers or family friends, people he wants to impress. Never once for a girlfriend."

My heart races. Heat pools low in my chest.

So that night, the first gala... I wasn't just a date. I *was* different.

I swallow, trying to play it off, but my cheeks are already pink.

Isabella's fingers move deftly through my hair, curling and pinning with practiced ease. Loose waves, soft volume, pearl pins glinting against the light. Then her brushes sweep across my face—primer, powder, a whisper of rose along my lips until I look like the very best version of myself.

Across the room, Ella's getting her eyeliner perfected, gossiping easily with the assistant. A nail tech files my nails into soft ovals, brushing pale blush polish over them until they shine.

It's indulgent. Luxurious. The kind of day I never let myself dream about because dreaming hurt too much.

And now? It's *real.*

When Isabella finishes, she leans in with a conspiratorial grin and slips a black envelope into my hand.

"This is from him."

My breath catches. I open it carefully, recognizing the sharp, deliberate strokes of War's handwriting instantly.

Beautiful doesn't even begin to cover how amazing you look.

Today is yours; every stop, every detail.

First hint: something sweet.

Head to the place that always smelled like sugar on your skin.

Maybe I'll be watching.

—W

I press the note to my chest, heart racing, lips splitting into a smile I can't hold back.

Ella chuckles from her chair, watching me. "Oh, you're gone. Completely gone."

I laugh, but my voice is shaky. "And happy about it."

The car hums softly as it winds through the city. Ella taps through playlists on her phone, humming under her breath, while I can't stop running my thumb over the edge of War's note.

Something sweet.

The answer hits me like a rush of sugar. "Smash and Sugar."

Ella grins, already in on the secret. "You got it."

By the time the car pulls to the curb, I'm practically buzzing. My *favorite* bakery. My spot. The place I used to sneak pastries from when War was too wrapped up in board meetings to notice I'd disappeared.

I step out, ready to bolt for the glass door—then freeze.

Because he's standing there.

Vaska.

Leaning against the window, twirling a knife between his fingers like it's a coin. Casual, dangerous, sharp grin playing at the corner of his mouth.

My heart stutters, but I force myself forward. Ella stiffens beside me, but Vaska just chuckles low in his chest and extends a small paper bag.

"Sweet tooth, krasavitsa," he drawls, the Russian lilt thick around the word. "Your man asked me to play delivery boy today."

I take the bag carefully, the knife catching light as he flips it into his palm again. Inside, neat rows of macarons in every color of blush and cream. Resting on top is another black envelope.

Vaska smirks as I slip it free. "Don't worry, little dove. I didn't read it."

I narrow my eyes, but my fingers are already tearing at the seal. War's handwriting floods my vision.

Sweetheart,

This one isn't about sugar. It's about you.

Think back to where I once put you on display, where every eye was on you, even when you didn't know it.

That's your next stop.

—W

I frown, confused at first. On display?

Ella leans over my shoulder. "What does he mean?"

"I thought you knew everything?"

She shakes her head. "I stopped listening after bakery."

Then it hits me. *The art gallery.*

My throat tightens. The gallery where War had that painting of me commissioned, hung under the lights for everyone to see.

The first time I realized he didn't just see *me*… he wanted the world to.

I clutch the note to my chest, breathless.

"The gallery," I whisper.

Ella smiles. "Guess we're headed to see your portrait, future Mrs. Beaumont."

The car pulls away from Smash and Sugar, and Ella immediately tears open the bag of macarons.

"Pass the pistachio," I laugh, nudging her as I peek into the envelope again just to reread War's handwriting.

She hands me one, biting into a raspberry with a sigh. "Okay, I know he was terrifying, but… that Vaska guy? Kind of hot."

I choke on a crumb. "Ella!"

"What?!" She grins, brushing sugar from her sundress. "Dangerous, yes. But hot. The knife twirling? *Very bad boy aesthetic.*"

I shake my head, laughing so hard I nearly drop my macaron. "You've officially lost it."

The car slows as we pull up to the grand glass façade of the gallery. My laughter fades into something softer, chest tight as memories roll in. The last time I was here, I stood in a gallery, staring up at my own face on canvas, larger than life. War's gift. His *declaration.*

The driver opens our doors, and as we step onto the marble steps, a sharply dressed woman is waiting for us. She's elegant, clipboard tucked to her side, smile polished.

"Miss Baker," she says warmly, pressing a black envelope into my hand. "On behalf of the gallery, congratulations."

"Thank you." I answer, bewildered.

But she's already stepping back, leaving me with the note.

I open it, pulse quickening.

Your art deserves more than a gallery.

It deserves to be free.

Today, your piece will be hung where it belongs: amongst your family.

—W

My brows knit. "Amongst my family? What does that even mean? He wants me to go back to Brokenwoods?"

Ella tilts her head, thinking. "Hung. Amongst your family. Obviously photos are hung. Where do you have pictures of your family?"

The realization hits me like a thunderclap. My old apartment.

The last place I stayed before I left him. Before I thought I had to go back to my family instead of building one with him.

My throat tightens. "My apartment. He furnished it... he hung all my portraits there."

Ella squeezes my hand, eyes shining. "Then that's where we're going next."

The car glides to a stop in front of my old building. My heart twists as I step out, so many memories embedded in these bricks, some sweet, some jagged.

Ella follows close behind, clutching the bag of macarons like it's her security blanket. "This is it?"

I nod, nerves buzzing under my skin. "Last place I lived before War"

We head into the lobby, up the elevator, the ride quiet except for Ella crunching on a soft macaron shell. When the doors slide open, I lead the way down the hall. My old door feels both foreign and achingly familiar.

I reach for my bag, then stop short. "I don't have the key."

Ella smirks. "Under the carpet?"

I laugh. "Yeah, right. I never kept it there."

She arches a brow. "Check."

I roll my eyes, checking anyway, just to humor her, then freeze. "You've got to be kidding me." My fingers close around cool metal. "It's here."

I shove the key into the lock, heart hammering, and push the door open.

The breath leaves me all at once.

It's beautiful.

The apartment has been transformed, every corner softened with white and blush peonies. *My flower.* Their scent wraps around me like a memory.

I move down the hallway, and my steps falter. Because there they are: the portraits of my family. My mother. My brothers. All framed, aligned neatly along the walls.

And hung amongst them: my portrait. The one from the gallery. My likeness now part of the family gallery, woven into where I belong.

My chest tightens. He didn't just give me my image in art. He gave me a place.

On the small table beneath it, another black envelope waits.

I tear it open, hands trembling.

You once swore you'd never go back here.

Today, I need you to.

Ask for Vincenzo.

—W

I glance at Ella, the name already on my lips. "La Serenata."

Her brows lift. "The restaurant?"

I nod, heart racing. "The restaurant."

Ella grins, slipping her arm through mine. "Guess dinner's on War."

La Serenata glows like it always has—soft golden lights spilling through the windows, violins drifting faintly from inside. The kind of place where every meal feels like an event. The kind of place I once swore I'd never set foot in again.

But tonight, my hand is steady as I push open the heavy door. Ella trails behind me, her sundress swishing, eyes wide as she takes it all in.

We approach the hostess stand, and I clear my throat. "We're here for Vincenzo."

The hostess blinks once, then her face warms with a smile. "Of course. One moment."

A minute later, a man in an immaculate suit emerges from the back. Soft brown hair, charming smile, posture like he's been running this room his entire life. *Vincenzo.*

"Ms. Baker," he greets me with a little bow, and from behind his back, he produces a velvet box, black with a satin ribbon. "From Mr. Beaumont."

My breath hitches as he sets it in my hands. Ella leans close, whispering, "If that's food, I'm stealing half."

I laugh, but my fingers tremble as I undo the ribbon. Inside, nestled against silk, are diamond earrings; brilliant, perfect, glittering under the restaurant lights.

Ella's gasp echoes mine. "Holy—*Olivia.* Those are huge."

There's a note tucked inside, folded small. I pull it free, my pulse racing.

For the woman who makes diamonds look dull.

Put these on, my sweet girl.

Then go to the place where it all started.

Where we first met.

—W

My throat closes around a rush of air.

I know exactly where that is.

Ella watches me, eyes shining. "Where?"

"Beaumont Enterprises." My voice is barely a whisper, but my chest is soaring.

Ella squeezes my arm, grinning ear to ear. "Then let's go get you engaged."

"He can't really want to propose here," I laugh nervously as the car pulls up to Beaumont Enterprises. The steel and glass rise sharp against the night sky, every floor lit like a beacon.

Ella just smirks. "Oh, he can. He's War Beaumont."

We ride the elevator up to the seventeenth floor. My stomach flips as the doors open to WesTech's wing. Conference Room A—the place where I first met him, full of tension and fire and intrigue neither of us wanted to name.

The door's already open.

Inside, Wesley leans casually against the table, a black box in his hands, his smirk just this side of infuriating.

"Olivia," he greets, pushing off the table. "Back where it all began."

I blink at him, startled. "You're in on this?"

"Of course I am." He grins wider, stepping closer. "The man knows how to delegate."

He opens the box to reveal a necklace, delicate platinum, diamonds that match the earrings glittering in perfect symmetry.

My breath catches. "It's beautiful."

"Turn around."

I do, hair swept aside as Wesley clasps the necklace around my throat. The cool metal settles against my skin, heavy with meaning.

He squeezes my shoulder lightly. "Good luck, Baker. Last chance to back out."

I laugh, breathless. "Not a chance."

He slips a black envelope into my hand. I unfold it.

Amongst the flowers, where I first showed you what forever could feel like.

Meet me there.

—W

Flowers.

I frown, then it hits me all at once.

The conservatory garden.

Our first weekend together, hidden under glass and strung lights, wrapped in roses and orchids. The place that felt like magic.

My chest swells. "The conservatory garden," I whisper.

Ella loops her arm through mine, eyes glinting with excitement. "Then let's go find your forever."

The car rolls to a stop outside the conservatory, its glass dome glittering under the night sky. My pulse is so loud it drowns out the hum of the engine.

"Come on," I say, grabbing my bag, but Ella doesn't move.

I frown. "Aren't you coming?"

She shakes her head, smiling soft and a little teary. "No. This is where you leave me. Good luck, future Mrs. Beaumont."

My throat tightens. Happy tears sting my eyes as I lean across the seat and crush her in a hug. "Thank you, for everything."

"Go," she whispers, nudging me toward the doors.

I step out, heels clicking against the stone path, and push the conservatory doors open.

Inside, it's breathtaking.

The garden is just as I remember it, quiet, lush, rare, but tonight it glows, dressed for forever. Candles flicker in glass lanterns. Roses and orchids spill over trellises. The cherry tree blooms again, just like that first weekend, pale petals drifting down in a soft, impossible rain.

And under it, waiting, is War.

He stands tall in a black suit, the sharp lines softened by the glow of string lights. His eyes find mine immediately, and for a moment the world falls away.

"Olivia," he says, voice rough, steadying. He steps closer, every inch of him sure. "You found me."

The words hit me deep, *too deep.*

"I was nothing but shadows when you walked in," he continues. "A man with too much steel, too many walls, too many ghosts. And then you—" He gestures around us, to the flowers, the light. "You brought starlight to every inch of my darkness. You turned every shadow into something I could finally stand in without fear."

My lips tremble. Tears spill over.

"I thought I was building an empire. But what I really built...what I *fought* for, was a place where you'd stay. Where you'd be mine. And tonight, I don't want a future without you. I don't ever want a *moment* without you."

He drops to one knee, a small velvet box in his hand, eyes burning into mine like a vow already spoken.

"Olivia Baker," he says, voice breaking for the first time. "Be my wife. Let me spend every day proving that forever is too short for us."

For a second, I can't breathe. My chest is too full; of light, of love, of *him.*

I drop down in front of him, dress pooling around my knees as I throw my arms around his neck. Laughter spills out of me, unsteady and real. "Of course I'll marry you," I whisper against his ear. "Like I'd ever say no."

War chuckles low in his chest, arms crushing me tighter. When I finally lean back, he's grinning, relief and triumph flashing in his eyes.

"Give me your hand," he murmurs.

I hold it out, trembling, and he slides the ring onto my finger, the one I picked out, solid, perfect, glittering under the conservatory lights.

He lifts my hand, kisses the ring, then presses his lips to mine. The kiss is sweet, slow, but underneath it hums that fire that's always been ours, untamed, undeniable, forever.

When he pulls back, his forehead rests against mine, voice dropping low.

"*All steps complete,*" he smirks triumphant.

"What?" I chuckle.

"It just means you're mine now. *Always.*"

Cherry blossoms drift down around us, beautiful and soft and I know there's no world, no lifetime, where I wouldn't be his.

ACKNOWLEDGEMENTS

Every book costs a little piece of me, and this one took more than most.

To Destiny, who reminded me I'm not crazy for dreaming big and writing wild, you're my heart, I mean it.

To Tianna, who checked in when I hadn't even checked in with myself. You are my light.

To Julia, who will always be my plot therapist and voice of reason when I want to burn it all down. Thank you.

To my mom, who believed I'd do something with all these characters talking in my head. (You were right.)

To my ARC readers: Thank you for helping me hold the pen steady. I kept going in preparation for you.

To my readers... How can I ever thank the people who make this all worth it? I'm never more astounded than I am by the way you love and support my words. I appreciate you. I thank you. I love you.

ABOUT THE AUTHOR

Amanda Zuelo writes emotionally charged romance filled with obsession, grit, and heart. From mafia empires to billionaire boardrooms, her interconnected worlds explore love, power, and the people brave enough to chase both.

When she's not building fictional legacies, Amanda is curating aesthetics, running her author brand, and plotting her next heartbreak on the page, always with a playlist and a cup of something strong. She lives for fierce heroines, morally gray men, and writing characters who make you feel everything.

ALSO BY AMANDA ZUELO

The Sovereigns Series

Ruins: An Arranged Marriage Mafia Romance

Santo Amato and Vasilisa Popov

Legacy: A Second Chance Mafia Romance

Angelo Amato and Adriana Castillo

www.ingramcontent.com/pod-product-compliance
Lightning Source LLC
Chambersburg PA
CBHW071752310726
48976CB00001BA/96